NO
PLACE
LIKE
YOU

also by jeannie choe

Best I Never Had Series

Best I Never Had

NO PLACE LIKE YOU

A ROMANCE NOVEL

JEANNIE CHOE

LN
♡P

No Place Like You
Paperback Edition
Copyright © 2025 by Jeannie Choe

Love N. Books Press
An Imprint of Wolfpack Publishing
1707 E. Diana Street
Tampa, FL 33610

www.lovenbookspress.com

Character illustrations by Martin Barnes
Internal graphics design by Rachel Chaya Design
Edited by My Brother's Editor

No Place Like You was originally self-published in 2024 by Jeannie Choe.

Paperback ISBN 979-8-89567-964-7
Ebook ISBN 979-8-89567-963-0
LCCN 2025931565

To anyone chasing their dream. This is going to sound awfully cliché, but don't give up. Just...don't.

"If you're creating anything at all, it's really dangerous to care about what people think."

— Kristin Wiig

And to my babies. In a world full of labels, you might find that you don't fit into one.
So create your own. And stand proud of who you are.

note from the author

Hello reader! If you're new here, welcome! And if you've already met Lucy and Dexter in Best I Never Had, welcome back!

This journey has been a rollercoaster of highs and lows. And one thing I can say about No Place Like You is that Lucy and Dexter's story was one of the highest of highs. Their chemistry flew off the pages and I am so excited for you to dive into their story.

Just a few notes before you start this book, I have some trigger warnings. If you've read my books in the past, you'll know that I usually direct you to my website for trigger warnings, but I wanted to do things a little differently this time. While I still want to be considerate of those who would like to go into this story blind, I also want to take a moment to acknowledge those who not only appreciate the trigger warnings, but depend on them to have a safe and enjoyable reading experience. I think every author and reader can agree that a safe reading experience is the best one. And while some triggers may not affect readers, there are many that do.

So thank you for being mindful of your own reading experience by being aware of your triggers and taking the responsibility to look up warnings before reading a book. And if you are still learning what your triggers are, as I am doing myself, I hope that any trauma that you experience from exposure to those new triggers is handled safely.

No Place Like You carries a lot of heart and sometimes, with heart comes pain. Because we as humans feel. We laugh, we cry, and we hurt. So while my intention is for my readers to have their heartstrings tugged at just a little bit, it is never my intention to resurface any past trauma that my readers are working through or have worked through.

So here are the triggers as listed. And if you have any questions or would like to discuss the presence of the triggers listed below in more detail to either help you prepare to read this book or decide that this book isn't for you, my emails and DM's are always open.

- Loss of a parent(s)
- Portrayal of cancer in a close family member
- Loss of a job/job security
- Lack of familial support for main character
- Open door/explicit sex scenes throughout

Thank you for giving my pride and joy a chance. Thank you for finding your way to these two characters who danced around in my mind and heart. And thank you for being here.

Always,
Jeannie

NO
PLACE
LIKE
YOU

1

three years ago

SATURDAY, 1:24 AM

Dexter: Lucy?

1:38 AM

Lucy: Yes, Dexter?

1:39 AM

Dexter: Just making sure you didn't give me the wrong number.

1:40 AM

Lucy: Crossed my mind.

1:41 AM

Dexter: Well, I'm glad it didn't stick.

And thank you for a very entertaining night.

I never knew beer pong could be so… strategic.

1:42 AM

Lucy: It's a competitive sport. Of course it's strategic.

1:42 AM

Dexter: I guess I thought it was more of a throw the ball and pray for luck kind of game.

1:43 AM

Lucy: Such amateur mentality.

BTW, I believe I won that last round.

1:44 AM

Dexter: Ref said I won, fair and square.

1:44 AM

Lucy: The ref was five tequila shots deep with a feather boa and heart shaped sunglasses.

1:45 AM

Dexter: Where did he find that boa?

1:47 AM

Lucy: I don't even know.

I demand a rematch. Or some other drinking game.

And a sober ref.

1:49 AM

Dexter: Like strip poker?

And I don't know how I feel about people watching.

It's a little creepy, no?

1:53 AM

Lucy: I meant a neutral party to make sure you don't cheat, not an audience.

I don't know how to play poker. Maybe Jenga or Twister.

1:53 AM

Dexter: Strip Twister sounds very interesting.
And slippery.

1:55 AM

Lucy: Just regular Twister, Dexter. Or Uno.

1:56 AM

Dexter: Strip Uno sounds like fun too.

1:58 AM

Lucy: OMG. Never mind. Just know, the next
drinking game we play,

I will be watching your every move. Like white
on rice, baby.

2:00 AM

Dexter: Jeez, Lucy. I know you find me
irresistible.

You don't need a drinking game as an excuse
to stare at me all night.

2:02 AM

Lucy: BYE.

SATURDAY, 9:58 PM

Lucy: You know I'm here for another day. I'm
going back to Seattle Monday morning.

10:01 PM

Dexter: I'm aware.

10:04 PM

Lucy: If you wanted to hang out or something,
I'm free tomorrow.

10:04 PM

Dexter: Dinner?

I'll pick you up at 7?

10:06 PM

Lucy: My sisters are taking me out. Some self-serve ramen place.

And can we keep this a little on the DL? I'll never hear the end of it if my sisters know.

10:08 PM

Dexter: Mum's the word.

10:10 PM

Lucy: Would breakfast work? I can be at your place in the morning.

10:10 PM

Dexter: Sure.

Should I pick up a deck of cards?

10:12 PM

Lucy: I don't know. Twister sounded more fun.

2

Dexter

three years ago

MY MOVE to Brooklyn two years ago isn't necessarily a memory I like to revisit often. It was stressful more than anything. Mainly due to reasons like trying to find a roommate who wasn't into conspiracy theories or didn't have a secret meth lab in their closet. Add on the trauma of furnishing my room with items from Goodwill that weren't infested with bodily fluids or bedbugs, and you got the grand slam of inhospitable welcomes. At the ripe young age of twenty-four, fresh-faced and working some temp job that might as well have paid me in clams, the glitz and glamour of moving to the city was a little intimidating. But my sister, Janet, made it memorable in her usual big sister fashion. She came to my apartment infested with cockroaches and smelling like stale chow mein with a bamboo plant and a white eight hundred thread count sheet set. The bamboo plant because she claimed it was good luck and the sheets because, according to her, I needed to balance the figurative "bachelor pad" neon sign I had hanging over my entryway with something other than my navy comforter and PS5. And while I appreciated the gesture, the sheets stayed tucked into the far corner of my closet, unused for a long time.

But today, in the early hours of Sunday morning, while stretching the elastic of that exact sheet set to fit around the curved edges of my mattress, I'm making a mental note to send Janet a thank you card. My intercom buzzes just then, and I sprint toward the door after smoothing my hand over the added duvet cover that felt like an actual Olympic sport trying to put on.

"Come on up," I call through the speaker. I peer at my apartment, making a quick sweep. I also need to extend that same thank you card to my roommate, Hayden, for being mysteriously absent from our apartment this early in the morning.

There's a light knock at my door, and I open it to find my guest.

"Hi," Lucy says a little breathlessly. Her teeth press into her lower lip, and a flush creeps up to her cheeks as she peers at me with her deep brown eyes. Eyes that light up with intrigue and something that leans toward a challenge with the quick and subtle flick of her right eyebrow.

"Hey." I open the door wider, letting her in.

She walks past me, her steps hesitant yet curious. "Is..."

"It's just us," I answer, although she didn't necessarily ask a question.

She turns to face me and nods. She stands there, silent, while her fingers tug at the highlighted blonde strands of her long hair. She's wearing sneakers today, a vast difference to the strappy heels she wore a few nights ago when I met her for the first time at a party at her sister's apartment. With those sexy ass heels that made her long legs look irresistible, we were the same height. A small, teeny tiny part of me misses them, but looking at her right now in her flat shoes and flowy sundress, I can't decide which look I like better.

"You know," she says after a beat with a wavering hint of conviction in her voice, "I don't even know your last name."

I take a cautious step toward her, finding that she's still pretty tall even without her heels while loving that I wouldn't have to stoop too low to kiss her. "It's Greer."

She nods again, slow and tentative, with a look of skepticism stamped on her face. Like I might be lying about my identity. And it makes me smirk, knowing how her nerves make her so adorable.

"Do you also want to know my date of birth? The last four of my social?"

"Oh no. I need all nine to dig up the *really* dirty stuff." Her lips twist to one side when a small smile peeks through her sarcasm, and she looks away from me. Her eyes nervously skitter across the room, and her brow furrows, almost as if she's trying to remember some minor detail like where she left her keys or if she left the stove on before leaving her house. "Look, I know I sounded all confident and flirty and all that jazz at the party the other night." She pauses to wriggle her fingers in the air, making nervous jazz hands. "But I'm really not."

"Not what?" I'm inches from her now, and I stroke her hand with my finger. I can feel her grow nervous, more fidgety and tense, but she doesn't lean away. Instead, she loops her finger through mine, making her thumb and my pinky the only parts of our bodies touching.

"Confident. Or flirty."

I lift an eyebrow. "I don't know," I argue. When I talk, a little low and drawn out, her gaze flicks to my lips. "That drinking game was pretty flirty. I believe you were the one who suggested the round of strip beer pong. Is that the usual impression you give people when you meet them for the first time?" I *tsk* my tongue against the roof of my mouth, working hard to hold back my smile.

"I was drunk, Dexter," she responds flatly. "And I'm on vacation. Visiting my sisters, who I haven't seen in ages."

"So..."

She huffs, annoyed, pinching my pinky as if to inflict pain while giving it a light tug. "So I was celebrating. Or just...having fun, I guess."

"And what was the excuse for the text messages last night?" Both of my eyebrows shoot up now, one joining the other. It's more suggestive than anything out of curiosity, but honestly, she started all of this with her inhibitions thrown out the window and her infectious laughter.

She opens her mouth, probably to throw some jab at me or to discourage *this*, but then shuts it. There's a moment that lingers between us. It's long enough for her to back out. To leave here and pretend like she wasn't the one who texted me back this morning after I suggested a game of strip Twister, claiming she would need a good twenty-minute warning to stretch.

Would right now be a good time to tell her I don't actually *own* the board game? Maybe not. Because I don't care if I have to paint the colorful dots directly onto my wood floor. All that matters is that she's here. Not across the bridge at her sisters' apartment, ignoring my messages or shutting me down with close-ended answers to my suggestive questions like, *What other games can you add the word "strip" to?*

"I'm going back home tomorrow," she blurts suddenly. She says it like she's trying to convince me to talk her out of this. To tell her us living thousands of miles apart is going to somehow wipe away my nagging curiosity of what she'd feel like when her bare skin is flush against my own.

"So you've mentioned."

She nods again. Third time, but who's counting. "So this…"

"Are you suggesting we start an LDR based on a shared interest in naked drinking games and tequila?"

"L…?"

"Long distance relationship," I answer when her voice trails, and her face scrunches into the cutest scowl.

"And here I thought only kids in junior high spoke in acronymic code." She finally laughs. Whatever nerves are apparent in the tight set of her jaw and her too round eyes dissolve for just a second.

I close the last inches of space between us and reach for her cheek, running my thumb across her lower lip. "I'm not expecting anything," I say close to her skin, feeling her warm breath meet mine.

I see her lashes flutter, fanning the skin I now know feels like silk, and a shallow exhale slips through her lips. "Good."

"So…I can kiss you now?" I say lowly, my gaze on her plump bottom lip, tracing the curves at the corners and enjoying too much the small recoiling bounce her lip has when I pull at it with my thumb and let go.

Her chin tilts downward in the slightest of nods, the act so subtle it feels hesitant. My arms wrap around her waist at the same time hers hook around my neck, and our lips collide. I don't mean to, but a low, desperate growl grumbles in my throat, right when her lips part and her tongue dips inside my mouth. She whimpers and runs her teeth along my bottom lip, taking a healthy nibble, and that sensation travels all the way down to my groin.

"You really wanted to kiss me," she says breathlessly against my ridiculously greedy mouth.

"You have no idea."

I turn toward my room, my feet stumbling over hers. My hand travels down to her thigh. And I take the moment to thank the saint of a human being who invented sundresses. Those thank you cards are piling up fast.

She hooks her knee over my hip, making her legs part open, and I rock into her, causing her to press herself against me. I start to see bits and pieces of her unravel. Those wound-up knots holding the remains of her reserve are unfurling, and I could spend all day watching her come apart like this. How her hands are no longer guarded and move with intent and motive. Or how she doesn't care that I can hear her moans and whimpers, making them leave her lips more often.

My thumb tucks into the single string of her thong, and it slips, snapping against her tight skin.

She pulls away. "Ow," she comments, not an ounce of pain in her voice.

"Sorry," I respond, my voice all gravely and rough. "It's in the way."

"You can ask nicely, and I'll take it off."

I bunch her dress around her hips and tug at the string again, but this time with two hands. When the rip of fabric fills the air, Lucy's eyes widen.

"Like I said," I say casually to her stunned face, dipping my lips to her jaw. "In." A kiss under her chin. "The." Another kiss on her pulse point. "Way."

"You totally owe me a new pair."

"I'll buy you the whole fucking store," I retort darkly. My voice drops about four octaves, and it makes me sound impatient and desperate and wild. Like I'd clean out the nearest La Perla in a heart-beat if it meant I could listen to her breathless voice against my ear.

Her head falls back at the same time the backs of her legs hit my bed, and her body falls onto my new old sheets with a thud.

"Are these Egyptian?"

"Hmm. Eight hundred thread count."

"I'm impressed," she says softly, catching her breath at the same time. "And here I thought they were going to be flannel."

"I guess I'm not like other guys."

She laughs. "You are so full of shit." The sweet sound of her giggle and the bounce in the column of her neck makes my heart stutter. *God, she's so beautiful.*

My lips continue their journey, meeting the sexy-as-fuck swell of her cleavage. Her hand flattens and tucks between the waistband of my sweatpants. And when her hand grips me, my entire body turns into Jell-O. My hand pulls at the fabric covering her breast, exposing a bare nipple. I take it in my mouth, and she moans, her hand moving in earnest inside my pants.

"This is just sex, right?" she says, a whimper ending her question when my tongue flicks her skin.

"Just sex."

3

Lucy

present day

HOLY SHIT.

"Nat. What is that?"

Silence. Nothing but wide smiles, stifled giggles, and *silence*.

I realize now that this FaceTime call isn't a simple video chat. One my sister texted me about the night before with a sudden urgency to be available the next day at 2:30 p.m., 5:30 p.m. her time, all while she told me, "I just want to see your face."

Stifled giggles continue to fill the silence. "What do you think it is?"

"I—is that...?"

More giggles. "An engagement ring?" Said engagement ring chooses that moment to reflect off the lights in Nat and her boyfriend of three years, Hayden's, apartment from her left hand. Like someone dramatically sprinkled a handful of glitter in front of the screen to time it with my stunned reaction. It's fucking gorgeous.

I nod vigorously. "Nat!" I squeal. "When did this happen?"

Nat turns to Hayden and grins. "Last week," she answers, her gaze swooning in Hayden's direction. "After Hayden's grand opening. We closed up for the night, and before we left, he asked me to marry him in his empty restaurant. He's been hiding this baby in his pocket for a few months." Her eyes twinkle with the far-off look of fairytale princesses, matching the one on Hayden's, while he looks at my sister as if she's the world.

"You guys!" I whine, letting the last word stretch for a few seconds. Hayden leans down to give Nat a tender peck at her temple, and my insides melt a little. *My sister's getting married!* "I'm so happy for you two!" I cry, and my voice cracks with a sledgehammer full of emotions.

"Is that Lucy?"

I hear a familiar voice at the same time both Nat and Hayden look over their shoulders. They lean toward the outer edges of the screen as Hayden's old roommate, Dexter, pokes his head in between them.

"Hey there, stranger," he calls in that low, throaty voice of his that can keep chocolate in a constant state of gooey softness.

The screen starts to wiggle, looking like Nat's laptop is being moved from its current position to elsewhere. I can see the entire span of the room, parts of the ceiling, and what looks like a blurred kitchen sink before the movement stops and I see Dexter, his hands braced against a countertop with a lopsided—and pleased—smile.

"How are you?"

I lightly scoff, turning my face away before letting a smile slip. Dexter's tongue pokes out and swipes across his lower lip, and that smile I couldn't hold back is joined by an eye roll. "I'm good, Dexter." My voice loses all of the sweetness and bounce it carried when I was talking to my sister.

"You changed your hair."

My hand lifts, my fingers raking through my short hair, a vast difference from when it was a shade darker than blonde and almost at elbow length when I first met him three years ago. Now, I've gone back to my natural dark color and had it cut to a near bob, stopping just above my shoulders.

"The bleached hair was getting a bit much to manage," I explain.

"It suits you." The corners of his mouth curl upward, and his eyes narrow in on mine, as if there isn't a screen and thousands of miles between us.

That smile, the one that says, *I know what you look like when you come,* is enough to make my mind spiral in about ten different directions. Sure, he knows what I look like when a body-rattling orgasm rips through me. And sure, I know the sounds he makes when a similar sensation tears through him too. But that was ages ago—three years, to be exact.

I lower my voice, leaning a little closer toward the screen. "Thank you, Dexter," I whisper, unsure of where my sister and her fiancé are. Whether they're standing elbow to elbow with Dexter or in the other room, I can't chance them hearing the guilt and secrecy oozing from my voice.

"What are the odds that I'd be here, visiting my old roommate, when you happened to be talking to Nat?" he teases, his chin resting in the palm of his hand. "Seems like fate had plans for us." His voice isn't hushed or discreet like mine. In fact, it's the complete opposite. He might as well have a sign taped to his back that says I'VE SLEPT WITH THIS WOMAN.

"Can I get my sister back, *please*?"

I jump at the same time I see Nat's thoroughly irritated face from the corner of the screen. Her small hands fling over him as his shoulder lifts to fight her off.

Dexter slaps her hand away. "We're talking."

"We were talking first!" Nat argues. I see her hand coming out from behind Dexter's waist to finally get a grip on the laptop before it's snatched out from under him. The screen starts to shake, and I get a close up of Nat's chin and nostrils. She walks into the only room in her small New York City apartment and closes the door behind her before sinking into an unmade bed. "Ugh, finally!"

"What's Dexter doing there anyway?" I ask, hoping I sound nonchalant. Maybe I should tack on a question about the weather or mention the random Yahoo! News article I read about the dangers of skipping your nightly floss routine to hide my impatient curiosity.

"I think he misses Hayden," she answers. She takes a quick peek over her shoulder. "He won't say it, but after Hayden moved out of his place, he's been randomly popping his head around here. I think he feels a little lonely even though he says he likes his privacy. Says he's been walking around naked a lot." She cringes.

"Oh." That's a little...*sad*. "So..."

"So?"

I roll my eyes. "Nat! You're engaged!"

She laughs, tilting a shoulder toward her cheek. "Miss blushing bride."

"I know it's only been a few days, but any plans for the big day?"

She sits up straighter, her hands splayed in front of her with her game face on. "Nothing official yet. But..." She pauses. "We're thinking Hawaii."

"Hawaii?!"

She nods. "Hayden's aunt has connections with the hotel she manages in Indiana, so we can get a pretty good deal on the venue and rooms. And we thought it would be nice to have a honeymoon doing a little island hopping. Plus, it's the perfect excuse to keep the wedding small. I don't want to make a big ol' fuss about it, and this way, we only invite the few people willing to make the trip."

I smile endearingly. "That actually sounds kind of perfect."

"Right? It'll give us a chance to take a nice vacation together. You, me, and Carmen."

"Yeah."

"I miss the three of us just hanging out," she adds. "I hardly see Carmen anymore since I moved out. And the only time I get to see your face is during these FaceTime calls."

"Has Carmen been picking up extra shifts again?" I ask, curious about our oldest sister, who's a quick trip across the bridge away from Nat.

She nods. "It's always something with that hospital. If they aren't short-staffed, then there's some big trauma that keeps her long past her shift."

I laugh. "Helping sick people. It's almost like Dr. Marquez signed up for it."

"I know, I know. I shouldn't be complaining. She's, you know, doctor-ing. But I just miss *us*."

"I miss you guys too," I tell her, wishing I could place a reassuring hand on her arm through the screen.

"How are things in Seattle?" she asks, her face lifting through a sad smile.

"They're fine," I tell her. "You know, same same."

"Are you at work?"

I peer over my shoulder, looking at the wall behind me bedecked with various coffee-related decor. A hand-drawn image of coffee beans to my right. A cross-stitched frame with the words "More Espresso, Less Depresso" to my left. "Yep, I'm on my break."

"And you chose to spend your ten minutes of freedom with *me*?" she asks with a sweet smile.

I laugh. "You said it was urgent," I tell her. "So what did Mom and Dad say? I bet Mom already set an appointment to go dress shopping with you. You better get out the tissues."

She rolls her eyes. "They're next," she answers. "And don't remind me. I love Mom to pieces, but her dramatics can be *so* over the top sometimes."

"Hmm," I hum, tapping my finger to my chin. "I wonder if that's where you get *your* dramatics from?"

"I am *not* dramatic," she tells me. "I'm just…*expressive*."

"Sure."

"Have you talked to Mom recently?" she asks.

"A few days ago," I tell her. "She told me about this job listing in my area she found off Craigslist. Who still uses Craigslist?"

"Mom, apparently."

I scoff. "C'yeah. Anyway," I continue, "as soon as I read 'must be bilingual in Farsi and English,' I deleted the email she sent me. I don't even think she reads the job description at this point. As long as they're in Seattle, she just zips them my way."

Nat laughs before her smile fades. "I talked to her last week. She, uh, mentioned something about an internship?"

My entire body freezes. "What?"

"I mean, she didn't go into detail, but she just briefly said you told her about it last month? From UW? She said you wanted to apply, but she convinced you it might not be the best idea right now."

"Oh, that," I say, holding back the deep sigh of relief from my chest. "Um, yeah. It was this internship at a photography agency. They're handling this huge ad campaign and filling some of the entry-level positions with interns. UW sent me the email to apply since I'm an alumni, but…whatever."

"That wasn't even your major," she points out.

I nod. "I know," I say, brushing off the tightness in my throat with indifference. "But I took some art electives in grad school, just for fun, I guess, so I think they thought I might be interested." I start to gnaw on my lower lip, hoping my nonchalance is believable.

She nods. "You know, she's just worried about you. After you got fired last year, she's focused on you finding a job. You know, like a *real* one. No offense."

I wince, recalling the sit-down I had with Ted from Human Resources informing me I was being "let go" from the marketing agency I'd been working at for two years, blaming the mass layoff on budget cuts and the current economic climate. I thought I was getting a raise or a promotion for all of my hard work. Or even a new desk chair. Not a cardboard box to fill with the contents of my desk. And I certainly didn't think those months of unemployment following my walk of shame out of the office would lead me right to Mr. Bean's Coffee and Tea and the bright Help Wanted sign in the window. "I know," I tell her.

"She said she doesn't want you getting your hopes up on an internship with no promise of a secure job. At least for now, you have Mr. Bean's. She doesn't want you to give *that* up since…you know, there isn't much else right now."

"Yeah, she—she said that." I couldn't disagree with my mom. But still, her reaction shocked me. My mom, and my dad, *never* tried to snuff whatever dreams and ambitions my sisters and I held in our hearts. When Nat wanted to take up figure skating at eight years old, my parents bought her her first pair of ice skates, only for her to ditch the dream of joining the next Winter Olympics a month later. They never got upset, always reminding us we don't know what we want until we at least try.

But this was different. Too much was on the line. My livelihood, my future. The stakes were higher. I wasn't sixteen, carrying around my high school yearbook department's loaner camera to take candid pictures of the student body. I wasn't in college, taking a few photography courses to see if it was something more than just a hobby while finishing my graduate degree. I couldn't be haughty or reckless about my future anymore.

"And, you know, maybe she's right." Nat pauses, reading the sullen dejection on my face as she tries to soften the blow with her gentle voice and cautious words. "I know you've always been into this whole photography thing, but maybe you can do that on the side. And if an opportunity like that comes up again, you'll be in a better place to take it."

But an opportunity like that doesn't come up every day.

Which is why I applied for it. Against my mom's wishes. With a big fat lie slapped on my face. Right alongside the emails from her and my sister backing my mom with heed and reason.

I didn't think I'd get it. In fact, I assumed the mass email informing University of Washington students and alumni about the internship was more spam related instead of a purposeful and thought-out offer. But it wasn't. And even though the extent of my photography experience in college was nothing beyond a few photography courses with a brief conversation with the professor about my art career, it was enough to get me in. And now, I'm starting on Monday, bright and early. In New York City, of all places.

There's banging on the door through the screen, followed by a light jump from Nat and a set of loose giggles. "And there's my fiancé's boyfriend. I better go before Dexter flings my laptop across the room." The door swings open just then, and Dexter hurdles toward Nat. "Dexter!"

The timer I set on my phone for my break dings just as the screen goes blank.

"Lucy."

I look up from the small round table I settled at to call Nat and Hayden to see Mr. Bean, the owner of Mr. Bean's Coffee and Tea, leaning over the counter to get my attention. "I have to leave a little early," he tells me. "You'll be okay until Vanessa gets here?"

"Sure." I shove my phone into my back pocket, rounding the counter where the glass display and register sits, and take the next

17

customer in line. I ring a few people up, pour various types of espresso drinks into disposable cups, and keep a watchful eye on the pastries in case I need to place a small Sold Out placard on the display. When the line dies down, giving me a moment to breathe, I reach for my phone in my pocket and open what I like to call my Anxiety Support Checklist on my notes app.

Email Elevate Media with the last of the HR paperwork before I start on Monday morning. Check.

Confirm my flight for Saturday at eleven a.m. out of Seattle International to JFK. Check.

Email the property manager for my new rental in Brooklyn to confirm the time of my arrival. Check.

Avoid running into my sisters while living in Brooklyn for three months.

Maybe if I invested in a wig or those thick-framed glasses with a plastic nose and mustache, I can check that one off. Spirit Halloween is open year-round, right? Or maybe I can order one off Amazon.

It's in the bag. A flimsy one full of holes and a broken strap, but a bag nonetheless.

With the late afternoon lull in customer traffic, my tasks dwindle down to restocking wooden coffee stirrers and sugar packets with the sporadic flow of customer traffic. Vanessa finally walks in close to four, looking a little frazzled.

"Hey," she says with an exhale. "Sorry I'm late." She ducks her head to fasten her apron around her neck before clocking in.

"No worries." I finish refilling the napkins and turn to her. "Mr. Bean took off. Something about his parrot's vet appointment."

"Maybe he'll finally get him to stop singing 'Rocket Man.'" We share a giggle before she adds, "You all ready for the Big Apple?"

"Physically? Almost. I just have a few things left to pack. Mentally? No."

She laughs. "Is one of your sisters meeting you when you get there?"

"Uh, no," I tell her hesitantly. "They, um, they don't know."

Vanessa jerks her head in my direction. "You didn't tell them?"

I shake my head.

"Why not?"

"I don't know," I tell her with a deep sigh. "I thought about it, but my mom already didn't want me to apply for this internship. I don't want them to accidentally slip and tell my mom. And I don't want them to lie to her either." I pause to look at her with a sad puppy dog face. "And I talked to Nat earlier. She thinks my mom's right. She said it's probably a good idea that I didn't apply for it. Thinks I'll just get my hopes up or something." I bury my face into my hands. Even my sister thinks this internship is a bad idea.

"Hey." I look up from my hands, and Vanessa has her chin in her palms, her elbows braced on the countertop, and her bright blue eyes peering up at me. "Just go and kill it. Break a leg or whatever. Worry about all of that family drama bullshit later."

I smile, though my lips immediately turn upside down into a sad pout. Vanessa stands upright and clicks away at the register before it opens with a heavy clunk. She lifts the drawer tray, where a large white envelope with my name is buried under a mess of invoices, and carefully plucks it out and slides it my way. "Let's hope this is the last time you get one of these from Mr. Bean."

I glide my fingers over my last check. "Fingers crossed."

4

Dexter

I'M speed walking through the busy streets of Manhattan, hurriedly dodging people left and right before I come to a stop in front of Buca's, my sister's favorite Italian restaurant. I didn't realize what time it was when I left Hayden's apartment, and now I have barely enough time to spare to make it to dinner with Janet and her boyfriend, Charles.

As soon as I walk in, I see them huddled over a table for four, the low candlelight making their faces glow under the dim light. Janet sees me and waves me over.

"We just ordered a bottle," Janet informs me, gesturing toward the freshly uncorked bottle of merlot and standing briefly to hug me. Charles stands too, shaking my hand before the three of us take our seats.

"Happy birthday, sis."

"Thanks, Dex." I watch as my big sister leans into her boyfriend of two years. He presses his cheek into her temple before turning to kiss her hairline. "Were you just getting off work? It's a little late."

I shake my head. "I was at Hayden's."

She smiles. "Have they made any plans for their wedding?"

"He briefly mentioned Hawaii," I answer. "But they just got

engaged last week. Plus, Hayden's pretty busy with the restaurant, and they're just barely settling into their new place."

"Well, I'm sure whatever they plan, it'll be nice. Natalia is going to make such a beautiful bride."

"Yeah," I say, casting an endearing smile in her direction.

The way she talks about one of my oldest friends and his fiancée makes my insides feel a little warm and fuzzy. She talks about him in the same way one would talk about a beloved relative. Like when a cousin gets into an Ivy League college. Or when an adventurous aunt goes on a cruise and ends up getting food poisoning from the all-you-can-eat lobster buffet.

When Hayden moved into my apartment three years ago, after my previous roommate up and left, leaving me high and dry with no one to handle his half of the rent, it became a different type of living situation with me and him. One that differed from the standard roommate/roommate affiliation. Our friendship and past, one that rooted back to our freshman year of college, made me realize how much I lacked those types of conversations with Janet. My sister and I didn't have family gossip to catch up on. We didn't have parents to come home to, ones who should be sitting at this very table with us, showering Janet with tacky greeting cards—the kind that sings when you open them—and an over-dramatized rendition of the traditional happy birthday song.

Instead, Janet and I used to catch up on our latest TV show obsession, usually something like *Supernatural* or *Peaky Blinders* for me and *Big Bang Theory* or *The Bachelor* for her. We discussed the weather ("Why is it so warm this February?") or work-related mishaps ("I swear, if Greasy Gavin steals another one of my pens, I'm going to report him to HR"). We didn't meander through family updates or relative gossip over brunch because we didn't *have* any family members to update on.

But now, we have Hayden. We have Hayden and Nat and their wedding and Hayden's restaurant and all of the in between that Janet asks about. We have family updates.

Our dinner continues, and at the end, a small strawberry cake with fresh cream arrives at our table, a single white candle lit at the center of it. We make a show of singing "Happy Birthday" to Janet, topped off with out-of-tune choruses and big hand gestures, before she takes a deep breath to blow out the candle.

Charles and I clap, quietly cheering on Janet as she smiles shyly.

"What did you wish for?" I ask, picking at the candle, now dripping with cooled wax, the burned tip of the wick letting off a ribbon of smoke.

"That the cake is as good as it looks," she answers smugly. She's interrupted by a fit of coughs she tries to cover. Charles's hand moves to her back, rubbing soothing circles between her shoulders before she reaches into her purse for an inhaler. She brings it to her mouth and squeezes out two puffs while taking in a deep inhale before tucking it back into her purse.

"Since when do you use an inhaler?" I ask, taking a sip of the remaining red wine in my glass.

"Since two weeks ago," she answers, picking up a fork to pick at her dessert. "I've been having some trouble breathing and this cough that won't go away, so I went to the doctor, and they prescribed me this for now."

"For now?" I ask. "Is there something else going on?"

"She's going to run some more tests," Janet explains. "It shouldn't be anything serious. She said it's most likely just a respiratory infection. It's probably from all the air-conditioned air at the gallery."

"Janet," I say, unable to hide the disappointment in my tone. "Why didn't you tell me?"

"That I have a cold?" she teases with a small scowl and an incredulous tilt of her head. "It's really not that serious."

I turn to Charles, silently pleading for him to take my side. Instead, he laughs it off. "She's taking care of herself," he says, wrapping his arm around her shoulders. "I'm making sure of it."

"See?" Janet chimes. "I'm in good hands. You don't need to worry."

I scowl before schooling my features, being careful to not come off as annoyed or rude, but the simple fact is that I *am* worried. I will *always* worry about her. Just the way she always worries about me.

"Would it help if I tell you that I haven't used this inhaler in four days?"

I shrug, rolling my eyes with a surrendering, "Sure."

"You know, I was filling out the paperwork at the doctor's office, and they have this long section asking about family history," she says, leaning forward as if she's telling me a secret. "And I realized I have no idea."

"What did it ask?"

"Just the standard stuff. Like if I have a family history of asthma, diabetes, high blood pressure, cancer." She pauses, glancing down at the stained tablecloth and the light bouncing off the handle of her fork. "I felt kinda dumb not knowing. You know?" she says, her voice sounding low and morose.

"Hey," I urge softly, calling for her attention. "It's not your fault you don't know. I don't know either."

She responds with a weak smile.

"But I think Grandpa had shingles when I was nine. I remember Mom told us we couldn't visit the summer before fourth grade because he was contagious."

Her smile deepens. "I don't think that's the kind of information they were looking for, but I'll keep that in mind the next time a genetic-slash-lineage related question arises. Maybe for my eHarmony profile."

"Hey!" Charles interjects, looking wounded.

Janet pecks a swift kiss on Charles's cheek. "I meant for when you're tired of me and want to date someone without a family history of shingles."

5

Lucy

SEATTLE HAS BEEN my home for almost five years. I took a year off after I finished my undergrad back home at Ohio State before I moved out to Seattle for grad school. I've made friends here, mostly grad school friends who were roommates and classmates, including Annabelle, who is still my roommate. I have a regular Starbucks I go to that knows exactly how I like my complicated caramel macchiato order and a mom-and-pop ice cream shop that sells my favorite mango-flavored sorbet.

I haven't left, aside from an occasional trip back home or to visit my sisters in New York City, and I can't complain. Which means leaving my home for three months is going to be a bit of an adjustment. There's going to be a lot of missing my friends, Annabelle's cat Jeremy, and the mango sorbet I can't find anywhere else.

"To Lucy," Annabelle calls, our shot glasses of tequila held over the bar top at Bottoms Up, the dingy dive bar a twelve-minute Uber ride away from our apartment.

"To Lucy!" Margo repeats, another UW survivor who joined me and Annabelle in the ranks as we drudged through a semester of organic chemistry before we tossed our caps in the air at graduation.

"To Lucy!" Alma, Annabelle's sister, chimes in. Alma snuck into our little friend group a year ago after she moved out to The Emerald City all the way from Texas following a rough breakup. Though she shot down Annabelle's offer to move in with us, claiming she didn't want to go back to the days when Annabelle stole her clothes and they fought over the TV remote, she spends most evenings on our couch, joining me and Annabelle for takeout while trash talking her ex.

The three of them smile brightly in my direction.

"Mmm!" Alma exclaims through pursed lips. "Another round!"

I hold up my hand in her direction and carefully place my hand on her bare shoulder, where the strands of her lusciously bouncy curls brush against my hand. Seriously, I don't know what kind of witchcraft she uses to get her hair that full and shiny. "Why don't we take it slow?"

"Nuh-uh," she argues, twisting at her waist to face me. "Nothing about tonight is going to be slow."

"I agree," Margo adds, the flush spreading over her deeply freckled face, making her look younger than her twenty-six years of age. "And you definitely dressed for the occasion, so we gotta take advantage."

I peer down at my dress, the silky green material swishing against my soft skin and the short hem barely reaching mid-thigh. I'd almost forgotten I had it. But when I pulled it out from the deep corner of my closet while I packed the last of my belongings into my large suitcase, the dress and the last memory I have when I wore it came rushing back.

"And I did not squeeze my big ass hips into this dress for us to 'take it easy.'" I look at Annabelle, her hands smoothing out her tight dress that clings to her like a second layer of skin, with an exasperated, pleading look. "I told you on the way over here," Annabelle adds breezily, ignoring my silent plea. "We're sending you off with a bang."

I roll my eyes. I should have known. These girls would never send me off with anything other than a night of binge drinking and the hangover of the century.

Another round of tequila is passed around, and we all take our glasses.

Annabelle raises her glass and stifles a laugh. "This one is to Lucy finding a hot man out in New York City who'll sweep her off her feet to his fancy penthouse and hand over his black Amex so she can spend all of his hot CEO money." She pauses to bring the glass to her lips. "Oh!" she exclaims before adding, "And takes her to his secret sex room to tie her up with his *sex* ropes and *sex* handcuffs."

I cackle. "*Oh-kaaay*, Miss Fifty Shades."

She shrugs. "What beats a sweaty fuck fest in a high rise with floor-to-ceiling windows on the large glass desk in his corner office because he can't wait to get you home to fuck you into oblivion on his ginormous king-size bed?"

"That is crazy specific," Alma comments, a look of disgust mixed with a hint of curiosity on her face. She quickly adjusts her neon pink dress that makes her stand out against the warm golden tone of her glowing skin before collecting all of our empty shot glasses.

Annabelle sighs. "Not specific enough."

I stifle a giggle.

"It just doesn't beat the real feel of a man's rough hands on your naked body," Annabelle adds wistfully. "To be manhandled? And fucking *dominated*?!"

"Okay!" Margo screeches, ducking her head and eyeing the growing crowd around us. "Why don't we save the sex talk for when we aren't in such a public space?"

We all fall silent.

"So what do we talk about?" Alma asks in a low voice.

A howl of laughter rips through the four of us.

"Okay, okay," I say, cutting into our laughter. "How about we talk in code?"

"All right," Annabelle agrees through a lime wedge in her mouth. She pulls the squeezed citrus from her lips. "I just want some sexy, six-foot-five-inch, two-hundred-and-sixty-pound man meat to...'squeeze' me." She lifts her wrung-out lime wedge in the air.

"It's been such a long time since I've been squeezed," I say, adding a small frown to the deep sigh ending my sentence.

"I believe I was squeezed two weeks ago," Alma adds. "Although, I wouldn't necessarily consider that squeezed. Maybe...pinched?" She holds her thumb and index finger in front of her, pressing them together with a look of disappointment on her face. "I want to be wrung out with not a single drop of liquid left in me. Like a chamois."

A look of forlornness glazes over our faces, mixing with the alcoholic haze buzzing through us.

The last time I was properly "squeezed" was three years ago.

I must have said that out loud because three sets of shocked eyes and gaping mouths are facing my direction.

"Three years?!" Annabelle screeches.

"You haven't had sex in three years?" Margo asks, lowering her voice.

"No, I mean, I-I've done *stuff*...I just..." I stutter.

"Three years?!" Annabelle repeats.

"With who?" I turn to Alma, who's waiting for my answer.

"What do you mean?" I ask, playing a little dumb at the same time a warmth starts to trail up my cheeks from that second tequila shot.

"Who 'squeezed' you three years ago?"

"Oh, no, not squeezed. I was properly wrung out." I giggle. "In fact...it's safe to say it was the best sex of my life."

Margo grips my arm. "Do we know him? Was it one of those douchey frat boy types from school? Or was it someone from your old work?"

"And more importantly, can we call him right now? Because you definitely need a repeat. *Three years*?!" Annabelle shrieks.

"He doesn't even live here." I wave my hand in their direction, assuring them a reunion isn't possible tonight. "He lives in New York."

"And how did this wringing out happen?"

"I met him when I was visiting my sister."

"So it was a one-night stand?"

"Uh, I guess?"

No one says anything, and I suddenly feel a little embarrassed. Is three years really that long? With my focus on finishing grad school, the shock of getting fired, and surviving on the basis that my life has felt so empty for the last year, mind-blowing sex was the last thing on my mind. And so far from reach, I might add.

"Can we talk about something else?"

"Yes," Margo answers. She reaches for my arm and gives me a reassuring squeeze. "How about more tequila?"

"Please," I say, suddenly wanting to forget how much I want to be wrung out by a specific someone.

6

Dexter

IT'S BEEN ABOUT three months since Hayden moved out. After a few years of Natalia coming and going from her place to ours, making herself comfortable while strolling around the apartment in Hayden's clothes, they were finally ready to find a place of their own. And while it's been nice to have a little bit of privacy until I find a new roommate, it gets a little quiet sometimes. A little too empty and cold, even in the heavy summer heat.

I'm sitting on my couch, filling the frigid silence with the TV volume on low and a televised showing of *World War Z* flashing on the screen while I mindlessly scroll through my phone. I stop when I see an Instagram story Lucy posted a mere thirty-eight minutes ago.

The same Lucy I saw earlier through a fifteen-inch laptop screen while my eyes glazed over her sideways scowl and sassy smirk.

The same Lucy I can't seem to expunge from my memory, no matter how many lousy first dates and Hinge setups I go on.

In the short video, Lucy is tossing back a small shot glass, her friends cheering around her. She screeches in a slurred voice, "*Squeeeeze* me, baby!" before everyone in the video breaks out into a fit of hysterical laughter. There's a series of stories from her night out, and it looks like she and her friends are celebrating something. I stop when

I see a five second snapshot of her in a green dress. It's the same green dress I met her in. I remember it because of how it draped across her thighs, the silky fabric brushing against her tanned and toned skin. She wore heels, and with her height, it brought her at eye level with me. Meaning, when we stood a little too close to each other, our mouths sat parallel. And if I'd angled my jaw a little to the right when her nose tilted in the opposite direction, we would've fit perfectly.

When I met her three years ago, I didn't think she could look sexier than she did in that green dress. But now, with her short hair baring her smooth shoulders and the dark color contrasting too well against her skin tone...she looks fucking stunning. It's an impulsive move when I tap on the message icon and hover my thumbs over the keyboard.

That dress looks familiar.

It's flirty and suggestive and a little dangerous considering I'm talking about more than just a simple dress. So much more.

It's just past two in the morning, which means the night is still young in Seattle. Which also means she may still be out, and she might see the message. Or maybe she won't even notice it until the morning when whatever remains of that liquid courage has seeped out of her, and she'll just ignore the message altogether.

My wondering is answered approximately seven minutes later when my phone buzzes in my hand with an incoming call from Lucy.

"Dexter!" I hear Lucy's slurred voice call through the phone. "So you like my dress?"

My brow quirks. So she's a little drunk. "Hi, Lucy," I call through the phone, my voice low and raspy.

"I don't think I've ever told you how *good* it is to hear the sound of your voice."

Okay, maybe she's a *lot* drunk. "You like the sound of my voice?"

"Can you keep a secret?" she whispers in a hushed tone instead of answering my question. I instinctively lean forward like I need to cup my ear to hear her better. "I have not had a good lay since you."

I sit up from my slouched position with my elbows resting on my knees. I should hang up. I should remind her how drunk she is, tell her she should call me when she's sober so she doesn't say things that make my insides tingle. *Jesus*, the tingling.

Why the fuck is there two thousand miles of distance between us? Why am I here? And why the fuck is she *there*?

"And why is that? Why can't I seem to get you out of my head?" she continues. "Instead, my options are narrowed down to my vibrator or these boys who can't even tell the difference between a good sneeze and an orgasm."

I stifle a laugh. She won't remember a single word of this conversation. Hell, she might not even remember calling me, but this is so much fun. While the miniature angel sitting on my shoulder coaxes me to do the right thing by giving me firm instructions to tell her good night like a gentleman would, its devil counterpart sitting on the opposite shoulder is egging me on. *Ask her why you're such a good lay*, it urges. And I almost want to give in. I almost want to hop on Google and type in "flights NYC to Seattle now."

"Lucy! Get off the phone! We're getting chicken wings!"

Lucy answers whoever she's talking to, hopefully one of her friends who'll get her home safe, with a high-pitched squeal and an elongated "*waaaaangs!*" And the line cuts.

She can't get me out of her head.

31

7

Lucy

MY STOMACH FEELS like the green blob from the movie *Flubber* has taken residence at the pit of it and it's trying to climb up my throat. I lift my head off my pillow only to be welcomed with the sight of my tumbled heels on the floor, right next to a small heap of green satin.

"Ughhh…" I moan, just as my alarm goes off. The fact that I have to be out the door by eight in the morning with all of my luggage stuffed into Annabelle's BMW causes the blob in my stomach to tumble. What was I thinking?

I drag myself off my bed and trudge to the kitchen, where Annabelle is shuffling two mugs on the counter next to a fresh pot of coffee.

"How are you up already?" I ask, walking past her to the fridge for a bottle of water.

She pokes a finger in my direction. "While you girls drank yourself silly, I stopped after the third tequila shot. There's no way I would've been able to drive you to the airport if I didn't."

She extends a mug to me, and I sigh with relief. It's not my usual Starbucks, but the toasty aroma of coffee is more than enough to shoo away my hangover, just a little bit.

I slump onto the barstool lined up against our breakfast counter. "How much did we drink?"

"I lost count after your guys' fourth round."

"I think I counted six and a half before the rest of the night became a blur." I slouch forward, burying my face into my hands. "Did I compare an orgasm to a sneeze?"

She laughs, taking a quick sip of her coffee. "I have no recollection of that."

A loud, grumbly groan sounds through my lips.

"I ordered something from the twenty-four-hour diner on seventeenth. I just got you an omelet."

"Oh, that sounds amazing." I lift my head up and smile at Annabelle. "What would I do without you?"

"Well, you're going to find out."

A deep frown tugs the corners of my lips downward. I'm going to miss Annabelle. I'm going to miss my girls. Our weekend brunches, late-night charcuterie parties complete with a chocolate fountain and pent-up gossip, and even the occasional mishap. Like when Jeremy got out through the balcony and the four of us spent the entire night practically scaling the building looking for him.

Who am I going to spend my weekends with for three months?

I certainly can't call up my sisters for a girls' night. Not when all I can see is Nat's face, looking at me like she pitied me while I lied to her, telling her this internship wasn't a big deal when it absolutely was. I downplayed the importance of it because she wouldn't understand. Because I didn't know how to tell her I'm willing to take the risks of leaving my secure job at Mr. Bean's for something that has a high probability of ending with nothing but three months of experience and still no job prospects. Or even worse, everyone there would tell me I didn't belong, and I should go back to taking heavily filtered images of aesthetically pleasing backdrops and Jeremy sleeping.

"You okay?" Annabelle asks when I've been staring into my coffee mug for a long stretch of silence.

"Yeah," I say with a sad face. "I guess I'm really nervous. This is so far beyond my comfort zone, and I'm worried I'll be in over my head. Plus, I'm going to really miss you guys." Jeremy chooses that moment to hop onto the kitchen counter, a place he is definitely not allowed. Neither Annabelle nor I shoo him off. Instead, I run a hand over this back as he arches into my touch. "And this little guy. I'm going miss him the most."

"Hey." Annabelle looks at me with kind, sympathetic eyes. "We've been over this. You got selected over hundreds of applicants. They didn't choose you with some random eeny, meeny, miny, moe name draw. There was a reason you got in." She pauses to firmly grip my hand. "Three months is going to fly by, and you're going to come back and become the next Annie Leibovitz."

I laugh and cast a grateful smile in her direction. "Seriously, what am I going to do without you?"

Annabelle is zipping through I-5 on the wet concrete of the highway with the bright early morning sun peeking through the clouds and hitting the streets like hundreds of beaming spotlights.

"You have everything?" Annabelle asks, switching lanes to bypass a slow-moving Jetta.

I nod, gnawing at the skin lining my thumb and peering down at my phone. "I just transferred you the money for rent," I explain, pressing the final transfer button on my banking app after confirming the balance on my account. "I'll transfer the rest when I get paid next month."

"It's such a godsend this internship is paid," she says, facing the windshield.

"Tell me about it," I answer, taking a quick peek inside my tote to make sure the plane ticket I'd printed out hadn't mysteriously disappeared since I tucked it in there two days ago. "And that Elevate helped me find a place with a steal of a rental agreement."

"It's another reason you were meant to do this."

"Yeah," I huff in agreement.

I want to tell her that all of that's bullshit. Fate or whatever the hell destiny or kismet is supposed to mean. Because none of that crap has ever worked in my favor. Or maybe it has but not in the way it's supposed to. Like getting fired from my fancy corporate job was a sign that I should be slinging espressos and baked goods for the rest of my life. Or that this internship was just an opportunity for failure to remind me of what my true fate is: behind the register at Mr. Bean's.

She pulls up to the curb to the terminal entrance to gate number four. We silently exit, and I grab a luggage cart before Annabelle helps me load it.

With my hand gripped on the metal handle, I turn to Annabelle. "Send me lots of pictures of Jeremy."

"I will," she says, pulling me into a big hug. "Have a safe flight. And maybe splurge on a vodka mix. A little hair of the dog might help."

I scrunch my face. "I'll stick with water," I answer, pulling away. "And maybe a bag of pretzels."

We both turn to face the entrance at the same time the glass doors slide open. "I'm really doing this, aren't I?"

"You sure are."

I face her one last time.

"You got this."

I nod. "I got this."

I give a sad little sigh in Annabelle's direction and walk into the airport. After an hour-long wait at the check-in counter and the glaring stare from the not so friendly TSA officer at the metal detector, I finally get to my gate. Once I'm there, I settle with a loud huff into a seat, tucking my carry-on bags close to me so they're not in the way of foot traffic.

I have my phone in my hand, aimlessly scrolling through my social media feeds, when it buzzes in my hand. "MOM" in big, scary, bold letters flashes across the screen.

"Hello?" I answer warily.

"Did I catch you at work?" I guess there's no need for formalities like *Hi, how are you?* when you're talking to your parents.

"Uh, no. I'm—it's my day off, Mom."

"Have you talked to Natalia recently?"

"Yeah, I talked to her last night."

"So you heard?" she exclaims. I can hear the excitement in her voice, her using a monumental amount of restraint to avoid ruining the news if it hadn't made it to my ears just yet.

I can't help the warmth spreading through my chest that has me smiling. "Yeah, she told me."

She squeals into the phone, and I truly can't remember the last time I spoke to her on the phone and she sounded this excited. It seems every time we talk, it's about how job searching is coming along or to tell me where to add "good at communicating" on my resume to make it stand out to future employers more. "I'm so happy for her!" she says giddily. I can almost picture her feet making a small hop and her fingers waving wildly in front of her.

"Me too," I answer with a smile. "Hayden's really amazing."

"I'm so proud of him too," she adds. "He's been doing so much with the restaurant, and now that they've moved in together and they're engaged, it's just so perfect for them."

"Yeah, I'm really happy for them."

"How are things with you? Did you get my email?" she blurts, abruptly changing the subject. "It was for that job listing near your place. I think they were holding a job fair next week." The shift in her voice is so apparent, I want to go back to talking about my sister when my mom sounded happier and carefree.

"Yeah, I got it," I answer, holding back the disheartened sigh rising in my chest. "I'll check it out."

"Good," she answers contently. "It sounded pretty promising. They had plenty of openings and—"

A loud and really difficult to disguise announcement sounds on the intercom. I panic-press the buttons on my phone, slamming my thumb across the screen in an attempt to mute the call before I bring it back to my ear.

"—and it's pretty close to you so you don't have to worry about a long commute."

I sigh. *She didn't hear it.* "Thanks, Mom," I finally answer after the announcement has passed and I unmute my phone. "I'll let you know how it goes."

"Okay," she answers softly and a little defeated.

I feel like the biggest pile of disappointment in the world. Why can't I just do something right in my life? Why can't I do something my parents could be proud of instead of slabbing on worry after worry onto their already full plates? Instead, we have to share phone calls about job hunts and resumes and whether or not I'll be able to pay rent next month. When will I be the one to shower her with good news like Nat?

"And, Lucy, I'm really glad you decided not to apply for that internship," she adds. My body freezes, and I hold my breath. "I don't mean to bring it up again, but I want you to keep your focus on finding a job. You know, internships aren't really promising. You'll probably end up getting coffee all day instead of doing actual work, and I don't want that for you. Maybe if you were still in college or something, but you're almost thirty now. You shouldn't be wasting your time doing grunt work for something so temporary. You're so much better than that."

"Yeah," I answer with a weak, dejected voice. "I get it, Mom. It's fine."

"I love you, baby. I just want what's best for you."

"I, um, have to go," I finally say after a long pause. My voice cracks, and I try to disguise it through a rough throat clearing. "I'll call you soon."

"Sure," she answers, her voice a little lighter. "I'll email you again if I find any more job leads."

"Yeah, thanks, Mom." I pause before adding, "And I love you too."

I hang up and grip my phone in my hand, hoping all of this—the internship, the fruitless job searches, the sporadic calls from my mom asking me about those job searches in a forced optimistic voice, attempting to sound supportive instead of worried—will all change.

8

Lucy

WHEN I ARRIVE AT JFK, I make quick work to gather my luggage and snag a cab. The forty-five-minute cab ride turns into an hour and a half with unexpected road closures and the expected rush hour traffic. The cab comes to a stop in front of a tall five-story brownstone, where there's a short flight of stairs leading up to a maroon-colored door with brass hardware that looks dull and rusted. I huff a sigh before lifting the retractable handles to my bags and dragging them up the stairs.

"You need some help?" I hear someone call.

When I turn to look over my shoulder, I see a man dressed in semi-casual business attire and a pair of hunter green loafers, sans socks, walking toward the same building I'm about to enter.

"Oh," I answer through a controlled breath, already winded from the first three steps. "I'm fine. Thank you."

"Well, let me at least get the door for you," he says, walking around me to the entrance. I make it up the final steps and angle my luggage to fit through the frame. I give a purse-lipped smile before looking at the narrow stairs, catching another glimpse of the too hard to miss green shoes and bare ankles below cropped dress pants. *Ugh,* that is such a weird fashion trend.

"Elevator's out," No Socks comments, adding insult to injury as he continues to watch me struggle.

I sigh. "Thanks," I deadpan.

He opens his mouth at the same time a small smile tips up the corners of his mouth when we're interrupted by a low thud. The door we just entered through reopens with a bang. A man who looks to be about four-foot-ten-inches tall waddles through the door and peers up at me. His eyes scatter over my luggage.

"Hi, Horace," No Socks calls.

"Gary," Horace mumbles. "I'm not here to make small talk. I had to rush here to meet a new tenant. Unless you need the downstairs shower drain snaked again."

"Uh, no. I'm good, Horace."

Horace harrumphs and fumbles with a set of keys on a large key ring.

I glance over at No Socks—or Gary, I guess—and my mouth suddenly feels dry.

"You don't happen to be the new tenant?" he asks, gesturing toward my luggage and my haggard appearance.

"I'm afraid so," I say in a low whisper.

At the same time Gary lets out a small smirk, Horace grumbles, "You Lucia?"

"Lucy," I correct.

He doesn't acknowledge my answer. Instead, he starts trudging up the steps with no indication for me to follow. But taking his lack of social cues and just general social indecency, I grab my luggage and follow.

"I'll see you around, Lucia." I look over my shoulder and get one last glimpse of Gary disappearing down a hallway.

After we come to a stop at the second floor, Horace rounds the corner down a narrow hallway. I maneuver with my luggage, and we finally stop in front of a door marked twenty-four. Horace remains silent, though ragged breaths filter through his nostrils from the trek up the stairs, while he unlocks the door using the same large jingly key holder he was playing with downstairs.

He continues through the threshold, his heavy steps thumping against the hard floor. He doesn't make it very far because it takes about four and a half steps to walk from one end of the smallest apartment I've ever seen in my life to the other. I know the listing said micro apartment, but this has got to be a new level of tiny living.

He lifts his index finger, vaguely gesturing toward the single window at the far wall. "Bed. Closet." He drags his finger across the room as if he has it pressed against a large touch screen at a kiosk. "Kitchen." He reaches into his pocket and retrieves a set of keys. "The bathroom's around the corner in the hallway. You need one of these keys to open it. The other two are for the door and the front entrance downstairs."

A rise of panic climbs up my throat. "I-I'm sorry. Where's the bathroom?"

He silently stalks out the front door and gestures his entire hand to the hallway on his right.

"It's not inside the apartment?"

He shakes his head. "It's communal," he curtly explains. "There's one on each floor, but you only have the key to this one." He lifts his hand again, pointing lazily at the bathroom I have yet to see. "You and about six other tenants."

"They didn't mention that in the listing."

"It's there," he says with an annoyed sigh. "But if there's an issue, you need to take it up with the property manager. I'm just the super here."

He juts out the keys in my direction, urging me to take them from him. "I'm on the first floor. Apartment twelve if you need anything." He gives a sympathetic nod before leaving. Perhaps he's offering a small gesture of compassion for this girl, wide-eyed like a deer in headlights as if she just landed in a foreign country where they eat octopus for breakfast.

Once Horace closes the door behind him, I'm left all alone in ninety-five square feet of living space.

I close my eyes and take in a long, cleansing breath. "This is only temporary," I whisper to myself. At least the place is furnished. Although, I don't know if a single hot plate and a mini fridge the size of a plastic crate would count as "furnished."

I unzip my suitcase, searching for the set of sheets I packed while inwardly thanking my past self for thinking long enough to pack essential linens. I spend the next hour settling in as best as I can. Tucking away my clothes in the closet, finding a safe spot for my electronics such as my MacBook and camera bag, and ending the hour realizing how badly I need to leave my apartment to stock up on household items.

After a quick Google search for the nearest Duane Reade, I gather my purse and sling it over my shoulder before grabbing my keys and walking out the door. I lock up with a tough jiggle, the door feeling a little loose even with the dead bolt in place, and hurry down the stairs.

"Lucia." I whip my head around right as I open the door to the building. I turn to see Gary stalking toward me with a small smirk. "You're still in one piece."

"It's Lucy," I correct, my hand still on the door, holding it open as I lean toward the outside air.

"My apologies," he drawls. "Lucy."

I smile politely, though awkwardly forced, before walking away.

"I'm Gary," he calls after me. "I'm in apartment nineteen if you ever need company."

I don't look back or offer my apartment number in exchange, merely waving a hand in the air while I continue down the small flight of steps. Taylor Swift's "Welcome to New York" starts playing in a loop in my head, causing me to hum lightly while I resist the urge to skip through the crowded sidewalks of Brooklyn.

9

Lucy

MONDAY MORNING ROLLS AROUND, and I've slept a total of three hours and forty-six minutes. In those few hours I actually slept, I kept having those dreams that reminded me of ones where I'm standing in the middle of the school cafeteria in nothing but my bra and underwear. Only, in the dreams I had last night, I was left holding my DSLR camera in my hand while feeling completely lost. I didn't know what buttons to push or what the dials even meant. In one specific dream that occurred just after midnight, I looked down at the black camera in my hands and found that it was a plastic one. The kind parents buy for their toddlers for sensory play. I fumbled with the red, yellow, and blue dials while everyone looked at me in shock.

What if after flying thousands of miles from the comforts of my comfortable two-bedroom apartment, I'm back where I was a year ago, jobless and jilted by the first big girl job I've ever had? What if after everything, I end up back at Mr. Bean's, standing behind a counter telling dedicated members of corporate America and moms with high-end strollers and tight yoga pants the daily pastry specials? Or worse, out of a job altogether? It's not like Mr. Bean left my position unfilled. He hired someone a week after I gave my notice. I really gave up the most stable thing in my life, Mr. Bean and his large, fancy espresso machine, to be an artist. Maybe my mom was right.

I attempt to push aside the flash memory of those dreams and trudge out of my apartment to use the bathroom. I found that during the early hours before six a.m., the bathrooms are more likely to be unoccupied. I also found that they're kept surprisingly clean. Apparently, there's a cardinal rule in place, one that's tacked onto the walls of every communal bathroom in the building, to clean up after yourself and to use as many cleaning supplies while bordering on gas chamber-like hazardous.

I further shove away those constantly intruding thoughts of failure as I get ready and walk out of my apartment to the nearest subway station. I try everything to keep my spirits up rather than down on my twenty-minute commute, following my phone's map app to the shoot location. I quietly mutter pep talk after pep talk, reminding myself I wasn't picked randomly for this. I earned my spot here. I'm doing this for a reason. It isn't about simply finding a job or making ends meet or even submitting an application to yet another job that fits my experience and credentials. It's about choosing my future. One I get to live to the fullest instead of merely surviving.

Still, that self-instilled confidence wavers the second I arrive at the eerie, abandoned-looking warehouse-style building that houses my new place of work for the next three months. I carefully walk into the building, aware of my surroundings while attempting to maintain my composure. I press the button to the elevator and wait as the lights above it flash in sequence, indicating its descent onto the ground floor.

I hear the same doors I walked through open and shut behind me, followed by the small taps of footsteps. When I turn to my side, a woman looking around my age and dressed in the similar business casual attire I have on stands next to me. We make quick eye contact and press our lips together in a polite smile before facing the elevator in front of us. Our movements move in synchrony, and I would probably let out a small giggle at the coincidence of it if I weren't so nervous.

"Are you here for the ad campaign with Elevate Media?" She tucks a lock of her jet-black hair behind her ear.

A soft and slightly relieved smile spreads across my face. "I am."

Her smile mirrors mine, and she juts out a hand in my direction. "I'm Elaine."

"Nice to meet you," I answer, slipping my hand into hers with a firm yet friendly handshake. "Lucy. I'm actually an intern."

"Oh! Me too!" she exclaims giddily. Her whole body slackens with a sigh of relief. "So are you from the area or…?" Her voice trails at the end as if treading cautiously with her question, unsure if it's okay to prod deeper.

"I'm from Seattle," I answer with an assuring smile. "I moved out here for the internship."

She presses a hand into her chest. "San Diego."

I nod, and she does too.

"Are you having trouble adjusting to the time difference? I didn't get to sleep until after two. My body is definitely still on West Coast time."

"It's been a bit of an adjustment," I answer, not necessarily a lie, but my lack of sleep had more to do with nerves rather than any form of jet lag.

The elevator arrives as our small talk dwindles down to comfortable smiles. We both enter, me following behind her as she presses the button to the fourth floor. We linger in silence, both fidgeting with our almost identical black camera bags slung over our shoulders and preparing ourselves for what's behind the elevator doors. When the loud ding announces our arrival, we're welcomed by the entire span of the fourth floor. And it's huge. The shiny concrete glistens off the strategically placed panel lights hanging from the ceiling as people scurry through the space. Racks of clothing flit across the room, and urgent chatter fills the silence sitting between me and Elaine. I tug the strap of my camera bag up my shoulder, and we take another step into the room.

"Names?"

Our steps come to halt as a man with dark curly hair and wire-framed glasses, looking highly stressed and frazzled, approaches us. He holds a metal clipboard in front of him, and his eyes urge us to answer his question.

"Uh...Lucy Marquez," I answer, a little thrown off with his abrasiveness.

"Elaine Cho," Elaine answers, following me. We exchange a quick look of disquiet and unease.

The man runs his finger down the paper tucked into the clipboard and hums quietly as he scans over the list. "Ah! Interns. Okay," he says, swiveling on his feet and looking at us over his shoulder. "We aren't shooting anything today," he calls, speed walking into the thick of the room. Elaine and I follow, trying to match his quick pace. "We're actually spending the next week or two prepping, meeting with models, and reviewing set and prop designs."

We finally stop at multiple racks of clothes lined up against an aesthetically pleasing brick wall sandwiched between two large pane windows. "We're randomly assigning tasks to most of the interns. You two are going to go through these racks. Sort by pants, skirts, shirts, jackets, etcetera. And then line them up by color."

Elaine and I shuffle closer to the racks.

"I'm assuming all of your paperwork was completed with HR via email?"

We both nod.

"You'll fill out a time card at the end of the day." He turns to leave before turning back to face us again. "And I'm Ryan, by the way. I'm the lead set manager. You'll meet Ivy later. She's the lead project manager for the whole ad campaign. You'll mainly report to me or Ivy. If you need anything, just look for me for now. I'll be around...there." He points to the far end, where a desk sits with a scattering of papers and a lone laptop. "Or there," he adds, gesturing vaguely in another direction. A small eye roll slips through his tense yet professional demeanor. "Hopefully you won't need me."

Elaine and I smile. "I think we've gotten enough work to fill the next few hours," I say, attempting to assure him.

He nods quickly and scurries off.

Elaine and I eye each other, carefully setting our tote bags and camera bags on an armchair closest to the clothing racks.

"I guess this beats getting coffee," I comment, squashing the assumption that that's what I would spend the next three months doing. Doing grunt work like picking up dry cleaning for a high administrative person or making coffee runs throughout the day.

Elaine lets out a small laugh. "You think we'll meet Kyle today?"

"Who?"

Elaine pops her head up from behind the rack she's sifting through. "Kyle Viotto? He's the artistic director handling the entire campaign. He's the reason I signed up for this whole internship. Left my shitty retail job at H&M to do this."

I smirk and jab my index finger to my chest. "Mr. Bean's Coffee and Tea."

Elaine laughs. "I guess we really had nothing to lose, huh?"

If only that were true. "So is this Kyle guy good?"

Her brows shoot up. "In the art world? He's like Beyoncé. He knows his shit and makes no room for modesty. He pushes boundaries left and right. It's probably why the ad agency contracted with Elevate just for this campaign."

"Has he been with the agency long?" I ask, my voice hushed.

She shakes her head. "No way they could afford to keep him on their payroll. He only takes on freelance work through Elevate. Usually for *big* campaigns like this one."

"Sounds pretty intimidating," I respond, my gaze lingering on the racks in front of me with worry.

Elaine nods in silent agreement. "He has a lot of connections, and I've talked to a few people who have worked with him on other designer campaigns. He has a lot to show for his work. We're going to get a lot out of this internship."

That impending failure feeling returns, and I feel like the walls are closing in on me. The pressure starts to build, and the importance of this internship thickens right in front of me. I have to do well. I just have to. I can't go back to job searches that skim the outer edges of my marketing experience and push more toward sales or dog walking or even another barista job.

"If we do well," I counter.

"Yep," Elaine shoots back. "Otherwise, it's back to coffee and tea for you and ringing up hipsters looking for ripped jeans and neon-colored blazers for me."

I brush off the reality of her statement with a loose chuckle. All while the fear of failure continues to brew and linger in my gut.

10

Dexter

I USED to watch Charlie Brown a lot as a kid. My favorite was *It's the Great Pumpkin, Charlie Brown*. I always remember how the grown-ups talked in the movie. They never said actual words. It was just a *whomp-whomp* noise that sounded like someone was talking to you while you had your ears covered.

Those are the exact sounds ringing through my head right now. I hear Janet's voice, all distorted and wonky, but I don't hear actual coherent words.

"My surgery is scheduled for next week. When I go in, we'll—"

"I-I don't understand," I finally say, cutting her off mid-sentence. She looks up at me, her hands wrapped around the frosty glass still full of strawberry and cream whipped together with a cherry on top. Jukebox music plays around us and the rectangular table in the middle of the small booth we're sitting in as I try to process what she just told me.

"It's stage three lung cancer," she elaborates after tossing the word "cancer" at me without so much as a warning. Then again, is there really a way to warm up to that word? That threatening, ominous word that feels like the world is crumbling underneath me.

"You don't even smoke."

"You don't have to be a smoker to have cancer."

"But you're healthy," I continue to argue. "I don't think I've ever even seen you have more than two glasses of wine. And you run a 5K, like, every Thanksgiving for that Turkey Trot thing. And—"

"Dex," she calls, regaining my attention. She doesn't say anything else. Instead, she looks at me with silently pleading eyes. And I feel like a complete asshole. So instead of continuing this demand for answers to questions that feel irrelevant at this point, I sigh.

"Sorry," I say with a deep breath. I take a long pull of my milkshake.

When Janet and I were kids, we traveled to Brooklyn from South Jersey often to visit our grandparents when they were alive. We were surrounded by smaller, quieter towns and beachy streets, so a visit to the city was always a big deal. We'd hop into my parent's minivan, duffel bags packed to the brim with pajamas and board games, and drive my parents crazy during the two-hour drive to Brooklyn. And because we spent as much time here as we could—three-day weekends, holidays, or long stretches of time over the summer—we grew attached to the one spot that made the best mint chocolate chip milkshakes and onion rings, The Lunch Car. Whether it was to get us out of the house when we became a little too stir-crazy or to appease a late-night, post-dinner snack craving, a thick, cheek-hollowing milkshake, a steamy serving of onion rings still glistening with hot oil, and our grandparents ushering us into an empty booth always did the trick.

But now, the same basket of onion rings, cooled and untouched, alongside the milkshake that suddenly tastes like cardboard, is doing nothing to soothe the numbness coursing through my head.

What makes things worse is that we don't have a cozy two-bedroom apartment to go back to after this where my grandma would most likely be baking some pie and my grandpa would return to whatever home improvement project he was working on that week. And for some reason, knowing we'll be working through this just the two of us makes it that much scarier. If there were ever a time I needed a mom or a dad, or even a gruff grandfather or a snuggly grandma, right now would be the time.

We sit in silence for a minute before Janet picks up an onion ring and takes a crunchy bite. "So what happens from here?" I ask, my gaze fixed on my milkshake.

My big sister has cancer.

She takes a deep, cleansing breath. "Like I said, my surgery's scheduled for next week. On the nineteenth," she explains, her voice in full problem-solving mode. "And then...most likely chemo."

I nod. I keep my eyes focused on the space in front of me, making it obvious I'm avoiding her. But then she reaches for my hand. She gives it a firm squeeze, and I finally look at her.

"Dexter," she urges. Her voice comes out shaky and scared.

"We're going to get through it," I assure her, though the shattered fragments of my composure are hanging by a thread. I might just break down right into the pool of liquifying whipped cream in front of me.

Her response is to nod, though the up and down movement of her head is slow and uncertain.

"Does Charles know?" I ask.

"Yeah," she answers, her voice sounding less guarded as we veer our conversation away from treatment and prognosis. Her phone chirps on the table just then. She turns it over in her hand and looks over whatever alert she has set on her phone. "I have to get back to the gallery."

I look at my watch. It's close to eight, well past her usual office hours. "It's late."

"I know," she says, gathering her things. "I have to get a few things before I go back home."

"I'll walk you."

She shakes her head. "I can get there on my own. And Charles is going to meet me there," she explains. "He's going to stay with me until I need to lock up."

"You sure?"

"Yeah, I'll be fine."

I sigh. "Okay," I answer, defeated. "I'll call you tomorrow."

"Can you do me a favor?"

I look at my sister. Her pleading, downturned eyes peer up at me, and her hand lightly grips my forearm. "Don't let this cancer define me," she says, a calm assertiveness in her voice. "I'm still me. This is just something I'm going to have to beat."

I choke back the enormous knot in my throat through a nod.

This is my big sister. The one I've been looking up to for my entire life. She's been my rock. When I graduated high school, she was the one standing front and center, waving a big sign with my face blown up and plastered on a poster board. She was the one who took me in when I first moved to the city, letting me crash on her couch for a week before I moved to my own place. She was the only one who was able to pull me out of myself when our parents died. What if I lose her? Who would I have? I would be all alone in this world. The version of myself that existed with Janet would be a distant memory, long forgotten with no one to relive those memories with.

I'm slowly walking back to my apartment, the heat dissipating into something cooler now that the day has eased into night. My gaze is settled on the concrete ground, aimlessly tracking the crooked cracks that trace between the divided squares. As I near the streets closer to my apartment, I get a text message from Janet letting me know she's safely at the gallery and that Charles is already there with her, to which I respond with a quick thumbs-up emoji.

As I'm shoving my phone back into my pocket, I look up into a storefront. It's a wine and cheese store. There are large cheese wheels on display at the window along with an entire wall of various wines on the opposite side. When I peer inside, I see people moving about the wine racks. Nothing out of the ordinary usual retail traffic. But then I see someone familiar perusing the large wine wall, right in between two wooden barrels showcasing triangle blocks of parmesan.

Is that...?

No, it can't be. She should be thousands of miles away. On the opposite coast.

Curiosity getting the better part of me, I enter the store. When I walk toward the wine wall, I stop.

It is her.

"Lucy?"

The last image I have of Lucy engraved in my mind is of her sitting at the edge of my bed, her bare back facing me with the light cascading from the windows onto my messy bed, creating shadows that outlined her curves. Her arms were holding up the thin, flat sheet to cover her front, and she thought I was dozing off into a lazy, post-coital slumber. But I wasn't. Instead, I was watching her through heavily lidded eyes. I peeked at the way her body rose from my bed and her blonde hair tumbled down to the middle of her back. I paid attention to how her body reacted when my fingers grazed over the two hollowed dimples between her hips, and she smiled at me over her shoulder. I swear, I would give my left arm to hear her giggle the way she did when I yanked her back onto the bed, the sheets tangling between us while she fell limp in my arms. And probably even my right arm to hear her moan the way she did when she wrapped her legs around my waist.

"Dexter!"

She's dressed in distressed jeans, a loose fitting T-shirt, and white Converse. The large wine bottle she was examining slackens in her grip as she turns to face me. I look around to see a couple of faces turn in our direction after Lucy practically shrieked my name, looking equal parts shocked and panicked.

"Are you visiting Nat?" I ask, sauntering a step closer to her.

"Uh...um," she stammers. Her eyes shift to the door, then back to the wine that's still in her hand. She places it back on the wooden racks, shoving it into the nearest available slot. "I-I, um..."

"Is everything okay?"

She sighs and starts gnawing on her bottom lip while refusing to meet my eyes. "Dexter," she finally says. "No one can know I'm here."

My head jerks back, and my expression twists sideways. "Huh?"

She doesn't answer me. She just shifts on her feet, looking so uncomfortable. Her hand comes up to her face, and she cups her cheek, her eyes turning down into the saddest set of puppy eyes.

"Lucy," I say softly, getting her attention. "What's going on?"

11

Lucy

WEEK ONE DOWN, about eleven more to go. But who's counting, right?

In case my dejected state isn't an obvious answer to that rhetorical question, the answer is me. I am. I'm mentally drawing a thick red line through every passing week until I can go back home.

Sigh. I miss Jeremy.

My first week at Elevate Media has been stressful, draining, and outright dissuading.

I finally met Kyle Viotto, and his presence on set was enough for me to doubt every bit of my skill while clinging on to the need to please him. He's just as Elaine described him. Talented and knowledgeable. But also curt and tough. He has enough rudeness in his presence for it to be considered complaining if I mentioned this character trait of his out loud. He's short with us interns, barely answering our questions without leaving any room for follow-up and forcing us to figure things out on our own.

Today, when I asked him what exposure setting he wanted the backlight at, he walked away without giving me an answer, barely giving me a sideways glance and leaving me a little baffled and offended. But what am I supposed to do? This is what I signed up for.

After spending the entire week running back and forth between shoots and outfit changes and proper lighting techniques, all of which I was gradually learning and slowly getting the hang of with Elaine by my side, I needed something to relax. So I ventured into Scarlet Vino, a wine and cheese store I've walked past a dozen times since my arrival to the city. With each brisk pass I made by the storefront, I told myself I would save the purchase of a forty-dollar bottle of wine on a day when I really needed it, and today was that day. The last thing I expected was to run into Dexter while deciding between the shiraz or the pinot noir.

Instead of walking out with a bag full of wine, quite possibly two or three bottles, and a healthy serving of havarti, I'm now sitting at the steps leading up to my rented apartment.

"So Nat and Hayden have no idea you're here?" Dexter asks, confirming the last bits of my story. I told him everything. From my decision to come to Brooklyn for this internship to the lies I told my sister right before coming here. And he sat next to me, listening patiently the whole time while I barely took the time in between my words to catch my breath.

I shake my head. "And they can't know."

He shifts in his seat, opening and closing his mouth as if worried he might say the wrong thing. "Lucy, you know Nat wouldn't be mad. She'd—"

"You know my parents help me pay my rent?" I blurt out, cutting him off. It just projectile vomits out of me after I held it down as far as I could. I've grown sick and nauseous with it, and I can't hold it back any longer.

The furrow between his brows deepens.

"My sisters don't know this," I continue. "My parents started doing it about four months after I lost my job. I was a few days late to pay my roommate, and I didn't know what else to do, so I told them I needed money. And even after I started working at the coffee house, they still helped me. Every week, my parents call me, asking if I've found a job yet. And I can hear the disappointment in their voices when I tell them no. They try so hard to hide it, and it kills me a little every time I have to tell them I haven't found anything. I'm worried—I think…They're getting tired of helping me out.

"Nat's out here doing things on her own. My mom's so happy she's engaged. You should've heard her talking about how happy and proud she is of both Nat and Hayden. Carmen's a *freaking* doctor, for crying out loud. My parents don't have to send them a dime. But me…I feel like such a damn failure."

I splay it all out in the open. This messy, muddled pile of runaway marbles, each one a symbolic representation of why I'll never be the person I thought I would be. One marble for the college degrees collecting dust in a drawer back home, wasting away and looking at me with shame. One for the guilt of having to take money from my parents. Another one for falling so low on the measuring stick of the adult I thought I was going to be when I moved out of my parents' house. And they're everywhere, scattering away from me, making it near impossible to wrangle them together so I can work through them properly.

"I know you think Nat would understand, but I'm not too sure. And I want to be the good little sister who listens to her parents and does what they say, but this internship…I couldn't turn it down. It's something I can really picture myself doing. And it's scary, but it's also really exciting and new. But if I end up back where I was before I came out here *without* even the cushion of my job at the coffee house, I don't know if I can face my parents and Nat while they tell me 'I told you so.'"

Dexter nods, showing a little more understanding this time. "I won't say anything," he finally says. We sit in silence for a minute before Dexter's lips shift into an arrogant little simper. "Your hair looks even better in person."

My hand lifts to the side of my head, feeling suddenly shy from his narrowed gaze. "Uh," I say, tucking my chin toward my chest, "thank you." My hand slowly glides down my neck before my fingers toy with my necklace.

"It looks good on you."

Our eyes lock. Suddenly, all the panic from running into someone who isn't supposed to know I'm here has subsided. A new type of panic, something that aligns a little closer to embarrassment, along with the realization that Dexter knows what I look like naked, has taken its place.

Did he always have that adorable mole at the corner of his right eye, making him look boyish yet dreamy? And how come I never noticed how, even in the dusky light shining above us from the street-lamps, his brown eyes look like honey? He smirks again, and a small peek of his teeth shows his pointy canines, only adding to the sweet charm that first attracted me to Dexter three years back. A lifetime ago.

Why the freaking heck does he have to be so good-looking? The perfect mixture of handsome and cute, making me want to rumple his hair while biting his lower lip. Seriously, *why?!*

Dexter reaches up and lightly tussles my hair, lifting a few strands between his fingertips. His hand comes close to the skin on my cheek, and I can feel his warmth skate over me. All of this, his close proximity, his hands inches from my face, and I'm suddenly back at his apart-ment, his hands gliding over my skin with purpose and knowledge. Like he already knew how I would react to his touch as he moved with a level of dexterity I didn't even bother to question.

"Well," I say a little too loudly, smacking my hands to my thigh. "It was great catching up, Dexter. I hope this doesn't become a regular thing."

Dexter leans back, looking at me as if I just told him the shirt he's wearing looks ugly on him, when in fact, it's the complete opposite. His shirt looks good on him. Too good. It's tight enough to show off his broad shoulders but not too tight that it seems he did it on purpose.

I seriously need to stop checking him out.

"So you're going to spend three months in Brooklyn and never see me again?"

I nod. "That's exactly it."

"Lucy," he calls with an incredulous plea in his voice.

"Well, hello, neighbor." I didn't realize how close Dexter and I are sitting next to each other, but it's suddenly so blatant when I turn to face my eagerly friendly neighbor and I can still feel Dexter's entire body inches from mine.

"Gary," I comment, sounding more like an acknowledgment rather than a greeting to his sudden appearance.

Dexter and I both stand, and I notice how in the process of moving down the last step and landing on the sidewalk, Dexter has inched even closer to my side.

"You remember my name. I'm feeling a little flattered." Gary winks at me, and I hold back the sudden grimace that crept up my face, hiding it with a forced smile. I should've pretended I didn't know his name and called him Gavin or Gilroy instead. Why men find the need to misinterpret something as simple as remembering their name as flirting is beyond me.

I move to the side, and instead of parting the way, Dexter steps even closer toward me. "You want me to walk you up?" he asks in a hushed voice.

I eye Gary still standing in front of us on the sidewalk as if waiting for an invitation. *Why is he still there?*

"No, I'm good. I'm just going to go...have some stale Cheez-Its," I answer, suddenly remembering I didn't get to buy the bottle of wine I was looking forward to after the shock of running into Dex.

Dexter takes one last sideways glance at Gary and faces me. "Call me while you're here," he whispers. "If you need anything."

I nod.

"I'll see you around, Luce."

"Bye, Dexter."

12

Dexter

"DEX," Charles calls from the hard, incredibly uncomfortable plastic chair across from me. When I look up, he's standing to greet the doctor, who just walked out of the double doors we've been boring our eyes into for the last four hours.

I stand too, following Charles's lead, just as Dr. Pham reaches us.

"How is she?" I ask.

"She's resting, still slowly coming out of anesthesia," she explains, gently patting a hand to the side of the brightly patterned scrub cap she has on her head. "We're going to keep her in the recovery area for a bit to monitor her."

Charles and I both nod with matching intense, solemn expressions on our faces.

"But she did well. No complications, and we were able to get in there and do what we needed to. I just want to warn you," she adds, "she's going to be weak and really out of it. She has a chest tube on her side, and it's going to cause quite a bit of discomfort."

"How long will she have that?" Charles asks.

"One to two weeks. So she'll have to go home with it after she's stable enough to be discharged from here."

Charles blanches for a second.

"But don't worry," Dr. Pham adds. "We'll give thorough instructions on how to empty it and what to look for in case the site gets infected."

"When can we see her?" I ask.

"Let's let her wake up a bit and get settled in the recovery room," she says, clasping her hands together in front of her. "The nurses will come and get you guys."

"Thank you, Doc," Charles says. Dr. Pham nods and smiles solemnly before she turns to walk away.

We glance at each other for a moment and stay silent.

Fuck. This is what it must feel like to come up for air. Air that's been sucked out of you. Air that's been drained and leached when you didn't think you had any left to give.

I feel like the day's been about twenty hours long, and it isn't even noon yet. We got to the hospital early in the morning after packing every essential in Janet's overnight bag to ensure she would be comfortable during her stay after her surgery. When they wheeled her to the surgery area, it was a waiting game. A long, ticking waiting game. Charles and I just sitting under water, waiting for the moment we're told we can breathe again.

"Dex." I hear the sound of my name. I look up to see Hayden making his way toward me. He's not moving urgently, but his steps aren't unhurried either. He's got a look of concern on his face, and his shoulders are squared with his hands in his pockets and his head ducked a little low.

"Hey."

"Any news yet?"

"Yeah, the doctor just came out and spoke to us," I answer. "She's being moved to the recovery area, and they're going to let us know when we can see her."

He nods. "Nat's heading over here in about an hour. She just had a few things she needed to finish up at work."

"You guys don't have to be here," I assure him, though it's nice to see a friendly face after staring at the drab industrial carpeting at my feet for most of the morning.

He frowns. "No, we want to be here."

When I told him about Janet and her cancer and her surgery, he called Janet himself. He and Nat talked to her about her treatment, and he was able to offer a less worried and somber ear. He didn't shut down like I did, the conversations about her health too difficult to have. He didn't become a ball of anxiety and frustration like Charles did, unable to keep his cool whenever she showed any sign of pain or weakness. Hayden just *listened*. He and Nat gave my sister something that Charles and I haven't mastered yet: calm reassurance.

We sit on the chairs around us when we realize we're sort of just hovering in the waiting area. Charles walks away to pace the hallway, something he's been doing every fifteen minutes, and it gives me and Hayden a moment to ourselves.

I lean forward and brace my elbows on my knees. "So, uh, how's wedding planning going?"

He throws a dubious look in my direction. "You want to talk about the wedding? Right now?"

I sigh. "Maybe a little distraction might help," I say, my voice tired and worn.

"You sure?"

I nod.

He takes a short pause, shifting the air into something lighter. "We booked everything for Hawaii," he tells me in a low tone, obviously not wanting to shift too much of my attention away from the current situation on hand. "Reception, flowers, hotel. Nat handled it all with my aunt and my mom."

"That was fast."

He nods. "You know you're going to be my best man, right?" he says softly after a long, pregnant pause.

"Yeah," I croak. I clear my throat and force myself to meet his eyes. "Yeah, of course." I smile at him even though I feel like crying right now. It's funny how while being thrown in the pits of wait and worry, it's the piece of good news that makes me want to cry.

He coughs into his fist. "And, uh," he adds, "Nat's just trying to get the guest list sorted. Making sure people get there when they're supposed to. We really just want to make sure family's there. Of course, you too." He nudges my shoulder with his.

That draws a smile out of me. "Your mom's going to be there, right?"

"Of course," he answers. "And Nat's parents and her sisters. Nat's been a little worried about Lucy, so she's looking forward to seeing her."

My brow furrows. "Why?" I didn't forget that Lucy's here in the city. In fact, I've been tempted more than once—okay, closer to, like, ten times—to pick up the phone and call her. Maybe even show up unannounced at her apartment? See if that weird neighbor of hers is still poking his head around her personal space? But she made it pretty clear she doesn't want to see me while she's here. Maybe if I stage an "accidental" run-in and visit that wine and cheese store again...

He exhales a deep sigh. "She's been out of work for a year," he explains. "She had to take this job at a coffee house last year, and now she was talking about some internship." He shakes his head at that last part. "Nat's mom convinced her not to apply for it. You know, doing grunt work like getting coffee and being an errand gofer isn't what she wants for Lucy. And it's a temp position. Who knows if it would've even amounted to anything."

I nod, listening while hoping I look as indifferent as possible.

"Anyway, I'm sure Nat'll be fine once she sees Lucy. She just worries since she's out in Seattle all alone. If she weren't so far away, then Nat could at least help her out or make sure she's making the right choices."

"She's an adult," I remind him. "I'm sure she's capable of making her own decisions."

He shrugs, my words rolling right off of him. Maybe Lucy was right. The wavering faith her family has in her isn't as rock solid as I thought. It's even bled into Hayden's mind, making him believe his future sister-in-law needs more support and guidance than he thinks.

If only he and Nat knew what she's made happen for herself in the past few weeks.

"Hey." Hayden and I both look up to see Charles rush back from the hallway. "We can go see her now."

Hayden and I both stand, and Hayden gently slaps a hand to my back. I guess the distraction actually helped.

13

Lucy

I ALWAYS KNEW the New York City heat was bad from my sisters complaining about it when July rolls around every year, but it's really one of those things you have to experience yourself to really understand. It's humid, like walking-around-with-a-steaming-damp-cloth-over-my-face type of humid. I've been here a little over a month now, and I desperately miss the gloomy Seattle clouds.

Today, when according to my phone's weather app, the humidity level is at an all-time high of sixty percent, is the day Kyle decided to venture down the alleys of Brooklyn to shoot an outdoor shot. My hair, sticking to my clammy skin and growing poofier and poofier with each passing hour, is tied up using the elastic tie fastened at my wrist. And now, the hair lining my forehead has started curling, making me look a lot more frazzled than I actually am.

"I want to take a nap in an ice bath after this," Elaine mutters, fanning herself with a stack of stapled papers. Her cheeks are flushed, and she lets out a deep breath.

Elaine has stuck close to my side since day one. We discovered a lot of similarities between us. We're the same age and both dabbled in marketing before taking the plunge into photography. It's her first time in New York City, and while I've visited before, it's a whole different experience living here. She took this internship to home in on her photography skills like me, but also to get a better grasp on advertising and the marketing approach to an ad campaign. I'm here to learn more about photography and different approaches to camerawork within commercial and fashion photography. We're both here to learn different things, but our goals run very parallel. And aside from our similar career goals, I've found that our personalities match well too. We're both fairly outgoing, open to casual conversation about our personal lives while we work, and lunchtime disputes are rare when it comes to deciding what to eat, which definitely sweetens the ropes binding our newly formed friendship.

"Or go sit in the nearest bank branch," I counter, tugging at the front of my shirt to keep it from sticking to my chest.

"You think they'd throw us out unless we're there to withdraw money?"

"I'll open a new checking account. I don't even give a shit at this point."

"It should be illegal to make us work outside on a day like this," Elaine adds. "And on a Saturday. For shame."

I laugh. "At least it's a short day. Hopefully we'll be out of here early."

There are four models lined up against the brick wall between two buildings. Messy graffiti and an overflowing dumpster sit at one end, and I can't decide if the stench of garbage or the image of a penis—aggressively spewing semen—adds to the edginess of this titillating shoot, or if it's the mixture of army print pants and black military boots.

I have my thick camera strap draped over my neck, most likely collecting sweat. After a few more shots, the models are instructed to step aside, making room for individual shots. I'm watching the three waiting for their turn, standing in the shade where a large industrial fan sits. They're crowding around it, taking small sips of water while attempting to cool down in the heat. One of them, a male model dressed in a black tank top, army print pants, and clunky black boots, plops himself on a folding chair, leaning back while emptying the rest of his water bottle. The light beams down just enough to cover the lower half of his body in the shade, the rest of him still in the sun. And the sweat already coating his bare arms and neck gives off a shiny sheen.

"Uh, Sebastian, right?" I ask, approaching him.

"Seb."

I smile a tight-lipped smile. "Right," I answer. "Do you think you could sit forward? Rest your elbows on your knees?"

He does as I say, ducking his head down while leaning toward me. "Like this?"

"Yeah," I say, lifting my camera in front of me. "And look up and sort of square your shoulders."

He follows my instructions without hesitation, something he's probably learned over time as a seasoned catalog model, and I take a step backward, including the colorful graffiti while making sure to leave out the phallic image painted in bright yellow. "Move your right foot about two inches forward. Yeah. Just like that."

My camera clicks. At this angle, only his face sits in the light, but for some reason, it makes the clothes on him stand out more. "Now relax your face. Drop your eyebrows. Almost like you're bored."

"What are you doing?" I glance to my side, my finger never leaving the shutter button while moving around Seb. Elaine is hovering over me, her observant gaze taking in the model as his eyes track my steps.

"Just...playing around. Seeing if I can get something good. Ryan said we could before we came out here, and Kyle's been asking us for input for each shoot, so maybe I can find something here."

"Seb!" All of our heads jerk toward Kyle, where his set sits sans model. I'm guessing it's Seb's turn because he stands from his spot and saunters over to where Kyle is.

"Thanks, Seb!" I call after him. He gives a small bow along with a flirty smile before he approaches Kyle. Kyle, on the other hand, keeps his eyes on me where I was playing around with Seb's look and the makeshift set in front of me. He takes a few moments before he leaves his camera sitting on a tripod and walks over to me.

"Did you get some shots of Seb in?" he asks brusquely.

"Uh, yes," I answer. "Ryan said we can experiment with some shoot ideas as long as the models aren't tied up with you."

"Can I see them?"

I glance quickly at Elaine, whose eyes are wide and just as nervous looking as mine. I remove the strap from my neck and hand my camera over to Kyle. He stares down at the small display screen, his thumb pressing the buttons to scroll through my most recent images.

He doesn't say anything. Not even a nod of approval or a disparaging scowl. Instead, the stone-like expression on his face remains the same, emotionless and uninterested. He gets to the last of the pictures, where he accidentally clicks too far ahead and lands on a picture of Jeremy sleeping, and hands my camera back to me. I, of course, cringe from embarrassment. Did he really have to see the picture of Jeremy cuddling my Winnie the Pooh sock?

"Hmm," he mumbles with that flat effect on his face, making him look bored. "Have those edited by Monday morning and send them to me."

"Sure."

He gives a curt nod and walks back to his camera. He starts positioning Seb how he wants, a hand against the brick wall, his head thrown back toward the sky, but it almost feels like I'm watching it happen from another dimension.

"He just asked you to send him your pictures," Elaine whispers.

"I know," I respond softly.

"And he didn't tell you they look like an ad for Lipitor in *The American Journal of Medicine*."

I shoot a look of confusion in Elaine's direction.

She shrugs. "My parents have high cholesterol." I laugh, but Elaine's face doesn't change. "Lucy! This is huge!"

"Shh," I hiss, peering around at the other interns and staff members. "He just wants me to edit them. It doesn't mean anything."

"Still," she urges. "He hasn't asked to see a single one of my pictures. And I took *plenty* last week when we were shooting the neon line. I really thought he was going to give me some feedback on the purple blazers, but he didn't even give me the time of day."

I smile apologetically, placing a gentle hand on her forearm. "Maybe you can get some pictures today and he'll take a look at them. He seems to be in a giving mood."

She ignores my optimism, as placatory as it is, and grabs my hand. "Come on," she urges, glancing at the dwindling staff as we approach our lunch break. "It's almost lunchtime, and we need to celebrate this new development."

"Are we finally going to try those chocolate cupcakes across the street?"

"I literally cannot think of a better excuse to get chocolate wasted on our lunch break."

I giggle. "Let's go."

My fingers clutch a plastic container holding my extra chocolate cupcake while I practically skip home. I'm still on a high from today after Kyle sternly reminded me to have my edited pictures to him first thing Monday morning. Normally, I would panic or hyperventilate or have some sort of palpitation-inducing reaction but today, all I did was tack on an extra cheesy grin when I responded with a cringe-worthy "alrighty" to Kyle's bemused expression. I think I even added some finger guns, but who cares?

The sun is slowly gliding across the clear blue sky, and the humid heat is finally cooling a bit. When I enter my building, the air feels much stuffier than outside, and I suddenly remember the small AC unit in my apartment may not be functioning at its full capacity, much like the toaster oven that doesn't go above three hundred degrees or the broken hinge of the closet door.

I sigh. *Only two more months.*

Once on the landing to the second floor, I peer around the corner to the hallway leading up to my apartment. The last thing I expect is for the light to be streaming into the hallway from my door.

Did I leave my door open? My heart drops into my stomach. When I rush to my apartment, I'm greeted with a zombie apocalypse level of damage. I wish I was being dramatic. Like someone would jump out of the armoire—which is surprisingly still standing—telling me to calm my tits, and I'd simply laugh the whole situation off. And maybe when

Jeannie Choe

I look back at this moment in five years, I'll realize that comparing my trashed apartment, with my dirtied clothes scattered on the floor and furniture knocked over as if a tornado ran through it, to a post-apocalyptic world is pretty dramatic. But I don't have that kind of logic at this moment. Instead, I feel like the cloud I floated home in has evaporated and I've fallen into the biggest pile of rubbish my life has ever created.

14

Dexter

"I NEVER THOUGHT I would live to see the day my big sister does drugs."

Janet shoves me, the bony points of her knuckles poking my shoulder when she punches me with her small fist. "I'm not doing *drugs*, asshole."

She pops a second medicinal cannabis gummy into her mouth, her mouth twisting to one side as she shoulders through the "interesting taste" she keeps commenting on. She extends the small jar in my direction, offering me one.

I shake my head. "I'm not the one going through chemo."

She rolls her eyes. "Marijuana can also be enjoyed by people who aren't dying from cancer," she points out.

I blanch at the mention of my sister dying, even if it came from her own mouth.

"Anyway, the dispensary dude said my insurance would cover it since it's being used medicinally."

"Well, hopefully it'll give you your appetite back," I comment, scanning my eyes over her wasting body. She'll be coming up on five weeks since she's had her surgery, but even with all of the cancer out, her doctor still recommended chemo.

The chemo was expected, something the doctor prepared her for, but on the day of her first treatment, she left her apartment in a puddle of tears and anxiety. She couldn't stop worrying about how she was going to react to the harsh meds in her body. And now with the treatment well in her system, the constant pain, and gradual changes in her appearance causing her to *look* like an actual cancer patient, those harsh hits on her mental wellbeing haven't gotten any better.

"Maybe," she muses, her lids falling heavy when a forceful wave of fatigue takes over her. She stretches through a yawn before grimacing through a sharp intake of breath.

"You okay?"

Her face tenses as she adjusts her position, shifting on the cushioned seats of her couch while wincing from the jerky movements. "Oh, you know. Just...chemo. And cancer. And blah blah blah."

Her most recent chemo session was yesterday. The first cycle of treatment is already coming to an end, and we're hoping for some good news for once. She came home throwing up into a plastic bag before she sucked on a popsicle to help with those pesky mouth sores and took a long nap. These chemo sessions are taxing on her. They're painful and tiring and leech all of the energy from her. She needs days to recover, and even then, she regains barely enough strength to get her through a workday. Luckily, she's been able to cut back on her work hours without losing her job completely, doing mainly admin work from home. She'd be devastated if she lost her job altogether on top of everything.

Still, she tries to keep a positive attitude through self-deprecating comments and wry jokes about her cancer. But I see her hiding behind that fickle mask of a smile as it occasionally slips, only for her to brush my concern off with indifference. I wish she would talk to me about what she's afraid of, how she feels, instead of constantly telling me she's fine.

As the much-needed medicinal cannabis makes its way through Janet's body and she relaxes a little from her high, my phone buzzes in my pocket. When I pull it out, I see Lucy's name flash on the screen.

"Hello?"

"Dexter," she calls. Her voice sounds weary, like she's a combination of scared and tired. "I'm so sorry to call you like this…"

Well, this can't be good. I stand from my soft, cushy spot on Janet's sofa and walk to her kitchen for privacy.

"Are you okay?" I ask.

"Umm…" she answers, a wavering in her voice that sounds like she's going to start crying if I ask her if she's okay again. "My apartment was robbed," she explains softly. "My whole place is a mess, and they took my MacBook. And this necklace my grandma gave me when I graduated is missing. And—" She starts crying, and the end of her sentence is cut off with a desperate sob. Her cries continue to ring through the phone, and I can't even explain the irrational rage coursing through me. "I'm so sorry. I didn't have anyone else to call."

Fuck! Fuck, fuck, *fuck.* I've never heard her cry, and it's absolutely gut-wrenching.

I sprint back to the living room and reach for my keys and wallet sitting on the coffee table littered with magazines and half-empty mugs of tea.

"I'll be right there."

When I reach the sidewalk at the bottom of Lucy's apartment building, I immediately spot her. The edge of her thumb is nudged between her teeth, and I can tell she's shivering even from the distance between us. She's talking to a police officer, who's taking notes on a small note pad, occasionally nodding while talking to Lucy in a calm, gentle voice.

"Well," I hear the officer say as I quietly reach Lucy's side, "it's not likely we'll find the suspect, but it's good to have it reported. I would file an insurance claim as soon as possible, and we'll keep our eyes and ears open for any leads."

It's then Lucy spots me, just as the officer turns to get into his car. Her eyes immediately start to water at the same time her chin trembles. I pull her into me, letting her fall against my chest, and her shivering skyrockets while my hands run up and down her back. I didn't realize how panicked and worried I was until I hold her.

"You're okay," I whisper. I breathe out a deep sigh into her hair, letting the stress ease off of me, and I impulsively press my lips to her temple. *Thank God she's okay.*

"I'm so sorry I had to call you," she blubbers into my shoulder. "I didn't know who else…"

I pull away from her, keeping my hands braced on her shoulders. When a lone tear trickles down her cheek, I wipe it with my thumb. "What happened?"

"I don't know," she says, the shivering now flowing through the shakiness of her voice. "The officer said my door was busted open. But now I don't even know if I forgot to lock it. And I didn't put away my things. I just left them out, and they—" Her voice is cut off by a sudden sob.

"Let's go up and get your things. Or what's left of them, anyway."

She looks at me, wiping her cheeks. A scowl of confusion creates a small frown to form on her lips. "Get my things?"

I'm about to do something impulsive, a little rash but circumspect considering what happened to her today. Because how am I supposed to let her stay here by herself tonight? What if the people who robbed her come back? Or that guy I ran into the last time I was here comes knocking at her door for sugar or some shit? That's a completely logical and rational reason she shouldn't stay here. It has *nothing* to do with a small inkling of jealousy. (*Way to convince yourself, Dex.*)

It doesn't matter. Jealous or not, she can't stay here tonight. Period. Her apartment is a literal crime scene, for crying out loud.

"Stay at my place tonight," I say softly, being careful not to come off as too pushy. "And we'll figure something out for you once you're calmer."

She lets out a loud sniff and quickly wipes another runaway tear. Instead of answering me, she turns and leads the way to her apartment. When we reach her door on the second floor, my heart drops at the scene left behind. Everything's been ransacked, and her clothes are strewn on the floor, loose tracks of dirt-covered shoe prints staining them. What little furniture furnished the smallest apartment I've ever seen is knocked over, looking like someone tossed it into the studio apartment rather than organized to maximize space. I see broken glass everywhere, a twin-sized mattress lying haphazardly off a bed frame, and a small toaster oven sitting on top of it.

"Lucy," I whisper. She's been living in this shit hole for over a month? Even with it being trashed, I can tell it's been hell living here before the robbery. I peer over at her as she slowly unzips a suitcase that's somehow magically come out of this ordeal unscathed. She looks almost embarrassed, refusing to meet my eyes while focusing on picking up her clothes off the floor instead. I continue my observation, scanning over what I assume is a "kitchen," making note of a small hot plate and sink the size of a textbook. "Where's your bathroom?" I ask, realizing that there's no other door in this space besides the one we walked through.

She gives me that sheepish, almost embarrassed look again. Instead of answering me, she points to the door left slightly open. Toward the hallway.

My eyebrows shoot up. "Like an outhouse?"

She smirks and rolls her eyes, the first hint of a smile finally peeking through her hellish day. "It's a communal bathroom," she explains.

I cup the back of my neck. "How come you didn't tell me you were living like this?"

"Like how?"

"Like a…" I hesitate, not wanting to come off as judgmental. "Like *this*." I wave my hands around me.

"It's fine, Dex." Her lips twist to one side, and she chews on the inside of her lip. Her face drops like she might start crying all over again, and I feel like such a jackass.

"Sorry, Luce." I take a step toward the wardrobe closet that's surprisingly still in one piece but left open and empty. "You have pretty good storage. And I'm sure you got a steal on the rent. That's hard to do in the city."

She nods, looking away from me and focusing her attention on packing her things.

"Look, I didn't mean that. I just know it can't be easy living in such a cramped apartment without even a proper bathroom, even if it's temporary."

"It's fine," she repeats herself, sounding so far from fine I want to punch myself in the gut.

She steps away from her suitcase, now slowly filling with wrinkled clothes and toiletries that were left undamaged. Her foot catches on the edge of the mattress, and she trips toward me. I reach out to her, catching her fall, and she lets out a small squeak. "Sorry," she whispers with her eyes downturned.

"Lucy," I say, trying to get her attention with her arms gripped in my hands.

"I'm sure the super will fix the door as soon as I get a hold of him. I just need to—"

"No," I argue.

She gives me an incredulous glare. "No?"

"I'm sorry about what I said before. I really am, but you can't stay here for another two months."

"Where the hell am I supposed to go?"

Stay with me, I think. I have the spare bedroom I'm going to put her up in tonight, the same one I haven't been able to fill since Hayden moved out. I want to blurt out the offer for her to stay with me while she's here, but I feel like it might be too rash for her to take as a sound offer. It definitely doesn't sound too rash on my end. In fact, it feels like the perfect solution.

I stay silent, holding back the *stay with me* whisper-chants in my head, and she doesn't say anything else, almost like her question was completely rhetorical and she just proved a point. Instead, she brushes off my concern with a breezy smile, something Janet would probably do. In fact, I'm noticing how Lucy and Janet are so alike. They're both so independent, they'd never let a man tell them what to do (believe me, Charles and I *know*), and they'd never intentionally burden anyone with their own troubles. I see it in the way Janet is shouldering through her chemo and the way Lucy moved all the way out here without telling her family, knowing they'd most likely overwhelm her with worry and skepticism. I must have done something right in my life to surround myself with strong women full of tenacity and spunk. But right now, it's definitely not working in my favor.

"Lucy," I urge again, hoping she'll see my point and hoping even harder that she herself will ask if she can stay with me instead of coming back to this hellhole.

"Dex, I appreciate you letting me stay at your place tonight, which is probably a smart thing to do considering this damn door doesn't even lock right anymore, but I'll be fine once it's fixed. Plus, like you said, this is temporary. I'm going back to Seattle once this internship is over, and I can pretend like I didn't spend my days sharing a toilet seat and shower stall with complete strangers." She says all of this to the floor, to her suitcase, to her toaster oven as she picks it up and places it on the nearest countertop. To every inanimate object in her room except to me.

I try to flip through a mental catalog of things that have worked on Janet in the past. All the things I did as a teenager to get her to do what I wanted. I *did* threaten to hawk a loogie at her once when she refused to give up the TV remote. Or maybe a bribe? I huff a sigh of frustration. None of that's going to work. I'm just going to have to stay quiet and let her work through this on her own.

The rest of the time spent in Lucy's apartment is silent. I replace the mattress onto the bed frame and upright the rest of the small appliances that made their way onto the floor. Lucy fills a garbage bag of ruined items, clothes, blankets, and towels. All items that she can thankfully replace. Except for that necklace. When she's packed away the last of her belongings into her suitcase and I've taken the broken glass in a dustpan down to the dumpster, we survey our work.

"Thanks for your help, Dexter." She huffs a small sigh and slings a large tote bag over her shoulder at the same time I grip the retractable handle on her suitcase.

I give a close-lipped smile and solemn nod. "Let's go," I say before turning to leave the apartment.

15

Lucy

"HOLY SHIT! ARE YOU OKAY?"

A deep sigh slips through my lips louder than I mean to. From my sprawled out position on the full-size bed in Dexter's spare bedroom, my elbows pressing into the soft mattress and my chin resting on the heels of my hands, I offer a sad smile to Annabelle through my phone screen.

"Yeah," I say through a deep exhale. "I'm fine."

I'm as fine as I can be, considering half of my belongings have either been ruined or stolen. Along with my MacBook. My *fucking* MacBook!

Every time I think of all the work I have saved in my laptop, the pictures, I want to crumble into a pile of mush. A gloopy, hundred-and-twenty-seven-pound Lucy mush pile. And I can't even afford to replace it right now. How am I supposed to get any work done without a laptop? I guess I should consider myself lucky I had my camera on me when I got robbed. I think if *that* were stolen along with my MacBook, I would've called it quits and taken the next flight home.

I peer at my luggage still standing upright with the handle retracted and realize how lucky I am that I had Dexter to call too. I considered calling my sisters, but then the idea of calling Dexter popped into my head, and it felt like the better alternative to ambushing my sisters with my presence in New York City *and* the burglary that left me a sobbing mess.

When he got to my apartment, it felt so right. He knew exactly what to say, how to comfort and console me. He even knew when to stay quiet and let me simmer with my own thoughts. Having him there while I dolefully picked up my ruined things made it less scary and daunting. And it was really sweet how he rolled up his sleeves and started collecting the mess with me.

"And who's this guy you called?" she asks, a hint of concern and suspicion cloaked over her face. "Don't tell me you hopped on Tinder in the month you've been gone."

"He's an old friend," I explain. "My sister's marrying his old roommate."

"Hold up." Annabelle stops me. "Is it...Mr. Wrung You Out Like a Dish Towel Three Years Ago?"

"I was hoping you wouldn't remember that conversation."

"How could I forget the best sex of your life?"

I whip my fingers to the volume on my phone. "Annabelle!"

"What? Those were your words, not mine," she answers innocently. She lets out a small giggle at the same time I give her a piqued shake of my head. "Does this mean a round two?"

"Absolutely *not*!"

"Why not?" she argues.

"Because, Annabelle," I scold. "We can't. What happened was a one-time thing. I was never supposed to see him again. But now, his best friend is marrying my sister. Which means I know his people and he knows my people. I can't do casual sex with men who know my people. I don't want to complicate things right now. *Especially* not right now. I need easy breezy, not...complicated messy-cated."

Annabelle smiles with a taunting bounce of her eyebrows, making a flush creep up my neck.

"Can we talk about something else?" I beg. "It was a meaningless hookup. Basically a one-night stand. I was drunk and stupid and, like, *really* horny. And I doubt he even thinks about it. I mean, it's been three *freaking* years. Of *course* he doesn't think about it! It would be near stalker status if he still thought about it. I mean, right? He can't still be thinking about it?"

"So did you still want to change the subject or..."

I sigh and slump my head back to face the ceiling, not even bothering to hide all the confusing thoughts running in what feels like a loop in my head. "He can't still be thinking about it," I repeat, more to myself this time.

"Well, *you* obviously still think about it," Annabelle comments observantly.

I lift my head enough to side-eye her with something that isn't quite disapproval but leans more toward ambiguous.

"I mean, you do, right?"

I finally give in and fully face her, shifting an inch closer to my phone screen. "All the damn time."

"Lucy!" Annabelle practically shrieks. "What are you doing on the phone with me? Why aren't you out there, jumping his bones?!"

"Annabelle," I plead. "What is wrong with you? Why do you act like everything wrong in my life can be fixed with a hot and sweaty fuck fest with someone I shouldn't be thinking about in *that* way?"

"I mean, it can't fix it, but it can make it easier to deal with," she answers, her thin argument dissolving into an unconvincing set of words, making me even more uneasy about invading Dexter's personal space.

"Ann—"

My words are interrupted by a rough cough that sounds like it's meant to get my attention rather than an act of clearing one's throat. I turn to see Dexter at the doorway, his hand on the doorknob that definitely didn't click when he opened it.

Shit! Did I leave it open?

"I ordered some food if you're hungry."

"Is that him?" I hear Annabelle whisper loudly through my phone. I panic-reach for my phone and fumble with it before turning down the volume on the call.

"I'll be right out," I answer, a guilt-stricken look on my face. My heart starts to pound in my chest, and my ears feel hot. *I really hope he didn't hear me.*

"I ordered Thai. I hope that's okay."

I avoid his eyes, keeping them trained on the floor instead. My gaze lingers on his bare feet, where his loose sweatpants stop right at his ankle. They shift on the wood floor, and his toes wiggle a little. The vulnerability of the exposed skin, so different from the confidence in his deep, gravelly voice, makes me feel fuzzy and warm inside.

So apparently, I have a thing for feet.

My eyes finally meet his, and I immediately regret it. How can one look, one single, second-long glance, cause everything in me to dissolve into mush? I just want to run to him and cry into his chest. Thank him for unexpectedly being my knight in shining armor.

"Of course," I answer.

Before he turns to leave, he takes one long, drawn out look at me. His eyes trail down the loose sleep shirt and short set I changed into after I showered, now a little stained with wet spots from the water dripping off my hair. My bare legs are crossed on the fluffy comforter, and my hands are tucked into the small space between my thighs.

Dexter closes the door slowly, and I turn back to face Annabelle. "Do you think he heard me?"

"I hope he did."

"I'll talk to you later," I say, ignoring her little comment. "Give Jeremy lots of kisses from me."

16

Dexter

SHE THINKS ABOUT US?

My stomach starts to do somersaults, flipping and rolling and twisting like it's entering some all-American gymnastics semifinals competition. I don't have time to process this new revelation that Lucy thinks about our one-time tryst. Or three-time tryst. It's surprising how much we were able to fit into a few hurried hours.

Lucy walks out of my spare bedroom, her steps slow and dragged while carrying the look of a guilty puppy dog on her face. I start to quietly sift through the takeout containers on my kitchen counter, gently spreading them out before opening and peeking inside to make sure everything I ordered arrived correctly.

The rustling of plastic and screech of Styrofoam rubbing against more Styrofoam fills the quiet as Lucy sidles up to my side.

She's freshly showered, and her hair is still damp. I can smell the clean soap scent surrounding her, almost like fresh laundry with a hint of something fruity. Like lemons and cherries. She looks at me with a small smile, and I can't help but feel protective of her. She sounded so weary and scared over the phone when she called me, and even more so defeated when I arrived at her apartment. I hate that she was in that place, where she felt so helpless. And I don't care that this overprotective impulse makes me want to hold and soothe her. I give in a little to that impulse and place a hand at the small of her back, where I can feel the smooth skin under the thin oversized shirt she has on.

"Thank you," she whispers.

"You're welcome," I whisper back. I shove away the urge to place a small kiss at her temple and remove my hand before I impulsively start rubbing circles into her skin. "So did you hear back from the property manager yet?"

She nods. "He finally called me back," she says with a tightness in her face making her look even more stressed. "He wants me to meet him back at the apartment tomorrow at eleven. I guess the super is out of town for the weekend. Probably why I couldn't get a hold of him."

I nod. The mere thought of her going back there runs a chill of unease through me. And those completely rational and reasonable reasons why I want her to stay with me start to float over my head again.

She would be safe.

She wouldn't have to play cheek buddies with someone else's ass in that fucking outhouse.

She'd never have to see that slimy neighbor again. What kind of a name is *Gary* anyway?

"I'll go with you," I tell her, knowing how serious my voice sounds. And it matches the energy drifting between us. Quiet with a hint of calm and an edge I can't place. Like a string pulled taut, somehow pulling me to and from her at the same time.

"Back to my apartment?"

I nod.

"It's okay, Dexter," she objects. Her finger flicks the empty brown paper bag that held all of the to-go boxes, and the hollowness inside of it makes the sharp paper sound loud, expressing her frustration and guilt. "You've done enough. And I really don't want to impose. Plus, I'm an adult. I should be able to do this on my own."

"I know," I say in agreement. "Just call it...moral support."

She doesn't argue further. Instead, a hint of a smile peeks through her bravado. Whatever mask she's been wearing all day to hide the aftermath of one helluva welcome party to the city and what I'm sure was a pretty jarring experience slides down her face for a second.

"Um, thank you, by the way." She taps at the aluminum tab of the Coke can I set out for her, along with a bottled water and a peach Perrier, unsure what her drink preferences are. "For coming when I called. Letting me stay here tonight." She pauses and looks up at me. "For the food."

"Sure," I answer softly.

"And, um…thank you for not making things, like, super awkward."

I feign ignorance with slightly puckered lips and a furrowed brow. "Why would things be awkward?"

A flash of disbelief and amusement swipes across her face. She rolls her eyes and purses her lips together, but it does nothing to hide the smile shouldering its way through the tilt at the corners of her mouth. "Dexter."

"Lucy," I mimic.

We stand there in a silent stand-off, our hands resting on our imaginary holsters. "Really?" she finally asks, obviously a rhetorical question. "You *know* why."

I can't help the wide grin creeping up my face. I try to hide it, pulling my lips between my teeth and crossing my arms at the same time I lean my hip against the counter. So she's choosing to address the elephant in the room.

My thoughts wander a little bit, letting that elephant shine in the spotlight for a moment. They veer toward a direction they really shouldn't be heading at this exact moment. Like the sounds of her moan when my mouth latched to the curved underside of her breast. Or her light giggle when I wrestled her against my sheets, her body molding to mine as if she were made for me. Or the harsh scrape of her nails digging into the skin on my back and shoulders.

"Oh, are you talking about the last time you saw me when you crept out of here like the Hamburglar in broad daylight?"

Her mouth gapes. "I did not sneak out of here!"

I cock my head to one side. "Really?"

"I-I...It wasn't like that," she stutters, and my smile grows. "I just didn't want to complicate things. I was leaving the next day."

"Okay," I say, the single two syllable word sounding more like an appeasement than anything else.

"Can we just be adults and agree to not make this awkward?" she asks, slicing a hand in between us.

I raise my hands, palms facing her in surrender. "*I* can," I tell her. "Can you?"

"Are you implying that I can't be mature and unbothered about being this..." She waves a hand back and forth between us. "*This*?"

I chuckle. "Not at all."

Her face shifts into an angry, determined scowl. "Good," she states, punctuating her word with a sweet, innocent smile, wiping away the animosity with a silent truce. "The food's getting cold." She takes the chopsticks with an affirming nod, and we start to eat in silence.

About ten minutes into our meal, when I notice Lucy hogging the pad thai, she breaks the silence. "You know I've never had Thai food?"

The noodles wrapped around my chopsticks stop midway to my mouth. "Never?"

She shakes her head.

"How is that possible?"

"I don't know," she says casually, even adding a shrug. "I guess I've never really thought to try it?"

"And?"

She eyes me over the lip of the white to-go container in her hand, the thin paperboard blocking how diligently she's working to shovel as much food into her mouth as she can. She lowers the box, revealing a thin sliver of noodle stuck to the corner of her mouth.

"It's okay." She casually places the box down, tapping the counter with her fingernail as she slides it toward me. "Did you want some?"

I roll my lower lip between my teeth, running my tongue over it to suppress the smile I can't help. "No, I'm good." I slide the box back to her. "You can have the rest."

Her face lights up. "Yeah?"

Aw, shucks. That's the silly little catchphrase that pops into my head. Aw. Shucks. Because her smile, with that small piece of oily noodle still tacked to the end of it, makes me blush while I look at her, all hopeful and sweet and so goddamn adorable. Aw *fucking* shucks.

She reaches for the box at the same time I grab a napkin. When she sees me inch closer to her, her eyes round. "What?"

I don't say anything. Instead, my hand slowly moves closer to her while her neck stiffens and her mouth slacks open. With a quick swipe, I clean off the corner of her mouth and smirk.

"Did I have something on my face?" she asks, rubbing the spot I just wiped with the back of her hand.

I nod, looking away from her because I'm getting really, *really* bad at hiding this stupid grin on my face.

She laughs. "And you let me just stand here, looking all silly with food on my face?"

"Way more fun than telling you," I say, low and playful.

She rolls her eyes, plucking the Coke can off the counter and veering toward the living room. I follow, taking my freshly opened beer bottle, and settle on the couch next to her. We get comfortable, the equivalent of a dog walking circles before lying down on a cushy spot, and I reach for the remote.

"Did you want to watch something?" I offer.

"Sure. Whatever you want." She's not even looking at me. Instead, she's busy finishing the rest of her meal while she scrapes the wooden chopsticks against the now nearly empty box.

I flip through the channels on my TV, doing a bit of channel surfing before I land on an episode of *Supernatural*.

"What is this?"

"*Supernatural*?"

Lucy shakes her head when I sit there gesturing toward the screen, where Sam and Dean are caught in a pickle, wrapped in chains and bindings.

"It's demon hunting. Ghosts and—"

"Who's that?" Lucy asks, interrupting my obscurely vague explanation of the show I've been watching regularly for a decade.

"That would be Sam," I answer, eyeing the way her gaze is glued to Sam Winchester's perfect jawline and wavy hair. "Or Jared Padalecki. He's the actor, if that's what you're asking."

She nods in approval with her eyes still laser focused on the screen. *Okay,* so I guess I'm just chopped liver over here.

"We could watch something else..." I point the remote in front of me.

"No, no," she argues, lifting a hand in my direction. "No, we can watch this."

"Are you sure? Because—"

She snatches the remote from my hand and shoves it in between the couch cushions. When Dean's pretty hazel eyes wink at an unsuspecting woman at a bar, I swear I see Lucy swoon.

"Who knew two fictional brothers with the genetic pool of Adonis is what would get your attention?"

"Huh?" she asks, finally giving *me* her attention after feeling as if I disappeared from her periphery when she discovered the Winchester brothers.

"Nothing, Lucy. Just enjoy the show."

The large pink elephant that was in the room, the same one that blew a trumpet-level disturbance filled with our sexual past, has gone silent. As if we threw it a handful of peanuts to keep it occupied while we diverted our attention to ghosts and goblins and all the scary things that go bump in the night.

17

Dexter

"WHERE DID YOU GO YESTERDAY?" Janet asks.

"Um, I, uh, had to go help a friend with something." I pause, unsure why my voice sounds so clumsy while on the phone with my sister. It's not like Janet would be upset that I left her place yesterday without so much as a wave goodbye. Maybe it's just Lucy's presence, unwittingly making me a little nervous and uncool. "She had an emergency."

"Oh," Janet answers from the other end.

I clear my throat through a rough cough. "Are you okay? How are you feeling?"

"I'm good," she says, sounding pretty convincing. "I surprisingly got a pretty good night's sleep. I think the changes my doctor made to my meds are actually helping."

My face softens, and the tautness in my shoulders I didn't even realize was resting there slackens. There's hope laced into her voice, like it's braided into all of the bad and the ugly she's had to live with as of late, making not only her optimistic, but me too.

"Yay," I exclaim quietly and Janet laughs.

Lucy walks into view just then. I've been in my kitchen, fixing myself a cup of coffee after I found that the orange juice in the fridge had gone bad, and calling Janet to check in on her.

Lucy's wearing a dress that falls just above her knees. It's a pale bluish color, one that looks like the color of the sky when the sun is starting to ease into dusk, and it's not as bright but more muted and subtle. Her shoulders are covered with sleeves that cap them, and she's finished off the entire look with an ensemble of necklaces, bracelets, and rings. It's nothing special. In fact, she's dressed down in something that looks as if she's running errands or having a casual lunch with friends, but she looks like a literal breath of fresh air.

She waves a hand in my direction, obviously noting that I have my phone pressed to my ear, and pads her way toward the coffee pot behind me, stepping softly in her white Converse sneakers.

"Uh, Jan," I say, my eyes on Lucy as she reaches for a mug from the wire dish rack, "I'll call you later. Maybe I can come by later this week. I'll bring over some ice cream and donuts."

"Not my weakness!" Janet exclaims through mock agony.

I laugh and catch Lucy looking in my direction. She tucks a strand of hair behind her ear, and the light streaming in from the windows catches against the small row of hoops looped through her earlobe.

"Bye, Janet." I place my phone down on the counter, and when I look at Lucy, we share an awkward smile.

"Personal call?"

"Um, yeah." I don't elaborate. It feels a little upsetting and grave to discuss my sister and her illness and why I felt the need to check in on her first thing in the morning. Luckily, Lucy doesn't prod any further. Instead, she glances at the small digital clock on the microwave and sips her coffee.

"We should probably head out in about fifteen minutes," I announce after we've been taking loud, warm slurps from our mugs.

She nods. "I'm ready whenever you are."

It takes about twenty minutes to get from my place to hers. Six subway stops and one car change later, Lucy and I are walking the last ten blocks to get to her building. When her building comes into view, we're met with a man in his early to mid-forties wearing business attire that looks too stuffy for a Sunday morning. His terse features,

Jeannie Choe

brow drawn together in disapproval, and a scowl set in the narrow lines of his frown make him look incredibly unapproachable even with his gaze focused on his phone held in his hand.

Lucy and I reach the building just as the man looks up from his phone. "Are you Lucia?"

"Lucy," she corrects. "Yes. Yes, I am."

He nods, does a reproving once-over at me, and turns to walk toward the building. I peer at Lucy, and her eyes widen. My hand automatically moves to the small of her back, guiding her up the steps.

"Let's get this over with," I whisper. The softness in my voice and the encouraging way my steps follow hers earns me a small smile.

When we reach her apartment door, the guy, whose name I have yet to find out, opens it with his own set of keys. The knob jiggles, and it almost falls out of the latch. He lets out a sigh of disapproval and walks through the entryway.

"I locked it best I could, but it was already a little loose when I moved in," Lucy starts to explain. "And the toaster oven was just done, so I threw it out, plus some—"

"Why didn't you tell the super that the door wasn't locking right?"

"What?"

"He could've come to fix it before someone broke in," he throws in, that deep scowl on his face transitioning into something that aligns with rage. "Now I have to deal with this mess."

"I'm sorry," I cut in. "But I don't see how—"

He huffs loudly, interrupting me. "Women," he mutters under his breath.

"Excuse me?!" Lucy roars and rears her face forward, and I have this impulse to hold her back. Not for her safety but for his.

"You wouldn't know the difference between a loose doorknob and a flimsy purse strap. You probably tried to fix it with some nail polish or lip gloss."

I take a step toward him, but Lucy's hand cuts across my chest. "I don't think it's *my* responsibility to make sure a damn lock is working *before* I move in. As the property manager, it's your responsibility to make sure the apartment is move-in ready. And I believe the listing said 'central air?'" She waves a hand to the lone window in the room, where a window AC unit is mounted. "There are a lot of defects in this place that needed to be taken care of before I was ever handed a set of keys, so false advertisement should be the least of your worries, but none of that falls on the tenant when all of those issues were present before I even set foot in here." She reaches into her purse, shifting through her things before brandishing a set of brass keys. "Here," she states firmly. "I won't be needing these." She slides the keys on the small kitchen counter, and the scrape of metal to laminate fills the tense silence.

"But you have a lease agreement," the guy says, his name still unknown to me, and to be honest, I don't think I care to know it at this point.

Lucy shakes her head. "It was a month-to-month agreement," she reminds him. "Which means there is no obligation on my end to stay here. And since my first month is up, I think I'll find somewhere else to stay."

The guy sort of gapes at her, and that scowl he wore so proudly has shifted into shock. "Bu-But you have to give a notice."

Lucy smiles her sweet smile. The one that holds a few secrets and tricks up her sleeve. "How about you take this as my notice, and I won't place a call to the city? That mold in the bathroom was getting pretty musty, and I'm sure they don't need to know exactly how much of it your tenants are being exposed to."

I cross my arms over my chest, and my smug smile matches Lucy's. Lucy offers a wave goodbye with a taunting wiggle of her fingers, marking her victory, and we walk toward the door.

"And the communal bathroom was definitely *not* on the listing!" she throws over her shoulder as we scurry down the stairs leading outside where we're hit in the face by the late morning warmth. Lucy grips my arm, and leads the way, taking a few hurried turns until the building is no longer in view.

"Ohmigod!" Lucy exclaims softly. "That was exhilarating."

"That was amazing," I add.

"I can't believe I just did that," she says, pressing a hand to her chest. I can almost see the adrenaline lift from her body like a rise of smoke. "Ohmigod, I can't believe I just did that."

"He deserved it."

"No, I mean, I can't believe I did that. I have nowhere to go," she says, her round eyes suddenly filling with dread. "I think I have to call Nat or Carmen."

I study her eyes. "Do you...want to?"

She looks at me, and the apprehension is written all over her face. "I might not have a choice." She peers at the ground like she's searching for an answer. Maybe a different solution to this problem that upended her living situation.

I grip her shoulder, calling for the last bits of her attention. "It'll be okay," I tell her, tilting my head to force her eyes to me. "I'm sure Nat'll be too happy to have you here to lecture you or tell you you made a big mistake about the internship."

"I guess, but...I just don't even know where to start." She pauses to nibble the edge of her thumb before she runs her fingers through her hair and lets out a deep, frustrating sigh. And I realize I may be wrong. It might not be okay. After my talk with Hayden and how it seems Lucy's entire family's been doubting her and this internship, it might not be the right choice to tell them. Especially when she already seems so vulnerable about her decision to move out here. What if she's met with disapproval and judgment? Or worse, with reprimand?

"Stay with me." Those three words that have been running through my head like a self-affirming mantra finally slip through my lips.

Lucy's face shifts into a twisted look of confusion. "What?"

"Stay with me."

"Like, until I go back to Seattle?"

I nod. "I mean, if you still want to tell Nat, you can, but do it on your own terms. You can think about how you want to tell her. Give yourself time to ease into it."

"Dexter, I don't want to..." she protests. "You have a life. People you...see. And—"

"Lucy, you're not imposing on anything, if that's what you're worried about. I have that spare bedroom you can take. You wouldn't be taking up any space that's currently occupied."

The inner corners of her eyebrows pinch together, and her lower lip juts out in a small, subtle pout as she mulls over my offer.

"Really, Lucy. Just stay with me."

"Okay." She says it so softly, I don't even hear it correctly the first time. I think maybe I simply hear her quietly exclaim "oh" as a reaction in place of the answer I'm hoping for. But it isn't. She's saying yes. "Yeah, okay," she repeats.

She's staying. In my apartment. In the room across the hall from mine. The same room I can see right into if both of our doors are left open.

She's *staying.*

My heart starts to hum inside my chest, and a swarm of butterflies flutters in my stomach. I'm nervous. I should have cleaned up a bit before I brought her over. Maybe vacuumed her room and lit a candle in there. I definitely should've thrown away the expired bottle of orange juice instead of putting it back in my fridge like I usually do.

The journey back to my apartment is quiet. We sit inside the cacophonous clanks and booms in the subway amid the rattling train cars and blaring announcements. We trudge up the stairs and round corners with her always half a step ahead of me and my eyes on her tight shoulders. We approach my building passing glances at each other with tense, forced smiles. The kind of smile you give a stranger on the street when you accidentally make eye contact.

When Lucy walks into my apartment, she lingers a bit by the entryway before carefully walking to my couch where she perches herself at the edge of the cushion.

"You hungry?"

She looks up at me as I hover over the coffee table and pick up some loose trash. "Um, sure," she answers.

"I can order a pizza," I tell her.

"Okay." Her voice sounds meek, and I realize how awkward and unresolved this situation is. We decided she'd come back home with me over a cursory agreement and her unexpected need for a roof over her head, and I almost feel like there needs to be a set of terms and conditions between us or she'll leave at the first wave of doubt or regret.

"Is everything okay?" I ask.

She straightens her back and her jaw sets in a solemn look of resolve. "I think we need to set some terms or ground rules."

"Terms?" I respond, finding it a little amusing that I was thinking something along the same lines.

"Yeah." She presses her lips together and exhales a firm sigh through her nose. "You're basically my landlord now and usually, when there's a landlord-tenant type situation, there's, like, a lease agreement."

"I'm not going to kick you out or change my mind, if that's what you're worried about."

"Still..."

"Okay. Whatever you need to feel comfortable while you're here."

"I'll pay rent at the first of the month like I was doing back at that... shoebox."

"Lucy, you don't have to do—"

She lifts her palm in my direction. "Dexter, I'm not going to take up a room and freeload off of you for the next two months."

The tone of her voice leaves me zero wiggle room. She's determined. "Fine."

"Also, if you have...guests over or something, just let me know. I'll make myself scarce. I don't want to put a damper on your social life."

I shrug. "I guess, but that's not really necessary."

She nods. "And lastly, if you're going to order pizza, I'm paying for half."

"No."

She frowns. "No?"

"No."

"But that's what roommates do," she argues. "You go halfsies on things."

"You said ground rules or whatever," I start to explain, shaking my head. "But you paying for lunch is a hard limit for me."

She holds back a smile. "Hard limit?"

"Yes."

She giggles. "I'd hate to push you beyond a hard limit," she says playfully. "Should we give you a safe word?"

My stern face of resolve softens, and a cheesy grin slices across my face. "I like pizza."

"Me too. Just no anchovies."

"I meant for a safe word."

She clamps her lips together, and her hand moves to her face in an attempt to hide her own smile that's growing more and more infectious by the minute.

"No anchovies," I say, my lips curving into something more suggestive than a simple smile. "Sausage okay?"

"And olives please."

I nod with a smile still stamped on my face, pressing my phone to my ear to place the order from the closest pizza shop saved in my contacts.

While we wait for the pizza to arrive, we both disappear into our rooms. It's still early, barely past noon. But with the AC on full blast and the enticing thought of a lazy Sunday afternoon, I change out of my stiff jeans and into something much more comfortable, sweatpants and a tattered undershirt, before I beeline to the kitchen to toss the bottle of orange juice and walk into the living room. I'm restacking some magazines and wooden coasters when Lucy reemerges. She must've had the same idea as I did because she's dressed down in attire just as leisurely and laid-back as mine. Her long legs are bare in her sleep shorts, stopping just at mid-thigh. She's wearing an oversized University of Washington shirt that covers most of her shorts, making her look like she's not wearing any bottoms at certain angles. Her feet are covered in fuzzy panda socks, and she's pulled back her hair in a small claw clip, showing off the rounded curves of her cheeks and narrow slopes of her jaw and neck.

"Food should be here soon," I tell her as we settle on the opposite ends of the couch, and she nods. She starts to fidget with a magazine on the coffee table, an issue of *People*, and she lifts an inquisitive eyebrow in my direction.

"Keeping up with your celebrity gossip?" she asks. "Maybe I

should come to you to get my fill on the latest Selena Gomez and Justin Bieber drama."

I chuckle. "My sister, Janet, left those last week."

"Janet." She says my sister's name like the sound of it results in a sudden epiphany.

"Yeah," I say, eyeing her curiously. "Why?"

"Oh, nothing. That's a pretty name."

"Yeah." We sit for a moment in awkward silence. Her fingers toy with the edges of the magazine, flicking the corners with her thumb. "So, how's the internship going?" I ask, cutting into the short period of quiet.

She slaps a hand to the cover of the magazine, delivering a defeated smack to Kim Kardashian's face. "It's...going."

I shift in my seat to face her, and she does the same.

"We had this shoot yesterday, and I was taking some shots of one of the models. The head photographer for the campaign saw some of them and asked me to have them edited by Monday. But now, I don't have a laptop. I'll have to try to get to work early tomorrow and see what I can do." She pauses, burying her face into her hands. "It just feels like..." She lifts her eyes to me. The inner corners of her brows turn up, and her lower lip juts out in the saddest little frown. "Whenever I take one step forward, I take two steps back. Maybe I should've listened to my mom."

I reach for her leg, the bony area of her shin since it's the closest part of her to me, and squeeze her gently.

"Hold on." I get up and go to my room to retrieve the one item that may add a cushion of support to the long list of mishaps and stress that've been thrown her way like a mean curveball. "I'm not trying to offer a solution because I know you're going to figure things out on your own, but maybe this'll help lighten the load a bit. God knows you've been through hell and back." I extend my MacBook in her direction. "Use this. I have my work laptop, and I only use this for personal things."

"Like a lifetime membership to Pornhub?" she asks with a sly smirk.

"More like my BDSM fanfic."

Her brow lifts in amusement. "Didn't know you had it in you."

I huff a laugh, and she eyes the laptop still in my possession. I nudge it closer to her. "I'm serious, Luce. Use it."

The sad furrow between her brow is replaced with a sweet, appreciative smile. "Thank you, Dexter. That's actually really, *really* helpful."

I wave a hand, brushing off her gratitude.

"And it means a lot that you'd share your most treasured possession with me."

"It's just a computer."

"I meant the fanfic."

I laugh at the same time Lucy gingerly takes my laptop from my hand. "Hey, I have a question."

Lucy looks at me with an innocent smile. "Hmm?"

"How do you know about Pornhub?"

Before she has a chance to answer, my intercom buzzes loudly, announcing the arrival of our lunch. Lucy giggles and shoves a hand into my chest, making me feel all warm and fuzzy inside. When all I do is smile back at her, the intercom buzzes again, this time more impatiently.

I wink at her. "Saved by the bell."

18

Dexter

MY CAFFEINE PREFERENCES are usually pretty straightforward. Black, no sugar or cream, piping hot. None of the fancy-shmancy foam crap on top or something sweet drizzled inside. And especially not in a twenty-ounce disposable plastic cup half filled with ice.

But here I am, Monday morning, my messenger bag slung over my shoulder, standing next to Lucy with her camera bag slung over hers and a matching set of Starbucks cups in our hands.

"Trust me, you're going to love it."

"What is it?" I ask, eyeing the cup like it's diseased.

"An upside-down venti iced caramel macchiato with oat milk and a light caramel drizzle."

"How do you not get an aneurysm every time you order that?"

She rolls her eyes. "And here." She offers a small paper bag holding something heavy and warm. "It's a coffee cake." I take her offering, the toasty cinnamon smell permeating through the packaging. "Coffee isn't one of the major food groups. You need some sustenance."

"And a sugar-packed pastry is the answer?"

"Carbs equal energy."

We take our first steps out of my apartment building, entering the busy streets while joining the rest of working-class America on just another regular Monday morning. But this Monday morning is different. It isn't starting with the usual drab commute to my office. It's starting with Lucy. With her perfectly styled hair and makeup looking subtle yet obvious that she took the time to apply early in the morning. With our day starting alongside each other and plans to end it together.

"I should be back home by about six, depending on what happens at today's shoot."

"Oh, I almost forgot." I shove a hand in my pocket, careful not to spill the coffee concoction in my other hand. "Here." I extend to Lucy a small set of keys. "Just in case you get home before I do."

She takes it in her hands, now a little cold and wet from condensation, and smiles gratefully. "Thank you."

"You're good finding your way to work?" I ask.

She holds up her phone and wiggles it in front of me. "I've got my handy dandy MTA app."

"Look at you, blending in with all the locals. I think we can officially revoke your tourist card."

Her face warms with a delighted blush, and my hand fists at my side when a sudden impulse to pinch her cheek has me lifting my fingers. We stand there a little awkwardly, not knowing what to do next.

"Well," she announces. "I guess I'll see you later?"

"Yeah," I say, throwing in a little smirk. "I'll be sure to text you when I'm jumping off the walls." I lift my cup in her direction, and she touches hers to mine.

"Cheers," she says softly with the sweetest smile. I watch as she turns and disappears into the sea of people.

"So my next infusion is in a few days, and I was wondering if you'd go with me."

Janet's voice filters through the AirPod shoved into my right ear while my busy hands scatter over my desk. The sounds of ringing phones and the usual office chatter linger outside my open office door.

"Of course," I answer.

"Charles was going to go with me, but he's been really busy at work. He said he would take the day off, but he's already taken so much time off, so I told him it's fine."

The stapled stacks of papers and the tablet holding various data and quarterly reports sent to me by my team and assistant become a jumble of hieroglyphics, all foreign and blurry. Even the company logo and the large block letters that spell Citadel Financial are no longer sharp and bold while my thoughts simmer over the idea of how sickly my sister's gotten over the past month.

This fucking sucks. We should be talking about Labor Day plans or the recent price hike for our shared Netflix subscription, not *fucking* chemo and *fucking* cancer. She doesn't deserve this. She deserves to be healthy and happy.

"Janet, you know you can ask me any time. I've gone with you before, and I really don't mind taking you to every single one."

The line goes silent, and I think maybe she got disconnected. But then I hear her sigh. "I, uh…I really wish I didn't need to ask you, Dex."

"Why?! Janet, I've seen you after those fucking treatments. You're literally going to hell and back with each infusion. I know you prefer to do things on your own, but you have to let me be by your side with this shit."

"Yeah," she says meekly. "No, you're right. I need you and Charles to help me out."

I nod, though she can't see me.

"But you don't need to cuss."

I scoff. "Whatever," I say flippantly. "Just…let me know when you have your infusion appointments. Or I'll hack into your phone and send myself alerts off your calendar or some shit."

"Gosh, I forget how bratty and mean you get when you don't get your way."

"I'm not any brattier than you're stubborn, big sister."

She giggles, and it feels like it's been forever since I've heard her laugh. And for a second, just a second, I push away the thought that she's sick. I just listen to the sound of her laugh and picture her smile. It's a shitty thing to do, to shove away the reality of her being sick and almost pretend like she isn't. That she's at the art gallery on the other side of town, doing her art world things. Because that's not the reality here.

"How are you feeling today?" I ask, my gaze shifting to the now almost empty Starbucks cup sitting at the edge of my desk.

"Better," she answers, actually sounding convincing. "I'm going to go into work in a little bit. Make some calls and help with contacting some local artists to fill the gallery."

"You up for it?"

"Yeah." I can almost picture her nodding her head, though she doesn't sound too sure. "I'm not meeting with anyone. And if I get too overwhelmed, I can call it an early day. I just want to try to do something so I don't feel so…"

"Stir crazy?"

"Useless."

"Janet, your body is fighting its biggest battle yet. I think you need to give yourself a little more credit."

A small, optimistic laugh cuts through the defeated tone of her voice, and it makes me smile.

"Fine then," she says, that smile still lingering in her softly spoken words. "I guess I'm just bored."

"Then maybe a little fresh air won't hurt. Just make sure you take it easy. Don't tire yourself out too much."

"I won't."

I pick up the coffee, the drops of condensation dripping on my desk and landing on the papers in front of me in fat blobs. "Have you ever had Starbucks?"

"You mean that large coffee conglomerate that's literally on every street corner of Manhattan? Why, no, Dexter. I haven't. Why do you ask?"

"Someone got me some, and it's not half bad." I tilt the cup back, taking a long sip as the hints of caramel mixing perfectly with the deep, bitter tones of espresso hit my taste buds.

"Please don't tell me this is the first time you've ever had Starbucks."

"No, I've had, like, coffee but never anything like this...iced caramel macchiato stuff."

"Who is she?"

"Who's who?"

"The girl that got you the coffee?"

My mouth hangs open in shock. *How did she know?* "Why do you assume it's a girl?"

"As if you had this sudden epiphany to try a caramel-infused espresso drink after having lived your twenty-nine years of life never trying one. Which, I might add, is basically sipping sugar straight through a straw."

"And what if I did?"

If I were to look up deadpanned in the dictionary, it would be very likely that I'd find Janet's face as it is right now alongside it. "We're doing this?"

"Doing what?" I ask, continuing this game of ignorance.

"Okay, fine. Don't tell me who she is. I'll have to do my own digging. Maybe pull me out of my useless boredom."

"Janet, really—" My denial, as false as it may be, is interrupted by a sharp knock at my door.

"Dexter," Jacob, my assistant, calls. "Margaret's holding a staff meeting with all of the department heads in fifteen minutes."

I click over to mute on my phone. "Is this about the quarterly reports you just sent me?"

He nods while eyeing the scattered mess on my desk. "I can brief you if you haven't had a chance to go over everything."

"Yeah." I look down at my phone screen, glancing at the twenty-three minutes and eight seconds—and counting—timer on the screen under Janet's contact info and number pad. I unmute the call. "Jan, I gotta go. Text me your appointment time, and I'll make sure to clear my day during your next...session." I look up and quickly glance at a waiting Jacob.

"Great, you can tell me more about this mystery Starbucks girl."
"Bye."
"Bah-yeee!"

19

Lucy

"OHMIGOD?! I can't believe that happened!"

I nod, my attention on adjusting the height to the softbox reflector to angle it toward the stark white backdrop while Elaine places the last of the camera lenses neatly organized on a foldable table and rushes to my side. "Yeah, it was pretty awful."

"So where are you staying?"

"A friend's," I answer meekly. "He, um, offered his spare room, so…" I just finished telling her the whirlwind of the weekend I had while she got lost on an impromptu trip to Washington Square Park.

"I can't believe you went through all of that," she sort of mumbles under her breath. She turns to face me. "You must have been so scared."

"Um, yeah…" I look up at her with a smile through the tightness lodged in my throat.

I've been trying to retrace the last forty-eight hours. The highs and lows. The expected and unexpected. The absolute last thing I thought I'd add on the list was "move in with Dexter." I would've expected a trip to the moon before that happened. Everything feels so…chaotic. Just when I caught a whiff—a minute resemblance—of decorum in my life, I feel like it's been snatched away from me.

How did I end up *here*? Robbed of my valuables, essentially homeless, and shacking up with an old…fling. Maybe I should just call my sisters. Maybe they'll be able to replace some of the calm that's gone wayward. But every time I even *think* about picking up my phone to call them or even taking a cab over to their apartments, my insides feel like they're going to flip inside out and teeny-tiny bubbles of anxiety start to pop inside of me. And now I'm reeling from this completely random and unwarranted attraction I have toward Dexter. I mean, I guess it's not *completely* unwarranted, considering we have history, but why did a spike of unease spear through my stomach when I thought he was talking to some *girl* yesterday? And why did it feel like a complete burst of relief when he told me it was his sister?

"You know, this shit wouldn't have happened in San Diego," Elaine fusses, jutting her index finger at me as she walks back to the table. "I can't wait for this to be over so I can go home. I miss the damn beach. And my car. Also, I think I sat in pee this morning on the subway."

I grimace just as my phone buzzes in my back pocket. When I look at the screen, I see a new message from Dexter. An image of him, his now empty Starbucks cup held up to his face, and a bright, cheesy smile fills the screen.

> Dexter: I think I can outrun a cheetah with the amount of caffeine running through me.

My wide grin matches his, and my insides melt a little. Okay, a lot.

I feel like I'm seeing his face in a completely new light, finding more things that make him cute and handsome and quite honestly, irresistible. Like the shadow from his Adam's apple somehow making him look masculine and strong. Or the way one eye squints more than the other, and it makes him look playful and flirty. And, of course, there's that little mole next to his eye that shifts into the small crinkles fanning out through his adorable smiles. I've been adding to the mental list of things I've started to find attractive in men. Bare feet, teeny-tiny moles, and now, Adam's apples. Or maybe it's just those things on Dexter that I find attractive.

> Me: I'll pick up a cheetah on the way home if you make sure to buy a stopwatch.

> Dexter: And a checkered flag.

> Me: Can't forget the checkered flag.

Home. Home *with* Dexter.

I didn't realize it when I typed out the single four-letter word, but there's so much weight to it. All of it filled with promise and comfort. I could get used to this. This feeling of security and something safe and easy.

In just two days, I've learned what it's like to coexist with someone. It isn't like this with Annabelle. We have our own lives, and we do our own things. Annabelle goes out for drinks after work with her lawyer friends. She spends two evenings a week with Alma at their uncle's house, where she brings back large Tupperware containers full of *pupusas*. I usually go to bed by ten after dozing on the couch for about an hour so I can wake up to start my early morning shift at Mr. Bean's.

But it's not like that with Dexter. He includes me in something as simple as doing the dishes or deciding how many episodes of *Supernatural* we can squeeze in before bedtime. He waited for me in the morning before walking out the door so we could leave together, and something tells me he's going to do the same tomorrow morning. I could get used to this, having someone to coexist with. Someone who would wait for me to make plans for the night. To split a sausage pizza or a large order of pad thai with.

No. I *can't* get used to this. Because this is absolutely temporary. Those dark, imaginary red lines I've been drawing through each passing week have been a comforting reminder that my flight back home is going to happen much sooner than later. I can't wait to go home. My *actual* home. I can't wait to snuggle up with Jeremy and tell Annabelle how delusional she was with her screwball suggestions to hook up with Dexter again. At the end of all this, I'll hop on my flight without even a second glance. Just like I planned.

> Dexter: Can't wait. I'll see you at home, Lucy.

And there go those red lines, drawn with a lighter hand and reluctance. Maybe one last glance before I leave. One last look back to see what I'm leaving behind. Just so I can see Dexter waving at me from the steps of his apartment building.

"Lucy?"

I look up to see Ryan hovering over the table Elaine was organizing, his expectant face eyeing the setup I was doing for today's shoot.

"Kyle wanted to go over the pictures from the shoot on Saturday. The ones he asked you to have ready."

I trip over a tripod leg, stumbling toward my tote bag. Ryan swoops toward me when my step hobbles a little before I catch my feet and stand upright. "Sorry," I say sheepishly. "I'm ready. Let me just grab my laptop."

I follow Ryan to where Kyle is stationed at a long six-feet foldable table. Sweat starts gathering in my armpits and under-boob region, making my bra chafe against my skin. Kyle doesn't look up when we approach him, and Ryan waits a beat before interrupting him.

"Kyle, you wanted to see Lucy?"

He nods, his gaze focused on the tablet screen in front of him. "Did you edit the pictures?" he asks, addressing me.

Ryan steps aside, and I open Dexter's laptop before setting it in front of Kyle. "I worked with a few different contrasts and exposures. For this one…" I pause, clicking open a picture of Seb leaned against the brick wall with half of his body glistening in sunlight and the other half hidden in the shade. "I used a more vintage style editing process and focused on bluish hues to contrast with his clothes."

He murmurs an acknowledging hum.

"And for this one," I add, clicking another picture of Seb leaned forward, the shade now covering his entire body with the light reflecting off the wall behind him, "I used a higher contrast to counteract the shaded area. I just thought it would make Seb pop a bit when he's surrounded by so many shadows."

Kyle hums again, turning the laptop screen so that it faces him fully. It forces me to relinquish control to him as his fingers skate across the flat mousepad. I stand there awkwardly, twiddling my fingers in front of me while attempting to read Kyle's facial expression. Is that furrow between his brows a good thing? Or is the way he just sighed through his nose a sign of disappointment?

"Okay," he finally says, looking up at me while gently pushing the laptop back in my direction. "Send those over to Ryan. He's going to send them to the rest of the project team, and we'll go over them before having the brand manager take a look."

I hold back the eager spring in my feet, refraining from hopping up and down. Hoping I don't look as impatient as I feel, I nod before turning to walk away.

"And Lucy," he calls. I turn to face him, suddenly scared he's going to change his mind. But he doesn't, and the constant trickle of letdowns and setbacks I've faced in the last month seems to fade away. "Good work."

"Oh! They have a chocolate peanut butter cupcake today!"

Elaine and I both light up in front of the bright display case carrying various flavors of cupcakes in front of us.

"Ohmigod, and a strawberry shortcake too."

It's our lunch break, and Elaine suggested we celebrate my little serendipitous milestone with a return trip to our new favorite dessert place while she claimed it wasn't serendipitous at all. That it was a result of my hard work and talent. We make our selections and head back toward the studio while I clutch my strawberry shortcake cupcake with a graham cracker crust and walk with a practical skip in my step.

As we approach the building, my phone buzzes in my pocket. I impulsively assume it's Dexter as we've been texting each other back and forth, with his last message before my break congratulating me on my most recent praise from Kyle. But when I look at my phone, I see Nat's name flash across the screen.

"Uh, why don't you go on up? I need to take this," I tell Elaine.

"Okay." She nods and presses the button to call the elevator.

"Hey, Nat."

"Hey! Are you busy?" she asks, her voice sounding distracted and echoey.

"Uh, I have a minute."

"Sorry, I have to put you on speaker," she explains. "I was in between meetings after lunch, and I just needed to talk to you before I forget."

"Okay. What's up?"

"So, I'm going back home in a few weeks. Mom wants to go wedding dress shopping."

I smile. "I called it."

"Yeah." She laughs. "We're going to finalize reservations and rooms for the hotel while I'm there. I was thinking you can stay in my room with me for the first few nights before the wedding."

"You aren't staying with Hayden?"

"We can't see each other on the wedding day!" she argues in a teasing voice. "It's bad luck."

"Okay," I respond through a laugh.

"Oh! I also wanted to try something fun while we're in Hawaii. Maybe snorkeling. Or ziplining!"

"You? Ziplining?"

She huffs. "Yes," she answers, a little annoyed. "Why?"

"Have you forgotten your debilitating fear of heights?" I tease.

"I'm trying to face my fears," she explains. "Plus, it'll be fun."

I chuckle.

"So I've been back and forth with Rita, and we decided about two months out—"

"Who's Rita?"

She exhales an exasperated sigh. "Hayden's aunt. Remember? I told you about her when we were talking about the reception? We're doing a garden style party. Twinkle lights and all."

"Right. Sorry," I tell her, remembering the last conversation we had where she word vomited everything she could about the wedding via a ninety-second phone call before she hopped into a crowded subway train.

"Anyway, we're keeping it small and intimate. Just a few family members who are willing to fly out, like Aunt Carlita and Jaqueline," she explains, referring to my dad's sister and our cousin. "And, of course, Mom and Dad and Hayden's mom, plus a few of Hayden's college friends like Dexter."

Dexter.

"Oh."

"So I'll go ahead and send you the link for the hotel and wedding dates so you know exactly when to book your flights," she continues. "Unless you want me to book yours too. You'll fly out of Seattle International, right?"

"Uh…" I hesitate, reminding myself I'm supposed to be in a completely different time zone right now. "It's fine. I can book my own flight."

"Are you sure? I can send you the money for it then."

I cringe. "Yes, I'm sure, Nat," I assure her.

"Really? I really don't mind helping you out. Those plane tickets can get pretty pricey."

"Nat—"

"Lucy," she interrupts. "I'm not trying to be overbearing or anything. Mom's doing enough of that, but I don't want to add to your stress. And I swear I'm not complaining. It's just…"

"What?"

She sighs. "Mom mentioned that…she wants you to move back home."

I groan. "Seriously?"

"She was just throwing it out there, but I think she's just as frustrated as you are about having so much trouble finding a job. And with the internship you mentioned—"

"I should've never brought that up," I say, cutting her off. A swirl of emotions starts to stir inside of me. I don't know whether to be upset or sad or just outright annoyed. "You know, she wasn't like this. She used to let us spread our wings and all that shit."

"I know. She's worried about you."

"I must bring it out of her," I huff. "Nat, I'm sorry you got caught up in all of this but seriously, I'm fine."

She stays quiet, and I wonder if she's shifted completely from being on my side to Team Mom. Maybe while she's telling me all of this as gently as possible, a part of her agrees with my mom. I just hope they don't stage some kind of intervention or something. "I'll talk to her when I see her," she finally says. "Maybe I can buy you some time before she flies over there and starts packing up your things."

"Oh god," I grumble. "I will seriously set up a barricade if she does that."

Nat laughs. "There was also another thing I wanted to ask you."

"Yeah?"

"I was wondering if you'd be my maid of honor. I mean, both you and Carmen would be my maid of honor, so I don't want to officially assign titles. That doesn't feel right. It would be just you two. And since Hayden has Dexter and one of his other college buddies, it works out perfectly."

The tension wrapped around my temple from Nat's mention of my mom's suggestion to move me back home has dissolved into pure joy. "Really?"

"Of course, *really*. I can't get married without my sisters up there. And I'll pay for everything. Your dress, your shoes. All—"

"Nat," I interrupt her. "I can pay for all of that."

"I really don't mind," she assures.

"No, Nat. I'm going to pay for my bridesmaid stuff. And I'm going to stand up there right next to you and hand you tissues and hold your bouquet." I pause before adding, "You just let me know whatever you need, and I'll be your little maid of honor minion."

She laughs. "Maybe you can help me find a dress both you and Carmen like once we decide on a color scheme. Nothing fancy, just something simple and classy."

"Yeah, anything you want."

"I gotta go," she says quickly. "I got a meeting I have to step into, and I'm meeting Hayden for his suit fitting before he needs to be back at the restaurant."

"Yeah, I'll talk to you later."

"Bye!"

20

Dexter

"HOW ARE YOU FEELING?"

A shallow sigh filters through the phone, followed by a pause. "You know, body ache this, nausea that," Janet answers, the glum tone of her voice doing nothing to hide her sarcasm. "But I haven't thrown up since the day before yesterday."

"Progress."

She gives a defeated chuckle, one that sounds more like a scoff. "I'm actually out with Charles tonight."

I turn away from the short pick-up counter at Pepper Thai, where I'm waiting for my order to be called. "You up for that? Like, being around people? I thought you weren't supposed to be out in crowds and stuff. Weakened immune system and all." She told me this the last time we spoke, brushing it off as a needless precaution from her doctor.

She makes a loud *pshh* sound through the phone. "I was getting stir crazy. All I do is go to chemo, stay at home and watch *Real Housewives*, and go to more chemo. I haven't even been back to the gallery since last week after my doctor told me to take a few extra days off. I was craving some strawberry milkshakes and onion rings, so Charles is treating me."

"At The Lunch Car? You're in Brooklyn?"

"Mm-hmm," she answers.

"Just be careful."

"I will!" she whines. "Do you have plans tonight? You want to join us?"

"I'm getting dinner right now and heading home."

"Then meet us here."

"I, uh…"

"Do you have a hot date? Is it Starbucks girl?"

I chuckle.

"You do, don't you!"

"Janet, I'll talk to you later. Tell Charles I said hi."

"You need to tell me who she is. You can't keep her a secret. I'll eventually find out!"

"Bye."

"Wait! Does she know you had an unhealthy obsession with Baby Spice when you were in third grade? Or that you wore diapers until you were five?!"

I hang up right as my order is ready. With my dinner held neatly in a brown paper bag, I walk the two blocks back to my apartment. It's become my evening routine. After a regular, uneventful workday, I take my usual commute home. I make a pit stop at Pepper Thai to pick up Lucy's latest favorite pad thai and mango sticky rice before being greeted by her back at my apartment.

This situation between us feels a little unresolved. Like the spinning wheel in the middle of the computer screen making you irrationally impatient. It's subtle, lingering in the moments she nudges a little closer to me on the couch or when our hands brush as we reach for the remote at the same time. I would say it's probably me being overly paranoid and unnecessarily wary, considering how *not* awkward we are with each other most of the time, but it's there. It's been there since Lucy uttered those four little words, and they've been playing in my head on repeat.

All the damn time.

It's like a record track playing some voodoo chant over and over and over again. One that I honestly don't even mind playing on a constant loop.

I shove those words into a small file cabinet in my head as I approach the steps leading up to my building, hoping they'll eventually fade away, knowing they most likely won't. While it might be fun and, quite honestly, a little daring to venture down the path to discover what she meant when she said it, I don't think she wants to have that conversation. So, as I choose to remain a gentleman and keep my mouth shut about those words I was definitely not meant to hear, I open my apartment door and beeline to the kitchen to set down the food. It's quiet aside from the muffled music playing in Lucy's room, something that sounds like Justin Bieber or the Jonas Brothers.

"Lucy! Dinner!" I call from the other side of Lucy's door, followed by a quick knock. I turn my feet toward the bathroom to quickly wash my hands before Lucy steps out of her room. But when I open the door, I find her there. Not in her room, where I imagined her singing along to pop music sung by outgrown teeny boppers. She's stepping out of the tub with the curtain drawn all the way back. She's naked. And wet. With flushed skin and steam floating around her. Oh, and did I mention *naked*?

"Ahh!"

My feet feel like they're set in cement. I just stand there, dumbfounded. I should look away instead of staring at those slippery curves lining down her hips or the perfect valley between her breasts. I should *definitely* look away. Pretend I didn't see anything. Or close the door and take the next train to Nova Scotia. Or...*something*.

She reaches for a towel and fumbles with it in her hands. "Dexter! Do you mind?!"

When Lucy's glare meets my deer in headlights, it's like all common sense returns to my body. I shut the door and turn my back against it. "Lucy. I'm sorry."

There's no answer. All I hear is some shuffling of feet and what sounds like clothes and towels being thrown around.

"I thought you were in your room so—"

"Dexter, it's fine."

"I didn't mean to stare."

"Ohmigod! Dexter!" she shrieks with the door muffling her voice. "I said it's fine. Please, just...Let me get dressed."

Great, now I'm the asshole who first, got his fill of her naked body and second, am not doing the one gentlemanly thing by letting her get dressed. "Yeah, sorry. I'm sorry."

Shit! As if things between us weren't ambiguous enough. That spinning wheel is back, and I have no idea how to get rid of it. It's not like I can press ctrl+alt+del and make things restart between us.

I'm pacing the kitchen, unsure of what to do with myself. What do I say when she comes out of the bathroom? *If* she comes out. I mean, she can't stay in there forever, right? Maybe I'll just pretend like nothing happened. Or offer to show her mine? Like a tit for tat kind of bargain?

I hear the bathroom door open as I'm sifting through the takeout containers, hoping I look busy and unbothered. I try to keep my eyes on the food in front of me, but when I see Lucy's polished toes peek from the hard floor, I falter.

"Lucy, I'm sorry. Really. I thought you were in your room. And I-I didn't mean to, you know, stare." I grimace, knowing I sound ridiculous with my excuses and half-assed explanations.

"It's fine," she assures, looking equally embarrassed and annoyed. "Nothing you haven't seen before."

Now that's unexpected. I stop what I'm doing to look up at her, a flicker of amusement lining my features. I bite back the smile on my face with my teeth pressed in my lower lip.

"What?" she asks a little tersely when I continue to stare at her. "It's true."

"Okay."

"Dexter," she calls when my smile widens, and I look away to avoid the stern look she's giving me. "I'm not saying let's make this a regular occurrence, but we can be adults about it, right?"

I smirk. "Better than my plan."

She gives me a wary look. "What was your plan?"

"Showing you mine. You know, to even the playing field."

She looks at me, her face twisting in an attempt to hide her laughter. A loud snort rattles through her throat when she ducks her head while covering her mouth. Little droplets of water land on her shirt from her wet hair, darkening the material with small spots, and I get a small whiff of her shampoo and body wash. "You are such a weenie."

I lean back when she pushes her hand to my shoulder, her body shaking with laughter. "I'm a weenie?"

"Total weenie," she confirms, her hand still pressed into me.

"*Wooow*," I answer, feigning shock while trying to ignore the warm, fuzzy feeling spreading across my chest. What is it about when she playfully shoves me that makes me feel all giddy and confident? Like I can move a boulder or do *The New York Times* crossword puzzle in one sitting. "I don't think I've ever heard anyone over the age of nine use that word before."

"Well, you know, if the shoe fits." She ignores the twist in my lips hiding my smirk, the practically menacing bounce in my brow, and even the shift in my body, angling my hips toward her as if offering an invitation.

"'If the shoe—'" My buzzer rings just then, interrupting this amorous back and forth.

I wasn't expecting company, so Lucy's face matches mine in confusion when we look at each other as I walk to the door. "Who is it?" I call, pressing the intercom buzzer as the staticky feedback distorts the outside noise filtering through the speaker.

"It's Janet!" I hear. Followed by "and Charles" in a deeper voice.

Aww, crap. "What are you guys doing here?"

"Bringing you dessert. Now let us up!"

I do as she asks, or rather, demands, and quickly turn to face Lucy. "Uh, it's my sister and her boyfriend."

"Oh."

"Uh…" I laugh nervously and cup the back of my neck, figuring out how awkwardly this is going to go, just as a sharp knock on my door interrupts us. "I'm. Sorry."

When I open it, Janet stands there, a Styrofoam to-go cup in her hand and the widest smile on her face.

"I couldn't head back home without bringing you a mint chip milk-shake," she says coolly while breezing past me. She stops when she sees Lucy at the counter. "Ah-ha! So you *do* have a hot date!"

Charles stands by my sister's side and wraps an arm around her shoulders. "Babe, you're killing his game."

"Oh, no. We're not—I mean, I'm not..." Lucy stutters.

"Janet, this is Lucy. She's...visiting from Seattle for, uh, work. And staying in the spare room."

"Hi," Lucy says with a small wave of her hand.

"Lucy, this is my sister Janet, who likes to come around unannounced like she pays rent."

"Don't be a dick. You should be thanking me for bringing you this liquid heaven." She extends the milkshake in my direction—a peace offering or a bribe, I don't even know—with an innocent smile. I look at her, examining her gaunt features. Her hair is beginning to thin, and she's wearing a lavender-colored scarf wrapped around her head. The skin around her eyes is a shade darker than the rest of her face, making her features look sallow and pale at the same time. And even though it's summer, she's wearing a thick cardigan wrapped around her small body because of the incessant chill rolling through her.

I take a step toward her while reaching for my drink. "Are you okay?" I ask, keeping my voice low and discreet.

"Yes. Why wouldn't I be?"

"I don't know...I just want to make sure. You're really okay?"

"Yeah."

When I don't say anything else, Janet rolls her eyes. "I'm going to go home and rest after this. I just wanted..."

"To be normal for a night?"

"Yes." She exhales a sigh that sounds like she's slightly annoyed. "Plus, you were on the way home. So please just, drink your damn milkshake and let me be."

Instead of prodding further or telling her to go home right away, I take a long, drawn out sip of my milkshake, savoring the dessert I would ride a tornado to get to. And even though my ability to share dwindles down to toddler-level selfishness when I have a mint chip milkshake from The Lunch Car in my hand, I can't resist offering Lucy some.

"You want some?" I say, low and carefully.

She hesitates.

"I don't have cooties."

She rolls her eyes and takes the drink from me. As she takes a sip, Janet makes a choked sound.

"Did you just let her have some of your milkshake?" she asks, her mouth slacked open in shock. "The milkshake I had to pry off your hands to sneak a sip? The same one you wanted hooked to an IV when you were ten?" She turns to Lucy. "I'm sorry I didn't bring you one. I really didn't believe that he had a date here. In fact, I can't remember the last time I've seen him with a girl."

"Oh, it's okay," Lucy says quietly with a shy smile.

"But since this greedy little jerk seems to be in a giving mood," she teases, "I guess it worked out. He must really like you."

Lucy smirks, and I roll my eyes. "Sorry," I whisper, leaning into Lucy a little closer.

"For what?" she whispers back. "I think your sister's better company than you. At least she doesn't ogle my naked body like a total pervert." Her brow shoots up, and her lips purse together, suppressing a cheeky smile.

I respond with a cocky smirk of my own. "I thought we were going to be adults about that."

"Oh—"

A sharp cough, more like an act of faux throat clearing—like a literal "ahem" sound—interrupts us. It's then I realize how my body's inched closer to Lucy, her own body angled to face me with her hips aligned with mine. We aren't even touching, and I can feel that we don't look like two platonic roommates discussing milkshake flavors or the week's weather forecast.

When I look over at Janet and Charles watching us, they both smirk and eye each other, passing along a silent tell. Something that silently whispers, *Did you see that?*

"Okay, Janet," I announce loudly. "I think it's time for you to head home."

Janet sighs, which transitions into a yawn, and Charles naturally wraps his arm around her waist in a way that shows he's holding her up instead of a small display of public affection.

"Fine," she answers. "I'm tired anyway. I guess I'll have to embarrass you another day."

"Thank you for stopping by," I urge, crowding both Janet and Charles toward my door. "Please use that device in your purse with the number pad and fancy screen to announce your visit next time so I don't have to set up security outside my building for future intrusions."

They're halfway out the door when Janet looks at me over the shoulder. "Or you can hang a sock on your doorknob. Or is it a tie?"

"Bye!"

I turn my back to the closed door at the same time a loud, staccato-like noise erupts from the Styrofoam cup in Lucy's hand. She pulls her lips away from the straw and smiles sheepishly. "I hope you weren't hoping for leftovers."

I smile. "It's fine."

I gesture toward the kitchen, where our takeout containers are still sitting there, untouched and growing cold. "Let's eat."

Lucy agrees, setting down the now empty disposable cup. "Your sister's funny."

"Yeah," I scoff. "She's got a great sense of humor."

She laughs. "She's your older sister?"

"Is it that obvious?"

"As the perpetual baby of the family? Yes."

"She's, uh...She's not doing too well."

Her brow furrows, and she reaches her hand to rest on my forearm. "I'm sorry."

I nod in answer, and she doesn't pry, which feels so much more comforting than her asking why my sister isn't doing well. And even though we continue in silence, letting the click of plastic utensils take up most of the noise, it feels less heavy than saying the words out loud.

21

Lucy

WARM THAI FOOD and *Supernatural* marathons are slowly becoming a nightly ritual between Dexter and I. We habitually start the day with Starbucks, something I insist on getting early in the morning. Mainly because he's the one splurging on dinner most nights, but also because he's the worst morning person I've ever met, and I beat him to getting the coffee before he even steps foot out of his room. By evening time, after Dexter gets home from work, about an hour after I do, we nestle into the couch cushions surrounded by our own little mess of dinner, dessert, and enough jump scare moments to make me squirm like a rodent caught in a mousetrap.

"They use that salt circle thing way too many times," I comment, my mouth full of mango sticky rice and the skin in my midsection pulled taut after helping myself to enough pad thai to feed a small army. "Haven't they learned?"

"Apparently not."

It's Friday night. No Saturday shoots for me tomorrow, which means Dexter and I have the whole weekend to do whatever the hell we want. To celebrate this weekend of freedom, we decided on an all night binge session of *Supernatural*. We included our usual Thai food order, always making sure to have mango sticky rice with our order, but tonight, I added a whole sundae station. Neapolitan ice cream, whipped cream, chocolate syrup, nuts, and sprinkles. The whole nine. The dwindling dessert supply, along with the large bowl of popcorn and the gradually creeping food coma, has me feeling the most worry-free and content I've felt in a long time.

A swarm of demons starts to occupy the TV screen, followed by doomy, threatening, ominous music, and I start to tense up under the throw blanket I grabbed for the exact purpose of hiding under. "Why do they have to do this? Can't the killing commence without the scary music and creepy jump scares?"

"Now where's the fun in that?"

I reach for the remote to hit pause. "I have to pee," I announce, tossing my blanket on the couch.

"What?!" he shrieks as I walk away. "It was getting to the big reveal! Castiel was about to tell Lucifer—"

"Don't tell me!" I shout over my shoulder as I shut the bathroom door behind me. When I return, Dexter's got his phone between his hands, his thumbs tapping a message on his screen. "Okay, I'm ready. My bladder complains when I'm stressed. I think they call it stress incontinence?"

"I don't think that's what that is." His brow furrows when a message pings through his phone, and that scowl deepens when he looks at it.

"Is everything okay?"

"Uh, yeah," he answers unconvincingly.

"Is it Janet?"

"No. It's uh…It's Hayden. He's just wondering if I wanted to come by the restaurant for dinner. I guess Nat went back home for the weekend? I think he just wants some company."

"Oh, right." We sit in silence for a minute, my eyes lingering on his phone screen where it lights up once again, and his gaze rests on me, watching the remorse make me squirm. I realize how much I'm disrupting his life. With friends, his privacy, and even the general flow of his daily routine. The guilt of it starts to blanket over the sweet scent of ice cream and chocolate syrup, and I feel horrible. "Dexter, you can go out if you want. I really don't mind being here alone."

He smiles at me, his eyes turning soft with kindness, and lays his phone on the couch cushion. "Hey. Don't worry about it. I prefer this." He gestures toward the TV screen. "Plus, I don't feel like being in a crowded restaurant tonight."

I run the pad of my thumb over my bottom lip to hide my smile. It feels a little selfish to keep Dexter to myself, but a part of me is relieved he'd rather stay home. I can't even begin to explain how nice it's been being Dexter's roommate. I come home, wanting to tell him things about my day. And not even big things. It's the little, insignificant details that no one else would care to know. Like how I fed a treat to a lazy cat at the register of a bodega during my lunch break. Or how, in an attempt to come off as amiable and even a little breezy while talking to Kyle, I tried to say awesome and cool at the same time, only to mix the two and it came out as "cawesome."

"I talked to Nat a few weeks ago. We talked about the wedding a bit. And Hawaii," I tell him, veering away from the creeping guilt clouding over the giddiness rolling inside of me.

"Yeah," he responds. "Hayden told me about it too. In about a month?"

"And it looks like I'm going to be the maid of honor. Me and Carmen, we're kind of splitting the role."

His smile brightens. "No way! Best man!" he exclaims, pointing a finger to his chest. He then high fives me, and my smile matches his. We've all but abandoned the show frozen on the screen with the glaring reminder of how easy this feels.

"It's actually around the time when my internship ends, so…"

"Oh, that kind of works out."

"Yeah." I play with my fingers, twisting at the ends of the blanket draped over my lap.

"Is that bad?"

"No. It's actually perfect," I answer, my brow pinching together. "It's just…when I talked to Nat, she kept telling me how she'd pay for everything. Like the bridesmaids stuff and my plane ticket. And then…" I pause before looking at him with shame. "She said my mom wants me to move back home."

"Why?"

"Because I'm still stuck at that coffee house—or, she *thinks* I am. And with all the job listings she sends me, nothing's panned out. I think when I brought up the internship, that was the final straw for her."

I stop to bury my face into my hands, and I feel Dexter's warm hand on my arm. "None of that's your fault."

"I guess," I say, chewing my lip. "It's just...Do you ever wish you could see into the future? And just know that whatever decision you're making is the right one?"

He nods, and the wrinkles on his forehead scrunch together. "All the time," he answers bleakly.

"Right," I agree, leaning toward him with a small pat on his knee. "Lately, I've been wishing that more and more. Like, if I could know this internship was the right choice and I'm not wasting my time being here...I just want to know if all of it will be worth it."

"You know, there's really no way to know those kinds of things."

"No, I know," I say softly.

"Can I say something, and you just not brush it off as me saying something nice or trying to get on your good side?"

I feel my body curl inwards like a tiny pill bug to protect myself, too uncomfortable with flattery and recognition.

"It takes a huge feat of bravery to do what you did. Uprooting your life and taking a chance on a talent you want to hone. Not everyone can say they took a shot at their dream. And even if none of this works out, which is impossible from where I stand, you can't say you didn't try."

I stay quiet, tightening into a cocoon of safety and doubt, something much more familiar than Dexter's warm blanket of sweet words.

Dexter stands from his seat and extends his hand toward me. "Come on."

I frown, a little confused but curious. "What?"

"We're going out."

"Like...to Hayden's restaurant?" I ask, still confused.

"No," he answers, brushing a hand in my direction. "Just... come on."

22

Dexter

SUMMER NIGHTS in New York City buzz like a live wire. It's like all winter and spring, New Yorkers hibernate, enjoying the warmth indoors in the midst of the biting cold, and when the chill finally thaws, we come out of our shell. When Lucy and I leave my apartment, we step into the still warm city night, blending into the crowded streets. We talk *Supernatural* theories. I listen to Lucy predict the ending to season eight as we move on to season nine based on her own hypotheses and her general preference for Sam Winchester. We talk about Hawaii, our roles as best man and maid of honor, who Hayden and Natalia's kids would take after. If they'd get Hayden's height or Natalia's deep brown eyes. The exact same ones Lucy has.

"So, are you going to tell me where we're going?" she asks, those brown eyes reflecting dim flickers of lights coming off the light posts and street signs. We've taken the subway to cross the bridge to the Upper East Side, and we're still walking through the streets, dodging people through intersections and moving about at a leisurely pace. Or as leisurely as Lucy's curiosity will allow.

"It's a surprise." I keep my chin held high and can feel Lucy's inquisitive gaze studying me. "Baring your eyes into my soul isn't going to get you the answer."

She shrugs as I turn to face her. "It doesn't hurt to try."

I stop walking when we approach a building where a doorman stands outside, his stark white gloves contrasting against his navy uniform and impassive smile. "Fourteen B. I believe Mr. Park called down for us."

The doorman's smile deepens as he reaches for the shiny gold handle on the heavy door. "Yes, Mr. Greer. Would you like me to show you to the elevator?"

I shake my head. "I'm okay."

He nods in response, and I turn to face Lucy looking bewildered and scared. "Okay, if you have a room lined with plastic tarp and torture weapons somewhere in this fancy building, I should warn you, I have pepper spray and a really sharp clicky pen in my purse."

I laugh and extend my hand in her direction. She eyes it warily before latching on to my arm. The pads of her fingers glide against my skin as her hand slinks into mine, and she smiles at me so adoringly. The apples of her cheeks round, and her eyes curve into little half moons. She sinks to my side with a level of ease I didn't notice until I realize how much of her guard is finally down. Those slabs of concrete she's built around her, the ones constructed with the stress of her internship and everything she's been keeping from her family, start to soften a little, opening up and letting me in.

As we hop in the elevator and it ascends, I feel Lucy's hand grip me tighter.

"Hayden and I have a friend we went to college with," I start to explain. "He lives in this building, and sometimes we use the roof access."

"Like to seduce a hot date?"

I smirk. "More like parties or to take a breather. Eighteen stories up will take you to a whole 'nother world."

"And are we meeting this friend up there?"

I shake my head. "He's in Greece with his wife. Babymoon. But he called the doorman for me."

"That's generous of him. What are you doing for him in return?"

I wink in her direction. "You don't want to know."

A bright ping announces our arrival to the rooftop, and when the doors slide open, a gust of cool air whooshes into the small space. Lucy's steps are hesitant, an obvious distinction to my sure ones as I lead the way toward the edge of the rooftop. Metal railings and air that feels about ten degrees cooler than on the ground surround us, and I hear Lucy suck in a breath.

"This is amazing."

The sounds of the city are muted up here. Even the headlights from the heavy city traffic and street signs lining the sidewalks look dull. It really does feel like we've stepped into a portal instead of an elevator to a fancy rooftop.

She turns to smile at me with a mischievous grin slicing through her face. "You're seriously going to tell me you've never brought another woman up here?"

I laugh, ducking my head toward my feet. "Not on a date or anything. More like to accompany me to birthday parties and the Fourth of July."

"Ah-ha! I knew it," she exclaims, pointing a finger at me. "The lengths you men go to get lucky. Please tell me you didn't challenge those poor women to a round of naked drinking games."

"Why? I thought you liked those games?"

She responds with a deep blush.

"Is that not how you remember it?" I ask, the playful grin on my face baiting for more from her memory. "Because I distinctly remember—"

"Okay! Yes!" she cuts me off, the redness traveling all the way to the tips of her ears. "I mean, it took a few servings of tequila to get there, but I guess…that's how things went."

We stay silent, the breeze blowing Lucy's hair away from her face like a curtain drawn open to let the sunlight in. With the summer heat feeling like a heavy down comforter instead of just humid air, we're both dressed in our summer best. A short sleeve shirt and bare arms. A flowy skirt and exposed legs. So when Lucy's knee brushes against my leg and my knuckles trail her arm from elbow to shoulder, it feels warmer than just a simple touch of skin against skin. It feels more like a syrupy, saccharine warmth that travels all the way down low in my belly.

"So these other women…" she says, avoiding my eyes. "Anyone… special?"

"No." My voice has gone deep, my eyes matching the somber cadence in the single, two-letter word. "I haven't really been with anyone since…you know." I gesture a hand between me and her.

"Since me?" Her voice squeaks, and her eyes round. Her body pulls away from me. Like she's scared this simple admission has more meaning behind it. And maybe it does.

"I mean, I've dated people, I guess, if that's what you call it. And I've fooled around or whatever, but…I haven't really *been* with anyone since we…"

She nods like she's agreeing with me. "Oh…"

It seems every one of our sentences ends in an ellipsis, filling the unsaid words with questions. Ones we don't know how to ask.

"Lucy, it isn't on purpose," I start to explain. "I guess I just really haven't met anyone I want to spend time with like you."

"Oh," she says again in a quiet whisper. Her eyes avoid mine, focusing on the metal railing in front of us instead. I see her jaw set and her lips twist to one side.

Maybe what I said was too personal, a little too intimate, and something that should've been reserved for a time after we've discussed things. But I wasn't sure if we were allowed to discuss such *things*. Until right now, when she slyly asked if there was anyone special in my life, I thought she'd set a pretty clear boundary. Now, that boundary she'd drawn in front of her like a brittle twig dragged across sand is becoming faint and confusing.

"I'm not trying to make you uncomfortable," I add. "Just know, it wasn't 'just sex' for me."

Her entire face shifts into a scared and worried pout. "But…"

"Hey," I say softly into the wind, making my voice drift and sound hesitant. "Forget I said anything. It's really not a big deal." My phone buzzes in my pocket, and it cuts into the moment, letting the words we're both holding back stay lodged in our throats. "Hello?"

"Hey." I hear Charles's low voice through the phone. He sounds tired and worried, making me worry just the same. "Dex, I had to take Janet to the hospital."

"What?!" I nearly shout. "Why?"

"She's had a low-grade fever since yesterday, and it spiked," he explains. "She called her doctor, and they told us to come in. Just as a precaution."

"Which hospital?" I ask. I look up to see Lucy start walking back toward the elevator to press the call button.

"New York Presbyterian."

"Okay. I'll be right there." I hang up and turn to face Lucy. "Janet's at the hospital."

She nods as if she already knows. "Let's go."

I don't bother to ask if she wants me to walk her home first. She's already decided she's coming with me. And even though I don't want to put a damper on her Friday night, it would make this situation a little less scary with her by my side.

We make quick work to catch a cab, staying silent through most of the ride by avoiding questions like what happened or if Janet's okay. Instead, we let the small talk from our cabbie and the muffled sounds of New York City traffic fill the quiet.

When we arrive at the emergency room, everything moves in a blur. I talk to people, a security guard and a receptionist, before finally being given a bed number in the ER. When I walk to the small room partitioned by a single curtain, I see Janet lying in a gurney, turned sideways in a half fetal position. The silk scarf she usually wears on her head, varying in different pastel colors, is no longer there, and I can see how much of her hair has been thinning. And with the oversized hospital gown she's practically swimming in, I can really see how thin she is.

I swallow through the constriction in my throat, forcing down the knot that has taken residence there since Charles called me, and step toward her.

"What happened?" I ask. She turns slowly, looking at me over the curve of her shoulder.

"Probably an infection. Bronchitis or something. We're still waiting on the doc to see me."

"You still haven't been seen yet?"

"They're pretty busy."

I huff, running a frustrated and aggressive hand through my hair.

"Hi, Lucy," Janet says weakly at Lucy hovering by my side. She smiles and blinks heavily in our direction.

Lucy waves her hand with a gentle smile. "Hi, Janet."

"Here," Charles calls, standing from his seat. "Have a seat. It shouldn't be too long. We called Dr. Pham, and she should be here soon." He pulls an additional chair from the corner of the room. Once Lucy and I have settled into the seats sitting side by side, Charles takes the empty spot at the foot of the gurney, putting him closer to my sister.

The four of us sit in silence. The machines at my sister's bedside aren't beeping, and the noise outside is somewhat muffled. We hear the occasional chatter filled with medical jargon passing by from the other side of the curtain, along with the coming and going of footsteps. While the quiet is probably the best for Janet to relax and maybe even squeeze in a small nap before things get chaotic, it's making the time go by slowly. I can feel the seconds tick and tick while the last five minutes feel like eternity. I start to fidget. My hands rub against the fabric on my thighs, and my knee bounces. I almost groan but stop myself when I see my sister's eyes fall heavy.

I feel Lucy's hand wrap around my arm, and I suddenly remember she's here. She's here, by my side, watching me slowly and painfully fall apart. She doesn't know what's going on, what the conditions of Janet's illness are that brought her here into the emergency room in the middle of the night. But she's here.

I finally look at her, and she looks at me. She runs her hand along the inside of my arm, and my hand covers her knee. Her lips press together into a small smile as if to silently say, *I'm sorry*. Not *I'm sorry we're here*, but *I'm sorry this is happening*. We stay like that, looking at each other and forgetting tonight. Forgetting about our cozy dinner at home and the impromptu visit across the bridge. About Lucy's doubts and reservations and wishing she could see the future. Even Janet laid up in a small gurney a few feet away from us. And it feels like it's just us two and I don't have to carry all of the scary and terrifying and heartbreaking things in my life. Like it's actually going to be okay.

"Janet Greer?"

All four heads in the room turn to look at the person who just entered. The woman, who isn't Dr. Pham, closes the curtain behind her and faces Janet with a calm, reassuring smile. "Dr. Pham is on her way," she explains, her back turned to me and Lucy. "But she asked me to check in on you and get some labs started."

From my side, I feel Lucy's hand grip me harder and her head lower, her eyes averting toward the ground.

"I'm Dr. Marquez," she goes on. She unravels her stethoscope from her white coat pocket and places the round drum on Janet's chest. "Any trouble breathing?"

"Um, a little," Janets answers. "Mostly when I move around a lot." She takes a deep inhale while Dr. Marquez continues her examination.

"Any pain?"

"When I cough," Janet answers. "I feel a little sore."

Dr. Marquez nods. "Dr. Pham mentioned you've had this cough for some time now, so the achiness is most likely from overusing those muscles," she explains. "We'll start with some Tylenol for now to get the fever down a bit, and respiratory will be here to start a quick breathing treatment. I'm going to send the nurse in to get things going, and then we'll go from there."

Janet nods, and Dr. Marquez stands upright to leave. "Just press the call button if you need anything."

"Thank you," Janet answers faintly.

In the midst of the back and forth between my sister and the doctor, I feel the relief spread through my body. If the doctor doesn't appear too worried, then my sister should be fine, right?

A slight tug of my shirt brings my attention to Lucy. She peers up at me, wide-eyed and full of panic.

"Are you okay?" I whisper.

Right as the words leave my mouth, Dr. Marquez turns on her feet and makes a quick glance at me and Lucy. When she does, she does a double take.

"Lucy?!"

23

Lucy

"HI, CARMEN," I say sheepishly.

"What are you doing here?" she demands. And then she looks down at where my hand is wrapped around Dexter's arm. She looks at him and then back at me. It feels like the time Nat and I got caught digging through Carmen's makeup. We were six and seven and so fascinated by our big sister's colorful eyeshadows and the weird spoolie brush dipped in the thick black tube of mascara, and our curiosity got us into big trouble. "Lucy. What's going on?"

Her face doesn't change amid her deepening scowl and my cowering. I shift in my seat, squirming on the vinyl covering with every set of eyes on me. Some confused, some concerned, but the one glaring at me looks pretty angry.

"Um, surprise?" I laugh a little awkwardly, but that disappears as soon as Carmen huffs a breath of annoyance. "Maybe we should talk outside," I finally say and stand. Dexter's hand reaches for mine and gives it a tight squeeze. As Carmen leaves the room, I turn to look at Dexter for one last nod of encouragement.

"You okay?" he whispers.

I nod. "Yeah, I'll be right back."

He nods back, and I turn to leave. I reach the hallway, where

Carmen's pacing the space between the nurses' station and the row of partitioned rooms. I reach her, my steps slow and nervous like that of a puppy dog that's been caught chewing on its owner's favorite pair of shoes.

"Lucy—"

"Carmen, please don't be mad."

Her tense body slumps a little, her shoulders sagging and the frustration on her face softening into concern. "Luce, I'm not mad. I'm just really confused. Is that someone you're seeing? Are you here visiting him?"

"No. No, it's nothing like that." I hesitate and then remember, this is Carmen. Not some scary ogre out here to eat me alive. Carmen. She's my big sister who's never once in my entire life judged me or made me feel small. "I moved out here about two months ago."

"Two *months*?! Lucy," she says, with an exasperated sigh. "Why?"

My eyes start to mist over so I look away, even more embarrassed now that I'm causing a scene. When she notices me on the brink of tears, she pulls me in for a deep hug, and I want to melt into a puddle of tears. Forget explaining everything to my big sister. Forget about all the lies I've been telling my family. I just want to fall to a heap on the floor.

"Come on," she says softly, running a hand up and down my back. "Let's go sit down somewhere and talk." She pulls away from me and wraps her arm around my shoulders, leading me toward a doorway marked EMPLOYEES ONLY.

Carmen looks at me over the faint rise of steam coming from the two coffee cups between us. It started off thick and white, like a smoke signal of warning alerting us to be cautious when consuming its contents. But now, since sitting down in the empty cafeteria twenty minutes ago with the low glow from the recessed lighting sitting above us, that steam has dissipated into something less hazardous, much like the air between me and my oldest sister.

I've just finished telling Carmen everything. I told her about the internship and how I couldn't pass up a once-in-a-lifetime opportunity, though she confessed she already knew through the grapevine, a.k.a. Mom. I told her about the money my parents have been sending me every month to help me with rent and bills. That one, as expected, she didn't know about. And while she tried to hide the disappointment in her face when I told her exactly how much my parents have been helping me, it slipped through the lines on her face with a small frown and furrowed brow. By the time I told her about the mishap that brought me to Dexter's apartment and the current state of Janet's health, those lines softened, as did the occasional hums and nods she gave.

"I'm sorry, Carmen."

"Lucy, why didn't you tell me?"

"How?" I ask, avoiding her eyes. "How was I supposed to tell you when Mom and Dad and even Nat told me not to apply for the internship? I mean, I understand they're thinking about me and they mean well, but this...I just couldn't pass it up. And it's been tough. The people I'm working with are really intimidating and knowledgeable, but I'm learning so much. And maybe I can actually make something out of this. But now, Mom wants me to move back home, and all I can think about is how desperate she is for me to find a job. And I—" My words are cut off by a sudden sob. It hits my chest with so much force, I don't even realize how dejected I sound. How wounded and hurt my words feel coming from my own lips. "I'm sorry I didn't tell you. I just...felt like such a disappointment."

I wipe away the tears falling off the edge of my chin, sniffling away my shame into my own self-wallowing penitence. Carmen stands from her chair, the metal legs scooting against the hard floor, before she moves around the table and pulls out the chair next to me. She tugs me into a deep hug, and I burrow my face into her shoulder.

"It's okay," she says into my hair. "I promise I'm not mad. I was just surprised. The last thing I expected when I walked into that room was to see my baby sister and her boyfriend—"

"Dexter's not my boyfriend," I blurt out.

"Oh."

"You know him. He's Hayden's friend? His old roommate?"

"Ohmigod," she says softly, rolling her eyes as if mystified at how she could've missed that minor detail. "I can't believe I forgot I know him."

I smirk, the first hint of a smile she's seen all night.

"And you called him instead of me? Or Nat?"

"Well, I ran into him my first week here," I explain. "So he found out about me being here by chance and it made sense for me to call him when..."

She nods with an understanding tilt of her chin. "Well, now I know," she says in that strong assertive voice she uses when telling me to buckle up or to help Mom set the table. "We're going to figure it out. Okay? I'm here for you. I'm going to help you get through this."

I feel the shift in her hands when she grabs my shoulders and in her eyes when a small frown presses her lips together. Like she's ready to come up with an eighteen-page PowerPoint game plan. She's coming to my aid, to big sister me like she always did when I was kid, ready to pull me out of whatever pickle I was in. But the thing is, this doesn't feel like a pickle she needs to *de*-pickle me out of. At least, not anymore. Every mishap that's come my way since I came out here, I've been managing on my own. It's almost as if Dexter's words have finally trickled their way into those aching parts of my heart, warming me from the inside out. Those ups and downs have been coming and going in a pattern with a track record that's been working in my favor. Or at the very least, not *not* in my favor. And maybe it wasn't all a fluke with a small serving of good luck. Maybe it's all evidence of my hard work. And this whole change, the internship and me moving thousands of miles away from home, happened so I could finally see this side of myself itching for a chance to shine.

I look at her with my tear-stained face and smile. A small, meek smile, but it's a smile. "I'm okay, Carmen. I've been learning to figure things out on my own since I got here. I mean, I've been doing it for over a month, and this has been kind of scary. You know, it's the first time I've done something this risky and so far out of my comfort zone, but I'm okay."

She tilts her head to the side, and I can't decipher if the look on her face is because she doesn't believe me or she can't stand the idea of me having to figure things out on my own.

"Really. I'll be fine," I add. "You don't need to worry."

"No, it's not that," she says, her thumb brushing my cheek as she cradles my face. "I just can't believe you did all of this. Move out here to the city, all on your own, and sign up for a job to do what you love. I'm so proud of you."

"Proud?"

She nods. "Of course," she assures. "And I understand why you didn't tell us, but if Mom and Dad knew everything you've done, they'd be proud of you too."

My chin starts to tremble again at the mention of our parents. The two people in the world whose opinion means the most to me. Why does life have to be so hard? Why can't I just skate through it without this constant feeling of never being good enough?

"But I get it," she adds, watching my eyes water once again. "They won't be mad at you, but I get it. So tell them on your own time. When you're ready."

We sit silent, an announcement echoing through the PA system and Carmen's fingers drumming along the hard tabletop. I start to worry about Janet in the ER, how Dexter's managing while waiting for more answers and test results. I should be back there with him.

"And staying with Dexter?" Carmen asks as if she's reading my mind. "Are you planning on staying there until you have to go back?"

"He's in between roommates right now, so he has a spare bedroom," I explain. "The plan is for me to stay with him till the internship is over."

"And that's it?"

I nod, but it doesn't feel like a nod at all. It feels more like if I could act out the answer *I don't know*, it would be through this hesitant up and down motion of my head. "I think so," I finally say.

She smiles at me as if she was already expecting this answer.

"It was at first, just him helping me out when my apartment got robbed," I continue. "But I feel so...at home with him. Like tonight, I was talking to him about the internship and how it's been a little stressful being away from home and all. And it didn't feel complicated telling him. It felt easy. Things are just like that with him. They're just...*easy.*"

I pause and bring my palm to my mouth. The image of Dexter, alone in his empty apartment, starts to fill my mind. Him going home by himself tonight, pacing his living room while his sister is lying in a hospital bed, worried sick. Or watching the next episode of *Supernatural* with a blasé look of boredom on his face reflecting the lights coming off the TV screen. And for some reason, I can't stand it. I can't stand the idea that he would be all alone. I would miss taking up that space in his home, filling the carved-out grooves of his couch or standing over the hard linoleum flooring of his kitchen while I scoop ice cream or pop popcorn. And maybe he would miss me too.

Carmen smirks. "It would be so you to come all this way to fall in love."

I huff and roll my eyes. "That is *not* happening."

24

Dexter

ANOTHER HOUR of waiting and tests and about a hundred different questions pertaining to Janet's chemo and her cancer history passes. It all goes by, minute by minute, while we wait for answers. By now, Janet's arm looks like it's been through hell and back. Her fever has been downgraded, thanks to the magic of Tylenol and a course of antibiotics started as soon as Dr. Pham saw her.

"We're going to admit you overnight," Dr. Pham says, standing by Janet's bedside with Charles clutching Janet's hand to his stomach. "We'll continue the antibiotics, and hopefully we can release you within the next few days. We'll see how your body reacts."

Janet nods, and both Charles and I exhale a deep sigh of frustration.

"Is there a reason why this happened? Or anything we can do to prevent this from happening again?" Charles asks. He rests his hand on Janet's shoulder and inches himself closer to her.

"Janet's immune system has become very weak with her chemo, which is expected like many in her condition, and it's made her highly susceptible to infections," Dr. Pham explains. "It's not uncommon for things like this to happen, and every person responds differently to different infections. Some are surprisingly able to get over it on their own, and most usually need some help with antibiotics. With Janet's case, her body wasn't able to fight it on her own.

"Getting a lot of rest is important. That, along with protecting what little you have left of your immune system. When you're tired, it makes your body more vulnerable in these types of situations." She turns to Janet, making sure this next part is specifically for her. "So, as much as I know you want to keep working and keep acting as if this disease isn't trying to kill you from the inside out, you need to rest."

I hear the curtain clink open, announcing another presence in the small, confined area. When I look up, I see Lucy, her solemn face full of concern, looking at me with a strained smile tugging back the corners of her lips.

"They're getting your bed ready," Dr. Pham continues. "Once we hear back from the floor, we'll get you admitted."

We all sullenly nod.

"And visiting hours are over, so most likely everyone will have to come back in the morning," she adds.

"Thank you, Doc," Janet says quietly, smiling sadly in Charles's direction.

Dr. Pham's gaze lingers on Janet and Charles for a second longer, and he lifts my sister's hand to his lips for a gentle, reassuring kiss. "But I'll see what I can do."

Another hour passed before Janet was finally wheeled away to her room. Dr. Pham was able to allow one visitor to be with her as she settled into her room. I encouraged Charles to stay, mainly so that I could get Lucy home, but also because I couldn't ask if I could be the one to stay when she looked at Charles with a sad smile before we came to the decision. So with the reluctant steps of my feet and the staggering in my heart that made me wish I could set up a small tent in the waiting room, I left.

Lucy and I are standing at the edge of the sidewalk outside the hospital, both of us making dithering gestures that lean toward flagging down a cab. Without the drone of street traffic this late at night, the quiet feels loud. And every ache in my chest, every twinge and tug, stands out like a beacon in the dark night.

"Dexter," I hear Lucy call from behind me. I turn to face her, and she looks at me with her downturned eyes and a tiny frown that makes me want to fall to a heap right on the hard concrete. She doesn't say anything, like offering me some false assurances that Janet's in good hands in her room up there or pretending to know the extent of Janet's illness through assumptions and the general knowledge that people don't die over silly infections.

I press the heels of my hands into my eyes as I feel the first of the tears start to gather. "She's all I have," I croak. "I don't know what I'm going to do if I lose her."

Lucy's body crashes into mine, and her arms wrap around me, caging me to her. My forehead falls into the crook of her neck, and I feel her press a small kiss to my temple. Her hands run up and down my back in a soothing way that makes me believe she has magic laced in them, something of the healing nature. Sirens call in the distance, reminding us where we are. The wailing grows louder and louder as an ambulance pulls into the bay outside the emergency room entrance we're standing next to.

I pull away, and our foreheads lean against each other where our breaths mingle. Her thumb brushes away the wetness on my cheek, and I grip her hips, letting my fingers curl over her waist and holding her tight like she might disappear.

"Let's go home," she whispers as my lips inch closer to her.

I nod and slowly pull away from her.

We walk at a slow, unhurried pace, our gazes on the ground in front of us, and the quiet, comfortable silence creating a small amount of distance between us. A stark reminder that I shouldn't have let my fingers slip under the loose hem of her shirt, where my fingers grazed over the small sliver of skin above the waistband of her skirt.

"She was diagnosed a couple of months ago," I say, cutting into the silence. "Lung cancer." I can feel Lucy look in my direction, but I keep my eyes on the sidewalk littered with old gum stains and weeds growing in between the cracks. "The doctors gave a pretty good prognosis, considering the severity of her cancer, but we've had our set of ups and downs since chemo started. I don't really...She's..."

I sigh and run a hand over my face. The things I want to tell her aren't light. They're heavy and substantial, and I don't know if I'm ready to have her carry that chunk of my burden. Because whatever I tell her, I can't *untell* her. But wouldn't it be amazing to not have to carry all of it on my own? If she could act as a pillar or a support beam or just anything so I don't feel so lost and lonely?

"I was fourteen when my mom and dad died," I say with a shaky voice. "Janet was nineteen. She was away at college. I was home by myself, watching some lame TV show I can't even remember anymore. My parents had gone out for the night to dinner for a friend's birthday party or something.

"I remember I walked out of my room to go to the kitchen. I was hungry, so I was about to microwave a burrito. And then I noticed lights out in the driveway. I thought it was my parents, but the lights were flashing red and blue. Someone knocked on the door, and my mom told me to never open the door, even if it was them knocking because they would always have a key, so I didn't know what to do.

"I heard police sirens outside when another police car parked in our driveway, and an officer told me to open the door. So I finally did and after that, I don't really remember much. It's like I skipped the part where they told me my parents were in an accident, and I was suddenly in the back of the cop car on the way to Janet's school an hour away. I don't even remember telling them what school Janet went to."

I pause when we hit an intersection, and we have to wait for a car to pass before crossing. Lucy takes that break in our trek to slide her hand into mine and squeeze my palm.

"She insisted she quit school, but I told her not to," I continue. "She'd gotten a scholarship to one of the best art schools in the state, and I didn't want her to lose that on top of everything else. So she agreed to move back home and commute to school. We got a hefty settlement from the insurance company, along with an even larger one from the drunk driver that killed my parents, so we were okay for a while." My throat feels tight and vulnerable. It shows when it cracks and the lodged ball in my throat feels too big to push down.

"We don't have anyone else. Our parents were only children, and our grandparents are all gone. Holidays and birthdays were usually pretty lonely for us when our parents were alive, and now…it's just me and Janet."

Lucy listens to me talk without interrupting. Without demanding more than I'm offering. And we continue to walk without any indication of wanting to hop into a cab or stop to discuss further logistics, like if we're going to take the subway or if we're really going to walk the second half of our journey on foot. Because that feels irrelevant at this moment. Whether we spend the next hour getting home or an entire week, time feels irrelevant.

I tell her about the last Christmas I had with my parents when I got a PlayStation 3 and powered through a seventy-two-hour Call of Duty marathon. I tell her about the time my dad taught Janet to drive, and she broke down when she hit a curb and sat sobbing in the car while I inhaled a bag of Cheetos in the back seat. She tells me about her own Christmas when she was fourteen and her dad gave her mom a brand new Volvo, which shocked the hell out of her and her sisters. She talks about her parents, how they met in college and moved out to Ohio for her mom's work before Nat was born. And the time she and her sisters spent a summer in Los Angeles with their dad's side of the family, where her grandmother gave them informal Spanish lessons over the sound of stone rubbing against stone from her *molcajete* and the clatter of pots and pans. Something Lucy's mom did when she was welcomed into the family as someone who otherwise would've been considered an outsider with her freckled cheeks and Irish roots. They learned traditions the way their mom did, through a language that no longer became foreign to them and an abundance of love and food.

We talk and talk while the streets remain quiet and the night starts to haze into light. We walk as if we have all the time in the world. As if Janet isn't laid up in a hospital bed and as if Lucy wasn't outed to her sister about moving out to New York City in secrecy. As if so many things aren't working against us. And maybe, for tonight, they aren't. Maybe things are slowly working in our favor, and they all led to us, right now.

By the end of it, when we've finally walked through the doors of my apartment and kicked off our shoes, it's officially morning. We slump onto the couch cushions with a heavy sigh and the light streaming through the windows. I turn the window AC unit on so we won't wake up in a few hours too sticky from the humid heat. Neither one of us moves to our separate bedrooms. Instead, we stay on the couch, where we linger against each other. Her shoulder nestles under the crook of my arm, my hand grazing over the warm skin of her knee. As our eyelids fall heavy, we shift so we lie side by side. She buries her face into my chest, and I rest my chin atop her head while we doze off into a sweet slumber.

25

Dexter

THE HARSH VIBRATION from my phone buzzing on the coffee table jolts me awake. But when I try to sit up, I realize my arm is pinned down. I start to tug at it when I see it's Lucy who has my arm pinned against the couch cushions. Her head is resting on my bicep, where her hair is fanned over her cheek. She nuzzles closer to me, making me lie back down and abandon getting up all together. I stretch my free arm toward my phone where it's still buzzing and circling a little dance on the hard surface, flicking it closer to me with my fingertips.

"Hello?" I croak.

"Dexter," Charles calls from the other end. "Did you get some sleep?"

"Uh, yeah. A few hours, I think." I peek down at Lucy, and she hums a sweet sigh against my chest. "What time is it?"

"Just after eleven."

Shit. I didn't mean to sleep in this late. It was supposed to be just a quick power nap so I could get back to the hospital as early as possible. I even forgot to set an alarm. When the reason for my brief oversight starts to shift beside me, my body softens. I sigh through a smile and watch the way Lucy's lashes flutter and her lips twitch. What's a few stolen moments with the woman I'm slowly falling for and a couple of extra hours of sleep? We both needed the rest anyway.

"I'm getting up right now. I'm going to head over to the hospital in a bit," I say in a hushed voice, hoping I don't sound too suspicious to Charles. I brush my cheek against Lucy's forehead before giving into the urge to press a kiss to her temple.

"I'm here now. Janet wanted a few things from home, so I'm going to head back out after lunch," he explains. "I'll only be an hour or two, but I was thinking maybe you could keep her company while I'm gone."

"Yeah, of course. Just give me a minute to shower, and I'll head right over."

"Great, thanks."

I hang up and chuck my phone back onto the coffee table. When the clack of my phone rattles through the room, Lucy jolts awake.

"Sorry."

She rubs her eyes and lifts her head. "What time is it?"

"Eleven. It's still pretty early considering we didn't get to sleep till after seven," I answer.

She shakes her head, looking a little disoriented, and slumps back into my arms. "Were you talking to Janet?"

"Charles. He was wondering if I could come to the hospital so I can keep Janet company while he runs back home to get a few things."

She nods against my chest and smooths her hand along my stomach before tucking it under my back. "I don't want to get up yet," she murmurs into my shirt.

I chuckle. "Then stay here. I'll be back."

She shakes her head and mumbles a muffled "mmhh" into my side. She grips my waist harder and tightens her hold on me. I smooth away the hair covering her face, and she peeps an eye in my direction. "I'll go with you. I just need a minute to get up," she says through a yawn at the same time my fingers curl around her nape. "I mean, if you want me to come with you, that is," she adds in a whisper. She looks up at me with her round eyes, and my thumb runs across her skin in a back-and-forth motion.

I nod. "Yeah, I want you to come with me."

"Okay," she says so softly, I feel like I imagine it.

She looks so beautiful, it's disarming, with her cheeks a little flushed from my own warmth to the faint sleep lines running across the side of her forehead. It's almost enough to tempt me into spooning against her and staying on this couch for the rest of the day.

Her chin tips up toward me, and I duck my head down to her. We freeze, and our faces sit no more than an inch away from each other. I can feel her pulse thread under my fingertips, and a shallow sigh slips through her parted lips while her fingers lift the hem of my shirt and run sweeping strokes against my hip.

"Would you hate me if I kissed you right now?"

She shakes her head. My thumb tugs at her chin, and her mouth slacks open further. No resistance, no qualms or misgivings suggesting she doesn't want this to happen. Her feathery lashes fan against her cheek, and her tongue pokes out to run along the bottom curve of her lip.

My fingers rake into her hair. I shudder a loose, shaky breath, and I feel like I can hear my heart thumping in my chest, all the way up to my ears, like an angry mallet hitting a drum.

"Please kiss me," she pleads. And any hint of a doubt, any possibility of this being a bad decision, is wiped out from under me. Like a fucking rug.

My lips meet hers, and we mold like two puzzle pieces sitting side by side. I didn't think it was possible, but my heart beats harder, faster, making me breathless. Our hands start to move. To her waist, to my back, to her bare thighs, to my cheek. And we grip each other as if touching and feeling were our newest forms of sustenance.

I press off the couch to lift myself and hover over her, making her sink into the plush cushions under us. I dip into the space she's hollowed out for me between her legs and part them wider with my thigh. Her knees bend at the same time her skirt falls back, and the heels of her feet frantically scrape against my lower back. My hand grips her waist and travels higher and higher, until my thumb tucks into the bottom band of her bra and grazes against the rounded under-swell of her breast.

I feel her hand claw at my back, tugging at the fabric bunching between my shoulders. I draw back to pull my shirt over my head, leaving my bare chest heaving in the space between us. She hurriedly lifts the hem of her own shirt, pulling it over her head and leaving her exposed in her lacy pink bra. Her head rests on the cushions, her wavy hair fanned around her perfect face and the shadows drifting over her skin making her look even more stunning in the morning light streaming in through the windows.

"So beautiful," I whisper, dropping my face to her jawline and planting small kisses to her warm skin. I trail my knuckles along the inside of her thigh, tickling the elastic hem of her panties and plucking it away from her soft skin. She responds to my strokes with a sharp intake of breath while the languorous, careful touches make her tremble underneath me.

"I just want to feel you," I say.

She nods, granting me permission. Her breathing becomes more feverish, and I swear I feel like I've evaporated into a cloud of bliss. My fingers continue to sweep and brush and tease, pulling her to the edge until she can't take it any longer. Until *I* can't take it any longer.

"I don't want to sound too obsessive," I groan. "But I've missed you."

She nods again. "Can you touch me already?"

Before the last word leaves her mouth, I move her underwear to the side and push my finger inside of her in one go, meeting zero resistance with how achingly wet she is. She gasps, her back arching off the couch. I haven't been ignoring the raging hardness of my dick poking at her stomach, but now, its presence is practically invasive. I feel like I'm going to explode.

She wraps her arm around my neck, pulling me toward her for a deep, lingering kiss. There're about a hundred different senses swirling around me. The feel of her throbbing around my finger, the scent of her filling my lungs, the taste of her coating my tongue, her soft skin shuddering under my touch. I use my free hand to yank down her bra, exposing a single breast. I bring the peaked nipple to my mouth, and another sharp gasp fills the room.

Her fingers thread through my hair and dig into my skin, causing my scalp to burn like fire. It feels like everything burns, creating this aching pain, reminding me I'll never get enough of Lucy. No matter what, I will always have this prickling, nagging reminder of how deeply she's pummeled her way into my heart.

"Dexter," she gasps. I suck harder, lapping her up while her entire body tenses underneath me. When I add another finger, moving in and out of her in earnest, she bucks against my hand. I curl my fingers, finding that when I do, she whimpers this adorable, needy little cry that makes me want to bury my face into her warm skin. "Yeah, right there," she whispers. "*Ohhh* my god. Keep doing that." I stroke her, watching her body react and using her gasps and moans to guide me. My thumb presses into her clit, and I all but lose it at the sight of her face. Distorted like she can't collect herself enough to form a clear thought, with her brow pinched and forehead creased. She sinks her teeth into my shoulder, and I feel like I missed the moment I sold my soul to the devil because there's no way this is happening right now without some sort of sacrificial ritual.

"Dexter, I'm—oh, fuck. *Fuck*!" She presses her forehead to my shoulder, right where she left her mark on my flesh, and I feel her ripple around my fingers. She tosses her head back against the cushion, with the long column of her neck pointed toward the ceiling, and I bury my face into the dip under her jawline.

Just as I pull my hand away and cup the wet heat between her legs, she lifts her head and looks at me with serious eyes, her blown pupils making her already dark eyes look even darker. Her hand moves between us, gliding down my bare stomach. She flicks the buttons to my pants with one quick snap, and her hand slides inside my boxers, reaching for my dick, which feels like it's made of concrete at this point. She starts to grip me, moving her hand up and down in a way that makes my entire body weak.

"Lucy," I groan, inhaling the deep scent of her sweet-smelling shampoo.

She continues to stroke me, her thumb running over the stream of precum at my tip, letting it smear over her hand. I start to hear the movements, the slippery friction of her tugging at my orgasm in the most effective way possible. Her breathing grows harsh and hot against my ear before she whispers, "I want you to come on me."

And that does it. Like a pubescent teenager getting his first handjob and jumping from joy at the thought of it. I let out an embarrassingly strangled grunt that makes me sound so goddamn vulnerable and desperate. We both look down as I come on her stomach, letting the pale, hot liquid pool on her skin, and my groans fill the air between us. I press my forehead to Lucy's and let a low "fuck" slip through my lips. She angles her mouth to the side, and our noses brush, regaining my attention on her perfect face.

"I've really missed you," I say in an aching whisper, realizing how many moments we've missed out on all these years.

"I've missed you too."

26

Lucy

MY GRANDPA HAD LEUKEMIA. It happened when I was nine. I remember Carmen had just finished her sophomore year of college and was finally settling into life as a college student. She told my parents she didn't know what she wanted to major in, leaving her status as "undeclared." It wasn't until she saw the state of my grandfather, sickly and powerless to this illness taking over his body, that she decided she wanted to study medicine. It fueled a passion inside her. She wanted to help people, to learn disease processes and how to cope with this stage of life.

Not all illness is a curse. There can come some sort of shining light from it. A silver lining. Whether it be a calling or a way to bring family together.

He survived, living another five years in remission before the cancer came back and he decided to forgo treatment. He wanted to live his last few months with us, with my mom and her brothers, with my grandma and the rest of his grandbabies. Those last moments, before morphine became his only source of reprieve, were beautiful. We did things for the last time, like bake brownies with my cousins or go watch a movie at the drive-in. The goodbye was bittersweet, knowing he would no longer be suffering and leaving behind a memory I'll always cherish because it was his time.

I can't help but think, as I remember my grandpa and our memories with my sisters, how it would be the complete opposite with Dexter and Janet. No amount of time would be enough for them to say a goodbye worth reminiscing. If Janet didn't survive, those last moments would never be enough for Dexter. He wouldn't even be able to consider any silver lining, like the relief of knowing her pain and suffering were over or that she'd done everything to fight this cancer. He would only focus on the fact that she's gone and he's alone.

"If you call the cafeteria ahead of time, they send over chocolate soft serve," Janet exclaims in excitement. We're sitting in Janet's hospital room, relieved that it's a private room with a good view of the East River instead of the hectic Manhattan traffic on the other side. A lot of her color is back, the gaunt, grayish tone of her skin having faded away into rosy cheeks and warm skin. Her eyes still have that sunken-in look from lack of sleep, which she blames on the constant interruption at night from round the clock antibiotics.

"Well," Dexter says, "maybe once you get out of here, you can have some real food. Not any of this mystery meat."

Janet stabs a small chunk of said mystery meat and savors the taste before she nudges away the rest of her meal tray. "It's actually not that bad," she comments. "I'm just getting a little bored."

"Which means you can finally get some of that rest Dr. Pham was telling you to get," Dexter comments sternly.

"I know," she agrees, flattening the sheets resting atop her legs. "But some reading material might be nice." She flashes an innocent smile at Dexter.

"How about some magazines?" Dexter offers, giving into her silent plea. "I saw some in the gift shop."

Janet gives a cursory nod, including a small lift of her shoulder, exposing the swollen edge of her chemo port right below her collarbone. "Sure."

Dexter stands, looking down at me in the seat next to his. "You'll be okay while I go downstairs for a minute?"

"Yeah," I say quietly, reaching for his arm to give a reassuring squeeze. "Take your time."

Once Dexter leaves, it's just me and Janet. Along with the monitors by her bedside displaying squiggly lines and neon green numbers and the low volume of the television playing an episode of *Shark Tank*.

"Thank you for coming to visit, Lucy."

"Of course," I tell her. "I hope I'm not intruding on your time with Dexter."

She waves a hand at me. "We'd probably be fighting over the TV remote anyway."

I let out a giggle, and Janet smiles. "I hope this isn't putting a damper on you two spending time together," she adds.

"Oh, of course not," I assure. I reactively reach my hand toward the rough blanket draped over her legs, finding her knee and noticing how bony it feels. "I-I can't imagine what you're going through—what Dexter's going through—and it means a lot that he'd include me. I mean, even if it's just to visit you here, it means a lot."

A moment of silence lingers between us, and I worry if maybe I spoke out of place. Maybe it was too personal. Maybe, in reality, I shouldn't be here, and I really am intruding on a space that's meant to be carved out for Janet and her brother. I *did* sort of invite myself. I look away, suddenly embarrassed.

But then Janet smiles, placing her cold hand on mine still resting on her bed. "It's been hard on him, I know." I look at her and notice a mistiness coating her eyes, along with her sad smile. "This all happened so fast. Cancer wasn't really in the cards for us."

My brow pinches together, and my lips purse. "It's a pretty shitty card you've been dealt."

"You know what I'm most scared about with this cancer?"

I shake my head.

"It's that...if I don't make it and this cancer wins, Dexter won't have anyone."

An enormous knot forms in my throat. It feels tight and stuck, no matter how hard I try to swallow it. Dexter told me this, that he has no one else besides Janet, but hearing it from her and making that possibility into a very likely probability crushes me.

"And I'm so scared to leave him here without anyone," she continues, a small tear trickling down her cheek. "I keep picturing him on holidays and birthdays, all alone with no one to spend them with, and it sort of kills me. And if I think about it long enough—" Her words are cut off by a sudden sob, and her hand covers her mouth as if to stop the rest of that sentence. Like if she doesn't say it out loud, then it won't happen, and she can pretend Dexter will be just fine without her.

"He won't," I say hoarsely, my voice sounding scared and weak. "He won't be alone."

I can't guarantee she'll be fine. I can't make false reassurances that this will pass and she'll wake up one day to realize she worried for nothing. But I can promise one thing: Dexter won't be alone.

Nat and I have a family, one that's expanding with her upcoming nuptials to Hayden, and one I hope will continue to grow. Dexter can fit into that family. We have room, enough to love and embrace him as the friend who pummeled his way into our lives. I can promise Janet that much.

She nods, wiping at another runaway tear, and huffs a laugh. "I guess you can add 'emotionally unstable' to the long list of cancer symptoms."

I smile back at her, but it's much bleaker than her forced laughter.

She clears her throat and busies her hands with the hem of her hospital gown. "So," she says clearly, smiling at me too kindly. "I hear your sister's marrying Hayden."

I nod, my smile a little brighter. "In a little over a month. We're all flying out to Hawaii for the wedding."

"Dexter too, right?" she asks, her question sounding more like a confirmation.

"I'm not sure," I answer. "He was, but with you being sick, he might—"

She throws a hand between us. "He's definitely going," she says sternly. "There's no way he's going to miss out on a trip to Hawaii because of me."

I chuckle.

"You know, the last time we were on a beach together was in Ocean City," Janet says in a hushed tone. We both smile and duck our heads toward each other. "He got *so* sunburned. He started blistering all over. Charles and I called him Mr. Bubble Wrap."

I snort a laugh.

"We spent the rest of the weekend hydrating him and rubbing aloe vera on his back." She cowers forward, laughing into her hand. "So you make sure he wears plenty of sunblock when you're out there."

"I will," I assure her through a laugh. Just then, Dexter stalks back into the room with a stack of magazines in his arms and a large Crunch bar on top. He gives us a wary look once he takes in our stifled smiles and lingering giggles.

"What were you guys talking about?"

"Nothing," Janet answers. "Just the efficiency of proper packaging materials and prolonged sun exposure."

"*Okaaay*," he answers, his eyes narrowing. "I got *Vogue*, *Cosmopolitan*, and a very interesting copy of *In Touch*."

Janet reaches for *In Touch*. "Oh, Brangelina reunion!"

He plucks out the Crunch bar before handing Janet the rest of the magazines. "And this"—he extends the chocolate bar in my direction after plopping back in his seat—"is for you, milady."

I beam at him and take my treat from his fingers. "Thank you."

We're interrupted by two short knocks at the door. "Sorry I'm late." Charles rushes to Janet's side, pecking her temple before placing the overnight bag in his hand on a nearby chair. "I got caught up on a quick work call, and it ran later than I thought."

"It's okay," Janet assures. "Dex and Lucy have been keeping me company." The two exchange looks, something that hints at *I told you so*.

We're interrupted by another knock on the door, followed by the entrance of a woman in red-wine-colored scrubs. She smiles kindly at Janet, bustling around her bedside table and pressing buttons on the blue box attached to a metal pole, where tubes and bulbous bags of clear fluid hang. "I'm just going to start your antibiotics and the anti-nausea medication we gave you this morning so you don't feel too sick again."

Another nurse enters the room, handing over some supplies like a fresh bag of mystery fluid and a random roll of tape. She lingers around, repositioning Janet so she's comfortable and wrapping a vinyl blood pressure cuff around Janet's arm. "This is Lisa," the nurse pushing a syringe into Janet's IV explains. "She's just going to grab a set of vitals for me and make sure you're comfortable."

It starts to get a little crowded in the small room. Charles moves around so he doesn't get in the way, and Dexter and I scoot our chairs further back against the wall under the TV. Dexter reaches for my hand and stands, looking at Charles while jutting a thumb toward the door and moving a finger between us, signaling our exit.

"You okay?" Dexter asks once we're in the hallway.

I nod. "I'm good."

He nods too in response, smiling softly at my fingers twisting in front of me. "You, uh…you hungry?"

We haven't eaten anything since the yogurt I inhaled before we left the apartment and the Gatorade Dexter bought at the vending machine. "Uh, yeah. A little." My stomach decides to protest just then with a deep growl. We both chuckle. "Okay, maybe more than just a little."

He gently slides his hand into mine and stares at it, our hands linked together with his thumb stroking my knuckles and his arm brushing mine. We haven't really talked about what happened earlier when we made each other come while in a post-sleep haze. And I'm sure we will at some point, but right now, I just want to focus on the low timbre in his voice and the balmy caresses against my skin. And how all of it makes me feel giddy and hopeful.

"Would you like to join me in the cafeteria?" he asks playfully. "I hear the mystery meat here is top notch."

I swear, I could throw my arms over his shoulders and kiss him. "It's a date."

Dexter

"So? What happened after that?"

I shrug, holding back a laugh while looking at Lucy's wide eyes and gaping mouth. I just finished telling her about the time my sister and I lured a stray dog home only to find out my parents' excuse for never letting us have one—that my dad had a heavy pet dander allergy—was in fact true, not a ruse to avoid responsibility for yet another living being.

"After six hours of hiding it in Janet's room, sneaking it scraps and praying to the gods it wouldn't make a peep, we got caught," I explain. "My dad's allergies got so bad, he had to go to the emergency room."

"Aww," she says, letting a fake frown shine through the laughter in her eyes.

"We named him Zac Michael Murray," I explain.

She responds with a confused tilt of her head.

"Janet had an obsession with *High School Musical* and *A Cinderella Story*," I explain. "So Zac Efron and Chad Michael Murray consumed much of her bedroom walls. And a surplus of cheetah print and magenta bedding."

A twinkle in Lucy's eyes takes over her laughter. "Our parents never let us have a dog either," she explains. "But we never resorted to some covert scheme to hide a dognapping."

"He came willingly," I defend. "It just involved some treats and baby talk."

"So no catcher's net?"

I shake my head. "No catcher's net."

We've been sitting off to a corner of the cafeteria, the buzzing sound of hospital workers and other visitors with the bright Visitor tag taped to their chest, like Lucy and I are both wearing right now, surrounding us. We ordered a plate of the mystery meat and steamed vegetables, and a saran wrapped turkey sandwich with potato chips just in case the mystery meat was as awful as it looked. Turns out, the mystery meat, labeled turkey loaf, was pretty good. The remnants of it and the leftover gravy that was poured over it in excess sit on the plate, while the sandwich remains in its plastic wrapping, the chips long gone.

I don't want to stay too long. Janet will probably wonder where we've gone, and, in all honesty, I want to make sure she's okay after she got her meds. But this…I don't want to walk away from this either. Lucy and I've spent the last hour exchanging stories like they've become some sort of interactional currency, one that hasn't seemed to deplete on my end or hers. In fact, the stories keep coming. When I think I've already learned so much about Lucy and her life and her childhood, she has more of herself to give. More opinions, more musings. More pieces of her that make me want even more.

"That was the last time we got in trouble. Like, deep, 'you're getting your PlayStation taken away and grounded for three weeks' sort of trouble," I say to the table. "And then…I don't really remember much about our parents after that. It's just bits and pieces that stay with me."

The mood shifts, and I stare at the space between my hand and hers, right next to the scattering of empty plates and crumpled utensil wrappers. Where if I inch just a little closer, I could feel her soothing touch graze over my skin. And maybe this is okay now. After last night and today, maybe we can gently and carefully push back those boundaries we set until we're both standing on the same side of the line.

Her brow furrows, and she looks at me, a mistiness coating her eyes and the bottom halves of her front teeth peeking through her lips. "The last time I got grounded was when Nat hit a mailbox on a late-night Dairy Queen run. We tried to hide the chipped paint on my dad's minivan with white nail polish. I guess the Alpine Snow shade was a little too white in contrast to Toyota's original finish."

That draws a chuckle out of me, the image of a panicking Nat and Lucy crouched over a crap paint job using nail polish and prayers.

"But, you know," she continues, "my parents got over it, we paid the damages using our allowance, and things went back to normal. We went back to Dairy Queen as soon as our sentence was up, and my parents just warned us to be careful." She pauses when her voice cracks. Her eyes start to water, and her mouth twitches into a reflexive frown. "Bu-But, you didn't get to…Things didn't go back to normal for you."

She pauses, looking away from me, and takes a deep breath. "I know you've had time to grieve, not that you're over it. I mean, you'd never be over losing both of your parents at the same time, but you've lived with it pretty much your whole life, and you and Janet grew up. I guess what I'm saying is…I'm so sorry, Dex. I can't imagine what you two went through, and it breaks my heart knowing you two only had each other…Everything Janet had to take on. Everything you had to learn on your own as a child—" Her words are cut off by a soft sob, and I scoot my chair closer to her. I wrap my arm around her, and she lays her head against my shoulder. Her tears start to fall, staining my shirt in fat droplets, and she lets out a loud sniff.

"Hey," I coax calmly. "I'm okay. I think I turned out pretty good considering. At least I'm not into recreational drugs or…pyramid schemes." I reach for a napkin and hand it to her. She takes it, dabbing at the loose stream of tears running down her face.

"I should be the one consoling you. Not the other way around," she says in a watery voice.

"Eh," I brush off. "It's nice to switch roles every once in a while. Makes me feel useful."

She huffs a sad laugh before a fresh wave of tears pools in her eyes. "It's not funny," she says, her mouth twitching into another involuntary frown.

"It's really okay," I say, smoothing a hand down her arm. "I mean, you're right, it was a lot to take on and we—it was tough. Like, really tough. But we figured it out, and we're okay now."

Lucy sobs again, and I just hold her to me. I know she said she should be the one consoling me considering the situation, but this feels so much more cathartic. Her mourning over my parents' death and the childhood I didn't get to have. She understands the extent of what Janet and I went through without me having to lay it out and explain it to her. The level of empathy she carries awes me.

"We should go check on Janet," she says, pulling away from me, drawing a loud sniff and wiping at her nose. "She's probably wondering where we went."

"Yeah," I answer, smiling at her. It shouldn't be this easy, this uncomplicated. But despite all of the underlying reasons Lucy and I shouldn't be in each other's arms, consoling each other surrounded by the scent of hospital disinfectant and the occasional interruption of PA announcements, it feels like just that: easy.

We collect our trash and walk back toward the elevator. I press a hand to her lower back, and she wraps her arm around my waist.

"Thanks for being here with me," I say, low enough for only her ears.

She turns to smile at me. "Thank you for bringing me."

When we get back to Janet's room, she's asleep. Charles is curled up in an uncomfortable ball in a chair at her bedside. Lucy and I glance at each other, unsure if we want to disturb either one of them. Just then, Janet stirs and notices us.

"Finally," she says weakly. "I thought you two found an empty hospital bed."

Lucy turns beet red, and I glare at my sister. "We were grabbing some food," I say flatly.

She smirks and stretches into a yawn. "Well, Dr. Pham came by. She said I can probably go home Monday. As long as she can transition me to oral meds instead of this fancy stuff." She gestures to the IV pole next to her. "She looked pretty happy with my progress."

"That's good," I say quietly, eyeing Charles and taking a few steps closer to her. Lucy follows, staying a step behind me as I perch at the edge of the bed. "How are you feeling?"

"Better. I don't feel as weak and achy like I did when we got here."

"You look better too," I say.

"Why don't you guys go on home," she says, her eyes moving between me and Lucy. "It's getting late anyway, and you can always come back tomorrow morning if you want."

I hesitate, and Lucy does too.

"Really," Janet assures. She points at the TV. "*Jurassic World* is playing next, and I'm going to ask the nurses for some orange Jell-O. I'll be in nap mode before the T-Rex fights the abominable rex."

"You mean the Indominus rex?"

She throws her hands in the air. "To-may-to, to-mah-to."

"I can stay the night so Charles can go home," I offer, still not wanting to leave.

"They probably won't even let you stay once visiting hours are over," she says glumly. "We got kinda lucky last night. I think they felt bad for the sad-looking cancer patient with an even sadder-looking boyfriend."

"Still," I offer. "We can stay until they kick us out."

She shakes her head. "Seriously. Go home, get some sleep, and I'll see you tomorrow."

I finally give in and stand, leaning down to place a small kiss on Janet's forehead. Lucy steps in front of me, hugging Janet before we both turn to leave. We exit through the same way we did the night before but without the fear and anguish I had then. It almost feels like a different lifetime. Like everything heavy and scary was temporarily placed in a box and shoved in a corner. And I know deep down I'll have to eventually unpack that box, reopen it, and place its contents back into the corners of my life where they're meant to be, but for now, this feels nice.

27

Lucy

DEXTER AND I make it back home, this time opting for a cab instead of the nine-mile walk to his apartment. Dexter leaves to get takeout—more Thai food—realizing the hospital food ran through us pretty quickly, and I hop in the shower. I take my time, shaving parts of me that were growing prickly and scrubbing my skin using the small sample jar of watermelon sugar scrub I save for special occasions. I deep condition my hair and exfoliate my face. I'm not expecting anything. At least, I shouldn't be. Whatever happened with Dexter earlier, it wouldn't be smart for us to move things further. I'm leaving soon, and it would make things so complicated. Worst case scenario, we'd resent each other, hating our predicament and, in the end, each other. Best case scenario, we'd break each other's hearts.

So maybe this level of pampering is more to give me time alone to think about me and Dexter instead of preparing for…more complications.

When I walk out of the bathroom, Dexter's already back. He's at the kitchen counter, two plates in front of him and multiple open to-go containers. His focus is on transferring the pad thai noodles to the plates. He moves the bean sprouts I usually pick out to his and adds the extra servings of shrimp to mine. There's already a serving of fried rice on the plate that's mine and white rice on his. He moves to the larb, scooping a healthy serving onto my plate and a small scoop to his, right next to the bean sprouts he removed from my plate. He digs into the paper bag and unwraps a set of chopsticks. He separates them, rubbing them together to remove all the splinters, and turns to open the fridge door to retrieve a fresh Coke can for me along with a bottle of beer for himself.

My heart soars just then. I could really fall for this man. I really could. I could risk it all, my heart, my sanity, all for the sake of this feeling. Having someone in my life who takes care of me the way Dexter does.

He looks up and sees me standing there, just watching him. He smiles a small smile and waves his hands in front of him proudly. "Dinner's ready."

I nod. "Thank you."

"Do you…want to eat in awkward silence or watch another episode of the Winchester brothers take on more demons?"

"I could use some awkward silence to wind down," I answer.

He chuckles, pulling out a stool from under the kitchen counter. We both sit in the dim kitchen lighting and eat in silence, minus the awkwardness. Because it isn't awkward between us at all. Whether we're swapping stories from our childhood or sitting quietly, comfort and ease seem to be a consistent norm between us.

"Uh…" Dexter's gruff voice cuts into the silence. "Have you booked your flight yet?"

I look up, twisting the chopsticks in my hand. "For Hawaii?"

He nods, and I shake my head. "But Nat sent me the hotel stuff. I'm going to stay in her room until the wedding, so I guess my room situation is settled."

"I—did you, like, want to fly out together?"

I look up at him to see his gaze focused on his food. His hair hangs off his head, and his brow is drawn up, making his forehead wrinkle. He pokes at his food, moving it around instead of actually eating it. His throat bobs, and his lips twist to one side. Is he nervous? Maybe worried I'll say no? Or maybe he's scared to discuss the future, whether it be travel plans or us.

"Um, yeah," I answer meekly.

"I mean, if you don't want to, or if the timing isn't right and you need to go back home early or—"

"Dexter," I interrupt. "We'll fly out together."

He lifts his head and peers at me with cautious eyes.

"I checked my schedule with the internship and the wedding, and it looks like I'll be done with the internship a week before the wedding," I explain. "So, I mean, I *could* go home, but it wouldn't be worth the flight just to fly out again a few days later."

"I guess we'll look into some flights then." A smile lifts the corners of his mouth, and I smile back before we continue to eat in silence.

He opens his mouth again. It looks like he wants to say something else, maybe some more details about which airline we should book or what strategy we'll use so we don't show up at the hotel at the same time. But instead of saying something, he lifts his beer to his lips and takes a long pull. I hear the liquid glug into his mouth, and the bubbles in my drink fizz inside the aluminum can. Somewhere in the distance, I hear music thumping through the walls of the apartment and a car honking its horn.

Maybe this awkward silence is really a thing. Though not the usual type of awkwardness most experience. Words feel caught on my tongue, questions I feel need to be cleared and absolved. But that suddenly feels scary, almost terrifying. So much so that this "awkward" silence feels like a reprieve.

When I wake the next morning, Dexter isn't there. The apartment is empty, and the silence filling it feels almost too quiet. Much like the awkward silence that lingered last night. We finished dinner and went to bed—our separate rooms—without discussing anything. Without scrolling through our phones to check out flight deals on Expedia.com or suggesting a night cap with a few episodes of *Supernatural*. We were both really tired, so it made sense that we embraced in a much-needed hug before going to bed, but then I fell asleep feeling so confused. We should have talked. I should have told him that what happened should never happen again and reiterate the multiple reasons it should never happen again. Like us living on opposite coasts or that if this didn't work out, it would complicate things. Hayden is his best friend. The best friend who's marrying my sister. If this went south, it wouldn't just involve me and him, it would involve family and friends.

I walk to the kitchen without bothering to change or run a brush through my hair first. It's Sunday, and since I don't have anywhere to go, mussed bed hair and stained pajama pants it is. When I get to the counter, I see a note scribbled on the back of an unopened credit card bill.

Coffee's in the fridge. I'll be back soon. Please miss me.

I smile, and it hurts. Not in the way that my cheeks are sore or my jaw strains. The ache is in my chest, where it fights the giddiness bursting from my heart.

Please miss me.

I don't need the request for me to realize the ache is there because I miss him. Not just now with him gone from the apartment for a short amount of time, but for how I'll miss him in the future. Once I go back home, there'll be no more notes scribbled on random scratches of paper. No more surprise cups of coffee waiting for me in the fridge. No more plates of food arranged exactly the way I like it. No more Dexter.

I let my smile dwindle into a confused frown, and I reach for the fridge. I find my usual caramel macchiato order sitting on the middle rack and just as quickly, the smile is back. He remembered my order.

I start sipping my coffee and return to my room. It's a mess, clothes strewn all over the place and my suitcase still an open heap on the floor. It feels like a good time to clean up. I start with my clothes, gathering a pile to start a load of laundry downstairs, and move on to my toiletries. When I get to the one bathroom Dexter and I have been sharing, I realize how much of my things have taken over his space. My razor that I used just last night lies at the edge of the tub. My curling iron is resting on the bathroom counter, unplugged, along with all of my eye shadows, makeup brushes, and skin care products. My shampoo, conditioner, body wash, even my overpriced loofa fill the space in the tub, shoving his own products to a small corner. All this, me invading his space, and he hasn't mentioned it once. It doesn't even feel like it annoys him but he's keeping his mouth shut to be polite. It feels like it truly doesn't bother him. Like him, living like this, with my presence so glaringly obvious, is just fine, and he'd gladly give up the space for the sake of my comfort.

With Annabelle, I was conscious of my mess, not wanting to make her uncomfortable. We both remained respectful of each other's space and haven't had any issues. And it's always worked for the both of us. But all of that flew out the window with Dexter. He shoved away the mindful consideration of living with another person from my head and allowed me to just be me. To be the messy, carefree Lucy who enjoys the process of getting ready and hours of uninterrupted primping.

My phone rings in my room, and I jolt for it, expecting it to be the one person who's been occupying my mind all morning. But it's Annabelle, along with a welcoming FaceTime call, and I smile, missing her and Jeremy.

"Hey, Ann!" I squeal as I answer, excited to see my friend. When the screen clears from the blurry image before the call comes through, I not only see Annabelle but Margo and Alma too. The three faces beam at me with the sun shining behind them.

"Lucy!" they all shriek at the same time. They start to giggle, looking behind them at what looks like an outdoor patio, mindful of their high-pitched voices in a public setting.

"What are you guys doing?" I ask, a little melancholy that I'm not there with them.

"We're having brunch," Alma answers, her thick-rimmed sunglasses covering her eyes. "And we *miss* you!"

"I miss you guys too." My lips turn down into a little frown. I miss them *so* much.

"How's the internship going?" Margo asks, shielding herself from the sun with her hand hovering above her forehead.

"It's going," I answer. "Learning loads."

"And the mystery man you're keeping from us?" Annabelle cuts in.

All three faces zone in on me, wide eyes and even wider smiles.

"I told them," Annabelle says without batting an eye. I roll my eyes, and that just makes them squeal like schoolgirls.

"There's nothing…going on."

"You paused," Annabelle points out boldly. "Why did you pause? Is it because you're lying? You know I can tell when you're lying."

"Okay," I fold. And that elicits another round of squeals. "There was—"

"Mind-blowing sex?" Annabelle interrupts.

"Ann!"

"Oh, I'm sorry." She rolls her eyes and raises her hands in the air with her palms facing me. "An intense wringing out until you're sucked dry."

I bury my face into my hands. "Oh my god."

Margo jumps in and smacks Annabelle's arm. "Would you just let her finish?" She turns to the screen, and her face softens. "Okay, we'll be quiet and let you tell us. So please, because we're dying to know over here."

"So there may have been some heavy making out, something in the second to third base region?"

Annabelle lets out a low chuckle and a sly smile while Margo and Alma stare at me with gaping mouths.

"I called this, by the way. So I think a triumphant 'I told you so' is in order."

I shake my head through a reluctant smile.

"So what does this mean?" Margo asks, ignoring Annabelle's smugness.

I shrug. "I don't know."

"Are you guys, like, friends with benefits?" Alma asks, a mixture of concern and curiosity on her face.

"No!" I practically shriek. "No, it's nothing like that. We haven't really talked it over."

"Are you going to talk it over?" she asks, the curiosity on her face now fully replaced with worry and disapproval. With her broken heart still mending from her breakup last year, I understand that she'd have some misgivings about the whole situation. Especially when it comes to the interest of someone she cares about.

"Probably."

All three have grown silent, and I realize they're reading into this correctly, from my apprehensive body language to the stress in my voice. They see how much this has been wearing me down, no matter how much I've tried to convince myself that this can't go anywhere.

"Uh, where is he?"

"He stepped out," I tell Annabelle, not wanting to dive into the fact that he's probably at the hospital visiting his sister. Those details feel more personal and something of Dexter that I don't know if I'm ready to share just yet.

We all stay quiet, politely smiling at each other before Margo chimes in. "Well, we're here if you need someone to talk to."

"Or to spill the dirty details," Annabelle adds. "We're definitely here for that too."

"But seriously," Alma says. "Talk to him." She pauses before adding, "And tell him if he breaks your heart, we're hopping on the next flight to New York to beat his ass."

I chuckle. "There will be no ass beating," I assure. "And I'm going to talk to him. Like an adult."

They're interrupted just then with the arrival of their food. Plates are placed in between them and off the screen, and it's my signal to hang up.

"You guys eat your food," I say once they've settled on which belongs to whom and who needs a refill on their mimosas. "I'll keep you updated."

They all lift their glasses to me, and I reach for my coffee, only a quarter left, and tilt it toward the screen. "Have an extra mimosa for me!"

We exchange prolonged farewells, adding extra syllables to the word "bye" and excess hand waves. When the screen goes dark, I have a sudden twinge in my stomach. I miss my girls. And as much as Dexter's made me feel at home here, I miss *my* home. My life, my friends, Jeremy and Annabelle. Even Vanessa and Mr. Bean. My mind starts to play a little tug of war, wondering what it'll feel like when I have to leave, excited that I get to finally go home but sad that I have to eventually say goodbye to Dexter.

I slide to the ground from the edge of the bed, where I perched myself while on the phone. I pick up the remaining items of clothing lying around and start folding them into a pile around me, hoping staying busy will keep those lingering thoughts of heavyhearted good-byes and a home I miss in the foggy parts of my brain where I can ignore them for now.

"Lucy?"

I look up at the open bedroom door just in time to see Dexter round the corner. He smiles when he sees me, taking in my appearance, all messy and unkempt. My bed head has transitioned itself into a small claw clip barely holding back the hair from my face. I now have a sticky coffee stain on the front of my shirt, and the smear of toothpaste I had on my cheek is most likely still there. But he looks at me like none of it's there. Like I spent the last hour dolling myself up with hair care products and a shiny new outfit.

"Hi," he says softly.

"Hey."

He closes the space between us and plops onto the ground next to me. "What are you doing?" he asks.

"Just cleaning up," I answer. "I've become quite a slob since I moved in."

He shrugs. "I kinda like it. Seeing little bits of you all over the apartment."

"Like my dirty razor in the tub?"

"Yeah," he answers with a smirk. "And the smell of your shampoo in the bathroom after you shower. I kinda like that too."

I nudge him with my shoulder. "Did you go see Janet?"

He nods. "It looks like the doctor's discharging her tomorrow. I'll probably take the day off, just to make sure she's settled at home and everything. I think Charles needs to go back to work so…"

"How's she feeling?"

"Better," he says, his voice a little brighter. "I was going to ask you if you wanted to go, but I thought maybe you should get some rest."

"It's okay," I say softly. "I'm sure it was nice for you two to have some alone time."

He smirks. "She asked about you."

And I smile too. "What did she say?"

"If I was going to ask you to be my girlfriend."

I chuckle, bringing a hand to my mouth. "Did you tell her you were planning on asking me after fourth period behind the bleachers?"

"It crossed my mind." We both laugh but that quickly dissolves, and a line between Dexter's brows deepens. "But I told her that I like you."

We sit there on the floor, with our eyes locked on each other. "I like you too."

He sighs, the kind of deep exhale that feels like he's been holding his breath. "So we sorta like each other."

"Looks like it." He nods. And I nod too, mirroring the up and down bobbing motion of his head. "But I'm only here for another month. And we have the wedding after. And that'll be nice but then..."

"But then you go back home."

"Yeah," I say, answering this lingering silent question hovering over us, making me wonder if there was more to this simple "yeah."

"So we go back to how things were?" he asks, a small frown set in the firm lines of his lips.

"No," I answer too quickly. It's instinct. I'm not even sure if the answer should've been yes, but saying no felt too natural. "I mean...I-I don't..."

"I don't want things to go back to how they were either." He hesitates and scrapes his nail against the smooth plane of skin in front of his ear. "I might be getting ahead of myself, but would you consider long distance? If this..."

"I don't know."

"Okay."

I sigh a shaky breath. "It's just that I've seen the horrors of it first hand," I explain. "A friend of mine dated this guy from Tampa, and when they broke up last year, it got really ugly. I saw how badly it affected her. And my parents did it for a while after college, and my mom tells me all the time about how it nearly tore them apart, so—"

"Hey," he interrupts. "I get it. We don't want to complicate things."

"Yeah."

There's a pause between us where it feels like a turning point, and I can almost hear the gears turning in our heads while we try to figure out a solution. Until I finally say, "So we don't label this between us." I say it firmly, leaving little room for doubt, no matter how unsure I still feel. "We do this one day at a time, and after the wedding, we..."

"We go on with our lives." A quick smile twitches at his lips, and it looks so mournful, like he's already thinking about the fallout from this. "And we'll take things slow?"

"Yes," I say assertively. "That's smart..."

"And responsible." I realize he's finishing my sentences.

I don't know if this is a good idea. In fact, it feels like a recipe for disaster. A disaster full of broken hearts and painful goodbyes. But I couldn't say yes when he asked if we should just go back to how things were. When the feel of his hands on my skin was nothing but a distant memory. Or when the thought of kissing him was something that I tucked away as a dream and flushed down the possibility of it happening again.

"Okay," I say, cutting into the silence that snuck up on us. I say okay because we don't have any other choice. Neither one of us wants to forget about what happened yesterday. We don't want to act as if we didn't light each other's skin on fire. Or that there isn't already a gaping hole in my chest from whatever future goodbyes we'll have to share. It'll only be for a month. And that's it.

He inches closer and wraps his arm around my waist to pull me into a long, deep embrace. I turn so that I face him, and our bodies lean against the side of the bed. He drags me to him, pulling me flush against his body. Whatever reservations I have festering in my heart about us, about my temporary living situation, fall into the shadows. Almost as if they're giving us a moment of privacy so I don't have to think about what can come of this.

"Is this okay?" he says into my hair. I nod, rubbing my nose against the fabric covering his shoulder and allowing myself a deep inhale of his scent. Something in my brain chemistry alters as I consume myself in him, convincing me things are going to work out the way they're supposed to.

When I pull away, he doesn't let me go. I look at him, our noses playing this little teasing game of cat and mouse. I brush my lips against his, and his eyes squeeze shut. His hands grip my waist tighter, and when I bring my hand to skate along his chest, I feel his heart thrum underneath my fingertips.

"This is okay too," I say, adding a small kiss to his lips. It's his turn to nod. I kiss him again, and this time, he kisses me back. It's gentle and slow, and for some reason, it feels a thousand times more intimate than our rushed kisses from before.

The second his tongue dips into my mouth, I rise to my knees and straddle his lap. Our kiss deepens, and my fingers thread through his hair, tugging at the roots. That draws a low moan from the back of his throat, and I feel his hand caress my back underneath my loose sleep shirt I haven't changed out of yet. He trails my skin, making me shiver. His other hand cups the back of my neck, and he grips me so hard, so fiercely, I feel like melting into a puddle of sticky ooze right on his lap. His fingers rake into my hair, and the weak, hopeless moan that squeezes from my lips is outright embarrassing.

He pulls away just then and looks at me, the brown in his eyes barely visible with his black pupils filling most of the color. "I meant it when I said we should take it slow."

"Yeah," I whisper, pressing my forehead to his. I push my hips down into him, and he groans.

"You know," he says, his voice strained. "Doing the responsible thing?"

"Yeah."

"I mean, it *would* be the responsible thing, right?"

"Yeah."

"You keep saying 'yeah.'"

"Ye—" We both pause to chuckle. "You're right." I climb off him and kneel to his side, my hands twisting on my lap. "I guess things sorta got out of hand?"

"Yeah." That makes us both laugh, this time with less tension.

I glance at the clock and turn back to face him. "I have to go downstairs to get my clothes out of the dryer. And maybe we'll figure out what to do for dinner after?"

"I'll go with you. To get your laundry," he offers.

I stand first and wait for him but as he gets up, he crouches back down. "I might need a minute," he says sheepishly.

I look at him, confused, but then he gestures a hand toward his lap, and I dissolve into a set of giggles, falling back to my knees. I cup his face with my hands and grip him, placing a small peck at the corner of his mouth. "You're so cute."

He groans. "That's not helping."

I laugh, and his head falls back onto the bed. "I'll wait outside for you," I say as I pull away and reluctantly stand.

28

Lucy

I SPEND the rest of Sunday evening folding laundry and eating more Thai food. I thought I'd be sick of it by now but with so many menu options and Dexter's agreement that there's nothing better than a meal completed with mango sticky rice, I couldn't be swayed to choose something else.

So we lounge on the couch, stuffing our faces and discussing all the times we missed each other. How I thought of him from thousands of miles away and how he found any excuse to bring me up in conversation with Nat and Hayden. Asking how I was doing, hoping he'd catch me on the phone with my sister. All those times when we could've just picked up the phone and called each other.

We finally book our flights to Hawaii. Dexter helps me look into shipping costs to send some of my things back home so I won't have to take my entire suitcase I've been living out of with me to Hawaii. He switches on his PlayStation while I fill out forms for the renter's insurance claim. The property manager emailed me the paperwork, finally sealing the deal to end my lease agreement. I was relieved when I got the email notification, since I still need the money to replace my laptop, and grateful I didn't have to reach out with legal threats or a bad Yelp review. I just hoped whatever I get from the insurance is enough to cover a new one.

Over the chaotic yet somehow comforting clicks of his PlayStation controller and the sun slowly eclipsing behind skyscrapers, I sit by Dexter's side and finish sending off everything to the insurance company. I online shop for a bridesmaids dress using the color swatches Nat sent me, and Dexter gives me his full attention every time I show him a new dress, following up each approving nod with comments like, "I like the straps on that one" or, "That one would look really nice on you." We call Janet after dinner time, checking in on her while she receives yet another round of antibiotics, and she smiles at us as we squish together to fit on the narrow phone screen.

By the end of the night, when we're both stifling yawns, we meander our way to our separate bedrooms. I don't want to leave his side, and it seems like he doesn't want to leave mine. He lingers at my doorway, loosely holding on to my hand and crowding me against the frame.

"So…we should do this again sometime."

I laugh, feeling like I'm floating on a big, fluffy cloud. He tucks his hand under my chin and brings my lips to his, and we both melt into this deep, lingering kiss that makes me flash through every kiss I've ever had, trying to remember if I've ever been kissed like this.

He presses his hand against the hard surface of the doorframe next to my right ear and looks at me, his gaze flitting to my lips and back to my eyes. "I'd like to say we could sleep in the same bed and behave but—"

"But probably not," I finish.

He smirks against my lips and nods. "I guess…good night?"

"Good night."

He licks his lips. "Good night."

I laugh. "You already said that."

"I know."

I shove my hands into his stomach. "Good night!"

"Okay, okay," he says, lifting his hands in surrender. "Good night."

I kiss him one last time. "Good night."

Monday morning rolls around, and I'm on a high. I spent the weekend fully pushing away the stress of this internship out of my mind, something I hadn't been able to do since I started, and I actually feel optimistic. I've put on a fresh new pair of rose-colored glasses—heart shaped ones, I might add—and things are looking up.

I start the day handling more responsibilities than I have before. Moving around v-flats and reflectors to direct lighting and deciding which models to assign specific design looks to. Managing set designs without approval from Ryan or Ivy or even Kyle. It's a lot of responsibilities, and while it feels overwhelming and scary, it feels like an exciting kind of scary.

I'm tasked with props today in addition to set designs, so I've spent the better part of my morning hunting down weathered wooden chairs and plush loveseats for our boho-chic meets haute couture photoshoot to take place next week.

"Lucy, can you settle a dispute?" I look up to Ajay, another member of our intern team who's a practical child at twenty-two years old and fresh out of college. He's a little annoyed and flustered as he approaches my table, and I look at him, a little leery. "Min Jun doesn't believe that my last girlfriend was a lingerie model."

I roll my eyes, and Min Jun, another intern who I swear is Ajay's counterpart in maturity level, throws his hands in the air next to Ajay. "See! Even Lucy doesn't believe you."

"Why? Is it so hard to believe that I could get a girl—"

"Yes," Min Jun interrupts, his deadpan look showing no amount of evidence would convince him otherwise.

I sigh, looking up from my laptop screen. "Do you have proof?"

Ajay looks at me, a little insulted, and Min Jun stands behind him with a smug grin. "Proof?"

"Yeah. Like a picture you two took together? Or a text message convo in your messages? Or maybe even an old Instagram post?"

Ajay hesitates. "We—I mean, she's kind of a private person. And we hardly texted when we dated because we were both really busy."

Min Jun and I share knowing glances, and Ajay huffs an exasperated sigh. "Whatever. I don't care if you guys believe me or not. *I* know we dated."

I smirk, watching them walk away before I return my attention to my work.

"Kyle is on a rampage," Elaine whispers sharply, rounding the large conference style table I'm working at.

I stop mid-click on an eBay link. "Why? What happened?"

"Apparently, the brand sent over the wrong set of clothes," she explains, tucking herself into the seat across from me. "And the set we're preparing for next week isn't the right design for the clothes that were sent over."

I bury my face into my hands and resist the urge to groan. "So I'm looking for all of these props for nothing?"

Her face shifts into an apologetic look, her teeth clenched through a sympathetic frown. "Sorry."

"I already placed an order for a step ladder and an emerald high back chair," I whine.

"Well, it'll be used for the shoot when they send over the right clothes."

I grit my teeth, pushing down my frustrations through a silent *it is what it is*, self-soothing pep talk. "I guess," I grumble.

"Who approved these orders?"

Elaine and I both lift our heads to Kyle Viotto standing at the head of the table, his fists pounded into the hard surface and a deep scowl of anger on his face. He has a tablet screen angled in our direction with the emerald high back chair I was just talking about.

"I did," I answer sheepishly. "I placed it this morning before I knew about the change in the shoot. I can order something else to fit the—"

"This doesn't work with the original design, regardless if the wrong looks were sent," he says harshly. He doesn't yell at me. Instead, his stern voice is unwavering, almost void of emotion, and that makes it all the more intense. "This is why we had that two-hour-long meeting about the brand's vision. Were you even paying attention?"

"Y-yes, I was," I stutter. "I'm sorry, Ky—"

"If you don't think you can work with the styles we have lined up for the shoot, then you need to reconsider whether or not you're the right person to be ordering props," he says, cutting me off. "There's a very specific vision that's a part of this entire campaign, and I need all of the staff, including the interns, to understand that. If you don't think you can, then you shouldn't be here."

I shouldn't be here.

"I'm sorry," I say again, tucking my head down.

Kyle turns to Ryan, who's been standing by Kyle's side the entire time. "I need to hold a staff meeting in an hour."

His voice trails off as he and Ryan walk away, leaving me and Elaine completely dumbfounded.

"Are you okay?" Elaine says softly, ducking her head.

I shake my head. "Yeah," I whisper, my body language the furthest thing from okay.

She looks at me in my current state, breathing shallowed breaths with a dazed look of complete disbelief. "Lucy," she calls in a reassuring voice. "It'll be fine. We can start looking for new props. I can help—"

"I need some air," I interrupt.

I think I hear Elaine call after me, but I'm not sure. I can't really hear anything over the loud thundering in my ear, chanting, *You don't belong here. You don't belong here.*

I barely make it out to the stairwell before the tears start flowing.

Every doubt, every validating proof that my place is back at home, steaming hot milk and grinding coffee beans, comes rushing back to me. What the hell am I doing? This is exactly what my mom was talking about. She knew it wouldn't amount to anything. Just three months of me questioning my worth while working my ass off. She was right. I should've never left.

"Lucy?"

I hear my name echo off the stairwell walls just as the heavy metal door opens to the fourth floor. I quickly wipe my cheeks, sniffling back my runny nose before turning around. Elaine stops at the top steps and takes the empty spot next to me.

"Ryan wants to brief us before the meeting," she says carefully.

I nod. "I'll be right there." I turn away and dab at my eyes using my shirt sleeve.

"Lucy," she says, trying to get my attention. I look at her through blurry tears. "It's a small bump in the road. I've had about four since our first day, and I think number five is about to happen at today's meeting."

I chuckle a little, a low, watery laugh that slips through the crack in my voice. "The makeup blunder on the model wasn't your fault."

"And neither was this prop issue."

My chin starts to tremble, and I clamp my teeth on my lower lip to stop it.

"We're still learning. And all of us have come a long way." She pauses to rub my back, her soothing hand moving between my shoulder blades. This causes a fresh wave of tears and a tight constriction to form in my throat. "Come on. Let's hope Kyle doesn't keep giving us that disappointed parent look for the rest of the day."

"You mean the one that makes me feel like I should be grounded for a month and have my phone privileges taken away?"

"That's the one."

29

Dexter

I'M RUSHING from the subway station to Janet's apartment, zigzagging through the sidewalks, narrowly sidestepping a couple arguing about where they should've met two hours ago. I'm rushing because I just got off the phone with Charles after he told me Janet is already at home. Not still at the hospital, where I was supposed to meet her and bring her home, but already settled in at the apartment she and Charles share.

Apparently, the doctors decided she was good to discharge early in the morning rather than later, which allowed for Charles to bring her home before he had to go to work.

"Janet! Buzz me up!" I call through the intercom when she finally answers my incessantly impatient press of her buzzer.

"Dex?! What are you doing here?"

"Charles told me you guys got home from the hospital, like, two hours ago," I practically yell. "Let me up!"

I start to grow frustrated, inwardly smacking the side of my head for having to go into the office this morning when Margaret asked for some reports a day earlier than she had originally requested. I should've told her it would have to wait a few hours until I saw Janet home. I should've just gone straight to the hospital. I feel like I keep fucking things up. Like every time I want to be there for Janet, she makes do without me. Her guilt in asking me to take her to her chemo sessions and Charles taking over and stepping in because I couldn't. And now this.

"Uhh...You think you can come back later?" she answers after a beat of hesitation.

My face twists in confusion. "What?! Why?" I ask. I sigh, that frustration inside of me bubbling over. Why the hell is she asking me to come back later? "Janet, just let me up."

She doesn't answer me, but the loud buzzing noise sounds through the speaker, along with the light click of the door being unlocked.

Why is she being so weird? I start to worry. Maybe she got some bad news before leaving the hospital. Maybe some test results showed the cancer was worse than she'd thought. Or her prognosis has gone downhill. My worry grows tenfold, and I take the steps two at a time. When I reach her apartment door and knock with about a hundred different scenarios full of more shitty bad news flashing through my mind, there's shuffling on the other side.

"I'll be right there!" I hear in a muffled tone. After a few more moments of shuffling and the pitter-patter of steps, the door clicks open with the door chain being pulled taut. Her face peeks through the small opening, and her eyes nervously shift side to side. "Dexter, I thought you weren't going to be here until after work."

"No," I answer, even more confused than when she didn't want to buzz me up. "I told Charles I took the day off. I would've been here sooner, but I had to take care of some things in the office that were a little urgent."

She still stands there, the door chain slashing a line of gold across her eyes.

"Is Charles at work?"

She nods. She still doesn't say anything, and now I'm getting really worried.

"Janet, you're kind of scaring me. Will you open the freaking door, please?"

She sighs deeply before closing the door shut. The soft clicking of locks and chains sound, and the door opens again. Janet looks at me sheepishly, and it's then I notice the right side of her head is shaved.

"What are you doing?" I ask.

She steps aside and lets me in. She doesn't answer my question but instead walks to the bathroom, where I follow her. I see long locks of hair scattered over the bathroom sink and a set of hair clippers plugged into the outlet.

"I didn't want anyone to see this," she says, her gaze on the floor. "But while I was in the hospital, it was just coming out in clumps and…This is just something I need to do on my own."

My heart wrenches in my chest, and I start to sob. "Janet," I cry hoarsely.

"Dex, it's okay." She reaches for my face and cups my jaw.

"I-I should be spending more time with you," I hiccup through the sobs I'm failing to hold back while tears start to fall like a damn's been broken. "Charles is taking on so much, and I can't even be here to bring you home from the hospital. Or *take* you to the hospital in the first place. I'm so thankful for Charles, but *I'm* your family, Jan. Not—"

"Charles is family, Dex," Janet interrupts. "He could've bailed the second I got sick, but he didn't. Who does that if not family?" She pauses, taking a deep sigh. "He isn't going anywhere. I know it sounds a little naive considering there's no ring on my finger or anything, but he *is* family."

She has a point. If Charles has done anything since Janet's diagnosis, it's proving his place in her life. Every hour he's taken away from work to take care of her, staying by her side while she was in the hospital, loving her no matter what. She's right. He *could've* bailed. Legally, he isn't tied to her in any way. Aside from this apartment they've settled into over the past year and a lingering guilt he may or may not have if he decided to break things off after the shock of his new role as a caretaker, there's nothing keeping him tied to her. I'm almost glad they aren't married because if they were, it would be about duty and vows and a silly piece of paper legally linking them together. But he's here because he truly loves her.

My face softens. I offer a sad smile, and she smiles back.

I stare at the long strands of hair in the sink. It's everywhere. On the counter, on the floor, on Janet, littered over her shirt and leggings. "You know," I start, still keeping my eyes on the scattered hairs, "I knew this was coming. I knew there was always going to be a possibility that your hair would fall out and you'd most likely choose to shave it, but...I didn't think I'd ever be prepared for it." She strokes her hand on my arm, and I finally look at her. "How are you doing this? How is it that I feel like I'm falling apart and you're still somehow in one piece?"

"I'm not," she assures, giving me a gentle squeeze. "I try not to think about it and hope I'm doing the right thing, making the right choices. There are so many days I want to give up. Skip my chemo appointments, avoid my doctor visits."

My vision goes blurry behind a fresh wave of tears.

"But I'm not ready to die," she adds. "I want to watch you meet someone and make a family of your own. I want to become crazy Aunt Janet with my messy finger paintings and paper-mache." She grins, and I can't help but let out a bubble of laughter at the thought of that life. Me, married with kids, creating a future with someone I actually plan to spend the rest of my life with.

"You're going to be waiting a long while for that to happen," I comment, rolling my eyes.

Her brows shoot up. "I don't think *that* long." She peers at me with wide eyes and a silent—yet somehow loud and clear—knowing grin.

I stare at her, a little perplexed. "Lucy?"

"Yes, Lucy. You loser." She flicks my forehead, and I flinch.

"Janet, don't—"

"Don't what?" she cuts me off. "Don't start picturing little Dexter Jr. with *the* perfect woman for you?"

"Janet!"

She rolls her eyes. "Whatever," she scoffs, turning away from me. "If you're going to keep lying to yourself that there's nothing going on there, then leave so I can finish this fancy DIY haircut of mine." She picks up the clippers, taking a deep, cleansing breath, and faces the mirror. I reach in front of her, carefully plucking the clippers out of her hand. She smiles, keeping her back to me, angling the section of hair still untouched in my direction. "Thank you. Getting that backside was a bitch."

She watches me through the mirror where I stand behind her. But instead of running the clippers through the rest of her hair, I bring the clippers to mine.

"Dex! What the hell are you doing?!"

"Trying out the DIY haircut of yours," I answer, my focus on my reflection in front of me, where Janet's shocked face sits in my periphery. The dark, loose strands start to fall from my head and join the rest around us, where I can't really distinguish which hairs are hers and which are mine. "And once I'm done here, we're going to finish that whack job you're doing."

"Dex..." She starts laughing. Like, really laughing, from deep within her belly. Her giggles sound so light and happy and carefree. And I laugh with her. I smile while the prickly hairs start to tickle my nose and the whirring sound from the hair clippers grows louder. When I shave off the last patches of my hair, I move on to Janet, scolding her to sit still while her shoulders shake through her laughter.

With the scattered locks of hair covering the bathroom floor, Janet and I talk about everything. From her cancer to the various head gear we're going to be sporting to future travel plans to go back home once Janet's chemo sessions are finished so we can enjoy the beach again.

I take the final few blocks from the subway station to my apartment, a small smile on my face while running a hand through my short hair. When Charles finally made it back home to Janet, the stunned look on his face confirmed the shock, seeing our matching hairstyles.

The whole thing felt like some sort of cancer right of passage. And for the first time in a long time, I watched Janet feel in control of her body. Like *she* decided she wanted to shave it all off instead of dealing with leaving strands of her hair all over Manhattan. And I know it sounds weird, considering she no longer has her dark brunette hair she's had her entire life, but she looks...like herself.

I walk into my apartment and find Lucy on the couch with the hood of a sweatshirt pulled over her head. One that looks a lot like mine. I smirk at the idea of her wearing my clothes, her scent lingering on the fabric and the warmth of her spreading through the fibers. I have a small bouquet of daisies in my hand, something I picked up on the way home because the bright yellow and white flowers reminded me of her.

"Hey," I call, just as she looks at me over her shoulder.

"He—" Her eyes widen as she takes me in, my new look and the loose trimmings of hair scattered over the front of my T-shirt. "You cut your hair?"

I chuckle, suddenly shy, and pull at the back of my neck. "I went to visit Janet, and she was…uh, she's been losing a lot of her hair, so…"

"She cut her hair?"

I nod. "Shaved it right off," I answer. "And I couldn't let her do it alone."

She stands from the couch and pads her bare feet in my direction. I haven't stepped further into the apartment than the entryway, and she lunges herself into my arms, making my back lightly bounce off the closed door behind me. I toss the flowers somewhere, the floor probably, and grip her firmly, nuzzling my nose into her neck.

"You're amazing. You know that?" she whispers into my ear, making goose bumps trail where her warm breath skirted over.

I smirk. "I don't know," I say into her hair. "I think I need to hear it a few more times to believe it."

She pulls away and hooks her arms around my neck. "You." A kiss. "Are." Another kiss. "Amazing." She kisses me again, but this time doesn't pull away. Instead, our lips tangle together, and my arms circle around her waist.

"That's pretty convincing." My lips start to travel down her neck, and she tilts her head back, her skin vibrating as a low moan hums in her throat. "How was your day?" I say into her soft skin.

"Better now." Her hands smooth down my chest to my stomach, reaching for the bottom hem of my shirt. God, the things I want to do to this woman.

I lead her backward, our feet clumsily finding their way to the couch, where we both fall onto the cushions. My hand curls behind her, under her hoodie—or *my* hoodie—and I dissolve into a puddle of bliss when I don't feel a restrictive bra strap in the middle of her back. Just her silky skin.

"We're still taking things slow, right?" I whisper against her lips.

She nods. "I actually wanted to talk to you about that." I pull away to look at her, and a desperate whimper, almost like she's protesting something, slips through her lips. "I know technically we've…you know, had sex," she says breathlessly, her fingers trailing along the metal clasp of my jeans.

"Okay," I answer when she pauses.

"But you said it wasn't 'just sex' for you," she continues, her chest rising and falling against mine. "And I feel like it wouldn't be 'just sex' for *me* this time around. And I don't think it would be a good idea to do *that* when…"

"Okay," I agree, my hand moving to her stomach now, where it trails along the bumpy ridges of her ribcage. She draws in a sharp intake of breath.

"Yeah?" A soft sigh ends her one-worded question, making her words lack the resolve they should have. I thumb her nipple, rolling it between my fingers, and she grinds her hips into me.

"Yes. Absolutely." I give a light pinch at the same time she dips her tongue in my mouth, taking a long, silky sweep. She withdraws, nibbling on my lip, and my growing erection presses into the soft space between her legs.

"Yeah," she adds. "So…it would probably be a smart thing to stop."

"Probably."

"In fact, I should probably just take a cold shower."

I stop kissing her. "Is that an invitation?"

She laughs, her shoulders bouncing as she nuzzles her face into my shoulder. "I swear, it's like telling a toddler he can't have any candy."

I shrug and smirk. "I mean, I need a shower anyway, and we *would* be saving water," I comment, trying my best to appear indifferent.

"Dexter," she whines, pressing a gentle, assuaging kiss on my cheek.

I sigh. "Okay," I answer with a soft, teasing pinch to her waist. "Go shower. I'll go grab some dinner."

She pouts a little and pushes her palms into my stomach. I can tell she feels bad about the situation we've just lodged ourselves into. One that feels sort of like an impasse or even a crossroads where no matter what we choose, consequences will be the death of us.

"It's fine, Luce," I assure her, tucking a loose strand of hair behind her ear. "Really."

"We're good?" she asks.

I place a small peck to the corner of her mouth. "Of course."

30

Lucy

"WOULD A RIESLING WORK?"

Dexter looks up at me over the rack of wine bottles dividing up between aisles. "We can get both the riesling and the chardonnay if you want. We can never have too much wine."

I beam at him, and he smiles back. We both turn to walk to the end of the aisle, where we meet.

"You know," I say softly, all smiles and bliss. "This is a very coupley thing we're doing here."

He raises his brows, amused. "Is it now?"

"Accepting an invite to your sister's apartment for dinner with her boyfriend while you volunteered to bring the wine?" I ask, our smiles now matching. "Very coupley."

He smirks. "She's just happy she finally has enough energy to cook an entire meal," he explains. "And her gnocchi is honestly to die for."

"I'm definitely not complaining," I say, pressing a light kiss to his lips. "I guess..."

"What?" he asks gently, a small dip furrowing between his brows.

I shake my head. "I can't wait."

This isn't the first coupley thing we've done together. Late-night milkshake runs at The Lunch Car, movie nights at home under a shared blanket, heavy make out sessions on the couch. In fact, most of our time spent together has been doing very coupley things. But this… It feels like more. Like us playing the role of boyfriend and girlfriend in front of other people, no matter that we haven't officially assigned each other such titles, makes it that much more coupley.

We grab our two bottles, white wine like Janet asked, and walk the remaining fifteen blocks to Janet and Charles's apartment.

"Hey, guys," Charles calls when he opens the door. "Janet's just setting the table."

Dexter steps to the side, letting me through first. As soon as I walk in, we're greeted by the warm scents of cheese and garlic and something warm and homey. Small tea candles are set on a table covered with a linen tablecloth, and Janet's hovering over it, a large platter in her hands holding a combination of tomato and basil leaves.

"Come on in!" she exclaims.

Janet smiles at us, and her eyes twinkle against the candlelight. She looks better than when I saw her in the hospital. Much better. Her face looks fuller, not gaunt or sullen. She looks happy. Like she's excited and looking forward to the next day. Dexter told me she's been wearing a scarf or the hair prosthetic she was finally approved for through her insurance, one she can apply on her own at home, but tonight she's wearing neither. Instead, she's proudly displaying the matching hairstyle she and Dexter have, and it looks so incredibly endearing to see them together.

Dexter also mentioned that Janet started attending meetings with a local cancer support group, which is where she learned about using her insurance to file a claim for a medical grade wig. It's the little things that have been adding to her spirit. Talking to people who are going through what she is, learning ways to get a part of herself back —her pre-cancer self—instead of feeling like she has a big cancer stamp on her forehead. And it shows tonight.

I'm seeing the change in Dexter too. With each morsel of Janet and his past and himself he shares with me, I see less of it weigh him down. I don't know if he feels the same way, but I almost feel like he's letting me share the load with him. And for some reason, it doesn't feel the least bit heavy for me. In fact, distributing some of the heaviness, like what he's afraid of or the worry of how he's going to manage if Janet loses this battle, makes things light. I can't imagine either one of us ever going back to carrying each of our own burdens by ourselves. He and I together, we created this large, still growing construction of scaffolding, all the metal poles adding to me and him while we continuously learn how to hold each other up.

Charles moves around Janet to push aside some plates and sets a small basket of bread on the table. He places a gentle hand on her shoulder, and she turns to smile at him. Dexter and I give them a moment, more to watch them than anything else. Because I know deep down, witnessing moments like this has become rare for Dexter. Moments where he gets to see his sister just *be*.

"Thank you," Janet says to Dexter as she takes the bottles from him.

"Sure," he answers. "Lucy picked the riesling."

Janet nods approvingly. "You have good taste."

I feel Dexter's warm hand press into my lower back as he pulls out a seat for me. Dinner moves along. Janet serves us with her gnocchi and pesto sauce, which tastes amazing, and we move through the bottles of wine, including a third Janet had tucked away on her small four bottle wine rack. By the time dinner's over, the four of us are relaxed and fending off a slowly creeping food coma.

"I didn't know you were a photographer," Janet comments over a few slices of cheesecake she's serving.

"Aspiring," I correct.

"She's a part of this huge ad campaign with a big brand, and they're already going to use her pictures for the campaign," Dexter interjects.

"Well, no," I cut in. I glance at Dexter, giving him pleading eyes while he smiles proudly. "It's not official yet. The art director handling the campaign asked me to turn in some of my edited pictures I've taken of the models. But I'm still learning a lot. My pictures aren't nearly where they should be for any sort of billboard or magazine spread, but I'm hoping maybe by the end of this internship, I'll be able to gain enough experience to turn in some quality work."

Dexter waves a hand in my direction. "She's being modest."

"And you've seen my work?" I say in a sharp whisper, turning to face him.

He shrugs. "You do use my laptop," he says in a low voice only meant for me.

"Are you looking through my stuff?"

"No," he answers, taking a pause on jabbing the crumbly cheesecake crust on his plate to give me a sheepish smile. "I, uh, needed to transfer some files over, and I saw them."

"Oh."

He eyes me carefully, like he's gauging whether or not that small detail will upset me—him catching an unguarded glimpse of something that may be a little too personal for his eyes. But all it does is make me realize how much of myself I don't mind Dexter seeing. I don't feel guarded or timid about anything with him. And maybe it has something to do with the fact that he's the only person who understands me for me. Not the Lucy who still works at a coffee house back home. Not the Lucy who holds so many misgivings about the future but puts on a show like I do for my friends and family. Just me.

"Do you like fashion photography? Or commercial photography?" Janet asks, pulling me away from the inquisitive gaze I tipped toward Dexter.

"Um, I think I'm still deciding," I answer. "I kind of like both so far, and I think I'm just learning too much right now to decide what I'm really into. Before this, I was doing marketing for an ad agency, so I don't have much experience in the photography field."

"But that marketing experience must have helped," she comments. "Must be why you're doing well with this ad campaign."

"Huh," I huffed, musing at the realization that she has a point. All those years spent in marketing gave me an eye for what consumers look for. What stands out, what appeals to the eye of the general public. I'm using that experience and channeling it toward my photography work now. Who would've thought?

"You know, I have an exhibition opening at the gallery coming up next Thursday," Janet announces. "You two should come by."

"Are you okay to do that?" Dexter asks.

"It's just one night," Janet answers. "And we have a handful of new artists who I spent a lot of time with to collaborate on this exhibition. One of them, I got really close with. Her work is amazing, and I can't miss her first show." She turns to me. "Maybe you can take some pictures? I know she would really appreciate that. You know, anything that isn't taken from a crappy camera phone."

I smile. "Sure," I say, tilting my head to the side. "I'd love to."

Hours later, after the last of the cheesecake was wrapped away in foil and the empty wine bottles clinked in the recycle bin, Dexter and I are on our way home. We spent the rest of the evening poring over old photo albums Janet had tucked away on her large floor-to-ceiling bookshelf, mainly to embarrass Dexter but also because I asked. When Janet mentioned science camp and advanced rocketry, I had to see them for myself. And when I caught a glimpse of eleven-year-old Dexter in protective goggles and a gap-toothed smile, I fell harder.

"You know, you were right," Dexter says, sliding his hand into mine.

"About what?"

"That was very coupley." He pulls my hand to his lips and kisses the knuckle on my middle finger. "And I liked it."

I giggle. Like a girly giggle with a hand to my mouth and my chin tucked down to my shoulder. I've been doing that a lot lately, becoming bashful when Dexter gives me the kind of attention only boyfriends do. Like when he makes a silly joke just for the sake of making me laugh or when he says something like he just did.

"I liked it too," I answer as he lets go of my hand and wraps his arm around my shoulders. "It felt very…comfy-cozy."

He laughs this time, the deep throatiness of his chuckle vibrating against me. I know moments like this are measured, each one being ticked off an already premade list of kisses and hugs and more kisses. We both know the end is coming at some point. Every moment between us is full of expiration dates. My internship, my sister's wedding, my flight back to Seattle. All of those have actual dates on a calendar, like on a milk carton or a tub of peanut butter. And the expiration date of our...relationship, if that's what we'd call this, is becoming more and more invasive with each passing day. At first, we knew and simply pushed it aside, where we could ignore it. But now, with only a month until the wedding, it's becoming harder to ignore.

We get home and get ready for bed. With the early days we have tomorrow and our usual routine pat down, we mosey our way to our separate bedrooms and reemerge shortly after in our night wear. Me in a long sleep shirt that stops at the top of my legs and him in just pajama pants. Bare chest and pajama pants. This isn't the first time I've seen him without a shirt, but each time I do, it takes my breath away a little bit. I love how I can see the faint ridges of the muscles on his stomach that make him soft and warm. Or the way the bulge of his biceps show how strong he is while knowing how gentle he feels when those arms wrap around me. There are also the grooves that line down his hips, centering the smattering of hair that runs from his belly button to below his waistline.

We move to the bathroom, where we wash up. Dexter stands over me while he brushes his teeth, and I continue my extensive seven step skin care routine as he watches. When I'm done and he's just waiting, I turn around to face him. "You know when Janet said my marketing experience must be helping me during this internship?"

"Hmm?" he hums with serious eyes.

"I really thought I came into this with zero experience and I was basically algae. Just, bottom of the food chain with absolutely nothing to offer. And Janet made me realize I actually brought some of my experience with me and maybe I'm not, you know...scum."

He pulls me to him, wrapping his arms around me and running his hands up and down my back. I press my face into his bare chest and bask in the feel of my skin against his. "First of all, you could never be scum," he says into my hair. "And second, Lucy, I'm not saying your work is amazing because I'm trying to get into your panties." I giggle when he pauses, and he uses that moment to peck my cheek. "You're going to find your pictures on the side of a bus one day."

I roll my eyes. "I'll be happy to make it out of this internship with my will still intact," I say bashfully. "But I guess," I add a little more resolutely, "just hearing all of that once in a while makes me feel like I actually might have a shot of doing something after this internship. Something big. At least, for *me*."

"Yeah," he says softly with a smile that teeters between pride and tenderness.

I push away from him and saunter into the hallway. My back is turned to him, and I don't feel him close behind me. When I look over my shoulder, I see that he's still at the doorway to the bathroom. He's leaning against the doorjamb, his arms crossed over his chest, and his eyes track the length of my body. "You're not going to bed?"

He takes a slow, cautious step toward me. "I will."

"Did you want me to stay up with you?"

He shakes his head. "Only if you want to."

I yawn. "Sure," I say as I raise my arms above my head. It causes my shirt to lift a little, and Dexter's eyes zone in on the exposed skin below the hem.

His hands grip my waist, and he nudges me toward the wall. "I really don't want to push you into anything. I want to be responsible adults here because I really do think it's the smart thing to do given our...situation, but Lucy, I'm still a man." He pauses to swallow. "A man who *knows* he has the sexiest woman in the world standing in front of him."

My eyes round, and the sleep that was creeping its way through my body vanishes. "Are you asking me to put some pants on?"

He chuckles and leans into me. "Absolutely not."

"So...no pants, huh?"

"No pants."

I stand on tiptoes and press into him for a long, lingering kiss. My mind starts to sift through ways to bend the rules of our abstinence pact, looking for illogical ways to call the whole thing superfluous or overly cautious. Maybe even finding a few cracks we can slip through without fully breaking the rules.

"I know we said 'no sex' and all," I say, mischief written all over the racy gleam in my eyes. "But we can do other stuff, right?"

Dexter's eyebrows shoot up toward his hairline. "What other stuff did you have in mind?" he asks in a low whisper against my lips.

I kiss him again, trailing my hands down his stomach and letting our tongues tangle in a knot of desperation and heat before dropping to my knees. I peer up at him, and the realization of what this "other stuff" is I'm implying settles in his dark gaze.

"Lucy," he groans. "You don't have to."

I tilt my head to the side and bat my eyelashes. "I want to." And before he can protest again, I spring his already hard erection free and take him in my mouth in one long, greedy pull.

"*Shit*," he hisses. One of his hands presses against the wall behind me, and the other threads through my hair. My tongue flattens against the underside of his dick, and he starts to hit the back of my throat, forcing gurgled gagging noises from me. I grip his base with my fist, twisting and turning as his hips jerk forward, and his fingers tug at my hair with urgency. I feel my head hit the wall behind me, and his palm cups my scalp to buffer the harsh thumps. But his movements don't get any gentler. Instead, he moves in a frenzy, letting my head bob between his legs while I watch the muscles in his arms and stomach and chest strain. And suddenly, I become obsessed with making him come.

"*Baby*," he says through a rough voice. "I'm going to come. If you don't—"

I respond by sucking harder, hollowing my cheeks and humming a low moan that vibrates between us. Dexter urgently yanks me to my feet and quickly tucks himself back into his pajamas.

"Was that not—did you not like that?"

A harsh breath slips through his lips, and he swallows hard. "*No*, Lucy. That was…That was *good*."

"Just good?" I ask, my eyes rounding with innocence.

"More than good," he answers, his voice like gravel tumbling in his throat. "I just think—"

I cut him off with a kiss, raking my nails from his nape to his scalp. Because I don't want to think right now. I don't want to peruse through all the reasons we shouldn't be doing this, only to realize how reckless we've let ourselves become over a night out and a few extra glasses of wine.

He responds with a kiss just as hungry as mine, and that obsession to see him lose control returns. Through the foggy mist of lust and sex, all I see is the both of us giving into every carnal desire we can think of. And with anyone else, I wouldn't even dream of losing control like this. I can't fathom being this exposed and vulnerable while wanting to peel back more layers of myself.

But Dexter's not just anyone.

I shove my hand into his pants and grip him, moving my hand up and down his length while pushing away the slowly creeping ache clawing at my chest. It doesn't take long before he presses his body to mine, gripping me through a harsh shudder and a deep groan loud enough to make my entire body rattle, showing how violently his orgasm tears through him.

I expect things to end there, with Dexter breathing harshly into my neck and my hand growing slick inside his boxer briefs, but it doesn't. He wraps his hand around my wrist, and he drags me into my room, kissing me fiercely as soon as we cross the threshold.

"I swear to God, Lucy," he growls, gripping my throat to force my gaze to his. His bare chest heaves up and down, and a darkness casts over his eyes, making him look possessive. "This is as far as we go. After this, we go back on what we agreed on, okay? Because I'm trying really, *really* hard to do good by you."

I nod.

"Good," he answers, his voice dark and stern. "Now go lie down." He jerks his chin toward my bed, and I comply, climbing toward the middle and carefully laying myself flat over the comforter. As soon as my head falls back, his fingers grip my ankles, and he drags me to the edge of the bed. And it's his turn to drop to his knees. He taps at my hips, indicating for me to lift them so he can remove my underwear, and slides them right off. He sighs, rubbing his cheek into my skin and placing a small, gentle kiss at the apex of my thigh.

"You know what I want to do?" Those coarse words spoken through the low grating tone of his voice trails all the way down to my stomach where a throbbing empty pit sits. Waiting. Craving. Begging.

"What's that?"

"I want to build a shrine for you." A swipe of hot, wet tongue. "For every square inch of your body." Another teasing flick. "For this sweet pussy I'm going to be dreaming about for eternity."

I smirk. "Wouldn't that be a sight." Just as I get the last word out, his lips latch onto me, making me jolt. His tongue moves with purpose and fervor, and when he lays his forearm across my hips, I writhe under his hold on me. His mouth is so goddamn...greedy. Like he's absolutely starved.

He lifts his head, and his eyes dart to mine. I suddenly feel like prey, and he's the predator. "This might be a little...forward, but do you happen to have a little friend in here?"

My head pops up from the bed. "What, like a leprechaun?"

He chuckles against my skin before sucking on the sensitive area to his right, making me squirm. "I meant like a special battery-operated toy..."

"Oh, you mean Dennis."

"You named your vibrator Dennis?"

"'Cause, ya know, he's such a menace."

He buries his face into my stomach, muffling a laugh. When he looks at me again, his face is bright red. "Where is this Dennis?"

"Nightstand drawer, on the right."

He bolts for the nightstand, and within seconds, he's at the edge of the bed again. "Have you been using this pretty often lately?"

I hesitate. "Um, maybe."

His jaw clenches, and his nostrils flare as if this single admission makes him realize how ravenous he's become since I moved in. How we've both become a ball of pent-up sexual energy with nothing but toys and hands to temporarily relieve some of that pressure. "With me in the next room?"

I silently nod before I hear the click of my bright blue toy, and the low buzzing sound echoes through the room. Dexter nudges it between my legs, and I flinch from how on edge I am.

"I swear, if this could be me instead..." I hear him whisper. And without further warning, he pushes the vibrator into me in one sweeping, slippery go. My back arches off the bed, and bright bursting spots begin to fill my vision. This feels a thousand times more erotic than when I do it myself. Dexter's hands guiding it in and out of me with purpose, using my squeaks and moans to show him how much pressure to use or how high or low to keep the vibration setting at. The rough stubble from Dexter's jaw grazes my skin, and when his tongue flicks my clit, a sharp gasp slips through my lips. It all feels like too much. His mouth starts to become violent, and my heels press into the mattress. I feel his hand snake up my stomach and firmly grip a breast, where he pinches a nipple. All of these sensations tip me over the edge, and I come with such intensity, I don't know where on earth my body is. Sitting on the top of the Empire State Building, back at home in Seattle, floating around on a cluster of big fluffy clouds—I have no fucking idea.

"*Dexter!*" I scream, twisting the sheets in my hands. He rides out my orgasm, moving the vibrator in and out of me until my body slumps into the bed. When my body's finally gone fully limp, Dexter peppers my skin with gentle kisses, and sags into the soft skin of my stomach with a satisfied hum.

This was supposed to satiate the sexual tension between us, but I feel like it's done the complete opposite. There's no way I'll ever get enough of this. My skin feels like it's buzzing like a live wire, and all I can think about is how we can go another round in two and a half minutes.

Instead of suggesting just that, I watch Dexter pad to his room. He returns a few minutes later, reemerging in clean pajama pants and an easy smile on his face. He has a towel in his hand, and he kneels next to me to gently wipe between my legs. Everything about him is tender and soft, and I start to feel that ache tug at my heart again.

"Do you need a fresh pair of panties?" he asks cheekily when he's done. "Since you left a nice little mess in the ones you were wearing…" His voice trails at the end, and he runs his tongue along the edges of his teeth like he's ready to devour me all over again.

I huff a laugh. "Sure." I lift a lazy finger toward the dresser. "Top left drawer."

He does as he's instructed and returns to my side to help my floppy limbs into the simple cotton panties he picked out. We climb under the sheets and lay there, wrapped in each other's arms in complete silence while fighting off a slowly creeping sleep before letting it win.

31

Dexter

I'VE ALWAYS KNOWN Lucy to be beautiful. From the moment I met her, I was hooked, with her deep brown eyes and her perfectly round face with full lips that felt like a flame and I was a helpless little moth. I've always been attracted to her, and over the past month, that attraction's gotten stronger. Something that's becoming harder and harder to ignore. And now, watching her dressed in a sleek black dress that wraps around her curves and the top criss-crossing across her chest to wrap around her neck makes me want to fall on my knees. And those shoulders. I didn't even think shoulders could be sexy, but I want to build a goddamn monument for hers.

She has her short hair styled in waves, and she's standing over the sink in the bathroom to hook on some gold earrings. She catches me watching her from the doorway and smiles. "What?" she asks.

"You look very pretty."

She saunters toward me, her shoes clicking on the hard floor. When she reaches me, our eyes at level with the added height of her sexy heels, she drapes her arms over my shoulders. "You don't look so bad yourself, handsome." She pauses, peering down at the floor before guardedly looking back up at me. "The heels don't bother you?"

I jerk my head back in confusion. "Are you kidding me? They're my favorite part of this whole thing you put together. That, and your shoulders," I add, not caring if she finds it weird that I like her shoulders of all things. I lower my lips to the hollow dip above her collarbone and place a gentle kiss before adding, "Why?"

She shrugs. "Some guys don't like that I'm...a little taller than most women," she answers. "When I wear heels, it usually makes me taller than them, or at least the same height, and..."

"Boys," I throw in, and she laughs shyly. I flick my eyes to the deep red painted on her lips. "I would kiss you right now, but I'd hate to ruin that lipstick."

"That, and we're late." She pats my chest and briskly walks past me before reaching for her small purse on the couch. "You ready?" she asks.

I pluck the keys off the small dish near the doorway and jingle them. "Ready whenever you are."

"Oh," Lucy exclaims softly. "I need my memory card."

Tonight's the night of Janet's gallery's show. Janet already texted me twice today to confirm Lucy and I are still going, the same amount of times Lucy reminded me this morning about the show. Since we have to take a cab across the bridge, we decided to grab a quick bite and head to the show after. So this is basically a date. I mean, not basically. It *is* a date. And for some reason, I feel nervous. Topped off with butterflies in my stomach and a lingering giddiness I can't seem to get rid of. It's another item added to the growing list of coupley things we've been doing. Like when Lucy had an early day from work two days ago and had lunch with me, meeting me in the lobby of my office while we opted for a small sandwich shop and iced coffee. Or when we went on a quick grocery run for paper towels and Cholula hot sauce and spent our time perusing various breakfast meats after Lucy told me she'd been craving maple sausage links only to realize we forgot the paper towels once we got back home. With each coupley thing we've been doing, I have to remind myself to not get too comfortable with the notion of being one-half of a couple. All of this is very temporary. Not temporary in a maybe sort of way but temporary in a definite sort of way.

Lucy returned from her room, her bulky camera bag looped over her shoulder and her small clutch in her hands. "Not so flattering for this fancy little outfit," she says, gesturing toward her bag.

I take it from her and hang it on my shoulder. "I got it."

Her brows furrow. "You sure?"

"Of course."

She smiles and smooths her hand down her dress. "Thank you."

After a trip across the bridge and a short meal with a few small appetizer plates to fill our stomachs, we make our way to the show. Once inside the gallery, we're greeted by Janet. She's swapped out her chunky oversized sweater for a simple navy blue dress and heels. A surgical mask covers half of her face, a precaution her doctor insisted on if she decides to go out in a large public area, and she's wearing her hair prosthetic, which looks pretty damn close to how her hair was before chemo took it all away.

"You guys came!" she exclaims, pulling Lucy in for a deep embrace.

"I told you we would," I say from behind Lucy. Janet hugs me next and ushers us inside toward where the cluster of people is gathered in front of various paintings hung throughout the gallery.

"That's Avery." Janet points to a girl who looks like she's still in high school standing in the middle of a small crowd, where she's smiling politely and nodding along to the conversations around her. She looks timid, a little uncomfortable with the amount of attention she's getting. "She's the artist I was talking to you about."

"How old is she?" I ask, dipping my head down a little.

"Nineteen," she answers. "She's still really new to the scene, but she's doing such amazing work." Janet flags her toward us, and she breaks away from the crowd. "Avery," she says when Avery reaches her side. "This is my brother Dexter and his girlfriend Lucy."

Lucy eyes me when Janet says the word "girlfriend," but that moment passes when Avery extends a nervous hand in our direction. Lucy takes it, offering a soft smile with her gentle handshake. "It's nice to meet you," she says calmly, without any overexcitement or intensity. "Janet has told us a lot about your work."

Avery blushes a bit and looks at Janet.

"I actually asked Lucy to take some pictures tonight," Janet says, reaching up to squeeze Avery's arm. "Just something to document your first big show."

Avery turns to Lucy and smiles. "Thank you," she says gratefully.

"Of course," Lucy answers. "And I'll be in complete stealth mode," she adds. "You won't even know I'm here. Candid shots are my favorite. There's such a genuine feeling to them, and I think it'd be perfect as a little memento for tonight."

Avery looks relieved when Lucy tells her this. But before we can say anything else, Avery and Janet are pulled to another part of the gallery by more people. They walk away, and Lucy retrieves her camera from the bag hung over my shoulder. We don't know exactly where Avery's paintings are located, but we find them fairly quickly. Her name is labeled on them, and after some browsing, we discover that her paintings have a very specific style that translates into all of her work.

Lucy takes a few pictures, catching people admiring and discussing in soft gallery voices the style of Avery's paintings and the color schematic she uses that's a bit unconventional but striking in contrast. She gets a few of Avery talking to people in front of her paintings, laughing and chatting a bit livelier, noticing that she's growing a bit more comfortable and coming out of her shell as the night goes on.

Lucy's a complete pro. She moves artfully, working around the lighting and chaos like it doesn't deter her from getting the shot she's looking for. When she quickly shows me a glimpse of her handiwork, she smiles proudly at my reaction. It looks stunning. With the gallery lights shining a spotlight on the main focal point, making it pop against the low shadows around it. But what stands out the most is the reaction of an onlooker admiring the artwork. She's staring up at the piece of art like she's been transfixed by the beauty of the colors and shapes, and it's conveyed through the image Lucy captured like I was there to see it for myself.

As she moves along from painting to painting, she urges me to leave her be so she can work and even tasks me with bringing Janet a drink and a plate of some cheese and crackers from the small bar in the far corner. I do as I'm told and catch Janet just as she's stepping away from making her rounds through the crowd.

"The boss said to bring you something," I say, lifting a small glass of white wine and the plate.

She lowers her mask and keeps a watchful eye on the crowd around her. "And the boss being..."

"Lucy."

"Ah, of course." She nods and takes my offerings.

"Thanks for inviting us," I say as I watch her practically inhale a cracker. Looks like she's getting a bit of her appetite back. "Lucy's having fun," I add.

"Thank you for bringing her," she says, nodding her head in Lucy's direction, where she has her camera pointed at us. She pulls her face away from behind the lens and smiles. I gesture a small wave, and she wiggles her fingers at me. "I like her, Dex."

I nod. "Yeah."

"I like her a lot," she adds.

We stay quiet, the weight of her words settling around us. I haven't kept anything from my sister. She knows the agreement Lucy and I settled on, the impermanence of our situation and what feels like a contract that can't be reversed or revisited. Yet when she tells me something so simple like how much she likes Lucy, not just for me but as a person, it feels like hope is weaved into her words. Like maybe we can hash out a new deal, one that won't end with a slew of promises ready to be broken with thousands of miles between us.

"Avery won't stop thanking me for having Lucy take her pictures," Janet says, breaking our silence. "She's really shy and didn't want to keep pulling out her phone or stop people to take pictures with her, but this is her first show and she wanted to remember it. And Lucy's really on stealth mode. I don't think Avery's even noticed that she has a little paparazzo lurking from the shadows."

"Yeah," I respond. "She's pretty amazing."

Lucy caught on to that, Avery's shyness and her difficulty in approaching people for something as simple as a picture. That's why she said she would go throughout the night unnoticed, so Avery didn't have to worry about having a camera shoved in her face. She has this way of accepting people for who they are without pushing them beyond their comfort zone. She's done that with me every time Janet's illness is brought up, and now she's doing it with a complete stranger. She didn't force Avery into situations where she would have to take awkward pictures. And every time I've wanted to expose more of myself to her, it was on my terms, whatever I was comfortable offering. It's no wonder things feel so effortless with her.

Janet finishes the last cube of cheese on her plate and looks around the room. "I'm going to finish up with some of the sales and head home." I turn around to look at the span of the gallery and find the crowd of people has dwindled down to only a handful lingering throughout some of the open spaces. "You guys should head home too."

"How about you? We can wait." The "we" slipped, and the significance of it passes through me with a hitch. An incredibly hard to ignore, yet brief hitch.

"Charles should be here any minute," she says, looking down at her watch. "He had to stay at the office a little late. You know, to make up for some of the time he took off. But he said he'd meet me here to take me home." Just then, we see Charles walk through the doors of the gallery and spot Janet. "Ah, speak of the devil."

"Okay," I answer, finding Lucy across the room chatting it up with a bartender while she waits on a drink. He smiles a little too widely at her, and she smiles back, tugging at the strap of her camera hanging around her neck. "I guess we'll call it a night too," I say to Janet while I keep my eyes across the room.

Janet's gaze follows mine, and I can practically feel her shake her head next to me. "Alrighty, lover boy," she says, patting my back. "Go get your girl."

I press my lips together, not even bothering to hide my undeniable jealous side, and swoop down to hug my sister just as Charles approaches our side. I nod a quick hello in his direction and walk my way to the bar.

"You have to check out the Met while you're here," I hear the bartender tell Lucy with a bounce of excitement in his voice. His hands are braced along the counter he's leaning against, and I fully notice the way his eyes trail the length of her body. "They have an amazing photography exhibit. As a photographer—"

He stops and clears his throat when he notices me sidle up to Lucy. I wrap my arm around her waist, and she turns to face me. "Hey!" she exclaims as her eyes light up and her smile brightens. "How's Janet?" she asks.

"She's got some things she needs to take care of in her office, but she's going to head out after that. Charles just got here, so he's going to take her home."

The bartender slides a drink in front of Lucy—a Coke, it looks like—and he eyes her carefully. Lucy nods a polite thank you to him and takes a long sip from the skinny black straw. "I got a little thirsty," she explains. "And I wanted something a little sweet. Want some?" She offers the straw she just drank out of in my direction, and I take a sip.

She grins at me, and I realize it doesn't matter if this bartender was flirting with her. Whether or not he offered a little extra attention in hopes to gain some of hers. Because she wasn't going to give it. He's not the one she's smiling at the way she's smiling at me right now. He's not the one she offered a sip of her drink, not even bothering to add a fresh straw or asking if I mind exchanging germs. She probably wouldn't have given him the time of day even if she were wearing a clock necklace like Flavor Flav had it not been for the necessity for some sort of refreshment on her end.

"You ready to go home?" I ask, taking the camera from her and gently placing it in the bag I've been carrying all night.

"God, yes," she breathes. "I have about an hour left in these heels before I Cinderella the hell out of them."

"Did you just turn Cinderella into a verb?"

"I did, didn't I?" she answers with a proud smile.

My brow shoots up. "That takes a special kind of talent."

She smiles, and her nose scrunches as she takes one last long sip of her drink. She turns the straw in my direction, letting me have the rest, and she places it on the bar top. "Thank you, Matt," she says politely to the bartender. He's not wearing a name badge or anything, so he must have told her his name. He probably even weaved in some lie about how he's not really a bartender but an actor about to make his big break on Broadway while using some cheesy pick-up line like, "So... you come here often?"

"Yeah, thank you, Matt," I add sardonically before we turn to leave. My hand rests on her lower back—okay, maybe a little lower, hovering closer to ass region—and we leave the gallery.

Once outside, Lucy turns to me. "Are you going to pee on me next, Mr. Jealous?"

I give a crooked smile, looking equally pleased and amused. So she *did* notice. "Now, that's just unsanitary," I answer. "How about we just get my name tattooed across your chest? You know, in big block letters."

She gives an assertive, unyielding shake of her head. "Nuh-uh," she says firmly. "It's olde English font or bust."

"Anything you want, baby."

We walk in silence, our hands lingering on each other and the city sounds mingling with the clicks of our footsteps. And a thought occurs to me. Something that makes me rethink why I acted like a possessive caveman who actually thought peeing on this woman wouldn't have been a bad idea. "If, uh, that was a little too much, I'm sorry."

She turns to face me with an adorable tilt in her head and a confused blink.

"I mean," I continue, "you, we—me and you—it's not like we're...I mean, I guess it's a little complicated between us, and if you wanted to talk to other people or—"

"Dex," she interrupts in a pleading voice.

"I just wanted to tell you I'm sorry if that was inappropriate."

She stops walking and turns to face me, giving my hand two quick tugs to get my attention. "Dexter," she says, leaning into me. "You're the only person I want to be 'talking to.'"

I feel like a slew of bright hot fireworks are bursting inside my chest. "Yeah?"

She nods, her smile matching mine. And then she shrugs a shoulder with that sly smirk she has when she's about to tease me with something impish and playful. "But I kinda like you all jealous and a little overprotective."

"Oh, do you?"

She giggles. "It's cute watching you get all huffy and puffy like you're about to ram horns with another man."

"I did not get all huffy and puffy!"

She tilts her head back and laughs, and I swear I fall harder for this woman.

32

Lucy

COUNTDOWN to zero hour has officially begun. It's the last week of my internship. A bit of a turning point, not just work wise but life wise. After this week, I'll be heading to Honolulu for Nat and Hayden's wedding. And after that, I'll be saying goodbye to Dexter and going back home, making good on our agreement that we'll go on with our lives. I've been ignoring the niggling, gnawing realization of what life will be like after this. Will it be drab, maybe a little monotonous and depressing? Or will I slide back into the life I had before I moved out here without a second thought? The latter felt practically laughable. How could I forget about my life here with Dexter as if we haven't grown too comfortable with each other?

Today, I haven't really had a second to think about this. I've thrown myself into work with the last days ahead of us. I've been grouped with Ajay and Min Jun to work with Ivy where she's overlooking a portion of the men's line and the final pieces sent over by the brand.

"Seb!" Ivy calls as Seb finishes with the makeup department. He sits up straighter in the director's chair he's sitting in and looks at Ivy. "I need you in about five minutes," she informs him. "We're about finished with the rest of the lighting." Seb gives a quick thumbs-up and turns to the makeup artist swiping a big, fluffy makeup brush over his forehead.

I move about the set, positioning the faded barstool under the lights to make sure it sits at the right angle. "Ivy," I call as Ivy stands behind a nearby folding table, hovering over a tablet with a stern look of focus on her face while her fingers swipe across the screen. "I'm just going to grab the fan and once we set it there, we should be good to go," I inform her as I point to the far right corner of the backdrop.

"Great," Ivy answers. She sets the tablet down on the table and walks toward me. "Kyle's pretty tied up right now. I was thinking you could run the shoot with Seb."

I pause brushing off a layer of dust off the barstool. "What?"

"You and Seb have a pretty decent rapport," she says, her voice calm and confident. "I think we'd get some pretty good shots if we have you shoot him."

She wants me to run this shoot?

"Ivy," I say, my voice pleading. "Will Kyle be okay with that? I mean, I don't know if I'm ready to take on that much responsibility." I feel a queasy tumble roll through my stomach, and my hands start to sweat. I don't know if I can do this. I don't know if I *should* do this.

"I agree, it is a lot. But I want to try this approach," she says. "I saw the pictures you took for the streetwear looks with Seb. You did a good job."

I hesitate and bite my lip. This is an amazing opportunity, and I'm completely taken aback she'd even consider me, but I'm not as confident as I should be taking on an entire shoot.

"You don't think I should just watch Kyle? Or maybe just wait for him until he can give me more direction?"

Ivy offers a reassuring smile. "Try it," she instructs. "I'll be here to guide you. If things don't feel right, which I can't imagine it will," she adds, "we'll have Kyle take over."

Seb saunters over from the makeup chair and slips into a bright fuchsia blazer. He perches himself on the stool, and Ajay hovers over him with the light meter, moving the device around him like she's scanning him with a metal detector. Seb flashes a smile at me and runs his hands over the front lapels of his blazer.

"You already know what to do," Ivy says calmly. "Just work your magic and make that handsome man more handsome than he already is."

I huff a nervous laugh. "I thought we were taking pictures of clothes here."

"That too." Ivy laughs and nods her head to my camera bag sitting on the folding table. "Now, come on. Before all that foundation melts off of his cheekbones."

"Don't forget to pack a bathing suit," Nat calls through the phone I have set on speaker. "And some sneakers too. In case we do something outdoorsy."

"Check and check." I pause, wrapping up the straps to my new neon pink bikini and tucking it into the corner of my suitcase. I'm ticking off my mental checklist, waving a finger over the must-have items already packed. The green bridesmaids dress that looks absolutely stunning on me with the satin material and curve hugging fit, black strappy sandals, a tropical dress for a luau, the laciest lingerie I have on hand. You know, in case...

"What time is your flight?" I ask, removing my thoughts from the "in case" sweeping through my preoccupied mind.

"Six a.m." she answers. "And we'll arrive close to noon, Honolulu time."

"Ugh, that's so early."

She groans. "I know. Which means we'll probably have dinner in about an hour, and we'll call it a night."

I look at the clock. "Nat, it's four."

"And that makes us senior citizens."

I laugh. "Not even husband and wife yet and acting like an old married couple."

Nat laughs too. "You'll be there on Wednesday?"

"Yep."

It's Saturday now. The last day of my internship was yesterday, and a group of us interns are heading out for the night to celebrate. While I have some free time this morning, I'm opting for overly prepared instead of last-minute procrastination by packing for Hawaii. I keep telling myself the reason I'm staying busy has nothing to do with the aching notion of having to say goodbye to this place, but I know deep down, it is. I hoped packing would help keep those thoughts at a safe distance, somewhere I can easily ignore them, but it's actually causing the opposite effect. Because now the closet that once hung all of my clothes looks nearly bare with mostly empty hangers. And my suitcase that was shoved into the corner sits open on the floor once again, much like when I first got here, and it's too much. The reminder that all of this signifies my expiration date inside Dexter's spare bedroom. Which also means no more Thai food, no more *Supernatural* marathons, no more coupley things. No more Dexter.

"Dexter's coming that day too," Nat announces, and it startles me a little bit, the mention of Dexter's name from my sister's lips. Almost like I just got caught red-handed.

"Oh," I say, hoping I sound indifferent about a piece of information I already know. I push a foot against the cardboard box with my address back home written in thick black ink across the top, ready to be hauled to the nearest FedEx. Another reminder that my time here is coming to an end.

"Yeah. I think Carmen's getting there on Tuesday. She just has to wait for David to get off work," she explains, referring to Carmen's boyfriend of nearly six years. "And a bunch of other people should be there the day before or the day of the wedding."

"Mm-hmm."

"Maybe we can spend one of the nights in our room," she randomly suggests. "Just eat junk food and watch *Bridesmaids* and *La La Land*. I miss doing that with you and Carmen."

"Nat." The lingering guilt from the lies I've been telling her, either by omission or avoidance, feels like it's all ready to spill out of me. A part of me feels like maybe I can finally tell her. With the past few months behind me, maybe she'd understand now, knowing how hard I worked and how much praise I've received from my superiors.

"Hmm?" she hums, sounding distracted.

"I..." I pause. "I, um..." The words don't come out. I don't know how to tell her I've been living in the same city as her, playing house with her future husband's best man while working at the exact internship she and my mom agreed I shouldn't apply to. That I've been falling for Dexter, hard. Enough for me to occasionally rethink going back home and play imaginary scenarios where I stay in Brooklyn. And I realize it's another goddamn *lie*. While I lied about one lie, I created a new one. One involving her and her future husband and their inner circle. Why do I keep doing this? The guilt starts to make my heart crumple into a tight ball, and all it does is force the truth down. "I can't wait to see you."

She squeals. "I can't believe that in *one* week, I'm going to be a married woman!"

I can't help the creeping grin on my face. "Mrs. Natalia Marshall." I sigh. "Who woulda thought."

We both dissolve into giggles.

Just then, I see Dexter round the corner, and his face softens into a gentle smile when he sees me.

"I'll see you soon, Nat," I say, my eyes on Dexter. He watches me, leaning one shoulder against the doorjamb with his arms crossed, and I look up at him from the floor.

"Yep," Nat answers. "See you in a few days!"

I hang up and toss my phone on the floor at the same time Dexter walks across the room and sinks into one of the few empty spots next to me.

"Packing?" he asks, gesturing toward the suitcase, the half-filled box, and the scattering of items ready to be stowed away, all a symbolic answer to his almost rhetorical question.

I nod. "Thought I would start now while I had some free time." He nods too, mirroring the morose up and down motion of my head. "Do...you need to pack too?" I ask, hoping to steer away from the jarring reality of me going home.

He nods again. "But I can do that later in the week," he says with a sad smile.

I finish stuffing away a stack of clothing into my suitcase. "Oh," I exclaim. "I almost forgot." I stand from the floor and retrieve Dexter's laptop from my bedside. I start it up, sidling up back next to him with the screen pointed in his direction. "I touched up the pictures from the gallery show."

"Oh," he says softly. He readjusts himself when I lean into his shoulder and makes room for me in the crook of his arm. We settle ourselves as I pull open the files.

"I need Janet's email to send them to her," I say, scanning through the pictures of Avery and Janet surrounded by the crowd at the show. I stop at a few images of Dexter and Janet, the ones I took of them from afar. They're laughing and talking, looking as if they don't have a care in the world. "These are a few of you and Janet I got."

Dexter takes the laptop from my hands, and his eyes are glued to the screen. I notice a small furrow fissure between his brow, and his lips form a straight line. "She looks just like my mom," he says softly.

"Oh," I whisper.

"I never noticed it before, but when she smiles like that...She has my mom's smile."

I don't know what to say. Do I apologize for unknowingly dredging up the memory of his mom? For reminding him his parents never had the chance to watch him and Janet grow up? Or do I console him? Remind him that while he doesn't have his parents, he still has Janet. But given Janet's current state, even that feels wrong. So I just sit there, watching him scroll through the pictures. He clicks along, going back and forth between images as if he's trying to memorize them. Every shadow and light, every pop of color or contrasting gray and white area. Like he wants to remember Janet like how she is in the pictures, happy and healthy looking. Without all of the obvious depictions of her illness, like the barely remaining hair on her scalp hidden underneath the hair prosthetic she wore, or the layers of makeup carefully applied to disguise the gaunt tones of her skin.

"Thank you," he finally says, tearing his eyes away from the screen to look at me. "Seriously, Lucy. Thank you for taking these. You don't know what this means to me."

"You're welcome."

"I meant it when I said you have something special here," he adds.

I blush a little, too uncomfortable with praise and recognition. "I'm heading out around nine," I say, changing the subject and gently laying the laptop on the bed. "I'm grabbing some drinks with some other interns and a few other people from work."

"Oh," he answers, a little deflated.

"Did you want to come?"

"You sure? You don't want to mingle with your crowd alone?"

I shake my head. "Keep me company," I urge.

He smirks.

"Is that too clingy?"

He shakes his head. "You could be sewed to my side, and you wouldn't be clingy."

33

Lucy

THE MUSIC'S loud and the chatter even louder at Butter, an upscale bar and lounge in the West Village. Dexter and I didn't mind the distance across the bridge or the extra hour we spent getting ready, mainly because we spent that time together. By the time we walk into the bar, hand in hand, most of my coworkers are already there.

I poke a finger in the direction to where Elaine is sitting at a table, talking to a few other interns, and nudge my head in the direction while looking at Dexter, letting him know my friends are here.

"You want a drink?" he calls over the noise, leaning closer to me. I get a good whiff of his woodsy, spicy cologne and take a moment to appreciate how he looks tonight. His hair is still short, making him look boyish with the adorable dip in his widow's peak. He's wearing a dark T-shirt, neatly pressed without a single thread of lint hanging off of him, and he's paired it with jeans and sneakers. I love that his arms are exposed, the muscles on his forearms and the slight bulge in his biceps out in the open for me to ogle. I dressed just as casually, opting for jeans and low heels with a strapless bustier top and large hoop earrings, and it makes me melt into a tiny puddle every time he trails his fingers over my bare shoulder or when his eyes linger over the curve of my cleavage rounding the top of my bustier.

I nod. "Just whatever you're having."

"I'll catch up with you," he says.

I turn just as Elaine spots me, and she waves her hand in the air to get my attention.

"You made it!" she exclaims, pulling me into a tight hug. "You need to catch up!" She lifts her hand and catches the attention of a waitress walking by. Elaine makes some gesture at the empty round of shot glasses in front of her, and the waitress nods at their already acquainted signal. "We're doing tequila," she informs me. "And Ajay is making a bet with Min Jun on how many girls' Instagrams he can get by the end of the night," she adds.

I grimace. "I forget that they're literal children."

"We were once twenty-two, Lucy. Best to let them make their own mistakes."

We both cackle a loud laugh just as Dexter returns to my side, two pink-tinted cocktails in his hand. "I got you a paloma," he says close to my ear.

"Thanks," I shout over the noise. I turn to Elaine, whose eyes ping-pong from me to Dexter and then back to me. "This is Dexter," I say over the table. "He's my roommate."

"Nice to meet you," she says, extending a hand toward him. Elaine smiles at him and then at me, her brows raised, and I smile back, resisting a small eye roll. "I guess you don't really need to catch up," she comments, eyeing the matching drinks in our hands.

Just then, Ivy shows up, greeting us with hugs and eager waves. "Sorry I'm late," she says with a deep sigh. "It was hell catching a cab."

"You got here just in time," Elaine says, taking the shot glasses from the waitress's tray as she lowers them to the table. "We're doing another round."

"Seven!" Ajay announces as he returns to our table.

"Six," Min Jun corrects. "That last girl gave you a fake handle."

"I've heard of fake numbers, but fake Instagram accounts?" Elaine says, feigning sympathy as she pats Ajay's shoulder. "Rough night?"

"I probably just typed it in wrong," he defends while reaching for a shot glass. "It's six more than you," he adds, handing the drink to Min Jun.

"The night's still young, my friend. I am taking it nice and slow," Min Jun argues, taking Ajay's offering. "Looking too eager is highly unattractive." Dexter coughs a laugh, and Min Jun raises his glass to him. "I'm right, right?"

"It's worth testing out the approach."

"I'm Min Jun," he says to Dexter. "And this little eager bunny is Ajay."

"Dexter," Dexter responds, shaking Min Jun's extended hand. "Nice to meet you guys."

It's getting more and more crowded by the minute, and Dexter squeezes himself between another rowdy table behind us and me. He places his hand on my back and leaves it there as we all take a glass.

A quick toss and a painful grimace later, and we're all sipping on our drinks while we chat up about our work life these past few months. Dexter's been lured away from the table by Min Jun and Ajay, whatever brotherhood or camaraderie they've developed in the short time since we've arrived turning into a fun night of more tequila shots and loud games of darts and pool.

"So what are your plans after this? Is anyone staying in New York City?" Ivy asks.

"I'm heading back to San Diego in a few days," Elaine answers. "I've been looking into some work in my area but if something opens up elsewhere, I might look into it. I'm not really tied down to anything right now."

"You should look into our LA offices. Elevate's headquarters is there, and they're expanding soon. More positions are going to open, and they might even expand to different cities."

"Yeah, Ryan mentioned that," Elaine answers. "It's on the top of my job hunt list. It would be nice to stay near home instead of relocating."

Ivy turns to me. "What about you, Lucy?"

My lips twist to one side. "I haven't really decided. I'll probably start looking into some entry-level work in Seattle. I've also been considering freelance until I get something more stable."

"If you guys ever need a reference or anything, let me know. I might even know some agencies in Seattle that have some entry-level positions open."

I perk up. "Really?"

"Of course," she answers. "I know you want to go toward the more commercial part of photography, and I have a lot of connections all over. I've been doing this a long time, over twenty years, and I've met a lot of people along the way."

"That would be amazing. Thank you."

Ivy smiles at me and winks, clinking her glass to mine.

Hours later, after the drinks have dwindled down to the occasional slowly sipped cocktails and the shot glasses stopped coming in round after round, Dexter and I are heading home.

"Did you have fun?"

Dexter drapes his arm over my shoulders. "I did."

I laugh, remembering how Min Jun challenged Dexter to a round of Quarters and he wiped the floor with the boys, leaving Min Jun and Ajay equally dumbfounded and impressed.

"You?"

I nod. "I'm going to miss them. Especially Elaine." I pause to tuck my hand into Dexter's back pocket. "You know, Ivy was telling me she might have some connections to other agencies in Seattle if I ever want to look into entry-level work somewhere."

"Really?" He squeezes me a little harder.

"Yeah," I say softly. "Actually, on one of the shoots last week, she had me take over, and I did the majority of the shoot. And it went really well. She liked my work."

"Of course she did," he answers, his smile brightening and his brows shooting up with excitement. "I'm not surprised one bit."

"I know I walked into this with a lot of doubt, but I really think I did some pretty good work." I pause, shrugging as Dexter's thumb runs over the curve of my shoulder. "And I've been thinking. I want to look into freelance work in Seattle. I'll reach out to Ivy too, and maybe I can finally find something stable."

His prideful smile doesn't waver while he looks at me with fondness. Our steps slow and become leisurely as we approach his building, and I become even more aware of his gaze.

"What?"

He shakes his head. "Nothing." I laugh a little awkwardly, and he plants a small kiss at the corner of my mouth. "You just amaze me."

I roll my eyes and shove a hand into his stomach.

"Lucy, I mean it." His arm pulls away from my shoulders, and he gently grips my nape, grabbing my attention to him. "You did all of this. You made things happen, and you need to give yourself some credit."

I stay quiet, and a ball starts to form in my throat. He's right. I *did* do this. I made things happen for *me*. I start to grin, turning the bashful smile into something much more assured and gratified. "You should start giving motivational speeches."

He chuckles and kisses me, his hands cupping my cheeks. I lean into him, my own hands gripping his waist, and we fall into the kiss. We let it linger and deepen and turn into a passionate type of kiss full of heat and fire. The kind that only has one end.

Dexter starts to stumble up the steps of his apartment, and I follow. He fumbles with his keys, not breaking our kiss once, and we ascend up the elevator, where I push him against the closed doors while thanking the elevator gods for giving us an empty elevator car. When we reach his floor, we're still a tangled mess of hands in hair and backs and necks. We burst through the door and finally stop when we reach the nearest wall. Dexter lifts me, pressing me against the cold surface, and takes possession of my lips. That's exactly what it feels like. Like he's claiming what's his. Almost like if he didn't and someone else did, he wouldn't be able to stand the thought of it.

"You're killing me with this thing you're wearing," he rasps into my skin.

"You mean my bustier."

"Whatever it is. You're making me want to give up an internal organ just to see you in it again."

I laugh as he trails kisses down my neck. His hands claw at my waist, and I feel his hot fingers tug at my exposed skin at my midsection. The back of my head hits the wall when his tongue dips in the hollow between my breasts, and I swear my legs turn into soft, not yet fully set Jell-O. "Dexter," I moan softly.

He starts to gently suck at my skin, and I lose all sense of control. Why aren't we having sex again? Why are we trying to be responsible adults here? My mind has a moment where I forget what a consequence is. Fallouts? Repercussions? To hell with those. They might as well be foreign words to me, something in Swahili or Mandarin. What's the other word? YOLO? That sounds more my language right now.

But then Dexter stops, and he presses his forehead into my chest. "We should stop, right?" he says breathlessly. I feel his chest heave up and down and his hand squeeze my ass a little tighter. I swallow hard and nuzzle my nose into the top of his head.

"Right?" he repeats, lifting his face to look at me. His eyes search mine like he's waiting. Waiting for me to say no. No, we shouldn't stop. No, we shouldn't be responsible anymore and we should just fuck each other senseless. No, we shouldn't think about the future, where we'll stand in just a week when we wouldn't be able to revisit this moment.

"You're right. We should stop." Because he's right. This wouldn't be like last time, where we pushed the boundaries of our "no sex" rule and orgasmed through the fine print of our clause. If we started something, there would be no end. Not tonight. I don't have the will power in me to stop, and I don't think he does either.

His face deflates, and he pulls away. "Okay," he whispers, gently placing me back on the floor.

We should talk about this. I know we already did and things felt resolute between us then, but now, that firm, straight line we drew is starting to blur. It's starting to wiggle and sway, making me question whether or not things were ever really resolved between us. Maybe when we decided things would just go back to how they were before we ran into each other at that wine and cheese shop, when he thought I was thousands of miles away and I was too focused on my internship to realize the proximity of him and my temporary rental, we decided it too prematurely. Maybe we should have taken into consideration how our feelings would deepen and grow.

He laughs awkwardly and rubs his hand over his head. "Sorry," he says sheepishly. "I guess things got a little out of hand." A pained look passes across his face, and he looks over his shoulder. At first, I think he's checking the door to make sure it's locked or looking at the time or something else superfluous to avoid the awkward moment settling between us, but then I realize he's avoiding me. I notice his jaw tick from the side of his face, and the pained look that passed by too quickly returns.

"Dexter."

"I'm going to bed," he announces softly, looking back at me with a sad smile. He gives me one last kiss, too fleeting and painful, and he turns to walk into his room.

34

Dexter

"THIS IS the number to the hotel," I explain to Janet, who's distractedly scanning over the screen of her laptop. I thrust the piece of paper in her direction, which she takes without even looking at me.

"They have parasailing! Please tell me you'll try it when you get there."

"Janet, are you even listening?"

She huffs, rolling her eyes at me. "I heard you," she whines. "I told you to stop worrying."

I sigh. "Maybe I shouldn't go. Hayden would understand. He knows what's going on with you and—"

"No! Dex, I'll be fine. My infusion session is scheduled for Friday. By the time you get back, I'll be recovered, and you can tell me all about swimming with the dolphins."

"I'm not swimming with any dolphins. I'm not parasailing," I say, standing from the seat next to Janet on her couch. I walk to the kitchen to help myself to a bottled water. "I'm doing my part as the best man at my best friend's wedding, and I'm coming home."

"You aren't even going to go on an ATV tour?"

"No." I plop back in my seat and take a long, refreshing chug. It's warm and humid outside, but because Janet's been running cold, shivering at the smallest breeze of air, the AC in her home has been set at a higher than acceptable temperature. But I don't complain, even as the small beads of sweat gather along my brow and my shirt clings to my back.

It's Tuesday evening, and Lucy and I leave for Honolulu in the morning. I stopped by Janet's place after work. Mainly to say goodbye before our trip but also to check on her and make sure she can reach me while I'm gone. She already saw Lucy over the weekend. It was Lucy's request that she see Janet, though sad goodbyes weren't exchanged. In fact, we didn't even tell Janet it would most likely be the last time she sees Lucy, and I feel like it was because neither one of us wanted to discuss Lucy's departure. Instead, we met up for dessert at The Lunch Car, where we sat for a few hours, along with Charles, and Janet gushed over the pictures Lucy sent her from the gallery show. I refrained from pointing out how much she looked like our mom in the pictures and instead let her gab on about how Avery was going to love them.

"How's Lucy been?" Janet asks, interrupting my thoughts on Lucy waiting for me back home. This is our last night together in my apartment, and while I can't wait to spend it with her, a part of me is dreading it.

I nod. "Good. I think she's ready to go back home. I'm sure she misses her own bed. And her roommate's cat."

A furrow fissures between Janet's brow, and she rolls up the thick sleeves of her sweater. "When is she leaving?"

"We're going to Hawaii, and then she's going back to Seattle from there."

"So she's not coming back here after the wedding?"

"No."

She stays quiet, her hands running over the edges of her laptop.

"What?" I ask.

"Are you okay? With her going back home?"

I shrug. "I don't really have a choice." I fidget with the water bottle in my hand. "She lives all the way across the country. I can't just ask her to move here on a whim. And I can't move over there, at least not without us discussing a future."

"So then discuss it."

I turn to face her, my face deadpan.

"What?" she says innocently.

"I can't have that kind of talk with her."

"Why not?"

"Because..."

"'Because' is not a reason, loser."

I sigh. "Because we already did."

"When?"

"A while back," I explain. "We decided we'd hang out and just let things happen, and when she leaves, we'd go back to how things were before she moved out here."

"So what were you guys? Friends with benefits?"

"Jan, no. We aren't even...It's not..." I stumble over a few words, letting the ambiguity of my silence do the talking.

"You two aren't having sex?"

"You know, it's really weird to have this conversation with you."

She rolls her eyes. "Stop being such a baby. We aren't talking about sex; we're talking about you and Lucy."

I rub a hand over my face and pause. This has all been sitting on my shoulders for a while now, weighing on me, with the load growing heavier and heavier each day. I wanted to talk to Lucy about it, maybe revisit our talk and see if we could renegotiate our terms or discuss an "after" once the wedding is past us. But then the other night happened, when I thought for a second maybe she wanted the same thing, and it was obvious she had no intention of revisiting anything. She's going back to Seattle, and I'm going to stay here in Brooklyn.

"She hasn't given me any kind of hint or clue or *anything* that she'd want to continue this beyond what we already discussed. I don't think she wants to complicate things. She's already talking about finding work when she gets back home. And what if..."

"But what if?"

I look at her. And what little pragmatic reasoning I have left dissolves. Because what if? What if I asked her to move out here permanently or I considered moving out to Seattle for the sake of being near her? What if the future of Lucy and Dex could go beyond the next few weeks? It could go on and on, indefinitely.

But then the whispers of that what-if start to fade away, making my heart fall while I picture my life without Lucy in it, imagining the fallout from the mere mention of a future. I couldn't bear it, her shooting me down while reminding me this was never meant to go beyond the days we agreed upon. This is how it was always meant to be. "She's going home after Hawaii, and I'm coming back to New York. That's it."

Janet leans forward, placing her hand on mine. "And you can tell me how snorkeling went when you get back?" she jokes morosely.

I shake my head. "I'll go to a luau," I reason.

She makes a disgusted look. "Lame!"

35

Lucy

I ZIP up my carry-on bag, a large black tote bag with neon green stitching and a wide zipper. My suitcase is packed to the brim, the last remnants of my belongings stuffed into every nook and cranny. I turn to look at my room, the emptiness of it sitting too loudly for me to ignore. The small bedside table missing my phone charger and hand lotion. The six-drawer dresser no longer holding my jewelry and perfume bottles on top. The bed, neatly made and without the messy pile of clothes I've been keeping in a heap at the foot of it. I no longer live here. My stay here has officially expired, and I'm moving on to the next chapter of my life.

I've been thinking about this moment a lot lately. The days and hours leading up to it. The anticipation of how it would feel to finally walk out of this room I've inhabited and made mine. There were moments when I thought maybe the melancholy that kept coming in waves would just disappear. And even moments when I thought I would be happy to leave, too eager to go home to feel anything other than excited. But now that the moment is actually here, it's worse than I expected. I almost want to unpack, shove all my things back where they belong, and curl up into a little ball underneath the blankets. Maybe even ask Dexter to join me.

Dexter.

He's the reason I feel like this. Not this room or the apartment or even the city. It's Dexter. He's the one I'm going to miss.

"You want me to take your suitcase?"

I'm pulled from my thoughts, my depressing, puppy face inducing thoughts, and look at Dexter standing at the doorway. He's standing there, his shoulders slightly hunched and his arms sitting awkwardly by his side like he's unsure. He gestures at my suitcase with a look of unease, and I nod.

"Yeah, it's all packed."

He takes it from me without another word and wheels it to the living room, where he has his own suitcase lined up against the back of the couch. We stand there in quiet, disconcerting silence as he sifts through some mail.

"Is Janet going to come by to check on your apartment?"

He nods. "Charles, actually. I asked him to come by once or twice to bring in the mail and make sure the place hasn't been taken over by rats. Or squatters."

I smirk, trying to lighten the mood.

"You aren't forgetting anything?"

I shake my head. "I triple checked."

He nods again and pulls at the back of his neck. "We still have another hour or so before we need to leave. You want to go grab some coffee?"

I smile. "Sure."

We leave our luggage by the door and exit the building. We walk carefully through the streets, too aware that this will be one of the last times we'll be leaving his apartment to do anything coupley. We won't be going out for drinks to meet up with work friends anymore. We won't be having dinner with Janet and Charles or stopping by Pepper Thai to pick up more takeout. We won't be having any more early morning coffee runs.

We walk in silence, Dexter's hand gripping mine while I feel him give me an occasional squeeze. We stop at the nearest Starbucks and enter the already crowded shop. The line is long, and we wait patiently while perusing the menu, even though I already know what I'm going to order.

When it's finally our turn, Dexter reaches into his wallet and peeps open the bifold. "I'll have two upside-down venti iced caramel macchiatos with oat milk and a light caramel drizzle," he tells the cashier while looking into his wallet as if he's reading off the order.

The cashier taps away at the screen in front of him and tells us the total before Dexter retrieves his card from his wallet and pays. After the quick transaction, we move on to the waiting area for our drinks.

"What is that?"

"What?"

I poke a finger at his pocket. "That thing you had in your wallet."

"Your drink order."

I look at him, confused. "Like, you wrote it down on a piece of paper?"

Instead of answering me, he takes his wallet out of his front pocket. When he opens it, he angles it toward me, showing me a piece of paper tucked into it. I expect to see my drink order messily scribbled on a Post-it Note or something equally haphazard yet considerate. But instead, it's so much more than that.

"Is this the order label off the side of the cup?"

He nods. "I picked it off the cup that first morning you bought me coffee," he explains, holding the wrinkled paper between his index finger and thumb. The typed-out text is worn and practically impossible to decipher. The words abbreviated to shortened terms like Vt Icd Carml Macch and my name in the similar bold font, all dated to two months ago.

"And you've kept it this whole time?"

"Yeah."

I stand there, completely dumbfounded.

"What?" Dexter asks, watching my gaped mouth and speechless state.

"I just…" I pause, taking a breath, a moment to collect my words. "I can't believe you would think to do that."

"I wanted to make sure I got your order right if I ever needed to get you coffee," he explains with a small shrug, as if it was completely normal to have my drink order wedged between his credit cards and a few five-dollar bills.

Dexter's name is called, and our identical drinks sit on the counter, waiting to be collected by us. He grabs a straw for me, opting to drink his using the straw-free spout, and we walk out of the busy coffee shop. Once we're outside, I stop on the sidewalk, letting people walk past me while I ease myself under an awning, away from the steady flow of foot traffic.

"Hey. Is everything okay?" Dexter asks, following my steps.

I nod while I push down the lodged knot in my throat. This was supposed to be temporary. I was only supposed to occupy Dexter's spare bedroom while I finished out the length of my internship, and I'm supposed to go home at the end of it. It's an agreement he and I both agreed on.

And now, he goes and does something so *un*-temporary. That piece of paper could sit in his wallet for all of eternity. It could stay stuck to the leather lining as a constant and forever reminder of what we had. I can remove all remnants of myself from his apartment. I can pack away my clothes, my belongings, my messiness, all of it, without leaving a single trace behind, but I can't take away that piece of paper from him. *He* put that there. *He* turned it into something permanent.

"Are you sure?"

I look at him, the inner corners of my eyebrows turned up almost like I'm pleading. Why did he have to go and do that? Why did he have to make me want, make me hope, for more from this?

"Dexter," I say, my eyes avoiding his. I start to choke on my words, and I feel like I'm going to burst into tears. "I, um…Everything you've done for me while I've been here has meant so much to me. And I just want to tell you…thank you. For everything."

He strokes his fingers along my arm, and my eyes start to mist over. A look sweeps across his face, something expectant, with his widened eyes and rosy smile, and he nods at the same time his hand clutches my fingers.

"I'm going to miss you," I finally add, and his face drops.

An acknowledging look replaces the hopeful one he had, and he tugs at my hand. "We should get going," he whispers softly.

The chaotic energy you find at any large airport surrounds me and Dexter as we head out of the terminal to where the taxi service line is located. Dexter has my luggage in one hand and his in the other, and I'm following along with my carry-on bag slung over my shoulder.

We stand under the large sign that reads TAXI in bold letters, accompanied by the silhouette image of a taxi car, and patiently wait in the line. My hand is wrapped around Dexter's bare arm, and his hand occasionally rubs against my lower back. We steal glances at each other, wondering if the silence between us is due to the exhaustion after a ten-hour flight or because we don't know what to say to each other.

Everything I want to tell him sits heavy on my heart. Words like "home" and "future" and even "love." I can't possibly be in love with him. How can I? How could I have fallen in love with Dexter in just two months?

But maybe I gave that small four-letter word too much power. Placed it high on a pedestal, where even a ten-foot ladder couldn't help me reach. Something I never thought was in the cards for me. I always thought love was more calculated, more intentional and purposeful. I didn't think love could just *happen*. Out of nowhere, completely unexpected.

But it's here. "Love" and "Dexter."

He just showed up. He blindsided me, and now I don't know how I'm supposed to go back to how things were before love fell in my lap.

"You take the first cab," Dexter says, insisting I get to the hotel ahead of him. "I can get the next one."

"Are you sure?" I ask, my thumb tapping against the retracted handle of my suitcase.

"Of course." He gently places his hand on mine and squeezes it. "I want to make sure you're already on the road before I go."

I reach up and wrap my arms around his neck. He lets out a deep sigh as he pulls me closer to him.

"I've gotten so used to touching you, I don't know how I'm going to do without it."

Dexter chuckles. "Am I that irresistible?"

I nod. "I also find kittens irresistible." My hand smooths against his flat chest. "And those fancy Christmas villages with tiny people dressed in winter coats and fake snow. And a bowl of picked out marshmallows from a box of Lucky Charms."

"I find you pretty irresistible too," he answers, his own hand smoothing along the hollow curve of my lower back. "Though much more irresistible than a bowl of marshmallows."

"Rainbow marshmallows," I correct. "The regular ones, not so much."

"I think I'm going to miss kissing you more than anything." And he does just that: kiss me. Deeply and slowly. As if we don't have a hotel to check into and friends and family to pretend we haven't spent the last two months playing house in front of.

A taxi pulls up at the same time I pull away. Dexter helps the cabbie load my suitcase into the trunk and opens the door for me. "I'll be right behind you," he says. He grips the doorframe to the cab, staring at his hand as if avoiding my eyes. "I'll probably wait a little bit so we don't pull up at the same time," he adds softly. He still doesn't look at me.

"Yeah," I whisper hoarsely.

He tears his eyes away from his hand, the door frame, the shiny surface of the car, everything to avoid me, and he finally looks at me. He offers a sad smile, something that silently whispers goodbye, and leans away from me.

I turn to get in the cab, and he closes the door behind me. When I look out the window, his eyes are still on me. We wave through the glass, his palm facing me and my hand pressed flat in his direction, and the cabbie drives off, leaving a hollowness in my chest that makes me feel...empty.

My phone buzzes in my purse just as the car turns and Dexter is no longer in sight, and I smile. That's probably him, calling me or texting me, telling me more about how much he misses me.

But instead of Dexter's name on my phone screen, I see Ryan's name.

"Hello?"

"Hey, Lucy," he calls, his voice distant as if he's on speaker. "Do you have a minute?"

"Uh, sure. What's up?"

"I just wanted to give you a heads up," he answers. "The internship mentioned there would be employment opportunities after it ended. They probably said something about that to you when you applied."

"Yeah, it was brought up," I answer when he pauses.

"Right. We want to offer you a position with Elevate."

Holy shit. "You're offering me a job?"

"Yeah. Kyle referred you after he went over some of your work," he explains. "He was really impressed. Now, I know you're out in Seattle, so we're taking that into consideration with relocating, since the head-quarters offices are in LA."

"Would I be at the LA offices?"

"Yeah, most likely," he answers. "But nothing's set in stone, so don't go apartment hunting just yet."

"Yeah," I say softly. This is actually happening. To me. *To me.*

"HR will discuss with you all the nitty gritty. And I'll follow up with an email with the formal offer."

"Right."

"But I wanted to let you know so you can think about it."

"Thank you, Ryan. It's a huge opportunity. I'm honored Kyle would think of me."

"You did some of the best work for the whole campaign," he says, validating something I thought was so far from the truth. I didn't think a future working for a company like Elevate would happen so soon, if ever. "I know Kyle doesn't really acknowledge your hard work, but a lot of your photographs were submitted for the final ads that are going to go out. Your pictures are going to be on billboards and magazines."

"Are you serious?"

He laughs in a way that's endearing and not condescending at all. "Yeah, Lucy."

I stay quiet, mulling over this realization. My work is worthy of industry level standards. I'll be able to find my pictures out in public. I'll be able to point them out and tell people I'm the one who took them.

"Anyway," Ryan calls when I stay quiet too long. "I'll be in touch, but shoot me an email if you have any questions."

"Thanks, Ryan," I answer.

"Yep." He hangs up, and I'm left speechless and somehow full of too many words at the same time.

"I just got a new job," I say to myself.

When I look up, I catch the eye of the cab driver through the rearview mirror.

"What was that?"

I look at him, and my face brightens with the widest smile. "I just got a job offer with an ad agency. Like a real, grown-up job. Not just as an intern."

"Congratulations," the driver mutters, offering a smile with his lifelessly spoken words.

"I'm going to have a real job," I gasp. "I don't have to find work at a shitty retail job or a coffee house. I don't have to *find* work, period."

I ignore the confused look on the driver's face and instead stare at my phone screen. My fingers immediately find Dexter's contact, hovering over the call icon.

I want to tell him. FaceTime him with a wide grin, bursting with excitement from the news. He's the first person I thought to call. Not my mom or Nat or even Annabelle. It's Dexter. But I shouldn't be calling him with every piece of good news like he holds that level of significance in my life. Because there is no more Dexter and Lucy. We let the idea of us go outside of the airport terminal, with our luggage gripped in our hands and those silent goodbyes whispered through sad smiles and a long, drawn out kiss.

"We're here."

I look up to see the cab has stopped in front of the hotel entrance. The cab driver is already at the trunk, hefting my luggage onto the ground as an attendant at the hotel takes it from him. I pay the driver, making sure to leave a good tip after he was the first one to hear my good news, now somewhat less enjoyable with no one really to share it with.

"Lucy!" I turn to see Nat hurtling toward me, her arms outstretched and the widest smile on her face. "You're here!"

Her feet finally stop when she collides into my body, making me stumble a step back. When Nat's arms circle me tighter, I swoop a little lower to embrace her. Something in my throat constricts, making me realize how much I've missed not only Nat but my entire family. Over her head, I see my parents and Hayden walk toward us, though at a more leisurely pace.

"I missed you so much!" Nat says, pulling away from me.

I finally have a chance to greet my parents already waiting on the sidelines. My mom steps forward first. Her reddish copper hair, natural and one absolutely none of us inherited, sweeps with the breeze, as does her Hawaiian dress littered with palm leaves and hibiscuses.

"Hi, baby," she croons, pulling me into a long hug. She cradles my face in her hands, and she does a once-over. Like she's checking me for any bumps or bruises or new and sudden employment opportunities I might be keeping from her. "You're okay?"

I study her face, paying attention to the fine lines that have now joined the excess of freckles over her glowing skin. Her bright green eyes shine at me with genuine concern for her youngest child as she eagerly waits for my answer. "I'm good, Mom."

She doesn't pry any further, and the stress and frustration that's built up over the months from her persistence and overbearance softens, replacing it all with the warmth flooding my heart now that I'm surrounded by family. "Oh, it's so good to see all my girls in the same place."

"It's good to see you too."

When she lets me go, it's my dad's turn. "Hi, Daddy."

"Hi, baby girl." He towers over me by a good six inches, probably where I get my height from considering my mom and Nat are basically miniature next to me. His shirt matches the patterns on my mom's dress, and I realize they most likely have a few matching outfits in their suitcases. Probably one with a bright birds of paradise print too.

"How's my little chicken nugget?" he asks, his bushy mustache and eyebrows, no longer jet black like they've always been but now leaning more toward salt-and-pepper territory, twitching with his warm smile.

"Not so much a nugget anymore," I say, resting my chin on his shoulder while tilting up on my tiptoes. "More like a chicken strip."

Nat tugs at my hand, ripping my luggage from it and handing it off to Hayden.

"Hey, Lucy," he calls with a salute-like wave.

I barely get to wave back before Nat swivels me on my feet and nudges me toward the lobby. "I'll take you up to our room," she explains. "Hayden's is just down the hall from ours."

"You guys are so weird," I say, peeking over my shoulder to see my parents and Hayden following behind us. "You know Mom and Dad already know you two have sex. This whole 'bad wedding juju' isn't fooling anyone."

She smacks my arm, and I flinch. "It's not just because of that," she hisses. "We want our wedding night to be special."

I mouth a silent *whatever*, refraining from holding my thumb and index fingers together to form a W.

"Plus, it'll give me a chance to hang out with you," she adds as we reach the elevator. She turns around to face our little group, with Hayden still dragging my luggage and the matching outfits on my parents causing a weird magic eye effect. "I'm going to get Lucy settled in. We'll meet downstairs at the lobby for dinner in about an hour?" she announces, reaching for my luggage from Hayden.

Hayden nods, reaching into his pocket to retrieve his phone. "Sure," he answers. "Dexter just texted me. He should be pulling up in a bit."

Right, Dexter.

"Perfect," Nat answers. "Wow, you two should've just taken a cab together from the airport."

My breath hitches in my throat. "Heh," I laugh nervously. "Yeah, that would've been convenient."

We part with no further mention of Dexter's and my travel plans aligning a little too coincidentally. My parents walk off in the direction of the gift shop for the antacids my dad desperately needs if he wants to enjoy his steak tonight, and Hayden plants a quick peck on Nat's temple before he turns toward the entrance again, tapping away on his phone. "Carmen and David are already here. They're taking a nap since they took the red-eye in this morning."

We take the elevator and stop on the seventh floor, and I silently follow Nat's lead. Once in our room, I kick off my shoes and slump into one of the two queen-sized beds. "Ugh. I think I could sleep for about nineteen hours and still be tired," I groan, worn from my flight.

"You deserve this vacation more than I do."

I lift up my head, resting back on my elbows.

"So, anything new with you?" she asks, acting a little too casual. She's hanging something in the closet where the safe that looks like a microwave is not so discreetly stored, and she's more talking to the inside of the closet than me. Her eyes are focused on whatever she's fidgeting with, and I realize she's casually fishing for information. For a new job lead or interview that was more promising than the past eight or so I've been on. I stay silent, and she finally reemerges from the closet, sinking into the other bed with her entire weight.

"Uh, not really," I finally answer her. "Just same ol'."

"Nothing on the job search front?"

I shake my head.

"Well, just enjoy this vacation," she says, propping her elbow on the bed and resting her chin on the heel of her hand. "Forget about job hunting and all that crap. I think even Mom will give you a break while we're on the island."

"But..." I say, the lingering guilt in me forcing a bit of the truth to surface.

"But what?"

I want to tell her about the job offer. About Ryan's phone call a mere twenty minutes ago and the entirety of the internship she and my mom were relieved I didn't apply to. Not to shove it in their faces with a bold "I told you so," but so they can both stop worrying.

"I have a...thing lined up. For when I get back," I finally say, my hands tracing lazy circles on the bed. I can tell her that, right? It's not giving too much away, and maybe it'll fend off the hound-dog-like resilience my mom and Nat have in my job search endeavor.

"You do?" she asks excitedly. She sits up and faces me, her butt perched at the edge of the bed. "Like, a good thing?"

I nod. "I don't really want to say too much," I explain. "Don't want to jinx it or anything, but I'll keep you updated when I hear back."

She jumps up and hops, clapping her hands together. "Oh yay!" she exclaims. "I'm so happy for you!"

I smile, and Nat embraces me, both of us falling into the cushy comforter. "Jeez, what are you going to do when I tell you I finally got a job?"

She pulls away, taking in my excited smile with a thoughtful nibble on her lower lip. "I've been a little annoying lately, haven't I?"

"How so?"

She sits up. "You know, hounding you about Mom's emails. Being her little sidekick, trying to pressure you into finding work?"

I sigh. "It's okay, Nat. I know a lot of that was Mom's doing."

"Still," she responds, shaking her head. "I didn't want Mom to be worried, but I also worry a little too. But I'll back off. I'll fend Mom off and remind her you're an independent woman. Maybe I'll even fix your email settings and reroute her emails to your spam folder."

I laugh when we're interrupted by a sharp knock on the door. Nat jerks up from the bed, abruptly ending our conversation to open the door. Carmen stands there, a little bushed and dazed. Her eyes light up when she sees me before we greet each other in an embrace. Our hug isn't like the one I had with Nat. It isn't tight or fierce like when Nat cut off my air supply. It's calm and reassuring. Like her gently moving hands are silently asking me how I am. How I've been since I ran into her, if I've been good or barely surviving. If those assumptions she made about me and Dexter were correct.

I nod. And Carmen nods back. I almost want to tell her she was right. That she could've bet money on my heart, and she'd be rich.

Nat flits around us, chattering on about her wedding dress and a quick run-through of the itinerary, along with strict instructions to not let her have any tequila while she's here.

"I mean it," she scolds, her words directed at me. "Not a single drop."

"Why are you telling *me* that?"

Jeannie Choe

"Because," she explains at the same time Carmen smirks. "It's always tequila when I'm around you. It's like you have a blood pact with Don Julio."

I roll my eyes. "Seriously?"

"Anyway, since the rehearsal isn't until Saturday, we're pretty much free to do whatever we want for the next few days."

Carmen lifts her phone to her face, her eyes scanning the screen. "'Your soon-to-be brother-in-law just asked me if I knew that the grocery stickers on produce are edible. Please save me.'" She angles her phone away from her so Nat and I can read the text message from David, and we stifle a set of giggles. "I think David might get trapped by Hayden into some pyramid scheme involving the Chiquita banana."

Nat giggles. "Hayden's so cute."

"Come on," Carmen calls. "We should get downstairs before your future husband starts listing all the fruits that are actually vegetables."

36

Dexter

I'M NOT TOO fond of adjustment periods. Those moments that feel unsure and even a little embarrassing. And you never know how long they're going to last. Like adjusting to a new job or a different commute than the one you usually take because of road closures or to avoid an ex after a bad breakup.

Adjusting to this, pretending like there's nothing going on between me and Lucy, acting as if I don't know how smooth her skin feels under my fingertips or what her laugh sounds like muffled against my chest. It takes everything in me to keep my distance instead of gravitating toward her, taking up room in her personal space, and asking her how she liked the lobster bisque. It's…an adjustment period.

"I was thinking snorkeling?" Hayden pipes in, his hand loosely draped over Nat's shoulders.

"Or kayaking?" Nat adds.

There's a collective set of nods surrounding the bride and groom that includes me, Lucy, Carmen and her boyfriend David, Nat's parents, and Hayden's mom. Nat's mom, looking like she contributed absolutely nothing in the genetic pool that consists of Nat and her sisters, leans toward Hayden's mom in hushed tones of whispers and secret smiles. Mr. Marquez—or as I've been calling him, sir—hovers over his wife with eyes that look exactly like Lucy's, dark and inquisitive, and chuckles every so often, his way of contributing to the conversation.

Hayden and Nat continue their discussion, mulling over whether or not Nat's fear of heights will interfere with ziplining or if we have enough time to fit in an ATV tour after the wedding rehearsal on Saturday.

A light gasp pulls me away from my own telepathic memo to them that yes, a fear of heights will definitely interfere with a day of ziplining. (Who are they kidding?)

"They have a mint and chip milkshake."

Did I conjure a mental image of me shaking a magic eight ball, whispering, "Will I sit next to Lucy at dinner?" before we sat down? I might have. I also may have waited a few beats to see where she would sit and brusquely nudged a passing waiter with my shoulder to force the question to be answered with an affirmative, "All signs point to yes." And now, watching the way her eyes twinkle against the low candlelight on the clothed tables and her finger pokes at the thick paper menu where the dessert list does, in fact, have a variety of milkshake flavors, I don't even care what crystal ball or wishing well allowed for this to happen. All I care about is that I'm sitting next to her.

"Well, look at that." She giggles, and I turn to angle my body in her direction. "You wanna go halfsies?"

She mirrors my posture, scooting toward me with her shoulders slouched forward and an intrigued look of adventure. "Can we do that?"

I smirk. "Like there's a police for that." I drape my arm over the back of her chair. "I'll even ask for two straws."

There's talking and laughter and even the light clink of silverware against ceramic plates, but it's all white noise. Lucy's discreet voice and cautious laughter is all I hear.

Her eyes round when my thumb brushes against the bare skin between her shoulder blades, where no one can see my hand. I add my index finger, and those light strokes feel like a match against the sandpapered side of the matchbox, hot and full of buzzing electricity.

Her back stiffens, and a light flush creeps up her neck to her cheeks.

"Don't," she whispers. There's disappointment in the one-word sentence. Along with a mix of sadness and, somewhere between the single syllable, intimacy.

A ball rolls down my throat, right where her eyes linger, and a closed-lipped sigh exhales through her nose.

"Sorry," I whisper.

I say it like I'm not sorry at all. Like I only said it because I got caught doing something I wasn't supposed to, like taking an extra Halloween candy when the sign clearly says Please Take One. I drop my hand from the back of her chair and rest it on the table instead, where it feels empty.

Our knees brush, and our bare arms graze. And I feel the rounded tip of her platform sandals tap against my sneakers. When I clench my hand into a fist, I know it looks like I'm angry. Or at the very least, experiencing some level of discomfort that aligns with irritation.

I fucking *hate* this. Having her sit next to me while everyone around us is all coupled up, touching and kissing each other whenever they please. It shouldn't be like this.

"Can I see you later?"

I see her hesitate, her eyes catching the way my knuckles turn white and my forearm flexes. "I can't. Nat's going to wonder where I am."

I sigh through a frustrated pout. "You can't tell her you, I don't know, went to check out the hotel gift shop?"

"In the middle of the night?"

"Or you were curious about the armadillo population out in the wild?"

"They have those here?"

My fist loosens, and we share a small, painful chuckle. "In the morning then? Before the sun rises."

"You? Up before the sun?" she teases. A sad smile twitches my lips, and her teeth press into her bottom lip before she finally says, "Maybe. While Nat's still sleeping?"

I nod, trying to shift her hesitance into yes territory. "I'll meet you out front."

"Okay."

"Dexter!" I turn to look behind Lucy, pushing away from her while realizing how closely we scooted up to each other, only to find Hayden's mom approaching me with a warm and genuine smile. "How are you?"

I stand, embracing her as she opens her arms. "I'm good. How are you, Mrs. Marshall?"

"How many times am I going to have to tell you kids? Marsha."

I smile shyly and look down to see Lucy looking up at us. "Um, have you met Lucy?"

"Oh no, I haven't." She turns to face Lucy, extending a hand out to her. "It's so nice of you to accompany Dexter to my Hayden's wedding."

"Uh, Mrs.—Marsha, Lucy's Natalia's sister."

"Oh!" She brings her hand to her mouth, embarrassed. "I'm so sorry. I just saw you two talking, and I assumed." She gently places her hand on Lucy's arm, and Lucy smiles back at her just as kindly.

"That's okay," Lucy assures. "I'm sorry we haven't met before."

"Well, it's nice to meet you now," Marsha gushes. "Keep an eye on this one," she adds. "I'm sure he can use the company."

I see the redness creep up to Lucy's cheeks, and as uncomfortable as this whole encounter is for her, she's so damn adorable, I don't even bother to deny what Marsha's suggesting.

"Dexter," Marsha says, calling for my attention with a gentle squeeze to my arm. "How's your sister doing?"

"Oh," I answer, a little thrown off in the change of subject. "She's hanging in there. You know, a born fighter and all." I smile a purse-lipped smile and nod.

She nods back, silently telling me I don't have to say anything else. And instead of prodding further, she pulls me into another embrace, but this one is tighter, full of reassurance and comfort. The nurturing kind of embrace only mothers can give.

Hayden must have told her about Janet and only did so out of concern for me, or even to get some sort of advice on how to deal with a friend struggling through the role as caretaker when their loved one is sick. I pull away with a tightness in my throat and the flooding reminder of my sister's condition. "Thank you," I finally say, though my voice is hoarse.

"Take care of yourself," she says, giving my arm another gentle squeeze. And then she turns to Lucy. "It was nice meeting you."

Marsha walks away, and I'm left with Lucy, my hand gripped on the back of her chair and her looking up at me with worry.

I wish it were just us two, somewhere private and quiet. Somewhere where we could just be us, unguarded and vulnerable and maybe even a little rash. Where we don't have to pretend. Where *I* don't have to pretend, and I don't have to act all apathetic or brave or whatever the hell I'm supposed to be.

I wish I could find a small closet, like a storage room or maybe even the walk-in refrigerator somewhere in the kitchen of this restaurant, and drag Lucy with me so I could tell her that I think it was so sweet of Hayden's mom to ask about Janet and how it made me appreciate my friendship with Hayden even more. Maybe even tell her how it made me think about my parents and my childhood home and how I've recently realized how distant I've become to the feeling of "home." Not home as a place but as a feeling or emotion, like joy or hope or sadness. I'm never going to *feel* home.

And then Lucy looks at me. She looks absolutely heartbroken. I get lost in her eyes for a little bit, the same ones misting over and glistening against the warm light, and I want to ask her if she knows what home feels like. If it feels like this, how it is with me and her, or is it just a place for her like it is for most. Just four walls that echo sharp footsteps and a roof that occasionally leaks.

37

Lucy

THERE'S nothing but a blue haze filtering into the cold hotel room when my alarm goes off in the morning. I set it to the quietest sound, birds chirping or something just as discreet, but I'm already awake.

I knew this wasn't going to be easy. Us going back to just Lucy and Dexter as separate people. Not one, not a couple. But I didn't think it would be this hard. I didn't realize how much I would *miss* him. I'm on a tropical island, but I want nothing more than to be back in Dexter's apartment, us hovering over takeout and the warm, uncomfortable New York City humid heat.

I slip on whatever was on top of my suitcase, a pair of jean shorts and a loose T-shirt, and quickly wash up in the bathroom. Nat is snoring softly, something she claims she never does, when I close the heavy hotel door and quickly walk to the elevator. When I get to the lobby, Dexter's already there. He stands from the cushioned armchair he was sitting in, where he's dressed in a tank top, his toned arms and impossible-not-to-stare-at biceps on display.

"Hi," I whisper when I reach him.

"Hey." He reaches for my hand, and my fingers slip through his easily.

Why are we doing this? Why are we torturing ourselves? I ask myself these questions at the same time I shove all of the rational reasons away. Somewhere where I don't have to be reminded that even this is temporary. After this week, once my sister is officially a married woman, I really won't know when I'll see Dexter again. It could be when Nat and Hayden have their kid's first birthday or some other milestone-type celebration. Or never. I could never see Dexter again. There's always the possibility of that being true because whatever future meeting we may or may not have will be through chance. Fate. And as Dexter guides me, tugging at my hand through our linked fingers and veering toward the sandy beach less than half a mile away from the hotel, my heart feels like someone placed a heavy rock on it. Just so I can feel it, the ache, the dull pressure, the heaviness.

Once we reach the sand, I take off my shoes, sinking my feet into the cold ground and letting it fill the spaces between my toes. Dexter follows suit, bending to remove his flip flops before taking my own shoes along with his and reaching for my hand with his free one.

We stay quiet, the sky slowly lighting up and warming the air in the process. When our feet sink a little less into the sand with each step and we reach the water's edge, we stop. We still don't say anything, but I hear our shoes drop with a clack and a thud. And Dexter's hands are on me. One in my hair, the other around my waist. And he kisses me.

I kiss him back, my arms wrapping around his neck. His tongue dips into my mouth, and I whimper, making his hands rough and urgent.

"I've been wanting to do that since dinner," he pants.

"I've been wanting to do that since I got in that cab."

He smiles against the corner of my mouth. "It's not a competition."

"If it was, you'd be losing. Miserably." I laugh, something weak and morose. And I remind myself I shouldn't be having those thoughts. Wanting to kiss Dexter. Wanting to sink right here into the ground until we're a hot mess of sand in places it shouldn't be. But what if we discussed this? Maybe I could move to Brooklyn. Maybe decline the job offer from Elevate, start fresh in a new city. But what about everything I worked for? The past three months would be for nothing.

"Are you okay?" he asks after I've stood there too long, silent and brooding, while he holds my face in his hands.

I nod.

"Are you sure?"

I contemplate staying quiet, keeping from him the one thing that could send our reasonings and too rational decisions off-kilter to one side where we could be reckless. But that doesn't feel right. Because he should know. He should know that when we both go back to our respective homes, it'll be because we chose soundly. We did the smart thing and let our brain take the reins instead of our hearts. "I got a job offer," I blurt out.

Dexter looks at me with wide eyes. "What?"

"Um, yeah. Ryan called and told me Elevate is going to send me an official offer letter soon," I explain. "It'll be at the LA headquarters, but nothing's been made official so..."

"When did this happen?"

"Yesterday. On the way to the hotel. Ryan called me up personally."

"So you're moving to LA?"

I nod. "Looks like it."

The realization settles over us, and the silence feels loud. After what feels like eternity, Dexter smiles at me. "That's great, Lucy," he whispers, his voice hoarse and heavy. "I'm so proud of you."

"Dexter..."

"Um," he interrupts, clearing his throat. "We should get back. With the time difference, everyone might already be up."

"Yeah," I agree meekly.

He picks up our shoes and links our hands together again, and we turn our backs to the ocean. We trudge because one cannot simply stroll or amble gracefully through sand. And when we reach the concrete where the sidewalk begins and the area is slowly filling with hotel employees organizing beach chairs and early risers enjoying their first day of a Hawaiian vacation, we pause, looking at our linked fingers. As if we're taking a moment of silence before we step through the portal back to reality.

Dexter turns to me, pulling me into him for a long, tight embrace. "Thank you for agreeing to see me," he whispers into my hair. "Can we just…make the most of this? I know we don't have much time, but whatever moments we can have, can I be a little selfish with you? And I promise I won't be all clingy from across the country once we go back home."

He pulls away to look at me, and a tear slips from the corner of my eye. I silently nod, and Dexter swipes his thumb across my cheek.

"Dexter, I…" My voice sounds shaky and wet. And whatever I was going to tell him is stopped by the gentlest kiss. One that lingers on my lips and mixes with the saltiness of my tears.

"Come on," Dexter says, letting me go. We quietly dust off our feet and put on our shoes before we continue back to the hotel in silence, keeping a good amount of space between us as we make our final steps into the lobby. Dexter taps my forearm, and I wiggle my fingers in his direction. And we part ways.

"I swear, Nat is going to give my dad a heart attack."

"I don't know who's more scared," Dexter whispers. "Your dad or Nat."

I gesture toward Nat flapping her hands in front of her to shake off her nerves. "Apple." I turn toward my dad, who's wiping a runaway bead of sweat off his forehead. "Tree."

I look at Dexter, only to come face to face with a bright smile that makes the skin at the corners of his eyes crinkle. "You know my mom's the one who puts up the Christmas lights on the roof?"

His brows shoot up. "I hear acrophobia is no joke."

"But apparently 'joke' enough to willingly go ziplining."

I adjust the helmet on my head, loosening the strap and clicking it in place under my chin. Dexter does the same. The helmet sits on his still short hair a little lopsided, and he looks adorable. A crooked grin cuts across his face, and his cheeks are flushed from the heat and the strenuous act of hiking up the hill. His deep brown eyes gleam when he takes in my appearance: harness criss-crossing across my torso and my hair matted to my sweaty forehead.

A crease forms between his brows, and his lips straighten into a frown of disapproval. "I don't think they did a very good job." He reaches for the buckles resting on my hips, his hands tugging at the straps and my body jerking with each pull.

I rest my fists on my hips. "I think you should leave that to the professionals."

"You can never be too sure with these things," he claims seriously. His fingers brush over the area of bare skin below my crop top more than once, and I smile through an eye roll.

The frown on his face changes, only one side lifting into a sideways smirk that says he knows exactly what he's doing. And I can't help the laugh that has me pushing a hand into him and my chin ducking downward. Dexter laughs too, and his hand slowly glides to my waist before he coolly rests his hand there.

When I look up, I catch a glimpse of my dad looking in our direction. Sweat is still trailing down the side of his face, but his eyes linger on my hand pressed against Dexter's chest and where Dexter's is on my side. I drop my hand, and Dexter peers over his shoulder, where he meets my dad's observant gaze.

Dexter clears his throat, stepping to my right and extending a hand in the universal "ladies first" signal. I reach Nat's side, where she's actually whining. "Why the hell are you putting yourself through this?"

She huffs. "I thought it would be fun."

"Babe, we can go back down," Hayden offers, standing on the other side of Nat. We all turn to look at the edge of the platform, where a woman has a running start to jump off the edge like she's casually cannonballing into the deep end of the pool. She shrieks before taking the final leap, and her body careens down the zipline. Nat's eyes turn to saucers the same time my dad crouches with his hands braced on his knees.

"No, no," Nat answers firmly. "I said I was doing this. We're doing this. Come on, Marshall," she says to Hayden, shoving him forward. "It's our turn."

"One iced macchiato they both back out." It's Dexter, his hushed words close to my ear so only I hear. And I wipe away the glum smile on my face as quickly as it appears at the sound of his husky voice and replace it with something more rousing.

I turn and jut out my hand in his direction. "Make it a mint and chip milkshake, and you have a deal."

38

Dexter

"NOW, THIS IS MUCH BETTER."

Hayden, David, and Ashton, our old college friend who flew in last night, eye Mr. Marquez, a driver held upright with his fingers tracing over the sole of the metal.

"I'll take eighteen holes over ziplining any day." He chuckles, positioning himself over the golf ball nestled on the tee. His shoulders square, and his feet settle into the lush grass before he launches the dimpled ball across the golf course.

After spending the prior day partaking in activities that gave us enough adrenaline to fuel a triathlon, we decided to spend today doing something more relaxing. So while the guys decided to hit the golf course, the women are having a spa day.

"If you get a hole in one, Dexter's the godfather."

Ashton peers at Hayden over his shoulder as he takes his turn and positions his tee. "And if I don't?"

"I get to be godfather," Hayden answers. "Duh."

"What?!" I argue. "I did not agree to this."

Ashton rolls his eyes. "You guys are going to have to consult Carly before making bets on who gets to spiritually guide my unborn child away from immoral sins like pirated music and refusing to use your turn signal."

"I have a sixteen-page PowerPoint explaining why illegally down-loading music is the eighth deadly sin," Hayden announces. "Choosing me would be the responsible choice."

Ashton shakes his head before taking a hefty swing, his amateur wrist action angling his ball to land in the thick of some bushes pointing east. He groans, and Hayden hisses a quiet "*yesss.*"

We start to make our way to the next hole, returning to our golf carts on the narrow pavement area of the course.

"Why don't you ride with me?" Mr. Marquez says, approaching my side. He towers over me by almost four extra inches as he nudges me toward one of the golf carts, the other already occupied by David, Hayden, and Ashton. I hook my golf bag over my shoulder and follow along.

"You and Hayden have been friends for a long time, I hear," he calls over the high-pitched whirring of the engine. I peer at him, his eyes on the road ahead of us and large hands gripped on the steering wheel.

It's not really a question, more like a statement of fact, but I nod.

"He seems like a good kid," he adds. "Natalia's last boyfriend, I didn't like him. Her mom loved him, but I didn't think he could take care of her."

I continue to listen silently as he takes a tight turn.

"My girls, they have quite a bit of spunk in them," he continues. "And they need someone who's patient. Someone who's going to encourage that spunk, not try to smother it."

That's exactly who Lucy is. She's got spunk and determination and so much courage and tenacity. But what's even more special about her is that she doesn't even know these things about herself. Her humility is what makes her so unbelievably amazing. She shines and glows without putting on a show. Without even trying, and that unassuming brightness burns so much brighter because of it.

And because of that, I can never ask her to give up everything she worked for, for me. I'm so goddamn proud of her. She deserves someone who would never hold her back, and I don't know if I can be unselfish enough to be that person for her. Already, I could see the guilt seep through Lucy's voice when she told me about the job offer. We should be celebrating, toasting her success in excess, but there was no room for that yesterday. Just a few loose tears and unspoken words.

"But Hayden...I think he might be up for the challenge." Mr. Marquez looks at me, waiting for a response.

"I think so too," I finally say. And that earns me a nod and a smile.

"As a father, you worry about these things. What kind of partner they bring home, if they're happy and safe."

He parks the cart at the same time the guys exit theirs ahead of us, heaving their heavy bags out onto the grass. The engine dies, and he turns to face me.

"I want to trust that my girls have pretty good judgment," he says sternly as he faces me. "And maybe having you and Hayden as a part of our family is a good thing. God bless the men who have to deal with their sass..." He pauses to let out a low whistle. "But I think you're up for the challenge too."

He walks away with his golf bag and leaves me in the cart equally speechless and hopeful.

When we get back to the hotel, a little sunburned and dehydrated, it's about time for dinner. And since Nat's parents want to take the girls out to dinner, just the five of them, the guys settle for room service or deli style food from the small convenient store next to the hotel gift shop. I chose the latter and linger on the display case holding various sandwiches ranging from egg salad to salami and pepperoni subs.

"Oh." I turn around from the line consisting of two other people ahead of me to find Lucy. Her face is glowing, giving off that freshly scrubbed look, and her wet hair is pulled back in one of those claw clips with the bottom ends trailing down her neck. "Hi."

"Hey." I step out of the line when a man approaches it with a tube of sunscreen in his hand. "Did you enjoy the spa?"

She nods, smiling proudly with her fingers splayed out in front of me, palms facing down. "I got my nails done."

I smile when I catch a glimpse of the pale pink polish glistening against the fluorescent lights and resist the urge to pinch her cheek. "They look very pretty."

"Thank you," she says, suddenly bashful. "Dinner?" She gestures toward the sandwich and Doritos in my hand.

I nod. And she nods too, pulling her lips between her teeth. "I hear listeria does wonders for sunburns, so..."

She laughs, pressing her index finger into my pink forearm, where it blanches white for a second and goes back to red. "Well, let's hope it does the trick because that pretty green dress I got does not contrast well with red for the occasion. Gives off a Christmas-y vibe."

There was a fifty-fifty chance we'd be partnered up at the ceremony, and it looks like the odds were in my favor when Nat and Hayden gave us our altar assignments. And I'd be lying to myself if I said I wasn't fist pumping into the air thinking about spending the walk down the aisle with Lucy's arm linked through mine.

"But I thought Christmas was good. You know, hot chocolate, presents? Snow?"

She scrunches her face and shakes her head. "Not for a tropical wedding. Too political."

"Ah," I answer, omitting the expected *I see*. I huff out a sigh. "I was actually going to text you."

"Oh?"

"Just to see if you wanted to, you know, grab your own serving of questionable deli meat and join me, but I heard your parents—"

"Lucy, don't forget the—oh, hey, Dex." I look to see Nat round the entrance to the store.

"Hi, Nat."

She turns to Lucy. "Dad needs more Tums too."

Lucy looks away and nods, plastering a forced smile in Nat's direction. "Yeah, it looks like they ran out," she says softly, pointing to the shelf carrying Tylenol and Advil and an empty spot where the Tums must've been.

"He probably bought their entire supply after all of that bacon and sausage at the breakfast buffet," she comments. "Did you still need your water?"

"Uh," Lucy mutters, eyeing me. "I just remembered I have an unopened one in our room."

"Okay, then let's go. Mom and Dad are waiting."

Lucy turns to me, that fake smile so obvious it makes me want to call her bluff. "We'll see you tomorrow, Dex."

"Bye!" Nat calls.

39

Lucy

"HOW ARE YOUR FEET?"

Nat peeks down to the marble floor just at the edge of the large glass door leading out to the luscious lawn, the tips of her freshly polished toes peeking through her peep-toe pumps. "They're fine. Why?"

"Just making sure they aren't getting cold."

She responds with an eye roll and a long gaze outside, where a white gazebo sits at the end of a makeshift walkway. Hayden stands at the end, listening intently to the wedding planner who looks frazzled as she's wrangling the groom and groomsmen, her hands waving in front of her like she's explaining something to a classroom full of kindergarteners at circle time. Hayden glances at Nat with an exasperated look, and his eyes cross as he makes a cheesy grin at his bride to be. "They're pretty warm."

I glance to Hayden's left, where Dexter and the other groomsman, Ashton, are standing. I look at Dexter, and he glances in our direction. Right where Nat, Carmen, my dad, and I are waiting patiently. He has his hands linked in front of him, one hand gripping the opposite wrist, and he lifts a hand and waves at me. It's subtle and quick, but it's only for me.

I smile, unable to resist the silly grin creeping up on my face, and wave back. He smirks, and we continue this silent staring contest, filled with secret smiles and bashful giggles.

"I didn't know you and Dexter were that close."

I jerk my head in Nat's direction. She's still looking toward the altar, where the men are now at their markers, indicating it'll soon be our turn to enter the garden.

"I mean," I say, a little flustered, "we've sort of kept in touch since the last time I was in New York."

A look of indifference covers her face. "Well, obviously. I just didn't know."

"But you know, he's been fun to hang out with while we're here."

Nat nods, but she doesn't say anything else. And I feel my ears getting hot. Should I tell her I think he's repulsive? Just so I can fend off the scent of something cooking between me and Dexter? Like something about him makes me think he has a tail or webbed toes? ("*I don't know, he just gives off a vibe.*")

"Okay, ladies." The wedding planner interrupts whatever absurd lie I'm about to spew and approaches us with a clap and an overly eager smile. "When the music cues, I'll give the signal and maid of honor number two will step off first, followed by maid of honor number one." She faces Nat. "Then you and father of the bride will count to fifteen and follow."

We all nod, Nat's attention shifting to the wedding planner's instructions. She takes a quick step to my dad's side, and the four of us do sort of a square dance like tango to take our places. Once Carmen has made her way to about halfway down the aisle, it's my cue. I step out onto the lush grass, where the sun is streaming down in shiny streaks across the lawn. I step slowly and carefully, pretending like there's actual music playing, and make sure to walk at a slow, steady pace. When I look ahead at the altar, I see Dexter still looking at me. His gaze is full of intent with a lingering smile twitching his lips.

I take my place on the side of the altar where further instructions will be given, like when to take the bouquet from the bride or when to hand her her little note paper where she wrote down her vows. Nat does her quick procession with our dad by her side, and they do the clumsy exchange where my dad gives my sister away. And the whole process feels so definite. This is actually happening. In less than twenty-four hours, my sister will no longer be just my sister. She'll be a married woman.

After the fake bits of an invisible officiant are over and Hayden and Nat are given the "you may now kiss the bride" green light, it's time for me to walk down the aisle again, but this time, with the best man. In true Hayden and Nat fashion, they wave at the empty crowd, where it'll be filled with the handful of guests scheduled to check in tonight and tomorrow morning. And it's my turn to link my arm through Dexter's. He crooks his elbow, offering it to me at the same time a warm blush heats my cheeks.

"Fancy seeing you here."

"Right?" I say, faking a shocked look of pleasant surprise. "I thought the next time we met, you'd be nursing a horrible case of food poisoning."

"I guess I should've had more faith in convenience store deli."

I nod in agreement. "Seriously. We need to find out where your trust issues stem from. Did you fall for a phishing email? Or you accidentally signed up for a shopping rewards program the last time you were at Bath & Body Works? If that's the case, I totally get it." I lift a brow with a teasing smirk, and Dexter chuckles, with his warm hand covering mine.

Our steps move parallel, his right foot somehow stepping forward at the same time as mine, and he looks at me with those downcast eyes, almost like he's pleading. Maybe to ask if I want to chance an episode of explosive diarrhea and toilet hugging by trying out the tuna sandwich tonight since the cold cuts are already deemed safe. Or maybe to ask me again to spend time with him. To isolate ourselves somewhere. The beach, a utility closet, a remote island, since we seem to be surrounded by them. And I almost want to say yes. Even though he hasn't asked me, I want to tell him to whisk me away somewhere. So we can pretend things aren't the way they are.

We reach the end of the aisle, and it's time for us to separate. There's a half of a second where we don't and we just stand there, but then we're jolted back to the wedding, the rehearsal, and the glaring heat in the ceremony area when the wedding planner scampers toward us.

"That was great, guys! Tomorrow, you do the exact same thing but with about forty people watching."

Nat and Hayden grin at each other. "So we're free to go?" Hayden asks with his eyes on my sister.

"Yup, you guys are free to go. Make sure you're on time tomorrow and get lots of sleep. Nothing looks more drab than a tired and sloppy wedding party."

Hayden clasps his hands together. "All right, guys," he announces to us. "First round's on me!"

"Hey." Carmen slinks into the seat next to me, linking her arm through mine.

"Hey." My voice lacks the usual chirp and energy. I could tell myself it's the day spent in the humid heat, walking up and down the journey to the altar, that leeched the energy out of me. Or even the hour spent greeting a few family members before my sisters, Hayden, David, Dexter, and I headed to the nearest bar equipped with an open karaoke night and a gorgeous oceanside terrace. I could even blame it on the inquisitive questions our cousin, Jacqueline, kept asking about who the handsome best man is and if he's single. (I should tell *her* he has webbed toes.) But I know deep down, my state of fatigue isn't because of any of those things. It's Dexter. Dexter, who hasn't left my side the entire day. Dexter, who manages to somehow keep me calm with his presence yet nervous with the reminder that our minutes are measured.

"How you holding up?" Carmen asks, watching me blankly stare at the round water rings on the raised table. There's a collection of empty shot glasses, beer bottles, and skinny cocktail straws strewn in front of us, all of it surrounded by the bustling noise one can only find in a dingy dive bar.

My brows scrunch. "I'm good. Why?"

"Just making sure." She turns away and looks at Dexter from across the room. He's leaned up against the bar, waiting on his drink order while looking at his phone with a deep scowl. "How's Janet?"

I sort of shrug. Not in a way that I don't know about Janet's wellbeing, but more so that I don't know how I feel talking about Dexter's sister. "She seemed okay before we left," I answer, realizing there are so many implicit words in that simple sentence. Confirming that I was with Dexter before we flew out to Hawaii and that there was a "we" at some point. Maybe still is.

Carmen responds with this silent look as if she's equally worried and sympathetic. I almost want to tell her everything, right then and there. That this "we" Dexter and I forged without either one of us realizing it is tearing me apart on the inside. That I don't know how I'm going to be able to go back home after everything and go on like my heart isn't fragile and a little broken.

Hayden and Nat reach our table, the two of them dizzy from a highly flirtatious game of pool, which Hayden let Nat graciously win. And it doesn't seem like Nat even noticed how he was pulling his shots with her heart eyes glazed over with love and vodka.

"Next game, me and you," Nat says, sloppily pointing an index finger at me. I almost want to ask her how many fingers she's holding up.

"Actually, I think as one of your maid of honors, it's my responsibility to get you back to our room."

She huffs. "It's not even nine!"

"Yet with your tolerance of a teething toddler, you are plastered."

"Fine," she forfeits. "I'll just drink water for the rest of the night." She plops onto the bar stool, Hayden's hand hovering somewhere between her butt and her arm to catch her fall. "Oh! Unless we can find some butter mochi."

I cringe, and Hayden shakes his head in my direction with a silent *don't ask* look, right when Dexter sinks into the seat next to me with a fresh bottle of beer.

"What'd I miss?"

I lean toward him. "Hayden let Nat win a game of pool, which she thinks she won fair and square, so she's considering signing up for the next local pool tournament, *Queen's Gambit* style, and now she's on a hunt to find some butter."

"Butter?"

I shrug. "I don't question the bride. I just follow along and hold up her dress while she pees." I take a quick sip of my margarita. "What about you?"

"Oh, I think Hayden can piss on his own just fine without me holding his junk."

"I meant while you were getting your drink. And *please* don't ever talk to me about my future brother-in-law's genitalia."

The pleased, little smirk he had on his face drops, and he pulls at the back of his neck. "I was just checking on Janet."

My face changes too, my lips twisting to one side and my eyes downturning into concern. "How is she?"

"Tired," he answers. "She had a chemo session yesterday, so she's just resting."

"But other than that?"

"Uh, yeah," he answers, his voice teetering between hesitant and a little annoyed. "She seems okay."

We stare at each other, wanting to say more, wanting to do more but unable to. Instead of saying something, I reach out and place my hand on his thigh. Under the table where no one can see, wanting to reassure him of...I don't even know what. There's nothing I can offer him right now. I can't even offer him comfort or anything beyond touches under hidden surfaces. So I focus on Janet because it's easier, neutral. "Well, tell her I said hi when you see her."

He huffs, that hint of annoyance showing a bit more now. "Yeah."

He turns away, facing the table where his forearms rest and a deep scowl cuts across his face. I see it when he frowns and his jaw twitches. He's upset, mad. That need to say something tugs at me, and I hesitate.

He pulls out his phone, staring at the screen held between his hands, and I look away. This is how it's meant to be anyway, right? Him there and me here. I should start getting used to it. But then my phone buzzes on the counter, and when I look down, I see Dexter's name flash on the screen. I discreetly unlock my phone, sliding it under the table and ducking my head down to read his message.

Dexter: Can we talk later?

I chance a quick glance in his direction. He's still looking down at his phone screen, focused like he's reading some fine print on a legal document.

Me: I can't.

It's the truth, for the most part anyway. It's Nat's last night with me in the same room until she moves on to the honeymoon suite with Hayden tomorrow after the wedding. But if I could sneak away for a few hours in the middle of the night, would it be that difficult? When she's sleeping...

But is that really the smartest thing to do right now? Should I be playing with the already tattered parts of my heart, clinging to the hope that we can continue this charade without thinking about the consequences? I mean, what's a completely shattered heart for the sake of a few more stolen moments?

Three dots appear, flashing in sequential order before they disappear and then reappear. And then they disappear altogether at the same time I notice Dexter shoving his phone back into his pocket.

In an instant, the wooden legs from the stool scrape loudly against the floor before Dexter bolts toward the bathroom. I look around the table, but no one's noticed. Hayden and Nat are still in la-la land, and Carmen and David are picking at a wire basket full of mozzarella sticks and onion rings. I quietly excuse myself, reaching for Carmen's arm to get her attention with a quick head jerk toward the bathrooms, and follow Dexter.

When I round the corner to where the bathrooms are, he's there. Not inside one of the unisex stalls but pacing the small space. He lifts his head and our eyes lock. We stay like that, waiting for the other to make a move. And it's Dexter who does first. He turns toward the exit sign leading toward the back door without a single word, and I follow.

"Did I do something wrong?" I ask when the door closes behind me. *God, I hope it doesn't lock from the inside.*

He has his back turned to me, and I can see his muscles tense through the thin material of his shirt. "No, Lucy. You haven't done anything wrong."

"You look upset. At me. Why are you upset?"

He finally turns, and for the first time since I ran into him at that wine and cheese store, I'm scared. I'm scared of what he might say. That he hates me, he never wants to see my face again. Or even worse, he feels the complete opposite, and he doesn't want to say goodbye. That he wants me to come back to New York with him and go back to this fantasy bubble in his small apartment that smells like him and a little like me now.

"I-I don't know," he answers, hesitant with his words.

"Is it Janet?"

"No, Lucy. It's not." He groans a frustrated groan, and his hands fist in front of him. "Janet's...She's worried about me. About you *and* me." He gestures his hand between us. "She told me I should talk to you. And...I don't even know *how* to do that when things..." He stops talking, and I want to put my hands on him. On his arm, on his face, anything to calm him down because he looks so shaken and angry.

But instead, I stay quiet. I feel like I can hear my heart beating in my ears, the blood rushing in loud swooshing noises through my head. He looks at me and studies me. He starts crowding toward me, forcing me to step back and hit the cold wall behind me.

"Look, Dexter. I'm sorry about everything. Once the wedding's done and we go back home, it'll be easier."

He laughs dryly. He laughs like I told him some silly little joke.

"What?" I respond flatly. "What is so funny?"

"You really think me being thousands of miles away from you is going to make this easier? You seriously think—"

"Then what? What do you want from me then?! You want me to drop my life and..." I can't say the next words. I just can't. It's too scary, too daunting when I'm already unsure about so many other things in my life.

"And what, Lucy? What?"

I stay quiet, and my chin trembles.

"What do you want to do? What do you want *me* to do?"

"I don't know," I whisper, my voice sounding weak and scared.

"Lucy—"

"I don't know!"

We're yelling at each other now, and there's no more anger in our voices. None of the aching, painful resentment that made everything spill to the surface. Instead, we're both so goddamn sad. So fucking heartbroken over something that was never meant to be.

He takes another cautious step toward me, one hand moving to my waist and the other leaning against the wall behind me. And he enters my space. The space that feels like it's always been his to invade. Like he never needed an invitation.

"Tell me what to do," he whispers close to my cheek. "I'll do it. Whatever you want, just tell me, and I'll do it."

This is where I tell him, right? To whisk me off to a private island so we can be alone and away from all the confusing and unsure thoughts in my head. To tell me everything's going to be just fine as long as we follow our hearts. But we can't. We can't act like life isn't going to keep happening around us. As if he doesn't have a home to get back to in New York City and I don't have my own in Seattle.

"I don't know, Dexter," I finally say, looking into his sad, desperate eyes.

His eyes close, and he scowls like he's angry and hurting at the same time. "Yeah," he whispers, exhaling a deep sigh through his nose.

"I'm sorry," I say with a shaky voice. "I'm sorry this happened. Maybe we shouldn't have—maybe we shouldn't have let things go this far. I'm so sorry it did." The shakiness is covering my entire body now. In my legs, my hands, and I keep trembling. I can't stop.

Dexter watches me. He watches me fall apart and start to cry. His eyes trail a tear that trickles down my cheek, and he gives into the impulse to touch me. He cups the side of my face and wipes at the tear with his thumb. "I'm sorry too."

40

Dexter

"YOU NERVOUS?"

Hayden's eyes stay on the mirror, the soft, glowing lights from the hotel bathroom making us look like we're about to have our photos taken for a Men's Wearhouse ad.

"Nah," he answers casually. "I just want this day to be over so I can be alone with Nat."

I cringe, and he backhands my gut. "I'm not talking about sex, asshole. I just…It's been family this, wedding shit that, and I haven't spent any alone time with her."

"Still, it's kind of nice to be around family." I finish adjusting my tie and run my hand through my hair, still a little too short to style it into anything other than a quick swipe of pomade pushed to the side.

He shrugs. "I guess. My mom's pretty excited. Said she'll finally have the daughter she never had."

I place a hard pat on his shoulder and walk out of the bathroom. We're getting dressed in his hotel room, and Ashton is set to arrive any minute so we can head down. It's Hayden's job to arrive on time, and it's my job to make sure he does it without looking like he's shitting a ton of bricks. And it seems I'm doing a pretty good job, with his suavely styled hair and his relaxed posture. I don't think he would even understand what cold feet are right now and simply claim it's nearly eighty degrees outside, too warm to have cold anything.

I, on the other hand, feel like shit. I didn't sleep. Instead, I tossed and turned all night, replaying everything that happened last night.

I shouldn't have gotten so frustrated and let those frustrations take over everything. My outburst, my anger, my desperate need to touch Lucy. But I couldn't help it. We had agreed this would be temporary. Nothing beyond the walls of my apartment and the sixty-four days we spent living under the same roof (yes, I counted). I had no right to act the way I did.

I hate that we left it the way we did, her struggling to open the door that locked behind us and walking away from me to the front entrance. We got confused looks from Carmen when we walked through the front door and not from the hallway leading to the bathroom. Lucy patiently ushered Nat away from the large pitcher of water, where she claimed she just needed to hydrate and she'd be fine, and walked her outside to a waiting cab with Hayden hopping into the back seat with them.

I didn't know what else to do. Should I have followed her? Told her I was sorry? That I didn't know what to do either but we could try to figure it out together? I didn't do any of that, of course. Instead, I waved a quick goodbye to Carmen, her confused face growing a little more concerned, and walked the two miles back to the hotel. And even with the near hour-long trek, I was restless. I couldn't stop thinking about everything. About Lucy and wanting more from her. About Janet and her vaguely obscure message telling me she feels tired over and over again. About Lucy's dad's ambiguous suggestion that I would make a great addition to their family.

A sharp knock brings Hayden to his feet after he comfortably sank into an armchair. When he opens the door, we find Ashton with a pregnant Carly by his side.

"Hey!" Hayden stoops to embrace Carly, gingerly wrapping his arms around her like she should be bubble wrapped.

"Hi," she says with a kind smile. "I was just dropping this guy off, and I'm heading downstairs."

"She just wants to see if you have any sour cream and onion Pringles since she ate all of ours."

She smacks his chest. "Don't out me!"

I reach for the small tube of Pringles from the minibar and extend it to her. Her face lights up, and she takes my offering. "I swear, I'm not usually this greedy. I blame it on the kid." She pokes a finger at her protruding belly. "I'll give you all the Pringles you want, just please don't make it hurt when you come out."

Ashton leans down to place a quick peck on Carly's temple and does the same at the top of her midsection before she leaves. "You ready?" he asks Hayden as the door closes behind him.

Hayden nods. "Let's get this show on the road."

Once we get to the entryway leading to the outdoor lawn on the far south side of the hotel, we're approached by a near desperate wedding planner. "Oh! Finally. You're here."

Hayden complies when she tugs at the sleeve of his jacket and pulls him away from entering guests. "Are we late?"

"No," she says briskly, stopping about ten feet away from the gazebo decorated with flowers and string lights that aren't lit. "I just get nervous when I don't know where the bride and groom are."

I follow suit, standing behind Hayden with Ashton behind me where we're again approached by another eager-looking person, this one much warmer and more welcoming. "Hi, baby," Hayden's mom cries, her arms outstretched toward Hayden. "You look so handsome."

Hayden accepts his mom's embrace, careful not to muss up his boutonniere. "You look great too, Mom."

She smiles warmly at Hayden, a twinkle in her eyes that I know will be there for the rest of the day. She then turns to me, her open arms identical to when she approached Hayden. "Thank you so much for being at Hayden's side today," she says, rubbing a hand up and down my back. "You mean so much to him."

"Mom," Hayden whines, and I smile in a way that this type of interaction is completely foreign to me, finding the whole exchange a little amusing. A son uncomfortable with his mom's affection and her ignoring his plea to stop embarrassing him.

"Of course, Mrs.—"

She interrupts me with a sideways glance.

"Marsha."

The smile on her face spreads wider, and she cups my chin. There's a sympathetic tilt of her head and a warm squeeze of her hand on my forearm before she moves to greet others entering the wedding space.

"I told her about Janet." I turn to face Hayden, and he smiles at me grimly. "I hope that's okay."

"Yeah, she mentioned her the other night, so I figured." Hayden pats my shoulder, and we silently stand there, realizing how much we mean to each other. Not just old college roommates. Not just friends who continue to stay in touch as we approach yet another milestone together. His wedding, Ashton becoming a father. We're building memories, friends becoming family. "Hey," I call. Hayden looks at me, tugging at the crisp white sleeve of his shirt. "I, uh, I'm sorry if I haven't...if I've been a bad friend lately. I know I've—"

"Hey," he interrupts, placing a gentle hand on my shoulder. "Don't worry about it."

I nod, choking back the swell of emotions rising inside me. "Still, I've been really...absent, and I don't mean to be." I didn't mean to be so inconsiderate of our friendship over the past few months, but since Lucy moved in, she's the only person I've wanted to spend my time with. And I know it sounds incredibly selfish, but when Lucy and I are together, it seems to be the only reprieve from all the bad things in my life. She's become this tall building of refuge and I feel safe and sheltered in her arms. And maybe it was okay to be a little selfish while she was there. Maybe all the things I was able to press pause on, I could. Even if it was just temporary.

"I know." He nods. "But we're good."

We share a moment of tight smiles and acknowledging gazes before the wedding planner, looking a little less frazzled, approaches us again. There's a flurry of hands and clicks of cameras going off before we're ushered to our spots. The seats are starting to fill, and a low violin has started to play offside to the ceremony. We walk out to the altar and stand at our marks. We wait patiently, Hayden fidgeting ahead of me, and the music starts to shift. Something more drawn out and deep. Everyone's voices hush down and people stand, turning toward the building where Nat is set to walk out from. We rehearsed this just the day before, the entire wedding party dressed in casual vacation wear with flushed faces from the heat. But all of that's a clouded memory when I see Lucy step out onto the grass.

She follows Carmen, who's already halfway down the aisle, carefully walking down the narrow pathway just like yesterday, but this time with a small bouquet of white flowers the size of my palm in her hands. Her short hair is styled with wavy curls, and the green dress I couldn't wait to see her in drapes off those bare shoulders I love so much with two thin straps. It flows down her sides, her curves outlined against the silky material, before it stops just below her knees.

From her glowing skin to the extra care she took doing her makeup, she looks so fucking beautiful. So beautiful, it hurts. It hurts in the way that I'll never be able to run my fingers through her hair, tousling it to the side so I can inhale the scent of her lingering on the side of her neck, or know how easily her dress would slip off her once I lower the straps and unzip the zipper.

She sees me staring, and she stares right back at me. I realize the last time I saw her was last night. When I got upset and watched her walk away. When all I wanted to do was kiss her and beg her to give us a chance. Even with thousands of miles separating us, with her new career path and my responsibilities back home with my sister, just to see where this could all go. And I suddenly regret all of it, wishing I had just kept my cool and pretended like I wasn't aching for her instead.

Her somber look matches mine, and she looks away, her gaze focused on the altar ahead of her. Things move along as a wedding is supposed to. Music plays, vows are exchanged, people ooh and ahh. But I don't pay attention to any of it because all I see is Lucy. A sad smile when Hayden dramatically dips Nat into their first kiss as husband and wife, a blank gaze as she steps closer to me, her eyes glued to my arm while unsure if she should take it. She does, of course, because that's what we rehearsed. But even with her by my side, her hand draped over the crook of my arm, it feels like she's thousands of miles away from me. Like she's already gone back to Seattle, and I'm back home in my empty apartment.

41

Lucy

ONE OF THE perks of having a small wedding is that it's intimate. It's less crowded, easing the pressure of the bride and groom having to greet every single guest so they can enjoy the food, cake, and live band. But the downfall of having such a small wedding, for me, at least, is that I can't get away from it. Not without anyone noticing. I can't just go back up to my room and climb under the covers, so I don't have to keep seeing Dexter in his perfect khaki blazer and dress pants with no socks that actually look really, *really* freaking good on him.

With the lure of my cushy bed upstairs dilly-dallying in my mind, I try to enjoy the wedding. It's beautiful. The wedding planner, Nat, and Rita did an amazing job transforming the outdoor garden into a small haven with lit up twinkling lights and the fragrant scent of plumerias wafting around us. And Hayden and Nat look so happy dancing on the dance floor, cutting cake, even casually sipping on a flute of champagne. I'm so happy for them.

"Does my little chicken nugget want to dance?" My dad leans across the clothed table we're sitting at, where we're watching Hayden dance with my mom and Nat dance with Ashton on the smallest dance floor I've ever seen. He extends his hand out to me, and I smile softly before taking it.

"Sure, Daddy."

We both stand, my hand still in his, and we walk to the dance floor. My mom smiles at us as my dad circles his arm around my waist and I sink into his wide chest.

"My babies are growing up."

I look up at him and laugh. "We've been grown up, Daddy."

"Not in my mind," he says with a wistful smile. "I thought you were always going to be that same little girl who couldn't wait to be dropped off at the mall on the weekends."

"You didn't give us the 'don't spend all your money at Forever 21' lecture Mom always gave," I tease. "And you actually dropped us off a block away instead of right at the entrance."

He chuckles. "But...I guess that was just wishful thinking on my end," he says hoarsely. "My girls being my little babies forever." I look up at him and see his eyes mist over. And that sad, nostalgic smile he has turns into a frown.

"Dad."

"Ignore me," he says, shaking his head and forcing a smile. "I think I've had one too many glasses of champagne."

We catch a glimpse of my mom swaying in a small, intimate circle with Nat and Carmen, and the three of them wave in our direction. My dad twirls me playfully, which draws a laugh from behind the smile I was forcing. When he pulls me back into the slow rhythm of the music, he lifts his head toward the tables, where a few guests are sitting instead of enjoying the dance floor and flowy wedding music.

"That Dexter boy's a good kid." He jerks his chin toward the table where Dexter's sitting. He has a fork in his hand, and he's poking at the uneaten slice of cake in front of him. His face has transitioned from a deep scowl to wounded since we sat down for the reception. A part of me wants to go to him, sit down next to him, and fill him in on the acrobatics entailed in helping Nat to the bathroom in the small break we had before the reception. But, of course, I've been keeping my distance.

"Yeah," I whisper.

"You know, it's never easy letting go of you girls," he says, peering down at me to get my attention. "But it eases my mind to know there are men out there willing to take on the responsibility of taking a part of my heart with them."

I start to choke on my tears. And I want to break down right into my dad's burly arms. I want to tell him how sorry I am. For being such a failure and becoming this black sheep of the family who can't even stand on her own two feet. I want to tell him that he and my mom don't need to worry about me anymore because I'm starting to realize my worth. I'm starting to realize that if I take the plunge, if I jump headfirst into what I'm scared of, I can have the time of my life. I can learn to *live*.

My heart feels so heavy right now. It feels like a weighted sack I'm dragging behind me rather than something beating inside of me. I don't need to feel like this anymore. I don't *want* to feel like this anymore. I want to feel light and carefree. I want my heart to lift me, not drag me down. And I'm realizing now, in those fleeting moments when my heart felt like it was soaring, it was when Dexter was by my side. He's the only person who's ever made me feel like I could fly. I could have the time of my life with him.

Dexter lifts his head, and our eyes meet. At first, we just stare at each other. Blank looks of expectancy, waiting for the other to react first. Unsure if this exchange is a good one, something hopeful and meaningful, or if this is just another reminder of where we stand.

"Talk to him." My dad's voice is low and discreet. And when I look at him, he smiles warmly at me. My body stops swaying with his, and I sort of gape at him. The ache in my chest that caused my throat to constrict returns front and center. My instinct is to deny everything, look confused and even a little offended, but I don't have it in me to lie about this. How I feel about Dexter isn't something I want to hide from him.

So I don't. Instead, I tell him the truth. "I'm scared," I whisper. "I think he's mad at me…and I'm scared he won't want to talk to me."

"Impossible. I've seen the way he looks at you, and he would never turn you away."

"How does he look at me?" I ask, a little curious and still scared.

"Like he would do anything to see you smile."

My eyes start to water, and I try so hard to hide the way those impending tears cause an involuntary frown to form on my lips.

"Love is a scary thing," he says warmly, tucking a finger under my chin. "But sometimes, diving headfirst into what you're afraid of can be the most thrilling thing you do in your life."

"What if…" I pause when my chin quivers. "What if I get my heart broken?"

"Oh, *mi* Lucia," he coaxes. "You won't know until you try."

42

Dexter

I CATCH Lucy's eyes just as she steps off the dance floor. She smiles at me, a little shy and discreet. And it's subtle, the quick glance inside the building. Away from the music and cake and twinkling lights making everything glow with hope.

She walks away, her steps brisk and purposeful. And when I notice that she's walking in the direction of where she was glancing, making me realize she's signaling me to follow her, I stand. I follow her steps, catching the tail ends of her green dress as she turns corners down hallways, all while the bustling noise from the wedding fades into the background. I finally stop when I see her pacing a small hallway, hidden like it's our own sanctuary.

We stand there, her at one end of the hallway where it's closed off, me at the other, and all of the frustration of what we are or what we're meant to be dissolves into something less achy. Something more promising.

"Hi," she whispers, her lip clamped between her teeth.

I take a few steps toward her at the same time she steps toward me, and we meet in the middle. "Hey."

And her hands are on me. Her arm hooks around my neck, and she kisses me, wrapping her warm, soft lips around mine. I follow her lead, hoping this isn't going to end in some half-empty feeling of ache and hollowness, and press her into the wall. She pushes her hips into me, and I groan against her mouth. Her hands rake up into my hair, and I swear, I want to marry this woman right now.

"I'm so sorry about last night," she finally says when she pulls away. "I'm so sorry about everything. You're the only person I've been honest to, and I hurt you because of it. And I don't want to hurt you—"

"I'm sorry," I interrupt. "We had already made things clear on where we stand, and I made it unnecessarily uncomfortable for the both of us. I didn't mean to lose it last night."

She shakes her head. "No, no, I get it," she assures. "There's a lot going on, and we really should have talked it out and…"

I nod. "I know."

She dips her mouth to the side and kisses me again. She kisses me like she's hungry, whimpering into my mouth and clawing at my back as if she were scraping her nails against my bare skin instead of my suit jacket. My hands travel down to her hips and they continue, trailing down her thigh until they reach her soft skin underneath her dress.

An echoing laughter followed by fading footsteps has her pushing me away, making the air cold and harsh on my swollen lips. "Nat won't be in my room tonight," she says breathlessly, eyeing the open end of the hallway. "So…"

I dip my face to her jaw, trailing my nose against her skin. Fuck, she smells so good. She took the time to spritz some perfume on her skin. Something that smells like cherries and roses—probably something she usually reserves for special occasions—and it's mind-blowing. She tilts her head back, allowing me access as I plant a wet kiss behind her ear. "Are you inviting me over to make pillow forts and tell scary stories?"

She giggles. "Among other things." She kisses me again, gripping my head and yanking me to her. "Do you, um, have, like, you know, protection?" she asks against my lips.

"I think I have a letter opener in my room."

Her shoulders shake with a laugh. "My knight in shining armor."

I clear my throat. "But, uh, the other stuff. I actually don't."

She pulls away, a little disappointed. "Oh."

"Sorry."

"No," she says soothingly while running a hand along my cheek. "I mean, I like that. You weren't expecting anything…"

I shake my head. "But the gift shop might still be open."

Her eyes light up. "Gift shop then?"

43

Lucy

DEXTER AND I said some half-assed goodbyes to Hayden and Nat before rushing out of the reception. Dexter went first with plans to stop by the gift shop, and I used the excuse of a faux headache before running up to my room. Carmen gave strict instructions to drink plenty of fluids—most likely assuming my "headache" was due to an overconsumption of champagne—and I smiled with a secret held on my tongue. Something that hinted toward the knowledge that hydration will be a part of my night, just the latter part of it.

I'm pacing the small space between the two queen beds in my room now. My heels are kicked off to the side, but I still have my dress on. Maybe I should brush my teeth. Or shave? That's what you're supposed to do when you're about to have sex, right? Like, primp or preen or some shit. I lift my arm to bring my nose to my right armpit and take a quick whiff. At least I'm good there.

Those panicky thoughts on grooming choices and hygienic care are interrupted when there's a light knock on my door. I can do this. Whatever it is Dexter and I are doing, I can do it. Whether we crash and burn or free-fall into the most thrilling experience in my life, I can do this. Because if I don't...

"Hey."

I tilt my head, my hand on the doorknob and my eyes lingering on the loosened knot of his tie, with his hand so casually tucked into his pants pocket. "Hi."

He walks into the room when I open the door a little wider, and I sort of watch him take everything in. The scattered mess of my makeup bag and loose jewelry on the desk where a small lamp sits dimly lit. My bathing suit and some clothes draped over an armchair sitting in the corner. He turns on his feet and faces me. I take a few steps toward him, one foot in front of the other like a scared yet curious kitten.

My heart feels like it's racing out of my chest. Like I'm simultaneously running through a haunted mansion maze and riding a rollercoaster at the same time. And yet, I just want to fall. Into Dexter's arms, into us, and every single possibility that could come between.

"I-you look..." he stutters, chuffing a shy laugh. "You look beautiful."

I take another step to him, placing my hand on the desk he's standing next to. "Thank you."

His hand covers mine. "I don't think I've told you that yet."

I smirk. "No, you haven't."

"Lucy," he whispers. His knuckles glide up my arm, and I feel like I could crumble to the ground. Like all I've ever wanted in my life is this, for Dexter to touch me and make me feel...*alive*. "You're so beautiful. Sometimes, when I think about how beautiful you are, it actually hurts." He pauses to run his thumb down the column of my neck, grazing over my thready pulse point. "I still can't believe you exist. And that I've touched you and kissed you. And that you let me."

I kiss him, sinking into him, because how can I not after hearing those words?

He works to turn me toward the desk, leaning my butt at the ledge, and steps into the space between my legs. He trails kisses on my shoulder, up my neck, and behind my ear. And I tilt my head to the side, letting him. I respond by nibbling on his earlobe, pulling the sensitive skin between my teeth, and he sighs against me.

"*God*, I just want to fuck the shit out of you." His words, all breathy and hot, travel down low. To the arch of my feet, making my toes curl and my back bend. I feel his touch travel up my thigh and stop when his fingers curl around my hip, firmly and possessively. He reaches behind me, pushing me closer to him as he presses his groin into me, and I feel how badly he wants me. He buries his nose into my skin, and I feel him take in a sharp intake of breath.

"Can I?"

"Can you what?" I ask, so fucking breathless.

"Can I fuck the shit out of you?"

"*Yes*," I whimper desperately.

A deep, guttural growl rumbles low in his chest, and he lifts me, wrapping my legs around his waist, and I feel dizzy when he swings me around.

We're a flurry of clothes warped around us in heaps. Everything lands on the floor in a mess, leaving us in our underwear. I fall back on the bed, and he crowds over me, his hands braced on the bed at my sides. His eyes linger on my body, over the intimate parts of me barely covered with my matching bra and underwear set, and he lets out a close-mouthed sigh.

"The things I've wanted to do to you…" His eyes follow the path of his fingers, starting from my knees, up higher and higher, his thumb pressing against my skin as he gives me a soft, seductive squeeze at my waist.

He sinks into me, and for a second, he just clutches me against him. His hand fists into the base of my hair, tugging at it, holding on to me like I might disappear. Like if he doesn't grapple at what he can, this will all just be a figment of his imagination.

"I'm here," I whisper into his shoulder, wrapping my arms around his waist. "I'm yours tonight."

He nods, the ends of his hair brushing against my cheek. "We have tonight, and if that's all we have, then I'll take it. I'll take whatever I can."

It's another reminder this is exactly what it's always been. Temporary. But he's right. Whatever part of ourselves we can give each other, we'll take it.

He lowers himself down my body, kissing my skin. He starts at my navel, trailing up my stomach to my chest. It's so sweet and so tender, I want to burst into tears. The silence sits heavy between us, but I feel completely and utterly cherished in the absence of words. He's moving slowly, taking his time while unraveling bits of me as he goes along. And I let him. I let him take parts of my heart with each stroke, each kiss, because it feels like it belongs to him anyway.

When he meets my lips, his hands move to my back, unhooking my bra and letting it slip off of me. And he just sort of stares at me, at my bare chest scattered with goose bumps all the way down to my lacy underwear covering parts of me that are begging for him to touch.

"To think..." he whispers with his gaze fixed on my body.

"What?" I ask, but it comes out all winded, like a harsh exhale instead of an actual word.

His hand moves to cover my breast, and I feel his fingers graze over my nipple. "That I thought I could've gone without *this*," he says. "Without seeing you or touching you." His hand travels down to my thong, and his fingers gingerly trail over the lace.

"Please don't rip those," I beg breathlessly. "They were a matching set, and it would be a shame to have them mismatch."

He laughs into my skin, nuzzling his nose against my neck. "We can't have that now, can we?"

His hands hook into the strap of my underwear before he tugs it down my thighs. He moves slowly, carefully, following my plea to take care of the fragile material. I do the same to him, pulling at the waist-band of his black boxer briefs, letting my hands graze over his bare ass, and he helps me the rest of the way.

He straightens his body, lifting me by my wrists until we're both on our knees with our arms wrapped around each other. He grips my waist, guiding me toward the head of the bed. Nudging me until my back is at his front, he places my hand on the headboard, clamping my fingers on the cushioned edges.

"Hold on," he urges. His arm hooks around my waist, and he tugs me closer to him. I feel him, his hardness pressing into my skin, his thighs flush against the back of my own. He continues kissing me gently and slowly. "I like you like this."

I smirk over my shoulder. "On my knees?"

"At my will." He glides his hand down my stomach, reaching

down until his fingers spread me, and I let out a sharp gasp. My hand covers his, unsure if it's to guide him or to stop him because the sensation of his touch is too much to bear.

He doesn't stop though. Instead, he continues, his finger gliding across my clit, making a jolt of electricity shoot right through me. I whimper loudly, turning my face to look at him and reaching over until my hand grips the back of his head. I pull him to me, kissing him and loving the way he follows my lead with desperation on his lips. His other hand reaches to cup my breast, his thumb rolling over my nipple, and it makes my back arch from the sudden sensation.

"Dexter," I plead. "Please, touch me. I need you to touch me. *Please.*"

He hooks his finger inside of me, and I sag against him. My head falls back on his shoulder, and I can feel his gaze travel down to where his palm cups me and his fingers move in and out of me. I start to feel a prickling quiver roll around low in my belly, and my breaths come out in short gasps.

"God, I could just watch you come like this."

I shake my head. "No," I protest.

"No?"

"I want..." He pushes a second finger into me, and all words left in my vocabulary disappear instantly.

"What do you want, baby? Tell me."

"I want..." A nibble on my ear interrupts my train of thought, almost as if he's doing this on purpose.

"Hmm?"

I turn to face him, looking at him as his eyes flare with heat. "I want you to fuck me." His hand stills. "I want you to make me come with your cock."

A sharp smack to my ass fills my lungs with a sudden gasp. And then he's gone. The air suddenly feels so cold, but I wait patiently as he reaches into the pockets of his pants to retrieve a condom. He rolls it on, moving efficiently before climbing back on the bed. He reaches across my bare chest and glides his open hand until he's gripped my throat, pushing me back toward him.

And then his voice stutters. "Lucy, I-I don't..."

I reach my arm around to grip his ass, pushing him toward me. "What?" I say, suddenly scared. Is he going to stop? I swear, I'm going to kill him if he does.

His eyes darken, looking down at my naked body. "I'm not going to last very long."

I can't help the low, relieved laugh that slips through my lips. "I thought you were going to back out."

"Oh, fuck no."

"Dexter, I don't care," I tell him. "We have all night."

He smirks against my ear, and I feel his hand moving between us, his knuckles grazing my ass as he takes himself in his hand and presses his tip into me. My entire body stills, waiting, anticipating. Like I'm at the edge of my seat with my knees bouncing and only my toes touching the ground. Like I've waited a century for this, and these next few seconds until he finally fucks me feels like an eternity.

When he pushes into me, I feel his entire body tremble. He groans and rolls his forehead between my shoulder blades. "Fuck, *Lucy.* I've been thinking about this, how it felt before, but this is far beyond what I imagined."

My teeth clamp onto my lower lip, and I shift, adjusting to him. He starts to pull out but then I stop him, my hand still on his bare skin, pressing him to me. "Wait," I say through a strained voice. "Just wait a minute."

"Are you okay?"

"Mm-hmm," I answer. "I just need a minute." I need a second to adjust to feeling so full. It feels like every spare part of me is filled with Dexter, and it feels almost too much. A shiver runs down my back when he trails his nose along my neck, and I nod. "Okay."

"You good?"

"Yeah."

"Good." And he pulls out before slamming back into me. I cry out at the same time he groans. *"Fuck!* Jesus Christ, you feel so good." Another sharp breath spills from my throat when he slams into me again. My body bounces forward, and he holds me tighter. Our bodies start to move in tandem, him bucking against me as I push into him.

He starts touching me again, his finger circling my clit, and I start to feel it spread everywhere, to all ten fingers and all ten toes.

My hand covers his while the other holds on to the headboard. He starts to fuck me hard and rough, while his tempo increases and his fingers work me into fucking euphoria. His hands don't stop touching me. One between my legs, the other running over my sensitive skin in desperate yet sensual strokes. It's mind-blowing how I can feel him all over, even on the parts of my body he's not touching. He's *everywhere*. And I just know after all of this is said and done, I'll still feel him.

Dexter wraps his arms around me tighter, and I feel that electricity start to cluster at the base of my spine, making me moan loudly and my body tense up.

"Dexter...I'm—*ohh*..."

"I know," he says, his low voice gravelly and thick. "I can feel you." And his hand grips my chin, turning my cheek to kiss me. "Oh *fuck*, Lucy. *Christ*, I can feel you coming."

"*Dexter!*" He kisses me fiercely, crushing my lips to his. My orgasm rattles through me, and somewhere between me coiling around Dexter and my entire body tensing underneath him, he comes too. I feel his entire body shudder, and those strong and sure thrusts become jerky and violent.

We sort of just stay how we are, our bodies heaving through large gulps of air. But his touches are sweet and soft as he caresses me. "I'm so glad we have all night."

I laugh. "Me too."

44

Lucy

WHEN I WAKE the next morning, Dexter's gone. The side of the bed where he fell asleep is empty. And for a second, I think this is it. What we had last night, it was the best way we could've said goodbye to each other. And maybe that's for the best. We had one last night together. One last amazing, life-altering night that'll forever be engraved in me. And I should thank him. For taking me as I am instead of expecting more. But my heart feels too heavy for anything other than a kind of grief that can only come from an incomplete goodbye.

A draft blows the sheer curtains into the room where the sliding door to the balcony was left open, and when I look outside through the glass, I see Dexter. His bare back is facing me, and he's sitting in one of the lounge chairs, looking out into the expansive view that includes the hotel grounds and the beach.

I rise from my spot in the bed, draping the sheet over my naked body, and step onto the carpeted floor. When I reach the glass door, sliding it open a little wider for me to walk through, I see Dexter shift his head to the side where I catch a glimpse of his handsome profile.

I saunter around him, meeting him at his front, and run my fingers through his hair. "Good morning," I croak through my morning voice.

"Good morning." He runs his hand along my covered hip and tugs at the loose sheet. I fall into his lap, my legs straddling his thighs, and the sheets drop. "I like waking up with you."

I nod, pressing my naked chest to his bare one. "It is kind of nice, isn't it?"

He nuzzles his face into my neck, and I love how he feels strong and soft at the same time with his arms wrapped around me. We don't say anything for a few moments, letting the sounds of the waves crashing on the beach and the gulls squawking take up space while we enjoy the last hours of our day together.

"When's your flight?" I ask, speaking softly into his hair.

"Three."

"We don't have much time."

He shakes his head. "No, we don't."

Words stay held on our tongues, like we're unsure of what to say next or what should be said. His fingers trail up and down my spine in slow, languorous strokes, and I continue raking my fingers through his hair. I hear people laugh and prattle on the ground floor, most likely early risers excited to get a head start on their vacation. More waves crashing, creating a steady rhythm that makes me relaxed and a little lazy. The cool breeze drifts around us, and we stay quiet and peaceful and completely serene.

Until Dexter finally speaks. "This feels like home."

I smirk. "I think a lot of people would say that about a tropical island."

I expect some retort from him, something along the lines of moving out here and living off coconuts and palm leaves, but he doesn't. Instead, he shakes his head against my chin before pulling away.

"No," he whispers, his eyes so serious it makes my heart flop. "I meant you. Us."

My heart starts to race and I feel like it's going to beat out of my chest, exposing how vulnerable and unguarded I am right now. And I don't care. I don't care that Dexter can see how much he means to me. Because I mean just as much to him. It just took a few leaps of faith to get us here.

"You feel like home."

"Dexter." My hands grip the side of his face and his slide up my body, tightening his arms around me. This is what love is. Completely unconditional, willing to do whatever, fight against any and all odds.

He grips my nape and forces me to look at him. "This is going to sound...irresponsible. And maybe I'm being a little selfish too..." He pauses, looking at me like his life depends on his next words. "I know we agreed we had last night. And it was wonderful, but...I want—it doesn't have to end here," he says through a hoarse voice. "We don't have to end things because we're going back to our separate lives."

My eyes ping-pong between his, and they fill with so much. So many different thoughts and scenarios that make me want to agree with him. To free-fall. He's asking for more. He's telling me he wants more. To no longer make this temporary but indefinite.

"There's no instruction manual. No how-to when it comes to long distance or whatever this would be between us, but we can figure it out together," he continues.

"But how? I mean, you have your life back in New York. And with Janet—"

"I know," he interrupts, sounding so sure of himself. "And you have LA and this new job. But it's okay. We'll work through it, one day at a time. Please, just trust me."

My entire body stills. A huge part of me wants to say yes. Because maybe we *can* figure it out. One day at a time. "Are you sure? I mean, really. You're really sure you want to do this?"

He cups my cheek, brushing his thumb against my skin. "I don't think I have a choice, Lucy," he says, his voice cracking when he says my name. "I don't think I'll be able to live with myself if we don't give it a shot."

I look at him, searching for a whisper of doubt or fear, thinking there must be some considering how much of his heart he's allowing to be vulnerable. But I don't find any. "You're serious about this."

He nods. "I am."

And I free-fall. "Okay."

His face lights up. "Yeah?"

I nod. "Yeah. One day at a time."

"I can't believe you're leaving already," Nat whines while she drags my suitcase behind her.

I smirk, hooking the strap to my tote bag over my shoulder. "You're leaving for Kauai in the morning, and I have a home to get back to."

Nat pouts and Hayden stands by her side with his arm draped over her shoulder. The white gold ring on his ring finger glints in the light, and Nat slips her fingers through his, her own ring sparkling in unison.

"I'll call you when we're back," Nat says sadly, pulling me in for an embrace. "Maybe I can fly you out or we can visit you over Labor Day weekend."

"Yeah, that'll be fun," I tell her, squeezing her back. I pull away and reach for my suitcase from her. She reluctantly hands it over as if her keeping an iron grip on it would prevent me from leaving.

"It's good both of your flights are at the same time," Hayden comments, gesturing toward Dexter standing next to me with his own suitcase in his hand.

Dexter nods, his steps already leading to the cab waiting in front of the hotel. We mused over whether or not we should be sharing a cab, wondering if it may appear a little suspicious, but ended up not even caring. We even threw in a little fib saying we found out during the rehearsal our flights were leaving around the same time.

Our flights weren't leaving at the same time. In fact, they were hours apart, but that didn't stop us from wanting to leave the hotel at the same time. Anything so we could get a few extra hours alone before parting ways.

Carmen already left early in the morning, and I said my goodbyes to my parents up in the hotel room where they were packing too, their flight leaving later this evening.

"Text me when you get home," Nat instructs. The attendant takes our luggage, helping the cab driver load everything into the trunk of the cab.

"I will." She pulls me in for another short embrace before we both stubbornly part.

"We'll see you back home?" Hayden asks Dexter.

Dexter nods. "When you guys get back," he says. "We'll catch up."

Nat pulls Dexter in a quick embrace, and I change places and hug Hayden too, prolonging our farewells for as long as we can. I enter the back seat, with Dexter close behind. He closes the door, and we hear Hayden thump the top of the car. We continue our waves and sad smiles through the window until the cab curves down the road and Hayden and Nat disappear.

I turn to face Dexter, and we both smile.

"Do you wish you would have stayed a little longer?" he asks.

I shake my head. "I wanted to see you off at the airport anyway."

He nods and lifts his arm for me to fit under it, letting a satisfying hum rumble through his chest.

We spend the cab ride to the airport with comfortable small talk. Like how much I'm going to cuddle Jeremy when I get home or the beautiful purple scarf he got for Janet from the gift shop. When the cab comes to a stop in front of the airport, we exit and check in. Once we've made it through the security check and walked to a part of the airport where foot traffic isn't too heavy, we sit on a row of chairs in front of Dexter's gate.

"I have some vacation hours saved up," he announces, his fingers linked through mine. "I can try to take a day off for a long weekend and fly out to you."

I smile at him with sad eyes. "That would be really nice."

We stay quiet for a moment longer. An announcement sounds on the intercom, announcing a boarding call from Honolulu to New York City. Dexter looks down at his ticket, where his seat call is marked, and we both stand.

"Text me when you're about to board. I might not get it until I land, but still, I'll feel better knowing you did."

"I will," I agree.

He takes my hand in his, lifting it so he kisses my knuckles, and his arms wrap around my waist. I let out a small sob, and I bury my face into his shoulder.

"We'll see each other soon," he tells me, the same tightness in his voice as mine. "And I'll call you every day. And we can FaceTime and text. There're so many things we can do to still be a part of our everyday lives."

"But I won't get to touch you," I cry. It's then a lone tear slips down my cheek, and he swipes it with his thumb. "I won't get to kiss you or come home to you."

"I know."

Another sob slips through, and I feel so silly. So silly for crying over a goodbye like this, with someone who I've only really gotten to know over the past few months. Someone who I never thought I would have to say goodbye to in a drafty airport surrounded by hundreds of weary travelers. "I'm sorry," I whisper, ducking my head and wiping more tears. "I'm making such a scene, and it's so embarrassing."

"No," he urges, gripping the sides of my face. "I told you, you're my home. And this is…it's killing me just the same." He pauses to swallow a lump in his throat, and when he talks again, it's raspy and weak. "But we're going to figure it out, Lucy. We have to."

When I finally look up at him, I realize he's having as much difficulty saying goodbye as I am. He may be keeping his composure, assuring me with future visits and focusing on the silver lining of our separation, but all of that's just on the surface.

I nod, a sad up and down motion of my head, and his hands stay cupped to my face. "You should go," I say softly.

He looks up at the gate, where the line of people boarding has started to grow thick. "We'll talk to each other soon."

We part, our fingers refusing to let go of each other until we have no choice but to pull apart. I watch as he stands in line, taking occasional glances back at me, and then he disappears.

45

Dexter

I'VE WATCHED a lot of those apocalyptic movies like zombies taking over the world or some other end of world type calamity, leaving behind only a smattering of survivors and life. But they never show what life after a catastrophe is like. The movie usually ends, leaving those moments where people have to pick up everything and somehow go on with their lives behind scrolling credits.

It's the aftermath.

That's what this feels like. Walking into my empty apartment, too quiet and dull without Lucy's presence, feels like I have to pick up the pieces of my heart and learn to live my life without her in it.

I already got a message from her, a quick snapshot of her in her window seat with the light streaming into the cabin. She looks so beautiful with the light reflecting off her glowing skin. And her sweet smile makes her look even more stunning, regardless of her red-rimmed eyes and inflamed tip of her nose.

I wander through the living room, looking at parts of my apartment. Like where she sat on my couch, editing her photos on my laptop. Or at the kitchen counter, standing in front of the microwave while she waited for a bag of popcorn to finish popping. I can't even bear to look in the empty spare bedroom. It's too much to see how she no longer occupies the space. I'll never be able to look at that room and not feel the gaping hole in my chest.

I walk into my room, where my sweatshirt is draped over the edge of the bed. It's the one Lucy wore a few times. I run my fingers over the material. It feels cold and bare. I bring it to my nose and take a deep inhale. While it doesn't feel like her anymore with the coldness taking over the warmth she weaved into the fibers, it smells like her.

How did I end up here? I feel so lost and empty.

I sit at the edge of my mattress, hoping the feeling of my own bed will help something familiar course through me. Something that reminds me I'm home and I should just settle back into my life as it was before, but I can't. Everything feels out of place.

This isn't home.

I'm back at the office Tuesday morning, still feeling a little discombobulated with the time differences and jet lag. I stopped by the nearest Starbucks on the way into work, ordering Lucy's usual order with the assistance of the handy dandy order sticker in my wallet. It's one of the things that makes me feel like I have some kind of connection to her from two thousand miles away. I've already sent Lucy a screenshot of my drink and a quick *I miss you* text message. I've refrained from telling her just how much I miss her. How I want to quit my job and move across the country to be near her. Even go as far as demanding space in her full-size bed and the apartment she shares with her roommate. Maybe even partaking in ownership of the cat.

"You got a tan." Margaret, my boss, eyes me curiously before she fixes her gaze on her screen, where I emailed her a file of data for her to review. She called me into her office for a quick catching-up since I was gone for almost a week. "Where did you go?"

"Hawaii," I answer with a nod. "I was the best man at my friend's wedding."

She smiles warmly. "That's nice." We stay silent a moment longer as her eyes return to her screen. "Everything looks good here. We're going to have our weekly staff meeting today instead of Thursday, so bring the material with you so you can present it to the team."

I nod again, a little curter than intended, and shut my laptop I had open on my lap.

"Was everything okay with Jacob filling in?" I ask, hoping there were no hiccups while I was gone.

"Yes, everything was fine," she answers. "But I'm glad you made it back in time for this week. We have a few things we need to cover before month end and while Jacob's been great, we need you here."

I smile politely. "Just let me know if there are any adjustments you need me to make on the report, and I'll go over them before the meeting."

"Great."

I stand to leave her office, but when I get to her door, I turn back to face her. "Actually, Margaret," I say hesitantly, watching her fingers tapping a mile away on her keyboard. "I, uh…"

She stops typing and crosses her arms in front of her. "Was there something else you wanted to discuss?"

I run my fingers through my hair. "Just something I was curious about," I answer, unsure if this is even okay to broach. "There's nothing set in stone or anything really even happening yet, but…" I pause, considering backing out. But with the distance between me and Lucy eating away at me, I can't just sit here, thousands of miles away from her, and not make any sort of plans. "I was wondering about transferring."

Her eyebrows shoot up. "Transferring?"

"More like relocating. Los Angeles," I clarify. "Like I said, nothing's been decided, but there have been some changes in my personal life. And I know we have a fairly large branch in Los Angeles, so I would like to have the option if needed."

She nods, nothing threatening or impolite, just an understanding that this isn't personal. "I can look to see if there are any openings in our LA branch, any positions that align with your current work here. Sometimes they post openings internally, so it'd be good if I reach out to them."

"I appreciate that. Thank you."

She studies me a minute, taking in the scowl that's been practically stitched to my face. "I hope whatever changes they are, they're good."

I smile gratefully, though I'm sure it's coming off as impassive. "Me too."

Janet's picking at her food. Not eating the now cold pad thai I didn't have the heart to eat alone without Lucy, but poking and moving it around on her plate.

"Not hungry?"

She shrugs. "Don't have much of an appetite."

I was away less than a week, and in that short time, it looks like she's lost even more weight. And she looks weaker, more tired. She wraps a blanket around her frail shoulders, though the heat drifting between us could incubate an unhatched chicken egg.

I look at the takeout containers on the coffee table in front of us, half of them untouched, and suddenly, I don't have much of an appetite either. The food, especially the perfectly sliced mangoes, reminds me too much of Lucy.

"When did you last talk to her?"

"On my way here," I say to the mangoes, not bothering to ask Janet who she's talking about.

We stay silent longer, Janet's body slinking lower and lower into the couch cushions, and I just sit there, unsure if I can go back home to the empty apartment that reminds me too much that Lucy isn't here. At least if I'm not home, I can pretend she's there, waiting for me in my oversized hoodie and the loose sleep shorts that show off her soft skin and smooth legs.

Our sporadic calls, text messages, and after hour FaceTimes that go late into the night have helped. It's helped me feel like we're still connected in some way instead of through the distance separating us. But it's not enough. Not by a mile.

"You should visit her," Janet calls through closed eyes. "Take a day or two off work and spend a weekend with her."

I sigh. "That's the plan." I already booked a flight after figuring out the details on when I can use some of my spare vacation hours from work. I had to clear it with Margaret too and make sure Jacob was up for taking on any unexpected emergencies, but we figured it out, this time. But I'm not sure how many more times I can do this, take time off work while hoping my boss will be cool enough to let me.

"What's the actual plan?"

"What do you mean?"

She opens an eye, peeking at me like Popeye. "Like, you're going to continue doing this long distance thing? Or..."

"There's really no or, Janet." I scowl, angry that there really, truly is no "or." It's this, this back and forth with no promise of a future until we decide on something we can both live with. For now, it has to be *this*.

She nods.

"But...um, I kind of talked to my boss the other day," I say hesitantly.

She responds with a quiet look of attentiveness, letting me finish.

"I was just asking about a lateral transfer to LA."

"Like Los Angeles?"

"Lucy got a job there. The internship she's been working for wants to hire her," I explain. "And—I mean, I'm not going to do it, but it's just...I want to know what my options are."

"Dexter." She sits up, inching closer to me. "You're serious about her."

I nod. "I'm in love with her."

"Did you tell her?"

"Tell her what?"

"That you love her."

I shake my head. "This is still really new to both of us. And I don't want to scare her."

"But you want to move in with her?"

"No," I argue, sounding a little annoyed and defensive. "I would get my own pl—I'm not thinking that far, Janet. It was just a question that popped in my mind when I was talking to my boss. That's all."

She stays quiet, my near outburst enough to shut down any further discussion of what my situation with Lucy may be.

"Besides," I continue, my voice calmer. "I'm not going anywhere while you're still in treatment."

And now it's her turn to get upset. "Dexter, stop that shit."

"What?"

"You can't let *my* health dictate *your* life."

"I'm not. But I'm not moving across the country when you're still actively fighting this."

"Dex—"

"No, Janet," I cut her off. "And besides, Lucy wouldn't let me. She'd want me to be here with you."

Janet smiles and reaches for my arm.

"I promise, I was just asking to have some peace of mind. That's all."

"Okay."

46

Lucy

"LOOK! IT'S GOLD." I wave my hands in front of my new MacBook, Vanna White style, and Dexter smiles through the phone screen.

"Looks nice," he comments. "It's one hell of an upgrade."

I nod enthusiastically. "I've already uploaded my pictures in it."

"Have they reached out to you again?" he asks, silently referring to Elevate Media.

I shake my head. "Not yet, but Ryan said it would take some time before someone contacts me. They probably have to draw up an actual offer letter and everything."

"Well, hopefully they don't keep you waiting too long. It feels like they're doing an awful lot of pussyfooting while you're just waiting for them to call you."

"I know," I say glumly. It's been a bit frustrating, waiting for Elevate to get back to me, and I'd be lying if I said it hasn't bothered me one bit. I'm eager to get things going. And a part of me feels like they might change their mind. What if they have some time to think things over only to realize I'm not the one they want to offer this job to?

"How was your first day back at Mr. Bean's?" he asks, changing the subject and pulling my thoughts away from those lingering doubts that never seem to disappear. While waiting on Elevate to get back to me, I put a hold on any future job searches. And since I still need to pay the bills, I reached out to Mr. Bean to see if I could temporarily have my old job back. He gladly agreed. Apparently, the last guy he hired to take my place broke the espresso machine on his first day and burned his hand on the steam wand. He quit after a week, leaving Mr. Bean short-staffed. I've been telling myself I didn't circle back to square one, I'm just waiting on Elevate, but with each passing day, it's been a little difficult to stay optimistic.

"It was fine," I answer. "A little busy, but nothing new. Just the same old coffee shop I worked at three months ago."

I nod, and he does too. And we look at each other, the silence lingering between us, reminding us for the hundredth time that he's there and I'm here. It's been like this between us. Drawn out FaceTime calls, meals eaten together through a screen, quick text messages throughout the day because we miss each other and the only way to communicate with the distance and time difference is through missed messages with hours between chats.

Our silence is interrupted when Jeremy saunters into the room, his demanding meows equally obnoxious and cute. He hops up on my bed where I'm sitting, and his snout enters the screen, where Dexter greets him.

"Hi, Jeremy."

Jeremy paws at the screen at the sound of his name before nuzzling his head into my hand.

"He's been a little clingier since I got back," I inform Dexter, leaning down to kiss Jeremy's nose. "But I'm not complaining."

"You know, I never thought I'd be jealous of a cat."

I laugh even though all I want is to pout. Dexter catches on to my somber smile, and his face changes into something more longing.

"How many more days until your visit?"

"Nineteen."

"Are you seriously counting?" I laugh.

"Of course!" He stands from his comfy spot on his bed, walking toward a calendar hanging on his bedroom wall. Sure enough, there's a row of red X's marked for the month and when he flips it, I see a big red circle on the day he's flying out to Seattle and a few scattered hearts surrounding it.

"You're so cute," I comment through a blush.

"Some find me more irresistible than rainbow marshmallows."

I giggle, and he laughs too. "So what's for dinner tonight?"

He reaches from behind the screen and procures a small paper bag. "Onion rings from The Lunch Car."

"And a milkshake?"

"Of course," he answers, holding up a disposable cup. "You?"

"The girls and I had a little movie night yesterday, and Margo brought over couscous," I say, holding up a small glass bowl. "So I'm having the leftovers, plus some chips and salsa."

"Nice," Dexter comments. He reaches into the bag and pulls out an onion ring before taking a large bite. He's eating dinner a little late and I'm eating a little early, but we're making these sacrifices. Sometimes it's something as menial as a meal eaten at odd hours and sometimes it's a slightly bigger cost, like losing hours of sleep or making excuses at work to prioritize our FaceTime calls.

"Cheers," I call, tilting my Coke can toward the screen at the same time he angles his milkshake toward me. He grins at me before taking a loud slurp. I smile through the screen and think for a minute that maybe this isn't so bad. Yeah, we might not get to see each other in person, but this is kind of nice for now while we adjust to this new norm. It's a temporary fix, and eventually we'll be in each other's arms. In nineteen days, to be exact.

The next few weeks continue, but the text messages and phone calls between me and Dexter grow fewer and fewer with each passing day. I pick up more shifts at Mr. Bean's to fill my time and start to refine my resume when I still haven't heard back from Elevate. I continue my life, joining Annabelle, Margo, and Alma for our usual weekend brunch and the occasional late-night bar hopping. I empty Jeremy's litter box and rewatch episodes of *Supernatural* while hunting down nearby Thai food places to curb my constant pad thai cravings.

Nat and Hayden called me from Maui, where they're spending another week feeding alpacas and visiting the botanical gardens before heading back home from their extended honeymoon. I filled Carmen in on how things were going post-internship. She continued to poke and prod about Janet and Dexter, asking if I was still talking to him. When I told her things between me and Dexter were sort of irresolute, she gave a troubled hum through the phone, followed by silence. It felt like she was taking the impartial side, not wanting to give advice that's too biased or inclined toward a path I may regret, but I could feel her concern through the words she chose to hold back.

I spoke to Dexter just last night. He'd gotten in late after taking Janet to her doctor's appointment. He looked so tired and stressed, and he barely had the energy to talk to me. Apparently, the doctor's visit didn't go too well. After some more tests, Janet's doctor agreed radiation therapy would be the best way to go now that her chemo sessions were coming to an end. It wasn't news—her doctor had forewarned her before she even started chemotherapy—but everyone was hoping radiation therapy was one she could forgo, including Dexter. This all meant more waiting, more treatments, more time being sick instead of being healthy.

I keep reminding myself I have to be patient. As soon as Dexter comes to Seattle, we'll be able to plan more visits. As soon as I start working with Elevate, we'll be able to decide how often we'll see each other with my new work schedule.

As soon as things get settled.

As soon as…As soon as…As soon as…

My heart sinks as I realize how there will be no end to these "as soon as." Because as soon as I start working with Elevate, Dexter will be elbow-deep in Janet's treatments. It'll only keep him in Brooklyn, while I have my own set of responsibilities that come with a new job. And then what? What happens to us?

All of this morose ruminating has been making my mind spiral. I'm starting to feel the distance between me and Dexter, and I can't tell if it's my mind playing games or if he's really growing further and further apart from me. What if he's gotten used to the idea of not having me around him all the time? In the next room or just a few steps away. What if he really doesn't mind that I'm not there anymore? Maybe he's even gone as far as realizing that all of this, our emotional back and forth, trying to stay connected through technology, isn't worth his time anymore. Or maybe I'm just waiting for the other shoe to drop, waiting for all of this to crumble with nothing left but my broken heart.

My wondering and contemplating are cut short when my phone buzzes in my hand, and my face lights up when I see Dexter's name flashing on the screen. I accept the call, switching over to FaceTime, and am welcomed by Dexter's tired face.

"Hi," I chirp through the phone.

"Hey." He sounds so weary and disheveled. His hair, now grown back to his old length, is rumpled, evidence he's been running his fingers through it. There're bags under his eyes, and the line separating his brows doesn't seem to relent, no matter how badly he tries to brighten up his expression.

"Is everything okay?"

"Yeah," he answers, nodding. "I mean, no, not really."

"What happened?"

He hesitates before letting out a frustrated sigh. "Uh...Lucy, I hate to do this..."

I hear, practically feel, the other shoe drop.

"But I don't think I can make it out next week."

And there it is. *Thunk.* "Oh."

He sighs and buries his face into his hands. "I'm so sorry," he says hoarsely.

"I mean, it's fine. Is everything—"

"Look, I've got to go," he interrupts, sounding a little distracted. I was about to ask him why he had to cancel his trip, a little worried it may be because of Janet, but he's been so open about any changes in her health, I feel like he would've told me. Or at the very least, he wouldn't shut me down like this.

"I'll call you soon. Okay?"

"Uh, yeah. Okay."

47

Lucy

HE DIDN'T CALL. He didn't text or email or send a barbershop quartet or a homing pigeon. Something, anything to let me know I still exist in his world instead of feeling like he swiped away all remnants of me from his memory. The day he was supposed to visit passes by with no answers like why he had to cancel his trip, and I'm left wondering so many things and equally regretting them.

I called him once and texted him twice, asking him if everything was okay. He let my call go to voicemail and finally answered my second text message with a single worded "yes." No explanation. No follow-up apology, not that I needed it if the reasons were valid, but it still feels so...unsettling.

Maybe it was stupid of me to fall headfirst into us, to free-fall while throwing every caution sign into the wind. Maybe it was foolish of me to believe that this could work and we could pretend distance would never be an issue as long as we figured it out, one day at a time.

I feel hollow, empty, while feeling like Dexter is the only person in the world who can make things right. But he's choosing not to be that person to me, not anymore.

My front door clicks open, and I hear Annabelle walk through the door. Jeremy jumps from the spot next to me on the couch and meows his way to Annabelle while I keep my eyes glued on the television screen.

"Uh...Did you brush your hair today?" Annabelle asks, taking in the scene around her. I'm slouched on the couch, my hair tangled up in knots, my oversized sleep shirt stained with Cheeto dust, and a family-sized bag of M&M's sitting on my lap. *Supernatural* is playing on the TV screen, and I'm pretty sure there's a loose Cheeto desperately seeking air somewhere in my shirt.

"Of course I did," I answer glumly, popping another M&M in my mouth. "Can't promise I'll do it again this week."

Annabelle's brows shoot up, and she perches at the edge of the couch. "Did you not go to work today?"

"It's my day off."

She stays silent a little longer, still taking in everything before she lays a hand on my arm. "Luce, what's going on?"

I ignore her question, hoping that if I do, she won't notice the way my eyes heavily mist over and my heart twists. Instead, I tug at my upper lip with the bottom row of my teeth to hide the slight tremble of my chin, trying to stop the tears before they start to flow like a river.

"I don't know," I finally say when Annabelle keeps her sympathetic eyes on me. "Dexter hasn't called me back since he told me he had to cancel his trip. And...maybe he's just over us, and he doesn't want to be with me anymore. Or he met someone else."

That last sentence nearly kills me. The thought that he might be with someone else, sharing the things we shared like all the coupley things we did, makes my heart ache so damn much. I pick at my shirt collar, covering my face with it and sobbing into the stained fabric. I see the loose Cheeto fall to the ground, and I don't know whether to be disgusted with myself or cry harder.

"Lucy," she coos, pulling me into a deep embrace, and I, of course, cry harder. "Fuck him. Fuck all men!" she exclaims with gusto.

I laugh a weak laugh into her arm and wipe the runaway trail of snot before I look at her. The sad look on my face confirms this isn't a simple "fuck all men" type of situation.

"Do you want to crack open the tub of mint and chip?"

I want to sob into the couch cushions. Annabelle doesn't know mint and chip ice cream would only remind me more of Dexter. About our late-night trips to The Lunch Car that included a basket of onion rings and stolen moments inside a private booth seat. He's everywhere and nowhere at the same time.

"Sure," I say weakly, unable to resist another reminder of Dexter.

Annabelle walks to the kitchen to retrieve the dessert I'll probably cry into just as my phone buzzes on the coffee table. I reach for it, wanting to ignore it altogether while secretly hoping it's Dexter. I guess I'm still clinging on to the hope that he hasn't completely forgotten about me. Maybe he's doing a courtesy call instead of ghosting me. But when I look at my phone screen, it isn't Dexter. It's Carmen.

"Hello," I call glumly over the sound of Annabelle opening and closing kitchen cabinets and ceramic bowls clinking in the background.

"Hey, Lucy."

"Hey, Carmen." I settle back into the cushions, dipping my hand back into the M&M's and scooping a healthy handful.

"Uh, have you talked to Dexter recently?"

I freeze at the sound of his name. "Not recently, no."

"Oh."

"Why? What happened?"

I hear her hesitate, a few muttered words, unfinished and cautious, slipping through before she stays quiet. Has she heard something? Maybe some trail of gossip from Nat or Hayden made it all the way to her. Something that aligns with him being out and about with someone else. Someone prettier and who has her shit together and cleans up after herself.

"Carmen, tell me." I brace myself for what she's about to tell me with my heart pounding in my chest.

She sighs. "Okay, I really shouldn't be telling you this, but I guess… Whatever."

"What?"

"I've been seeing him here at the hospital."

All the puzzle pieces start to finally fall into place. "Janet."

"Yeah."

"Of course," I whisper. "God, I'm so *stupid*. How bad is it?"

"I don't really know. I'm not her direct provider. And even if I was, I'm really not allowed to say," she explains. "But he's been here for a few weeks. Like, in and out, of course, but I've been seeing him pretty consistently for almost two weeks now."

That's why he had to cancel his trip.

"I gotta go."

"Lucy—"

"I'll call you," I assure. "I promise I'll call you soon."

48

Dexter

MY SISTER'S DYING.

I've been trying to avoid the truth for such a long time, hoping this cancer isn't as serious as it really is, focusing on the fact that my sister still laughs and tells jokes and teases me. Because that's Janet. That's who she is. So how can she be dying? How can someone so full of life, despite that life being sucked out of her, be dying?

The robotic beeping and flashing numbers remind me of this. As does the plastic breathing tube down Janet's throat and the waxy appearance of her skin, now grayish and paper thin.

It didn't matter that she was careful, or that she quit her job to focus on maintaining what little of her health she had left. She got sick. Again, and this time, she isn't responding to the same treatments like she did the last time. It's almost like she's giving up.

"Any changes?"

I look up at the doorway where Charles stands. He's been in and out of the hospital for the past two weeks, just like me, and I finally urged him to go home. To shower, to do anything besides be surrounded by the four walls we've been confined in. It was only a few hours he'd been gone, but it was enough time to cause a lingering stretch of anxiety to take over me.

I shake my head. "The nurses just came in, gave her some more meds. Said they'll be back in a few hours, I guess."

He takes the seat next to mine. "If you need to go home for a bit, maybe get some real food instead of the crap in the cafeteria…"

I shake my head. "I'm fine."

"Dex," he says. "Go home. Take a shower. Take a long nap somewhere besides these lousy plastic chairs. I'll be here."

I sigh. A shower sounds so good right about now.

He sees me hesitate. "Go," he urges again.

"I'll make it quick." I stand, pulling a long stretch from the uncomfortable seats, and press a quick kiss to my sister's temple before walking out of the room. My steps are sluggish, and I'm unsure of what to do with myself without watching my sister as the machines help her breathe and stay alive.

I should at least take the time to call Lucy. I felt horrible after telling her I wouldn't be able to make it out to see her. I should've told her why I had to cancel my trip, but everything was happening so fast. And saying the words out loud, telling her that my sister almost went into septic shock and is fighting her biggest fight yet…I couldn't do it.

I feel so damn helpless. I can't do anything here. I'm just watching my sister, hoping she makes it out of this alive. Hoping that I'll see her one day, happy and lively, walking around her gallery all busy and energetic. I wish I could just talk to her one last time, let her know that I'm so sorry things had to be this way. That I wish it would have been me instead of her. How am I supposed to go on without her? I'm going to be completely alone, and I'm so fucking scared.

God, I wish Lucy were here. Even just to silently hold my hand or even wait for me back at my apartment. Just to know she's there, waiting for me to come home.

"Dexter." It's like I summoned her. Wanting to hold her, hear her voice, touch her. She's here.

"Lucy."

She runs to me from the other end of the hallway, not caring that there are other people around us turning their heads as they watch her crash into me. Her body meets mine with so much force I feel like the impact causes everything to dissolve. My sister laid up in the hospital bed, Lucy being too far away from me, me missing her every single hour of every single day.

"What are you doing here? How did you know?"

"Carmen called," she explains. Her hands run over my face, and she holds on to me with so much tenderness, I want to forget everything. I only want to think about Lucy and that she's here. "She told me she's been seeing you coming and going from the hospital, so she assumed Janet must be here."

"And you flew out here?"

"Of course," she answers.

"Lucy..." I say with a shaky voice. And I start to break down. I grasp her and bury my face into her shoulder, crying and sobbing. My entire body shakes, but she doesn't let me go. Instead, she holds me closer, running a hand up and down my back.

"I'm here," she says softly, clutching my head closer to her. "I'm here."

"I know," I sob. *She's really here.*

"It's okay, honey," she whispers as she shushes me. And while it's supposed to calm me, it has the opposite effect.

"*God*, I missed you so much," I cry. "I wanted to come to you but..."

She shushes me again. "I know. It's okay." And she just holds me. It's everything I ever needed in my entire life.

Fifteen minutes later, I still haven't gone home. Instead, Lucy and I've settled into a corner of the hospital where an empty visitor lounge sits. She's sitting in the seat next to mine, her knees drawn up to her chin, and I'm just staring at her. Marveling at her existence. Because she's here. She came here. For me.

"So what did the doctor say?"

"They're going to keep her on the ventilator until she can start breathing on her own," I explain. "They have her sedated right now, just something to help her feel less anxious and more comfortable, and she's starting to respond to the meds. Finally."

"So she's sort of out of it?"

I nod. "In and out."

"Dexter, why didn't you tell me?"

I sigh heavily. "I guess I was scared to say it out loud, and I didn't know if I would be able to keep it together while I told you," I explain. She inches closer, resting her hand on my thigh. "And I didn't want you to worry."

"When you stopped answering me...I thought maybe things were over between us."

I look up in shock. She couldn't have possibly thought that.

"I thought maybe you met someone else, or you didn't want to bother wasting your time dealing with us since things were so complicated," she continues. Her eyes start to water, and her voice trembles. "I didn't know all of this was happening."

"Lucy," I urge, just as a single tear slips from the corner of her eye. "No, no. I could never."

She nods. "I know that now. I just got really scared for a moment. But Dexter...I'm so sorry. I should've known it was Janet. I should've known you were going through all of this."

"Lucy, I'm so sorry," I say softly. I reach up to pull her face toward me and kiss her. Tears start streaming down her cheeks, and it makes our kiss wet and sad. "I didn't think it would—I didn't think. I should have called and let you know what was going on."

"No, it's okay. Really. It was just my stupid brain playing games on me, and I should've known better. I guess I was just...scared."

We sit there, both realizing how much we need this. How badly we need to stay open with each other. Our relationship has its own hurdles with the distance between us, and neither one of us communicating along the way didn't help. We don't have the luxury of living in the same city, where we don't have to wonder what's going on when we don't talk to each other for a day or two. We don't have the option to pop over to the other's apartment on a whim or make last minute plans to have dinner or watch a movie.

And then I realize how she'll probably go back home in a few days, or maybe in a few hours. I don't know how much time I have with her, and my heart starts to ache all over again. I don't want to talk about what should be and what can be between us right now. I don't even know if I'm ready to discuss her travel plans, like when she's heading back to the airport or what time her flight is. I'm definitely not ready to say goodbye to her just yet.

"So you left your things at Carmen's?" I ask, trying to figure out how to get her settled back into my apartment during the short time she's here.

"Yeah," she answers. "I brought what I could for now, and I'll probably go back to Seattle sometime soon to get the rest of my things—"

"What are you talking about?"

She takes a deep sigh, gnawing on her lip. "I'm going to stay with her for a while. At least until things get more stable with Janet. And then we can figure things out after that once—"

"You're staying?"

"Yeah."

"For how long?"

"I'm moving here."

"Like, *moving*, moving?"

She nods.

"Lucy, you can't," I plead. "You have that job offer coming to you. You can't uproot your life like that for me."

Her face twists into a frustrated scowl. "Why not? I was going to do it for a job. Why can't I do it for you? You matter more to me than any job. I can talk to Elevate. Maybe I can do something remote or part-time while traveling out to LA or something."

"Lucy, they won't—"

"Then I'll find another job!" She jolts from her seat and starts pacing the small space in front of me. "I don't know, Dexter! I'm trying to figure this out. I'm grasping at straws because I can't keep doing this. I can't live on the other side of the country and pretend like the distance isn't killing me. I've tried to be rational and responsible, but I'm so tired of it. It hurts too damn much. My place is with you, nowhere else. No job is going to change that."

I stand, pulling her to me, and I feel her sink against my chest. She's really willing to give up her life and be here with me. Without asking for any conditions, no tit for tat kind of deal like she'll only move in with me if I keep the thermostat at seventy-three degrees.

She's willing to risk everything and uproot her entire life to be here with me, despite the inconvenience of it.

"It's killing me too," I say softly as she pulls away to look at me. "It hasn't been easy since I got back from Hawaii, and I think I'd rather punch myself in the nuts right now than tell you to change your mind."

She huffs a sad laugh, and I see a small smile twitch at the corners of her mouth. "No, don't do that," she says with a shaky voice.

My hands move to her neck and the sides of her cheek and her hair. My fingers graze over her like I'm sifting through everything to make sure this is really happening. I'm double, triple checking because it feels like magic. Something that'll disappear into a fancy top hat or be swiped away from under a white cloth. But it's not. It's not some evil trick played on my already fragile heart. It's real. All of it.

"Are you sure about this?"

She nods. "Yes, I'm sure."

"Yeah, okay," I finally say. "We'll figure things out. If I need to follow you to LA, I'll do that."

"You will?"

"Yeah. Once things stabilize with Janet and…" I pause, unsure how to finish that sentence. "You can stay with me in the meantime."

Her face twists a little. "You don't have to," she says. "Carmen already told me I could stay with her."

I shake my head. No, she can't be here and *not* stay with me. I can't stand the idea of knowing we could be living under the same roof, using the same bathroom to brush our teeth in and get ready for the day, but choosing *not* to. We have a choice this time. We can *choose* to be together without worrying about circumstances or conveniences like work or burgled apartments. "Lucy, no—"

"I didn't come here assuming you'd want me to move in with you. I'm not expecting…" She pauses to take a deep breath. "It's a lot to ask of you."

"No, it's not," I urge, gripping her a little tighter. "I *want* you to move in with me. I want you to sleep in my bed. I want you to wake up next to me, and I want to come home to you."

She considers my offer, gnawing on her lip. "I know we've been pretty throw-caution-to-the-wind about a lot of things, but this feels like a pretty big step."

"I know," I agree. "Trust me, I'm not taking it lightly. I mean it when I say I want you to move in with me."

She hesitates, and I take the opportunity to kiss the back of her hand, hoping it'll sway her.

"Okay," she finally agrees.

"Yeah?" I ask, my face lighting up. It feels like my whole body lights up, like the entire weight of so many things shifts. And it feels a little foreign, a little alien and unfamiliar. I realize I haven't felt this way since I last saw her. With everything that's been going on with Janet and being in and out of the hospital, everything's been piling on top of me, and it took Lucy coming back into my life for me to realize there's a small stream of hope at the end of the tunnel.

"Yeah," she answers, smiling at me with her beautiful smile.

"Okay, then," I say, so giddy I could kick my feet into the air. "Let's go get your things."

49

Lucy

MY FINGERS TEAR at the sliced bread in my hands, and I pop a small piece into my mouth. I reach for the glass of water sitting in front of me, the condensation dripping into the fancy white cloth draped over the table, and gulp down almost half of it.

"Are you nervous?"

I turn to Dexter sitting next to me and huff a tense laugh. "Understatement of the century." He chuckles smugly and rubs a hand over my shoulder opposite to him. I take a deep, cleansing breath and warily lift an eyebrow in his direction. "Why aren't you nervous?"

He shrugs. "What are they going to do? Ground us?"

I roll my eyes and look over at the entrance to the restaurant just as I see Hayden and Nat walk through the heavy glass doors. My heart rate kicks up several notches, and I swear my armpits feel damp.

Dexter and I both stand from our seats at the same time Nat approaches our table, and she and Hayden have the same confused looks on their faces.

"Lucy? What are you doing here?"

Dexter gently places a hand at my back. I know it's to reassure me, but it only adds to the anxiety crawling through me when Nat notices his hand placement.

"Seriously, what are you doing here?" she asks again when I don't answer.

"Why don't you have a seat," I urge. She and Hayden take the seats sitting across from me and Dexter, and they both eye us like they're bracing themselves for bad news.

A waiter approaches our table, placing menus in front of us while murmuring items off the wine list.

"I'm sorry," Nat tells the waiter, looking impatient and annoyed. "Can we have a moment, please?" The waiter silently nods and walks away, leaving Nat to glare in my direction. "Lucy, please tell me what's going on."

I play with the bread on my plate before I look at her and sit up straighter. "So, I, uh…I guess I should start with the fact that I don't work at Mr. Bean's anymore. Those early mornings were wreaking havoc on my skin with how little sleep I was getting anyway. And you know how much I struggle with those gross bags under my eyes when I get anything less than eight hours of sleep. So it's been a total godsend for my skin. I can practically hear the little voices coming from my pores going, 'Thank you, Lucy! You saved our lives!'" I say that last part in a high-pitched voice like a cartoon character, and Nat looks at me like I've lost my mind.

"You've come all the way here from Seattle to tell me you don't work at the coffee shop anymore?"

Okay, maybe starting with a joke was a bad idea.

"And why are you here with Dexter?"

I sigh and look over at Dexter. He reaches for my hand resting on the table, right where everyone can see, and he gives me a gentle squeeze.

"I, uh…I've been in New York. For the past three months."

"What?!"

"I rented this micro apartment. Like, ninety square feet, and it came with a hot plate and everything. And then it got robbed. It was horrible. They broke down my door, stole my MacBook, and ruined that sweater I borrowed from you. You know, the baby blue cable knit one with the cherry print? So I, um, called Dexter because we-we, uh, ran into each other." Nat looks at Dexter like she forgot he was there. He waves and smiles one of those nervous smiles where his bottom teeth are more exposed than his top before she throws a glare at him. "And he let me stay with him until I went to Hawaii for your wedding."

"I'm so confused. You just randomly woke up one day and decided to quit your job and move to the city without telling me?"

"Not exactly."

"Okay," she says, her wide eyes demanding answers. "So…"

I pause, hesitating to tell her the next part. I turn to look at Dexter, and he gives me an encouraging nod. "Remember that internship I told you about?" I ask. "The one Mom told me not to apply to?"

"Yeah."

"Well, I applied for it, even though she didn't want me to. And I got in. So I quit my job and moved out here since it was for this big ad campaign and they were shooting in Brooklyn."

Her face softens when she realizes why I didn't say anything. She reaches across the table for my hand and clutches my fingers. "Lucy."

"And I'm so happy I did because it was so amazing," I continue through a sudden burst of emotions making my voice waver. "I learned so much, and they're going to offer me a job. Like, a real job. And I don't have to keep filling out those stupid job applications and send my resume to a hundred different places I don't even want to work at."

I look up at Nat and see her looking at me with apologetic eyes.

"I'm so sorry, Nat. I wanted to tell you, but when you told me it was good I didn't apply…I didn't know how to tell you without letting you down. I was already such a disappointment to Mom and Dad. I couldn't keep disappointing more people."

"Lucy…" she cries softly. "I didn't mean…I'm so sorry. I was only thinking about what was best for you. I didn't mean to make you feel like you were letting me or anyone down."

"It's not your fault," I assure through a shaky voice. "I just couldn't pass up on this opportunity, and I knew Mom wouldn't understand. I was scared and worried at the time, but I understand now, this was something I needed to figure out on my own."

A rumble of laughter at a table nearby brings us back to reality, where we realize we're in a public space and people can see our tears and sad faces. We both quickly dab at our eyes with our fingers, Hayden and Dexter looking over us in awkward silence, before Nat smiles at me. "Okay," she says, letting out an embarrassed chuckle. "So, um…why are you here with Dexter?" she asks, looking between me and Dexter.

Silence falls over the table. "We're sort of a, uh…thing," Dexter finally says, answering her question for me.

"What?!" This time, Hayden jumps in. He leans forward, bracing his hands on the table, and looks at us in shock.

"Surprise," I say sheepishly.

Nat starts laughing, her tears long forgotten, and she clutches Hayden's arm. "I told you so," she says in a sing-song voice to Hayden. She faces me with a wide grin. "I told him I saw something between you two in Hawaii."

"So, uh…um, when did this happen?" Hayden stutters, waving a loose hand across the table.

"While she was staying with me," Dexter answers. He peers at me thoughtfully before adding, "Actually, I guess it happened way before that."

"What do you mean, before that?" Nat asks with a confused look on her face.

"We sort of…hooked up, like, three years ago."

"When?!" Nat shrieks, and a few heads turn in our direction. I swear, this up and down of her emotions is going to give her whiplash.

"When I was visiting," I answer.

"But how? When did you…" Nat stares off into space like she's trying to pluck out a moment somewhere in her timeline that involved me and Dexter and us two hooking up.

"After we met at that party you had at your apartment."

"Ohmigod," she whispers. Her hands move to her mouth, and she gapes at us in shock. "I can't believe you didn't tell me."

Dexter sits up and leans his face toward Nat in an attempt to gain her wavering attention. "Look, Nat. We didn't mean to keep things from you guys, but things were a little complicated between us. Lucy was living all the way in Seattle, and I've been here. We didn't know what was going to—"

"Wait a minute," Nat interrupts, raising a hand in front of her. "What do you mean *was*?" She turns to look at me for an answer.

"I moved out here. While you two were on your honeymoon," I explain. "I'm staying with Dexter for now. At least until I figure things out work wise."

She's speechless. I can see it in the way her head swivels to face Dexter, then Hayden, and then back to me with her mouth hanging open.

"We talked about moving to LA since Lucy's work is going to be there, but I can't right now, not while Janet starts her radiation therapy, but we're figuring things out a day at a time."

"Is she okay?" Hayden asks.

Dexter nods. "She got admitted again, but she's stable now. It was kind of scary at first, but she's finally off the ventilator, and they moved her out of the ICU. I think her doctor's going to discharge her in a week or so, depending on some more test results."

We've been shuttling back and forth from Dexter's apartment to the hospital since I moved and settled in. I watched as Janet regained a lot of her strength and her doctors grew more hopeful about her prognosis. She was ecstatic when we told her I moved into Dexter's apartment, and she's been calling or texting me every day since. While she isn't in the clear in any way, it's still a good sign that she's fighting this. She needs as much of her strength as possible before she starts her radiation therapy after she's discharged.

I look at Nat and watch as she still continues to process everything. "I already talked to Mom," I start to explain. "She knows I'm out here with Dexter. I told her about the job and everything, and she's really happy about it. And she's so relieved we're all in the same city."

"Ohmigod," Nat says through a sharp gasp. "We're all living in the city." She grins at me, and her eyes light up. "You, me, and Carmen. We all live in the same freaking city. We're in the same time zone, and I don't have to fly across the country to see you!"

I laugh. "Yeah," I say, grinning at her.

"We have to tell Carmen! We should go straight to her place after this. She's going to be so excited!"

"Oh," I say. "About that…"

50

Lucy

six months later

"THE CHAMPAGNE IS IN THE FREEZER," I yell to Dexter from Janet's living room. "You should take it out now. It's been in there for about an hour."

"What?" He emerges from the kitchen, a half-deflated balloon in his hand and his voice sounding like one of the chipmunks.

Nat and I both dissolve into giggles while Nat pins one side of the large banner that reads CONGRATULATIONS in big block letters. I'm on the other side, my arms getting tired while we determine the banner's level. "I said to get the champagne out of the freezer," I tell Dexter. "And don't get high off the helium. Or your voice will stay that way."

He sucks in a healthy serving of helium. "That's an urban myth," he claims in his silly voice as he turns toward the kitchen.

I tack the corner of the sign and step down from the chair I was standing on, admiring my handiwork. "Now we just need to set up the food once Hayden gets here with it," I say to Nat.

She glances at the clock. "What time did Charles say they were heading over?"

"In about an hour," I answer. "He's treating Janet to some cronuts as her first post-treatment treat, and then they're coming home. I just told him not to seem too eager or she's going to catch on."

After two weeks in the hospital and once Janet's recovery stabilized her enough to be discharged, she came home on oxygen and further follow-up visits. She completed eight weeks of radiation therapy, fighting an unfair fight, one that felt like the opponent always had an upper leg. And she won. After more waiting, more tests, and even more waiting, we got the final verdict two days ago: remission. She's still weak, recovering from the aftereffects of her hospitalization and radiation therapy, but she's returning back to her old self. Enjoying company, laughing and joking with me, teasing Dexter about his pouty heartbroken state before I moved in with him.

There's a buzz on the intercom, and we all jump. "They're early!" Dexter screams, bolting out of the kitchen to the door.

"Honey," I call, trying to calm him down. "They aren't going to use the buzzer in their own apartment. It's probably Hayden with the food."

Dexter smiles sheepishly at me. "Oh, right." He buzzes the door and surveys the room. The balloons—the ones Dexter didn't inhale— are scattered throughout. The banner, gold and glittery, is placed so it's the first thing Janet sees when she walks through the door. And we've set up the cake on the coffee table, the words "Fuck Cancer" written in cursive over the frosting.

There's a low knock at the door, and when Dexter opens it, we find Hayden, his arms full of three large aluminum trays carrying something that smells absolutely delicious. "*Jeez.* I almost got attacked by a wiener dog that had the face of a pitbull. That was a really weird mix."

He strains against the weight before he slumps the trays on the kitchen counter, and he and Nat busy themselves to organize them neatly over the space.

"Thank you for helping," Dexter croons into my ear, sidling up behind me with his arm wrapped around my waist.

"As if I would miss this."

He plants a kiss on my neck. "Still, you must be so tired after your flight."

I turn to wrap my arms around his neck. "Totally worth it."

"Ew!" We both turn toward the kitchen, where we catch Nat launching a disposable plastic cup in our direction, and it lands square on Dexter's head. "No making out with my sister!"

"How about after this we go home and take a nice long nap?" Dexter asks, ignoring my sister.

"A nap? Or..."

He smirks. "I mean, we can do other—"

I clamp a hand over his mouth. "She's going to throw the whole champagne bottle at you next."

"I really don't care," he claims, planting a kiss on my mouth, proving that my sister's threats mean squat to him. "I only get to have you for a week before you go back to LA."

This is what our lives have been like for the past six months. After Elevate finally reached out to me with a job offer, I countered with conditions. I told Ryan I wouldn't be able to relocate to Los Angeles. I told him I'd be willing to work out what I can to work for the company while preparing myself for the possibility that they might turn me down. But, as it turns out, Elevate was set to open a corporate location in Manhattan...in thirteen months. So Ryan and his team agreed to have me start at the Manhattan branch when it opens. I'll be handling so much more than I thought with so many future projects for me to head. Ryan and the HR team explained how I'd be managing some of those projects, and in the meantime, I could take on projects in LA so I'm prepared when the new branch opens.

So until that happens, I've been shuttling back and forth from Brooklyn to Los Angeles. Dexter and I spent Christmas in New York City and New Year's in LA together. We flew back home with Hayden, Nat, Carmen, and David just after the holidays to celebrate my parents' fortieth wedding anniversary, and now I'm back here to commemorate Janet's new lease on life.

"So I have an idea," I say in a low voice.

"Does it involve your vibrator? I charged it after you left—"

"No," I scold, though unable to hide my laugh. He laughs too. That boyish smile I missed before Janet got the news that she was finally in remission is back, front and center. "I was thinking, maybe you can come to LA with me?"

"Next week?"

"Just the weekend," I clarify. "I can take you to that new croffle shop near The Grove."

"How they mixed a croissant and a waffle together baffles me. Like that wiener-pitbull mix."

"So yeah?"

"Yeah," he answers, his brows bouncing up and down.

"Really?"

He smiles, pulling me closer to him. "Have you not learned yet that I can't say no to you?"

"Dex," Hayden calls from the kitchen. Dexter pulls away to face Hayden. "You just got a message. It's Charles. They're on their way."

He turns to me, grinning widely. "Let's get this celebration started."

51

Lucy

two years later

"HOW MUCH LONGER?"

I stop pacing my small bathroom and pause at the sink to peer down at the timer on my phone. "Forty-seven seconds."

"Ugh! How long does it *freaking* take to absorb some pee?!" Nat complains, dramatically burying her face into her hands. She crouches forward with her butt perched on the edge of the bathtub, and her left foot taps up and down.

I chuckle. "Thirty-nine seconds."

"I blame Hayden," she deadpans.

"*Riiight*," I respond sarcastically. "Because you had zero contribution in the conception of this possible baby."

"Shut up."

"Geez." If this is any indication of what Nat would be like pregnant, it's going to be a long nine months. *If* this timer goes off any time soon.

Just then, the thrill of a bell goes off on my phone.

"Is it time?"

I nod. We both slowly walk toward the toilet tank where the pregnancy test sits, approaching it like we're hunting a frightened bunny.

Nat suddenly jolts backward. "I can't look!"

"Nat!"

"No! Look at it for me!"

"Oh. My. *God*," I groan. "You're so dramatic."

"What am I going to tell Hayden?"

"Well, we don't know, do we? We have to look at the test before we know what to tell him."

She shakes her head dramatically. "Just look at it for me. I can't do it."

I roll my eyes. I feel Nat start a round of jumping jacks behind me to settle her nerves. I take a deep breath, suddenly realizing that I'm nervous too. *My sister's going to have a baby!*

I blow out a deep exhale. I have to keep my cool. Especially with Simone Biles doing a double backflip behind me. When I look down at the porcelain tank, I dart my eyes to the teeny-tiny digital screen on the white and blue stick, just in time to catch the word "pregnant" flashing in front of me.

"Oh my god."

"*What?!* What, what?!" Nat shrieks.

I grip the pregnancy test in my fist, ignoring the fact that my sister peed on it, and swivel on my feet to face Nat. "You're pregnant!"

"What?!"

I shove the test in her face at the same time she holds my fist in her hands and reads the result. "Oh my god."

"Nat!"

"I think I'm going to throw up," she says, panic glazing over her eyes.

"What? Here," I urge, ushering her back to the toilet.

As she's about to cower over the seat, we hear the door open from my living room. The opening and closing of the front door is followed by boisterous laughter and loud chitter-chatter. Hayden and Nat came over so the guys could go out for some drinks while Nat stayed home with me to catch up over takeout. About an hour into Nat nibbling on her cheese pizza, she confessed to me that her period had been over a week late. And that caused a domino effect of events. Me excited at the thought of my sister and her husband having a baby, us frantically running to the nearest bodega for a pregnancy test and the pack of Starburst Nat was eyeing at the counter, her yelling at me to give her some privacy while she peed on the stick even though she's used the bathroom plenty of times with me in it.

"They're back," I say. Nat looks up at me, and I swear she's going to cry. "Nat, he's not going to be mad."

"I know," she responds tearfully.

"Then what's the problem?"

"This wasn't planned," she says just as her eyes start to mist over. "I'm not ready to be a mom."

"Lucy!" I hear Dexter call from the other side of the door. "Are you guys in there?" A light knock follows his question.

"Come on," I say gently.

Nat wipes her tears and watches me walk toward the door. Instead of following me, she plops herself on the edge of the tub again. "Can you send him in?"

I take in her tearful state, hoping this sudden burst of emotions has more to do with hormones than an actual fear of telling Hayden they're going to have a baby. She and I both know Hayden will be ecstatic over the news. Nat might think she's not ready to be a mom, but I know Hayden's ready to be a dad. I see it every time we see Carmen and David and Hayden beelines for the newest addition to the Marquez clan, baby Silas.

He doesn't turn his cheek whenever Silas spits up curdled breast milk over the front of his shirt or when Silas's poopy diaper demands a change. Instead, he showers him with raspberries to his soft stomach and hours of cuddle time while he naps in Hayden's arms to give Carmen and David a break. He loves that kid as if he were his own.

I turn toward the door and open it carefully, finding both Dexter and Hayden on the other side looking confused and worried.

"Is Nat in there?" Hayden asks.

I nod. "She wants to talk to you," I tell him solemnly.

His head jerks back in confusion. "Like, in here?" he asks, pointing his hand toward the door behind me. I nod again, and he looks at

Dexter like he might know what's going on. When Dexter shrugs, he looks back at me. "Is everything okay?"

"Just go in there before she has another freak-out."

Hayden walks past me, carefully opening the door. I get a peek of Nat sitting at the same spot I left her, and Hayden gently closes the door behind him.

I look at Dexter with a wide smile, and I know the whole shift in my demeanor is confusing. "What's going on?"

I do a little hop and rub my fists together in front of me. I squeal a little, and Dexter laughs. "I can't say," I answer, letting a loud giggle slip.

"What?" he asks with a laugh. "Seriously, what's going on?"

Just then, we're interrupted by a roaring "WHAT?!" from inside the bathroom. We both glance at the closed door and face each other again.

"Okay, maybe I can tell you now." I hear both Nat and Hayden laugh, and Dexter's eyes widen. "I'm going to be an aunt. Well, I mean, again. I'm going to be an aunt again."

Dexter's mouth cracks into a smile that matches mine. "No way!"

I nod, and Dexter scoops me up in a tight hug, twirling me until I grow dizzy. We both laugh ourselves silly before Dexter sets me down. Just then, the door to the bathroom clicks open, followed by a proudly beaming Hayden and a timid Nat trailing behind him.

"So I guess you guys already heard the news," Hayden announces. Dexter rushes to Hayden, the two embracing in a cheesy hug. I can't help but roll my eyes and smirk. Nat does the same, laughing at her husband and his best friend hopping on their two feet from excitement.

"Are you okay?" I ask, sidling up to Nat.

She nods and rolls her eyes, silently telling me she's definitely aware of how badly she overreacted five minutes ago.

"We have to celebrate," Hayden announces. "And I have to call my mom. And your parents too," he adds, looking at Nat with a wide, blissful grin that hasn't shifted once since he walked out of the bathroom.

"Should we wait?" Nat asks, tugging at Hayden's hand. "I mean, isn't there like a grace period? Or a trimester rule we need to follow?"

"Yeah," I chime in. "I think Carmen waited until she was ten weeks before she told everyone."

"What?!" Hayden argues cheerfully, that smile still unwavering. "This isn't like waiting thirty minutes to swim after we eat. I want to tell everyone!" He reaches down and pulls my sister into a deep, bursting embrace, and I worry a little that Nat is going to pop like a tick from him squeezing her so hard. "I want everyone to know my wife is going to have my baby."

She smiles at him, and I see her eyes mist over. "We're having a baby," I hear her whisper. She giggles, and Hayden follows, crouching down so their foreheads rest against each other.

"Yeah," he responds, his voice low like hers. "We're having a baby."

"I can't believe I'm going to be an uncle."

I pull back my side of the comforter in our dimly lit room. It's long after midnight, and Nat and Hayden left an hour ago after we drank multiple glasses of champagne and orange juice for Nat as we clinked the glass flutes too many times for us to count.

I reach for the hand lotion at my bedside and squirt a small dollop onto my hand. "Well, technically, no."

Dexter throws me a wounded look. "What are you talking about?"

I grin slyly before explaining. "You aren't *technically* an uncle."

Dexter rolls his eyes. "I think my best friend having a baby falls under 'uncle' category."

"Yeah, but I'll always one up you in that department," I say smugly. "Technically."

He looks up at me, the blanket pulled up to his stomach, where he's settled in under the sheets. "Oh, really," he taunts. "So it's a little competition now."

"Absolutely." I dip my feet under the blankets first, and the rest of me follows. Dexter flinches a little when my cold toes touch his legs, but it's followed by a forceful tug of my waist to him.

"I bet the baby will call me 'uncle' before he or she calls you 'aunty.'"

"That's a pretty risky wager for someone who isn't technically an uncle."

"I guess I'm pretty confident I'll be a better uncle than you'll be an aunt."

My brow shoots up. "Okay, Mr. Cocky," I answer, my lips pursed together in disapproval. "What are we wagering?"

He hums, putting on a show of thought and pondering. "We gotta make it big. Something worth the stakes."

"Agreed," I say, playing along. "How about a lifetime of foot massages?"

He shakes his head in disagreement. "No, something bigger."

"What's bigger than nightly foot massages?" I nudge my slowly warming feet into the groove behind his knee. "For a lifetime."

He continues this contemplation, ruminating through all of his options, when he snaps his fingers. "I got it."

I laugh. "What?"

"If this kid calls me 'uncle' first, you marry me."

I laugh harder. "Seriously?"

His face doesn't change into something lighter or playful. In fact, the seriousness in his eyes grows darker, making me wonder if there's more to this little wager we're tossing back and forth. "Yeah." He says that single syllable, four-letter word like it carries something more than a far-off agreement to spend the rest of our lives together. "Marry me."

"Like, if you win, right?"

He pauses before answering, his eyes lighting up with something that leans toward hope. "Or sooner."

"Wait, what?"

He hops off the bed, leaving me equally confused and dumbfounded. After rummaging through his sock drawer, he returns to his soft, squishy spot next to me and unfolds his large palm to reveal a small velvet square box. The wires in my brain start to short-circuit. Is he showing me something? Maybe some sort of antique trinket that needs to be stored in a box that looks like something that may hold a ring? You know, for safekeeping? Maybe he found it on the ground.

Yeah, that's it. He found it outside on the sidewalk and inside is some expensive-looking jewelry, earrings or a broach, and he wants my help to find its owner.

"Dexter, what is this?" My trembling fingers reach for his hand, but I stop, unsure if it's real. If maybe this is just a figment of my imagination and the thing in Dexter's hand is nothing but a tube of ChapStick or my little claw clip I left at his bedside table. But even after I blink what feels like a hundred times, it's still there. The soft, fuzzy box lined with gold trim around the edges is still sitting in the middle of his open hand.

Dexter uses his free hand to pry it open slowly. The soft creaking of the hinges sounds louder than it actually is in our room filled with my messy heap of clothing on a blush-colored armchair and the pictures of our families lined up on our dresser. All pictures I've taken that he had printed and framed, filling our home with memories he never had before I moved in with him.

Inside the box is the most beautiful diamond ring I've ever seen. It's round and simple, no big show of a cluster of diamonds or a thick, gaudy band that'll look too flashy on my bare and unembellished hands. Just one really, really big rock showcasing how perfectly easy our love has been.

"I got this a month ago," he says softly, watching my wide-eyed look of shock as I finally register what's in front of me. "I didn't plan some over-the-top proposal or anything. It didn't really feel like...us. So I've been waiting for the right moment because...I guess being spontaneous with you made more sense."

My eyes start to water. "Dexter, I...I, um—"

"Marry me," he repeats. "Tomorrow, next week, next year, I don't care when. But be mine forever."

"Really? I mean, are you sure?"

"Yes," he answers with a laugh. "Of course I'm sure."

"Like, you've thought this through? Maybe you should think about it some more. A pros and cons list can't hurt."

A sweet, shaky sigh slips through his lips that sounds like he's exhaling a breath of fondness for my flustered state. "Lucy," he says, tucking a finger under my chin to lift my face toward him. "Remember when you came back to the city? When you came to me in the hospital?"

"Yeah?" I answer with a shaky voice.

"The second I saw you in the hallway running toward me, I knew I wanted to spend the rest of my life with you."

A single tear trickles down my cheek, and Dexter swipes it away with his thumb. I smile at him, and he smiles back, causing us to sit in silence. I'm going to marry this man. He wants me for the rest of his life. "I guess you are going to be an uncle after all."

"Is that a yes?" he asks, his eyes lighting up with excitement.

I laugh through my tears. "Yeah."

a look at

Take Me Back to the Start

Her first love was unforgettable. Losing him was unbearable. Seeing him again might be undoable.

Christine "Teeny" Diaz thought she had life figured out—married young, built a career, played the part of the perfect wife. But now, at thirty-six, she's facing a failed marriage, a shattered heart, and a past she's tried to bury. Until Everett Hayes walks back into her life.

Once the boy next door, Everett was her first love—the one who left without knowing the secret she carried. Now, thrown together for her brother's wedding, old wounds reopen, and memories resurface: stolen kisses, late-night diner runs, the way he made her feel like the only girl in the world. But the truth she never told him still stands between them.

Everett never forgot Teeny, never stopped wondering what could have been. Now that fate has brought them back together, he's determined to prove that their love was never meant to be left behind. But when long-buried secrets come to light, Teeny must decide if the pain of the past is too much to risk a future with the only man she's ever truly loved.

AVAILABLE MAY 2025

acknowledgments

Jumping right into this…

My biggest thanks, one that will always come first, is to my readers. To *all* the readers. The readers picking up their first chapter book at their school library. The readers browsing the romance section at their local bookstore. The readers staying up until two a.m., reading just one more chapter. Without each and every one of you, no author would write the stories they write. But to *my* readers… Thank. You. Thank you for watching me become a debut author, putting into the world this new, very fragile story that I wasn't sure would be well received. Thank you for watching me through the awkward teenage phase as Best I Never Had was released and I was still learning how to navigate this author world. And thank you for sticking by me through yet another release. I'm still learning and growing, and I hope with all of my heart to see all of you along the way, watching my storytelling grow and blossom.

To my Bookstagram friends who fill my DMs, and in turn, fill my heart, your warm messages and kind words keep me going. I love all of you. And a special thanks to Katy, Anna, April, Hazel (for our nightly writing sprint sessions), Kaye, Keelan, and Danielle. You guys are my shining star.

To my dearest friends, Amy, Jessica, Cheann, Rose, Mhel, Bea. My life wouldn't be complete without my girl gang.

To my family. My Hunny and B. and C. For understanding my sacrifices weren't easily made. For loving me no matter what. For knowing how important my dream is while keeping in mind that it doesn't change my dedication to our little team. I will always support all of you, just as you always support me. We're in this together.

And lastly, certainly not least, my village. Thank you to my editor Katie, who has been with me since book one. Your knowledge and skill has taught me so much as a writer, and I can't even begin to tell you how much I value our relationship. To Sam at Ink and Laurel, your skill overwhelms me. I can't even put to words how blown away I am by not only your artistry, but by your professionalism as well. And to Shaye and Lindsey at Good Girls PR. I've worked with PR teams in the past and I have never had an experience quite like yours. I don't feel like just another author on a roster, I feel like a valued client. I feel like an author whose needs are not only being met, but considered in every way possible.

And (I know I already said "lastly," but I have to sneak this in here), Lucy and Dexter. I love them. I love their softness and wit. I love their pain and their healing. I just love them.

—Jeannie Choe

JEANNIE CHOE
ROMANCE AUTHOR

Specializing in new adult contemporary romance novels, Jeannie Choe offers stories ranging from angsty and emotional to heartfelt and outright adorable. Because who doesn't love a happily ever after filled with squeal-inducing moments of romantic gestures?

Living off an endless number of paperbacks, cold brews, and 2000's rom-coms, Jeannie lives in Southern California spending her days with her family and two attention-seeking elder dachshunds.

www.jeanniechoeauthor.com